TOO
MUCH LIP

ALSO BY MELISSA LUCASHENKO

Steam Pigs (1997)

Killing Darcy (1998)

Hard Yards (1999)

Too Flash (2002)

Mullumbimby (2013)

TOO MUCH LIP

A Novel

MELISSA LUCASHENKO

HarperVia

An Imprint of HarperCollinsPublishers

HarperCollins books may be purchased for educational, business, or sales promotional use. For information, please email the Special Markets Department at SPsales@harpercollins.com.

Originally published in 2018 by University of Queensland Press, P. O. Box 6042, St. Lucia, Queensland 4067, Australia. Reprinted in 2018, 2019.

FIRST HARPERCOLLINS EDITION PUBLISHED IN 2020

Designed by Terry McGrath

Library of Congress Cataloging-in-Publication Data

Names: Lucashenko, Melissa, 1967- author.
Title: Too much lip / Melissa Lucashenko.
Description: First edition. | New York : HarperVia, 2020 |
Identifiers: LCCN 2020021739 (print) | LCCN 2020021740 (ebook) | ISBN 9780063032538 (hardback) | ISBN 9780063032545 (trade paperback) | ISBN 9780063032552 (ebook) | ISBN 9780063032569
Subjects: GSAFD: Black humor (Literature)
Classification: LCC PR9619.3.L73 T66 2020 (print) | LCC PR9619.3.L73 (ebook) | DDC 823/.914—dc23
LC record available at https://lccn.loc.gov/2020021739
LC ebook record available at https://lccn.loc.gov/2020021740

20 21 22 23 24 LSC 10 9 8 7 6 5 4 3 2 1

For my brother David, who swam a river to save my life

She was charged with shooting the accused, who in giving evidence against her, made no secret of what his intentions were towards the woman. She, he said, was only a gin, and he could do what he liked with her.

"District Court, Criminal Sittings"
Brisbane Telegraph, January 31, 1908

Owen Addison, 1943

It was Owen's first time in the big country town that thought it was a city. The boy had never heard a tram rattle along a paved street, never before seen a raised boxing ring waiting for him empty and ominous under blazing electric light. The number of whitefellas in the world was a revelation. Dugai burst out of every door, their pale faces staring at him, strangers to a man. *The great yellow hope*, he heard one of them say to the flash piece of mutton hanging off his arm. Owen swallowed. At home his enemies were clear: Reverend O'Sullivan, the gunjibals, the Welfare. But where was the snake hidden in this particular paddock?

There.

Over in the corner, a stout gunjie with a flaming red beard. Three more beside him, all wearing the unfamiliar blue serge of the Queensland Police Force. His mum's voice rang in his ears: *Keep your jang shut tight, son. It's your job to keep the god botherers away. So keep quiet—and mind ya bloody win.* Her arms flung around him so tight his breath was forced high into his throat. His arms roped around her, too, trembling. Pride bursting in his chest: *I'm a man, fighting to keep us free. Me, Sissy, Bon.* And the terror of it all falling on his head at fourteen.

The red beard strolled over, smiling a smile to chill the marrow of your black bones. He shook Mr. Lewis's hand.

"Corbett's the name. So this is him, is it?" he asked, swivelling to pin Owen beneath his gaze. "The new Jack Johnson?" Owen stiffened.

Melbourne had rioted after the Negro Johnson had won. Men had died. And Mr. Lewis was a banana farmer; he knew nothing about gunjies.

"Oh, Owen's no flash Yank," Mr. Lewis said mildly. "He's just a handy half-caste from Rivertown."

"Is that right, boy?" The sergeant seized upon the adjective. "*Handy*, are ya?"

"Try to be." Owen's chin jutted.

The sergeant gazed at him, unsatisfied. He leaned closer and his copper's breath blew hot in Owen's ear.

"You might be thought something pretty over the border," he said softly. "But the last coon that got too handy round here swung for it. Got that?" He stepped back laughing, as though he'd made a fine and private joke. After a moment of incomprehension, Owen's bladder jerked in fear. He wanted to kill the man standing in front of him, but there was his mother to think of. And Reverend O'Sullivan, sniffing after his sisters' souls.

"Yessir," Owen mumbled, though he didn't. He'd heard the word a hundred times in approval from older men. Handy with a horse. Handy sort of a lad. Handy with his fists. Now, somehow, in the instant between Mr. Lewis uttering the word and it ricocheting back at him, *handy* had become a steel trap.

Owen's job was clear. Keep the gunjibals away by winning in the grimy tents of country towns, by boxing his way to the title Mr. Lewis said was his for the taking. By being the native pride of Rivertown, so authority had no excuse to come hunting down his sisters and him. But if Queensland didn't like its blacks handy—if Queensland lynched them for it—then was he supposed to win this match, or not? It was a question gnawing at him when he ducked between the taut white ropes. Still consuming him when the copper's eyes bored into him on his corner stool, warning him away from handiness. And paralyzing him until the instant his opponent, a red-haired chunk of a lad, was announced as "our own Johnny Corbett."

Owen knew then what he had to do to win. Could guess, too, in a general sort of way, what the Silver Gloves would cost him. He bent and spat into the zinc bucket, his pulse hammering in his neck. Then the lad rose to stand lean and tall and black beneath the blazing lights, which multiplied his shadow in four directions. All fear evaporated. This was the moment he had been born for, oh yes. His Old People hadn't made him into a man for nothing. Owen made sure the newspaper fella was watching and swung to face the baying crowd. He whooped loudly and slammed his gloved hands together above his head. "Second round," he called, "I'll lay your Queenslander out in two." The room howled as Owen turned back to look Johnny Corbett fair in the eye. There was no mystery here. The snake in the room was him, and by Christ he was ready to strike.

———————

Owen survived the retribution that followed his victory. He went home a hero, stunned by the new kinds of violence in the world, and refusing point-blank to satisfy any of Mr. Lewis's questions about his shattered face, his bloodied legs. He had understood early in the night that the price of his life would be silence. And when Owen died, a very old man in a house far away to the south, there were seven decades of agony caged in him, held down by liquor and a steely pride, and by various acts of bastardry his family could never quite manage to forget. But he had held one thing dear. Since the night the sergeant locked the cell door behind them, laughing with the other white men waiting there, nobody—not his wife, nor his brother, nor any of his descendants—would ever see Owen Addison cry. He had left his tears behind on the cracked cement floor of a Queensland watch house.

PART ONE

LESS IS LESS

Chapter One

A stranger rode into town, only it wasn't a stranger, it was Kerry, come to say goodbye to Pop before he fell off that perch he'd been clinging to real stubborn way for so long. Cancer, Ken reckoned, never mind cancer, ya couldn't kill the old bastard with an axe. But ah, no good. The call come last night. Get yerself home, chop chop.

Kerry dropped into second as she cruised past the corner store, clocking the *whitenormalsavages*, a dozen blue eyeballs popping fair outta their moogle heads at the sight of her. Skinniest dark girl on a shiny new Softail, heart attack city, truesgod. So yeah, let's go for it, eh, you mob. Let's all have a real good dorrie at the blackfella du jour. Kerry resisted the urge to elevate both middle fingers as she rode past the astounded locals, past the produce store. Past Frankie's Mechanical. Past the vacant lot with its waist-high weeds hiding a generation's worth of fag ends, torn condom wrappers, and empty bottles. Past the landmark pub, which hadn't changed in a century and wasn't about to start now, thanks very much all the same. And when Kerry had made it to the other end of Main Street, that was about it for Durrongo ("Place of Centrelink fraud," according to Ken), population 320. Now, as ever, if you wanted anything more complicated than a beer, a bale of hay, or a loaf of last week's bread from Kath at the general inconvenience store, you had to make tracks for Patto, half an hour up the highway.

As Durrongo petered out, Kerry throttled back. She stopped at the T-junction of Main and Mount Monk Road and straightened first one stiff leg, then the other, letting her toes point skyward in heavy black leather boots. Twenty thousand bucks of American heritage engineering shifted in her hands as she did. Right boot out: a small tilt to the left. Left boot out: a small tilt to the right. Then, in a futile gesture towards flying under the gossip radar for at least the afternoon, Kerry turned the bike off. Silence expanded around her. She flipped her visor up and flinched, late December bouncing straight up at her off the tar. Eleven in the morning and already the road soft beneath her boot heels. Sweat broke out on her forehead as she gazed around the empty intersection and the paddocks beyond it.

"Been a fair while," Kerry murmured to nobody and to everybody. "Been a fair old while." She let out a sharp bark of laughter. There was no telling what today might bring, or who might be alive at the end of it. Same as any other fucking day in Durrongo, in other words, only more so.

———

Three waark flapped down onto the road beside her, drawn to the flattened remains of a king brown, which looked to have lost a fight with Scruffy McCarthy's cattle truck.

The birds stared at Kerry, cawing obnoxiously before they turned to their snake, and promptly ripped it in half. The biggest crow seized the open-jawed front end of the carcass and hopped with glee to the grassy verge. Hungry, it plunged hard into the rotting head, seeking out the reptile's soft brain, and then looked up, totally baffled. The fanged snake skull had gotten wedged hard onto the bird's beak. The crow shook its head, first in surprise and then in anger, but to no avail. Kerry watched, fascinated and appalled. Would the crow manage to free itself? Or would the mundoolun have the last grim laugh, its hard, tiny skull locking the crow's beak shut until the bird starved to death? The eaters and the eaten of Durrongo, having it out at the crossroads. You don't see old mate Freddy McCubbin painting that, do ya? Talk about down on his fucking luck.

The other crows noticed their companion's plight.

"Hahaha, looks like a mutant, half a bird and half a snake," mocked the one on the left.

"Are you sssssssssssstuck?" asked the other, falling about with delight at its own wit.

I'm not the only one in Durrongo plagued by arseholes then, Kerry noted.

"Yugam baugal jang! Wahlu wiya galli!" the luckless crow complained. *My beak's no good. You could help a bird.*

Kerry looked around the deserted road.

"Yugam baugal jang! Buiyala galli! Yugam yan moogle Goorie Brisbanyu?" *You could help, instead of sitting up there like a mug lair from the city.*

Kerry looked around again. The waark hopped up and down in rage.

Then the second crow chimed in, dripping scorn.

"It's no good to ya, fang-face. Can't talk lingo! Can't even find its way home! Turned right at the Cal River when it shoulda kept going straight. It's as moogle as you look."

"How the hell do you lot know where I've been?" Kerry retorted. Back in town five minutes and the bloody wildlife keeping tabs on her already. The second crow preened as it gave her a self-important sideways glance.

"Us waark see all that happens. We see the platypus in his burrow at midnight. We see the dingo bitch in her lair under the new moon; we see—"

The third crow butted in, impatient.

"Oh, shuttup ya bloody blowhard. Make me sick, truesgod! Old Grandfather Pelican went and told our aunty second cousin he seen ya get lost at the bridge. Goodest blackfella!" The third crow sharpened its beak on the bitumen in contempt. Kerry turned to the trapped bird, pulling her hair up into a tight ponytail to get it off her neck. Because Jesus Christ Almighty, the heat.

"I'll help if you fly up here," she offered, tapping her handlebar. The other crows instantly began to shriek in alarm.

The snake-crow tilted its mutant head at her.

"Gulganelehla Bundjalung." *Speak Bundjalung*. A test of good character.

"Bundjalung ngaoi yugam baugal," she said. *My Bundjalung is crap*. The bird hesitated.

"It's a trap, a trap, a trap!" the other crows screeched.

The sun beat down on four black heads as one minute passed, and then another. Kerry shrugged and kicked the Harley to life again, the enormous vee-engine booming like a bitch over the thistle-studded paddocks.

"Well, suit yerself, bunji. I'm not sitting here getting cooked to death."

With a last suspicious glance at her, the crow took two fast hops and then was airborne. Its so-called friends took off as well, bullying each other all the way across the paddock to the dead gum standing by the creek.

Kerry sat for another troubled moment, feeling certain the crow was going to spend several hideous days before starvation claimed it. But she hadn't ridden three hours to worry about a doomed waark. She was here to deliver her final goodbye to Pop, and then fuck off quick bloody smart back over the border to Queensland, well away from anything resembling Durrongo.

————————

Revving the throttle, she looked straight in front of her, down a long gravel driveway to the house that jack shit built. It huddled beneath the spreading arms of a large leopard tree. Same old fibro walls. Same old iron roof with rust creeping into a few more panels each wet season. The lawn bore a lopsided Mohawk from where the mower had died or been stolen or where Ken had run out of the minimal motivation he'd had to begin with. Gazing at the front veranda where the old nickel bath used to live, Kerry felt her scalp begin to itch. She hauled her helmet off and scratched furiously at her sweaty head.

Ken still hadn't replaced the busted louvre beside the front door. More accurately, Kerry squinted, he'd replaced it with a strip of roughly hacked ply, and this had become a permanent memorial to the window his stubby had flown through upon discovering a $125 council parking fine in the mail. The offending Falcon stood in exactly the same spot Kerry had seen it last Christmas. Beside it another two old bombs kept the rusting XD company. Kerry guffawed. Jerry, she thought, still scratching the long-dead nits of childhood, they shoulda named him Jerry—everything the prick does is Jerry-built. My biggest blue-eyed brother. Such a fucking boon to the tribe.

Suddenly not caring about the local gossips and their hurricane tongues—for she would be long gone this time tomorrow—Kerry revved the Hog. In their distant gum tree, the crows cawed in mocking response. Kerry revved the bike again, louder, and gave an evil grin. That's a warning to yez all. Big dorrie locals, paranoid crows, flattened brown snakes, the big brothers of the world. Or maybe it's just a real deadly welcome home to meself. Cos ready or not, here I come. She threaded her helmet onto her left forearm and released the clutch. Plummeted down the drive to where Pretty Mary was continuing her life's work cursing the inhabitants of Durrongo, as if anyone with two eyes in their head to see with couldn't have told her the fucking place was cursed to hell and back already.

In Sydney, Martina closed her eyes, not believing what she'd just heard from the state director of sales.

"Tom," she said very carefully, "I'm really not that interested. Things are going right off in Metro South, so thanks but no thanks."

"Eight weeks, Martina. Ten at the most. It's just till Jim Buckley's replacement wraps things up in Auckland. You could probably even do it from Byron. Come to the party, and I promise you, you'll be at the top of the list of applicants for the next Metro agency."

Martina paused. *Applicants! Supplicants* would be a better word. There was a limit, however, to how often you could say no to senior management. Fuck. Tom had no idea what he was asking of her.

"I heard Glen Plummer's retiring."

Martina opened her eyes wide. Glen had owned the premier real estate agency in Sydney's inner south for thirty years. She did some rapid mental arithmetic as her pulse quickened. Two months exiled to Shitsville for an outside shot at her dream.

"The boss smiles on team players, Martina."

Martina grimaced. She'd never been an arselicker. But for a chance to buy her own agency, she'd pucker up with the best of them.

"Eight weeks, tops. And Buckley pays my airfares and accommodation."

"Good girl. I knew I could count on you. We'll need you there Monday."

———

Kerry shrugged off her blue backpack and apologized to the terrified ginger cat crouching under Ken's car. Poor puss. But the noise of the Harley didn't worry Elvis one bit. A small cunning mutt of no discernible heritage, he raged at the bike from the top of the stairs, finding it a worthy adversary. When he recognized Kerry, Elvis leaped off the veranda and beat his half-a-tail wildly in greeting, all the while conspiring to get past her and piss on the bike's front wheel. On his third attempt, the dog nearly made it, hopping sideways on three legs with the fourth poised high in anticipation. Kerry whirled to head him off at the pass. Stymied, but with the cork already out of the bottle, Elvis ended up spraying the length of her leather boot instead. She screeched in disgust as she flung him away from her. "Go piss on ya owner's boots, ya dirty little unit," she added. Elvis made landfall heavily and ran yelping towards the chicken pen as Ken appeared at the back door.

"I see Elvis has left the building," he observed.

"Small-dog syndrome. Has to mark everything he sees." Kerry lifted her drenched boot to demonstrate. "The dirty little cunt."

Ken laughed as he took in the extremely interesting fact of his baby sister on a late-model Harley. "He's got anger issues," he said, raking his fingers through his mullet.

"Show me someone who don't, brah, and I'll lick their crack for em," Kerry joked.

Ken leaned over the veranda rail, six foot two and heavy with muscle from years of basketball and footy. Sweat glistened on his corded neck. Enough had already trickled south to turn his navy tank top, fresh that morning, to a clammy charcoal. Kerry squinted up at her oldest brother. He'd stacked on the weight since he got out. Now, with his long flat nose and graying hair, Ken was looking more like a giant overgrown koala every time she saw him.

"Bugger me, two visits in a year." He grinned, his busted teeth showing. "Stalking us now are ya?"

"Don't get used to it." Kerry was climbing the stairs.

Ken nodded down at the Hog.

"Might have to take this for a burn."

"It's hot. I flogged it on the Goldie last night," Kerry said, deflecting his suggestion and pushing past him to dump her backpack on the kitchen table. Safe in full view. Beside the fridge an upright fan was blowing a gale of hot air around the small fibro house.

Kerry looked around at the changes in a home where nothing ever, ever changed. A narrow hospital bed had been squeezed into the lounge room, beneath the louvres that looked out onto Scruffy McCarthy's bull paddock. So Pretty Mary had moved Pop back indoors, then. A notorious snorer, Pop had been exiled for decades to the Viscount caravan that sat out the back, rusting beside the chook shed in a forest of dockweed and fourth-rate yarndi.

Home at last, thought Kerry. Great godamighty, he's home at last. Though Pop had appreciated the privacy of the caravan, he had never quite felt it reflected his status as patriarch of the mob. Now, nearing death, he was back squarely in the center of things, with everybody knowing his business. And I wonder just how well that's going down, Kerry mused.

Upended beside the empty bed was a red Crazy Clark's crate, piled high with pill packets, betting slips, and Homebrand ginger ale cans. Form guides and well-thumbed racing mags littered the sheet and every other flat surface. On the TV leggy thoroughbreds were walking around a saddling yard.

Just inside the back door a *Watchtower* magazine lay on the kitchen table, untouched inside its clear plastic wrapper. Kerry picked it up and gammon crossed herself with it for Ken's benefit.

"Bless me, Father, for I'm a lezzo and a crim!" she laughed.

"Don't let Mum hear ya say that," Ken warned. "She's gorn natural-born Christian again."

"The JWs in Durrongo, ah, fuck me roan." She tossed the magazine back onto the table and began unlacing her boots. The smell of her feet would give a baby a nosebleed, but that was too bloody bad.

"It's all go round here, I tells ya. There'll be quinoa salad at the pub next," Ken answered, deadpan. "Keep that door shut, will ya? The flies are gonna carry this feed off, the dirty little black shits," he added, returning to the stove.

"Got one of them for me?" With her chin Kerry indicated the stubby holder in Ken's left hand. He was on beers, thank Christ. Her brother hesitated for a split second, a hesitation so brief it would have been invisible to anyone not a Salter. Ken wanted Kerry to drink with him, naturally, because he wanted everyone to drink with him, all the time. If, in this particular instance, Kerry drank with him, it added unspoken weight to the fantasy that being on your third beer at eleven in the morning was nothing remarkable, something anyone—even your little sister—might do. But on the flip side, there was only half a six-pack and one single solitary tallie in the fridge, with payday two days away, and both his credit cards maxed out since who could fucking remember when. A third, complicating factor was the distinct possibility that Kerry, who had come into possession of a Harley-Davidson Softail since he'd last seen her, might have arrived bearing gifts. Hard cash, even. And so Ken hesitated.

Suddenly overcome with irritation that he had to be hospitable when he was on the bones of his arse, he grabbed a stubby from the fridge. Without warning, he flicked it backhanded to Kerry. Acting on pure reflex, she jerked sharply sideways to keep the bottle from crashing onto the worn linoleum; her hands met around the slippery brown glass. Triumphant, she straightened and casually knocked the bottle cap off on the table edge with an emphatic thump of her right fist. *You'll have to get up earlier in the morning than that to fuck with me, mate.*

Ken turned back to the stove.

"Cheers, big ears." As the icy liquid hit the back of her throat Kerry realized how parched she was. Must have been pushing 104 F in the middle of the road, arguing with them bloody waark. "Fuck, that hits the spot. Judge Judy home?" Kerry meant her mother.

"She took Pop up to see the specialist." Ken was stirring ham- per on the stove and swatting furiously at the half dozen flies that had slipped inside with Kerry. "His head was shocken again last night."

Ken's ancient blue Falcon stood not five short steps from the veranda; the spiderweb of its permanently busted windscreen was visible from where Kerry sat. As a former captain of the Patto footy team several years running, Ken had an understanding with the local constabulary and usually got away with trivial shit like that.

"On the bus." Kerry's voice was flat. Dangerously so, since Ken had long held the monopoly on anger in the Salter family. But Kerry didn't give a rat's. She couldn't see Ken busting her up today.

"Yeah-on-the-bus." Ken swung around fast and eyeballed her.

He's literally twice my size, Kerry thought, instantly on high alert. But it's okay. Chill. He's only on beers. A spot of bright yellow grease dropped from Ken's spatula onto the floor. "So fucken what?" he challenged, chin thrust forward, the ropy veins in his neck beginning to swell.

If a person was anything close to smart, she'd backtrack now, kowtowing all the way. Yes, sir. No, sir. Three bags full, sir. But Kerry had been away in the city, hanging with a crew of hardheaded Logan dykes.

"It's a million bloody degrees out there."

Death stare from Ken.

Why did I even come back? Why put meself through it again? Am I some sort of simple bitch?

"She won't ride in my car cos the brakes are shot. I fucken *offered*!"

Ken scowled, then—luckily—noticed the grease spot. He grabbed a paper towel from the sink, and Kerry looked away to the photos on the TV cabinet, all telling their ancient family-approved lies. A sepia Granny Ruth as a young woman, smiling wide on her father Chinky Joe's arm, long before she was claimed by the flooded Richmond River. Dad Charlie, all of twenty, in his khakis, off to Nui Dat. Herself and Ken and their cousin Chris at a supermarket booth in the nineties, skinny brown kids in school uniforms. Kerry's younger brother, Black Superman, a throwback on their father's hip, so dark the pair of them looked like a different breed altogether. Mum, very beautiful at an early Lismore show, back when she really was Pretty Mary. Donna, the palest of the litter, with that fair skin that used to make Dad Charlie joke about the milkman leaving more than just full cream milk behind. Ken, young and fit in a trophied state basketball team. His lad, Donny, holding a surfboard on a rare weekend trip to Bruns. And off to the side, Donna again, blowing out birthday candles; a dead ringer for Amy Winehouse and sixteen forever.

"Air-con's gone in the Falcon anyway. They're better off on the bus, day like this."

Ken could have driven Pop himself, left Mum home, but no. *Arsehole.*

"Whatever."

A rigid silence fell. Kerry leaned against the kitchen doorframe. She used a pointed purple fingernail, one last memento of Allie, to shred the label on her beer bottle, seesawing between impotent rage and guilt that she had left her mother to suffer in Ken's orbit for so long.

"The ambulance took em." Ken turned the stove off and flapped a tea towel in a hopeless gesture at driving some of the heat out the screen door. "Ya think I'd put em on the bus when the poor old prick's on his last legs? Jesus, gimme some credit."

That was the thing with Kenny Koala. You could never be quite sure which version you were dealing with.

"Yeah, yeah, yeah." Kerry plonked herself down at the kitchen table and pushed aside a stack of betting slips and *Watchtowers* to clear a space. She idly flicked through the tarot pack Pretty Mary kept handy for daily consultations. Should I, or should I not, fuck off back home to Logan right this minute?

"So how bad is he?"

"Driving me up the bloody wall. He's demented. Keeps asking the same thing over and over again until you're just about ready to knock him on the head yerself . . ."

Kerry glanced up from the Ace of Cups and the Tower. Christ. Look in the dictionary under self-centered.

"I meant, what do the doctors reckon? How long's he got?"

Ken laughed mirthlessly.

"*Keep taking these for the pain, Mr. Addison.* Could be weeks, could be months. He coulda checked out half an hour ago and be lying in the ambulance doing the dead man's tour of Coolie. It's all a bloody bingo game, eh. He just wants to get his bets on, or sleep. Can't blame him, the poor bastard. Except when he wants the same bet on forty fucken times a day."

Ken plonked two sizzling plates of hamper and onions on the table and slid one towards Kerry. Then he added bulk bread, slathered with Norco butter. No mystery where them extra kilos had come from.

"Mmm. Heart attack on a plate. Yer good for something after all."

Ken grinned. "Who loves ya, baby?"

"Fuck knows. I ask myself that on a regular basis."

Ken was nonplussed. "What's happened to Allie?"

Kerry wolfed her feed, blinking away the sudden threat of tears. She didn't want pity. Much less scrutiny. And she especially didn't want Ken on her back about her seriously fucked-up choices of the past few years. Ah Christ.

"Brisbane Women's. On remand."

"Fuck sake!"

"It's all gotten kinda . . . complicated."

"Have another bad hair day, did she?"

Uncharacteristically shame, Kerry didn't look up from her plate. Allie had made the papers two years ago for putting a Woodridge hairdresser in hospital ("I *told* the dumb bitch not to take too much off"). Then, several weeks ago, exactly as predicted by Pretty Mary, Allie had graduated in spectacular fashion from hot-wiring Commodores and felony assault. Kerry had lain in bed every night since and flashed back to Allie's pale blue backpack flying over the tall hedge between them, seconds before the sirens started up. Manna from heaven, except for the price, which was steep, and cruel, and as unexpected as the backpack itself.

"I fucken wish. She went off her meds and decided to knock over the Springwood TAB with Tyrone's replica. There was cop cars at Maccas. She's lucky they didn't blow her fucking head off."

Kerry now had Ken's undivided attention.

"Armed rob? Yeah . . . I can see that being *complicated*."

They both laughed in disbelief.

"It's fucking hectic as," Kerry said.

"You in on it?" Ken asked coolly. Kerry gave him a look.

"I told ya. It was a brain snap."

The wrinkle lines around Ken's eyes had fanned out, longer and deeper than they were last Christmas, Kerry saw. He was getting old fast, the way Goorie blokes did, especially in little shitbox joints like Durrongo. Deep into middle age at thirty-five, decrepit at forty-five; you do the math.

"Armed rob ain't as easy as people like to make out," announced Ken. "Blokes think, oh, I'll get a shottie off some dude in a pub, turn up and do the job, and fuck off quick without anyone getting killed. But there's a lotta preparation involved, if ya doing it right. Them cunts that buy a gun in the morning and pull the job that afternoon, they're the same blokes ya see, year in and year out, in the visits room at Grafton, waiting to see their kids."

Kerry gazed at her brother. It never ceased to amaze her how men could flap their gums and have absolutely no doubt that women would hang on their every word. That everything coming out of their mouths was pure genius.

"What's the lawyer reckon, anyway?" Ken continued.

Kerry held up one splayed hand and kept shovelling kai with the other. Ken winced. Sucked his teeth.

"I'm guessing that ain't five months."

Her mouth full, Kerry swung her head wordlessly from side to side, a sad Ekka clown. Ken sucked his teeth again. Five years made his pissy little stretches seem like nothing at all.

"Fuuuck. That's all kinds a crazy. But at least you're still out walking around." He paused for a long, thoughtful slug of beer. "Bloody nice bike you got ya hands on." Did you dog her, he meant. Roll over to the cops then take the bungoo and run south on a shiny new Softail. Kerry smiled bitterly. She wiped her mouth, then gestured with her fork to the window, the big world beyond it, precious freedom stretching every direction you could look. So long as she stayed under the radar.

"I didn't know fuck all about it till the lawyer rung up. She just had one of her stupid bloody bipolar episodes."

Ken folded a piece of bread in half and popped it in his mouth, considering Kerry's dubious claim to innocence. When he spoke he was abrupt.

"Ya sound like ya bailin' on her. Youse split up?"

"We're not splittin' up," Kerry retorted angrily, although they were. Allie's last phone call had winded her.

Nah, bitch, you put the pedal to the metal and fucked off on me. It's ride or die, remember?

"I just . . . Five years is five years, eh? It's a bloody long time. And she might even cop more . . ." She stared down again at the smears on her plate. The words sounded nonsensical, spoken aloud. Five years. How could Allie possibly stay in the one place for five years? As if she'd suddenly turned into a house, or a tree. She belonged in the world, cuddled up behind Kerry on the Hog, or sitting on a forklift at Aldi, shifting pallets of soft drink and baked beans. Dancing up a storm at The Beat of a Friday night. Her arrest and all that came with it felt like some gigantic stupid mistake, fixable if only they could explain the misunderstanding to the magistrates and gunjies of the world. If only Allie could see she'd had no choice but to cut.

"Without a scrape? Welcome to my world." Ken had a talent for losing girlfriends.

"It's a long time without a partner, full stop."

"Long fucken time to be sitting in the big house worrying where ya missus is, too."

Ken was getting proper goolied up. He'd done a lot more time than Kerry over the years. Lost his missus and kids over it. Jealousy had undone him. The mind games the screws played, the bullshit gossip of the other blokes sending him to any number of wrong destinations, like Google Maps directing them Jap tourists into the cool blue waters of Quandamooka. His anger was misplaced, but Kerry couldn't bring herself to say so. Admitting out loud that she'd been dumped would make it real.

"Long time to be walking around outside waiting for that tap on yer shoulder too," Kerry countered.

"So you were there." Ken pounced. "I knew it."

Kerry laughed him off.

"Black doob don't have to be guilty of nothing to have the booliman after her, brah. Anyway, forget all that. How's the neph?"

Ken stood and snatched a fresh stubby out of the fridge. He twisted the top off and flung the cap at the sink. It rattled for two laps. Kerry froze, and then very carefully lowered her head to start eating again, hoping that Ken would shift his focus to the food, to her chewing, to the harmless movement of her fork and elbow, or something else, anything else, to do with her, and away from whatever Donny had done this time. Oh, I hate this walking on eggshells shit, hate it, hate it, hate it.

"Donald Duck will be asleep. As per usual. Donny!" Ken bellowed down the hallway, before adding tightly, "Lazy little cunt."

"I might take him for a swim later, eh," she said, placating Ken with *might. Should take him* would have worked too. Not *will* though. All actual decisions about Donny, even tiny ones, were Ken's to make.

"Yeah, good luck with that," he retorted. "This place is like a fucking coma ward. Pop in bed with the remote welded to the nags. Mum sits doing her cards and reading about the Second Coming of Christ our Lord, and I'm just about ready to harvest Donny for his organs if the useless prick don't move his arse soon. Talk about Limpet Dreaming."

Kerry laughed. If Ken felt like he was a comedian, he was less likely to lose his shit. Plus the organ harvest thing was pretty funny. She finished eating, put her rinsed plate in the sink, then wandered past her precious backpack and down the hall. She stuck her head in the end bedroom. A tan teenager lay, a corpse on the bottom bunk bed, torn cotton sheet over his bony backside. Overhead, a ceiling fan was threatening to lift the entire house into the stratosphere. Kerry turned it down and kicked the teenager's foot, none too gently.

"Oi. Wake up."

There was no response. A thrill of ridiculous fear ran through Kerry; maybe the kid really was dead.

She peered down at him. Nothing moved. Alarmed, she grabbed him by the shoulder and shook him, hard.

"Piss orf," Donny mumbled, mostly asleep, turning to curl and face the *National Geographic* posters on the wall. Other teenage boys had sleaze and machismo in their rooms. Donny had Invertebrates of Australia and a taxonomy of coastal mammals.

"Nice way to talk to yer Aunt Kerry."

The boy lifted himself onto an elbow and pawed at his face. Two gray-green eyes blinked at her beneath a peroxided fringe.

"Sorry, Aunty."

Kerry sat and put an arm around him. "Ya better be! Give us a hug. Crikey, where's the rest of ya gone?"

Donny stiffened slightly but suffered her embrace. He even put a narrow arm around her shoulder for a second. She sipped at her beer, trying to sound casual. The kid was skeletal. Sunken cheeks. Wrists you could wrap two fingers around.

"You getting up? I'm gonna go jump in Granny Ava's waterhole, chuck a line in. Might even see The Doctor if we get lucky, eh?"

Donny just shrugged a hopeless shrug. Kerry frowned. Donny loved the river as much as she did. Something was very wrong if he didn't want to go there in a stinking hot December.

"Come on," she teased. "Ya worried about eels, eh? Them fellas won't eat much!" Donny bent the corners of his mouth like he was trying to remember how to smile. Kerry stood up.

"I'm not taking no for an answer, lad. I swum in that creek every day for years and look at me!" Kerry made a mock supermodel's pose at him before quickly checking down the hall for any movement from Ken towards her bag. But Donny was flat on the bunk again, eyes shut. At the bedroom door, Kerry twisted her mouth sideways.

"You chuck the snooze button on, then. But I'll be back dreckly to haul ya skinny black mooya over there," she warned.

In the kitchen, Ken was washing up the frypan, sloshing its yellow beads of oil into soapy water. Kerry could have sworn her backpack sat at a faintly different angle on the table. Her stomach churned. Ah, don't be such a gutless wonder.

"You move my bag?" she summoned the nerve to ask.

"Hey?" Her big brother seemed genuinely surprised, then immediately interested. "Why, what's in it?"

The only safe thing was to make a joke of it. Kerry sprang towards Ken, covering half the distance between them in a split second, her right hand extended claw-like towards his face. She hissed like a demon.

"Debil debil business!" she croaked at him in a witch's voice, her eyes weird. Ken took a large step backwards and laughed uneasily.

"Fuck off with that womba shit," he said.

"Nothing," said Kerry in her normal voice, her claw becoming a hand again. "It's just some bits of scrap metal I found. Copper pipe and that."

"Scrap metal my arse."

"Ah, ya got me. It's big fat wads of cash. And ice. All the usual goodies," Kerry said.

"Fuck that shit, I've barred ice from Durrongo. The whole pub knows—they bring it here, I'll flog em silly. Gimme Johnnie Walker any day."

"Show me where I can lift some, I will."

"Thought you promised Mum you were going straight?" Ken said.

"That's right, I forgot. I'm a fucking angel of innocence these days, just ask Allie." Kerry drained her stubby and tossed it in the white swing-top bin, where it crashed onto Ken's empties with a tinkle of breaking glass. "She's doing hard time and I'm the one that gets rehabilitated—go figure."

"Whatever floats ya boat." Ken started wiping down the kitchen table. "Just don't let Mum catch ya with a hot bike."

Kerry hooked her hands onto the top of the kitchen doorway and looked out at the bombs clustered beneath the leopard tree. She got it, alright. Since leaving at seventeen she'd barely darkened the family door. Unlike Pretty Mary, Ken lost no sleep about the prospect of his sister doing more time. She knew what his take on it would be: your first stretch was the worst, and Kerry was staunch. More importantly, as far as Ken was concerned, once you left Salter country, once you headed over the Margin Ranges and left Mount Monk and the Cal River behind, well, you were on ya own. If Kerry wanted to go to the city and live like there was no tomorrow, then let her, big brother would have said. He had enough on his plate with a dying grandfather, an anorexic son, and a town that had always had its doubts about blackfellas from the get-go. Kerry could do all manner of crime till the cows came home—all the better, in fact, if it meant she might occasionally have some cash to splash in his direction back over the border, down Mexico way. That's what he would have said, if she'd cared enough to ask.

"Well, I'm gonna go visit them Old People," Kerry said.

"We're outta milk," Ken told her, "and a bottle of Jack wouldn't go astray, neither."

"Yeah, no worries. I'll wave me magic wand and pick up a few ounces while I'm at it," Kerry said, heavily sarcastic. Let Ken think she was cashed up and that'd be it. She grabbed her backpack, well aware of his gaze following her all the way down the hall into the bathroom. She sat on the toilet lid and looked at the bag's light blue nylon panels and tight-stretched seams. The ancestors stored their most precious things in secret tree trunks and on distant cave ledges. Was there a hollow log anywhere in Durrongo that she could trust? Kerry weighed the bag in her left hand. There was no simple answer. For now, wherever she went, the bag would have to follow.

Chapter Two

Martina glanced over from the steering wheel and instinctively knew to ignore the call flashing on her iPhone. A client who was almost ready to sign was a pretty damn delicate animal, but if she knew anything about real estate after fifteen years in the game—and she most certainly did—it was when to pick up a call, and when to keep the buyer waiting just that little bit longer. It was a gift. Some agents had it and some didn't. She'd definitely call the Marsdens back—in a half hour. Long enough to get their juices really stirred up about buying on the fabled north coast of New South Wales. Long enough that they could convince themselves just that tiny bit more that the crumbling weatherboard house at the base of Mount Monk, well over an hour from the nearest beach, was exactly the sea change they so desperately wanted it to be. She'd seen it all. Ex-husbands lying to ex-wives. Current wives lying to current husbands. Adult children selling parental homes out from under frail, bewildered pensioners who had no idea what was happening. In comparison, this deal was a straightforward *caveat emptor*. If the Marsdens didn't have the common sense to realize that a country creek was a force of nature that rose and fell with the seasons, well. Not her circus, not her monkeys. Oh, she'd satisfy the law, technically, murmur something nonthreatening about the way the creek—*Of course you realize*—came up from time to time. But not until they were well fastened on the gleaming silver hook of the Far North Coast, and far too in love with the half-rotted ruin to back away from the deal. Which was now approximately twenty-five minutes away, in her estimation.

"You just hold your horses, my friends," she told the flashing screen. "*Martina* will decide who comes to Durrongo Shire and the circumstances in which they come." There was no need to exert herself too much. The Marsdens—him an electrician, she a teacher aide about to deliver a bawling sprog any tick of the clock—were schmucks from Gloucester with a battered HiLux and a dream. She would make less than four grand on the house they were buying, as she had explained at length to Jim Buckley last week. Martina was doing Jim a giant favor even listing the bloody dump, considering he couldn't sell it himself without the Corruption Commission sniffing around. That's one house signed already out of five—*I told you they'd get snapped up, and anyway, you're not in Newport now,* the mayor had retorted. More's the pity, she thought but didn't come out and say, since technically being given temporary management of the Patterson district office was a promotion. *Technically.* Two months and she'd be back on Sydney Harbour with a corner office and never have to risk looking at another bloody Brangus again. She might have started out-country, but those days were far behind her and she had the Prada sunnies to prove it.

Martina drew hard on her cigarette and wound down the window a crack to blow smoke outside. The white swirl was gone in an instant, and as it cleared, she noticed a young hitchhiker on the far side of the two-lane highway. She noted the shape of the man's wide shoulders beneath a camo rucksack, and the way his thighs curved below his yellow and blue footy shorts. Young and built for action. If she'd been going the other way she might well have made an exception to her rule—no hitchhikers and no freeloaders—and stopped. The man had a gym body, high cheekbones, a mass of light brown curls spilling from beneath one of those silly straw cowboy hats they sold at music festivals. The basic Aussie spunk, before screaming kids, middle-aged spread, and general disillusion with life set in. She liked the red straw hat too, that light touch. Oh, we could make beautiful love, my friend. She laughed at the man in her rear-view mirror. You know we could. You can leave your hat on, cowboy. Yee hah!

Her phone flashed again. It was Will. The next three seconds were consumed by an unfavorable mental comparison of Will v. The Hitchhiker. Blond and English had never really been her style. And the Essex accent that had at first amused her was now beginning to seriously irritate.

"Hey, baby," Martina purred.

"Hey, what's happening in the boondocks? You still the only wog in the village?" Will asked.

"The only Homo sapiens in the fucking village, more like. I miss you, honey. I need my man beside me." Martina laid it on with a trowel. "When are you coming up?"

"You know I booked Watego's for Boxing Day. It's going *off* down here!"

"A fortnight's way too long, babe." Martina pouted. As Will began to argue, her phone showed a second call interrupting. The Marsdens, yet again. Martina paused and stubbed her cigarette out before tossing it. She rewound the window and made a fast decision. It was time to reel these suckers in.

"Gotta go sell a house, babe. Call me in ten to congratulate me."

She hung up. Will wasn't going anywhere. Neither were the Marsdens, for that matter, but four grand was four grand, and she wasn't in Patterson for the good of her health.

———

Kerry floated on her back in the Caledonian River, looking skyward through the limbs of Granny Ava's hoop pine. The oldest tree on Ava's Island was a giant, throwing shade across the entire width of the river. All the years Kerry had been away, this place was where her mind had flown to. Many a night at Trinder Park or at Brisbane Women's Correctional Centre had really been spent beneath Granny Ava's pine. Not dozens, or hundreds, but thousands of times she had come in her imagination to this spot on the island where the fruit bats nested and where cormorants perched on fallen logs, their wings high, surrendering to invisible enemies. The family had practically lived here when Granny Ruth was still around. In and out of the river all day long. Cooking snags on little fires; yabbying and fishing the summer away. Taking fallen blossoms and pretty shells to Granny Ava's grave, hidden in the forest alongside where her husband, Grandad Chinky Joe, lay with only a plain piece of granite to mark his passing. And none of them knowing, back then, that Granny Ruth would be lost to the Richmond River in '91, and would never lie here beside her parents the way she should have.

Kerry gazed up at the geometric shapes made by the crossed branches of the hoop pine and the neighboring gums. Around her she could hear the swirling fresh water brushing against the river stones before it spiralled away downstream, and the *pock pock* of native frogs deep in philosophy. If anywhere had healed her, it was this place; the Salter holy water flowed past Mount Monk and Durrongo, on down the flood plain through Patterson, and then across to the ocean at faraway Brunswick Heads. Her native church was built right here of rock and sand and feather and bark and moss. Bless me, Father, she thought as the water lapped her temples, for I have gone to the city and sinned there, and then sinned some more by not returning home. Not that she believed in sin. Not really, not like Pretty Mary did. People did what they needed to to survive, that's all. Or what they thought they had to. Sometimes it was good, and sometimes it wasn't. And sometimes the planets went berserk and a little blue backpack sailed over a hedge into your waiting arms, and everything went to the shithouse, real fast.

On the bank opposite, Donny squatted on a boulder, throwing twigs into the water and watching them bob on the current that would turn in another hour and begin drifting back downstream to the distant coast. Kerry could clearly see each of her neph's individual ribs where they met his jutting vertebrae. Squatting there blond-headed with his knees under his chin, looking into the water and shadowed dark by the eucalyptus, he looked like a photo of some skinny old-time desert blackfella. But Donny wasn't gaunt from desert genetics and drought. He was just an innocent bag of Goorie bones looking for a reason to exist. Kerry felt a surge of something like hatred for Ken. But you can't *make* somebody love their kids. Can't grab a forty-year-old thug and shake paternal feeling into him. And the thinner and weaker Donny got, the more harshly Ken would judge him. If the lad was a tattooed car thief with a smart mouth and a police record, Ken might take him to the pub, show him off with an arm slung around his neck. But Donny was a social liability in Durrongo: too quiet, too gentle. Too interested in insects and birds, until the time Ken had thrown all his ornithology CDs on the fire one June morning in a rage, calling him a piss-weak little white cunt who needed to get a life. After that, Donny shrank into his computer, where he was safe, and where Ken couldn't reach him with his sarcasm. A computer was a coffin you crawled into to wait for death, Kerry thought, consumed with guilt that she had not been around, even after Pretty Mary rang in a state and told her about the CDs. But she was here now. She would make the kid come swimming and fishing, and for long rides on the Harley, force him to be in the world. Hug him and love him up until he remembered who he really was. Until he somehow found somewhere it was safe to be Donny.

Untroubled by any such human angst, a magpie carolled from the next bend, and was answered by its mate standing on the grassy bank, watching Kerry turn with the current.

"Donster!"

The boy looked up at her.

"That magpie—male or female?"

Donny didn't need to look.

"Daughter to the other one."

Kerry laughed in genuine delight. "You da man, Donny. You da man!"

A faint change in expression; something in the vicinity of a smile.

"Real pretty here, eh, punyarra jagan? Don't ya reckon?"

Donny shrugged, then changed his mind, nodded. "Yeah. It's nice. Peaceful."

"Them Old People's looking out for us; I can feel Granny Ava watching. I'd be here every day if I was you, growing gills."

Silence. Kerry waited a few moments, then rolled facedown to hold her breath as long as she could, watching the blurry wet world go by beneath her.

The bend on the river was the most sacred place the Salters knew. Right there, she thought, where the shadow of the hoop pine is blackening the water and the sand. That's where Granny Ava swam to save two lives, and made it, and now here we all are. If there had been no hoop pine root there to pull herself out of the river by. Had the resident bull sharks been less agreeable that day. Had the horses of the dugai been more willing to enter the cold August water. Any of these, and there would be no Kerry floating in the sun, gazing down at the silver flashes of school mullet beneath her. No Granny Ruth, no Pretty Mary, no Ken, no Black Superman, no Donny, no nobody. There's a pretty simple lesson, then: when the men with guns come after you, you go and you go fucking hard and you don't look back. Kerry remembered the moment she first heard her great-grandmother's legend. Nine years old, in the corner of the front veranda, forgotten, with her head in a comic book. Aunty Tall Mary, who was helping to shell peas on the front steps, had been talking about the Yugambeh massacres farther north. How the mob feasted by invitation on poisoned flour at Mudgeeraba, and how these days butter wouldn't melt in the white descendants' mouths.

They shot Granny Ava, Pretty Mary had cried out bitterly. Used their muskets on her and made the river run red, but she kept going, oh, she was a strong old girl that one, truesgod, and lucky too. Her Dad knew, see. Old King Bobby. He looked after her. Sung that necklace they give him and made it a weapon. Take more'n muskets to stop that clever old fella. Granny climbed out alive on the island with his song around her neck. Picked up a big rock and chucked it over the water, telling them dugais to go to buggery. Stood there bleeding onto her own dirt, swearing em proper, trying to make em swim across to her. She always said that if she was gonna finish up she'd finish up on her own country facing the dugai square on. She wanted em to see her face at the end, see. But they give up before she did. Scared of a bitta cold river water. And lucky for them they was. Lucky for us too, maybe.

Lucky, both women had agreed over the shelling of the peas. And Kerry sat puzzled in the corner, thinking: How is that luck? To be hunted down and shot. To face certain death armed with no more than a rock and a charmed necklace. Where does luck come into that?

There was more.

Them dugais took off but they left their mark that day, see, Pretty Mary whispered. She ceased her shelling to grip the steel bowl tight in two hands, rocking back and forth with it clasped between her knees. Cos Granny Ava was big belly with Mum that day, ready to pop, and when Mum was born that night, the bullet marks on Granny come out on the baby. Come out in the pattern of the Union Jack. Mum wore the mark all her life. And now us Salters are scarred by that musket forever, Pretty Mary said sorrowfully. She let go of the bowl and used her index finger to mark the dust of the window glass beside her. Dab. Dab. Dab. Twelve small smudges to imitate the queen's flag.

True? asked Tall Mary, astonished.

Truesgod, Pretty Mary confirmed.

It's not right, said Tall Mary fiercely. *They never ever paid for it! Never! Somebody gotta pay!*

Branded like bullocks was all Pretty Mary said.

In the corner, Kerry had stared into her comic as she tried and failed to grasp this new story. She'd always understood that Granny Ava hadn't really died. She was the bend in the river. She was the grave lying deep in the forest behind the giant pine. Was the tree itself. She was the presence constantly invoked whenever an example was required of discipline, courage, tenacity, culture. Granny Ava would have. Granny Ava never. Granny Ava would be rolling in her. Now, suddenly, this shocking picture of Granny Ava being shot by dugais expanded to fill the pages of Kerry's book, the air around her, the veranda. It tangled in her head, until she had to push it away and make it a lie, or else explode with the knowledge.

Ah gammon, I don't believe ya, she cried from the corner, with the bluntness of a clever child.

Tall Mary sucked her teeth in alarm. *Too much lip, this little gin!* she observed.

Pretty Mary, the world's most modest woman, startled at the realization that she had been overheard and gave her daughter a strange look. Then, horrifyingly, she put down her bowl of peas, pulled up her dress, and yanked down her knicker elastic to show her daughter the mark that appeared just once in every generation. Kerry saw a neat familiar pattern marked out on Pretty Mary's brown skin, a crossed rectangle of purple blotches, and then gazed out across the paddock, feeling strangely disconnected from her body and knowing that nobody at school would ever, ever believe it. "God Save Our Gracious Queen." She had heard Principal Taylor sing it under his breath as the faded blue cloth with the Union Jack in the corner jerked up the tall steel pole every Monday morning. That day on the veranda Kerry learned the reality about being a Salter; it was not simply that you were black, and different, but that the differences couldn't even be spoken of sensibly. You could tell the gospel truth to white people and be thought a crazy liar, and there was no way of bridging the gap. Some things could never be told. Some secrets could hardly even be held inside your nine-year-old mind.

I was born with it, like Granny Ruth before me. Donna too, said Pretty Mary quietly. *So best you believe it, bub. Cos it coulda been you wearing the dugai brand all ya born days.*

For weeks afterwards, Kerry stared at Donna, wondering where history could possibly have marked her sister that she had never noticed in nine years of sharing a room, a bath, very often a bed. Something stopped her asking outright, though. It was as if, having once been proven wrong by a softly spoken mother, there was nothing that she couldn't be wrong about. Her sister could be revealed as a werewolf. Her brother could turn out to be a black snake. It might be better to watch in silence and think things through; words were dangerously powerful and nothing much good came of them.

Kerry flipped over now in the gentle current of the river, gasping for breath. As her heart slowed, she lay floating easily again, a bony black starfish, and she listened. Midday shone hot on her face, until behind her eyelids she saw only a red blur. Her T-shirt billowed up around her stomach, exposing her black undies and making her glad that she'd picked the most isolated of their childhood swimming holes to jump in the river and think. The Harley was parked on the opposite bank near where Donny squatted. Her jeans were draped over the seat, and the backpack was hooked safe in view on the handlebars. For the first time since she'd crossed the New South Wales border that morning, Kerry felt at ease. There was nobody but her and Donny around for at least a couple of kays, the distance down the secret dirt track that led to the highway.

Above her, giant blue gums soared high on either edge of the river, their hollow branches tantalizing her, completely safe but completely inaccessible too. There were weathered stumps all around in the scrub, though. Dozens of them, left over from the dairying days when pasture was suddenly infinitely more valuable than eucalyptus, and the broadaxes came out swinging with a vengeance. Kerry shifted to tread water, making her own mark in the surface patterns of the river. Her pulse beat fast as she took in the many indistinguishable stumps on the river flat opposite. It could work; it would work. There were enough stumps to make it a viable proposition. She could get a watertight container, tape it up in thick plastic, and bury it deep inside the rotted heartwood of one stump, anonymous among the multitude. Sprinkle the top with fine dirt and weathered gum leaves, then walk backwards sweeping the ground with a branch. Nobody would ever know. Kerry smiled in triumph. She'd come back alone tonight, and make her first and only deposit in the Caledonian River Bank.

"Whaddya reckon?" she called out with sudden enthusiasm, her problem solved. "Beat Warcraft?" Donny was shivering on his rock now, arms wrapped around his sticks of legs for warmth. "Hey, go stand in the sun before ya die of pneumonia and we hafta go to all the trouble of digging ya a hole next to Granny."

"Aunty," Donny obliged, crabwalking sideways into the sun, "how come they didn't bury her in the cemetery?"

"Cos this was her *home*, bub," Kerry answered, startled by the idea of Granny resting anywhere else but on her island. "Grandad worked so long for the Nunnes I think everyone probably turned a blind eye, no pun intended. She had to be here, same as Dad and Grandad Chinky Joe—and Pop too, when it's his time. Ya gotta go back to where ya from."

"I thought Pop didn't really know his own country."

"Well, no. But sometimes a country kinda grabs a person, see. And this place grabbed him through Dad Charlie marrying Mum. Pop come up here from Rivertown and just never went back south again."

"Can ya get buried anywhere, then?"

Kerry squinted at Donny. Was the kid thinking about doing himself in?

"Nah. But back in them days, if an old Goorie up and died in the bush, see, nobody in town would've cared much. So Granny Ava and Grandad Joe got away with it. And with Dad Charlie it was ashes, and you can scatter them anywhere—so long as nobody knows."

Kerry paused. Donny hadn't even been remotely thought of when Dad Charlie had clutched his chest in the kitchen and fallen in 1999. Ken had already chucked school to play basketball for the Brisbane Bullets on weekends and party hard on the Goldie all week. Pretty Mary blamed Donna for her husband's death, but sometimes Kerry wondered how much of it was really down to Ken. Dad must have been waiting for the night Ken would disappear too, shotgunned by the bikies he was buying drugs off in Surfers, or murdered by the Westville KKK. And the strain proved too much in the end, Dad crushed by overwork and heartbreak at fifty, leaving Pretty Mary alone to raise her and Black Superman. Pop Owen had done what he could to take his son's place, but ah, how could he replace Dad Charlie? How could anyone? Kerry swam slowly across the river to Donny, and despite the heat of the day she shivered off the guilt, the questions. Dead was dead, and that was the end of it. Don't look back. She gestured at a golden wattle in blossom.

"Let's get some flowers to put on the graves, eh?"

Kerry was climbing out of the water to do just that when a trio of cockatoos rocketed, screeching, out of a strangler fig. A dog barked in the distance, and then Kerry heard the faint buzz of a four-wheel drive barrelling along on the gravel track. *Fuck*. Dugais coming. And her precious bag just hanging there for anyone to grab. She clambered over the slippery rocks, hurrying, but fell heavily in her haste. She gave a cry of pain as her elbow met hard, hot granite.

"What's up?" Donny turned to ask.

"I've got warrants out. Quick—move!" she urged, flailing at him in a panic with her good arm. She would have to leave the backpack where it was on the bike and pray not to be robbed, not to be dis-covered trespassing on private land, wrapped up in her suspiciously black skin.

All there was time to do before the 4WD burst noisily around the corner was drag Donny into the thick undergrowth. The two of them hid together behind a large gray stump, hidden by masses of lantana and high crofton weed. Scratched on her legs by lantana stems and bothered by insects she didn't dare swat, her elbow on fire, Kerry lay on her wet stomach and watched in dismay as Jim Buck-ley pulled up in the clearing. His late model LandCruiser ute was decked out with all the expensive shit: roof racks, snorkel, the top-shelf type of square towbar, and fat white-inscribed tires that each individually held more tread than all of Ken's tires combined. Along the ute doors ran the spray-painted legend: *Jim's Conveyancing, Earth-works, and Development*. A pigger bitch grinned bossily in the tray. She was a pedigree hulk of a dog, supremely confident of her place in the scheme of things, a confidence that was only mildly shaken when Jim and his passenger—a fifty-something bloke in expensive cream trousers and a John Deere cap—got out and wandered off without unchaining her.

Kerry's gut tightened.

The men strolled across and puzzled over the Harley. Jim stared at the bike in clear affront, then flipped up the legs of Kerry's flaccid jeans. John Deere Cap made a crack about a shallow grave, and both men chuckled. Lucky, Kerry thought, that there's nothing there to tell them I'm female and a very different kind of target. The bag hung from the handlebar, a cheap generic nylon thing, square with the bounty it held. *Oh sweet Jesus, leave it alone.* Buckley paused, looking without touching. Holding her breath, Kerry caught some commentary about "trespass" and "development approval" before the men wandered off to inspect the river. Keep walking, you dumb cunts. Surely, *surely*, they would have to notice two sets of wet foot-prints on the grass, or on the rocks she'd fallen on just a minute ago.

Yet all they did was gesture—well, Jim pointed and John Deere Cap nodded—and squint around at the scrub. Could she breathe yet? Was it safe? (It would never be safe, not with outstanding warrants for possession and assault of the police.)

"Good water, mostly clear land. Run forty head, easy," said Jim. "Maybe fifty. If it's cattle you're thinking." He looked curiously at the man. John Deere Cap didn't reveal his position on cattle. Instead he assessed the slope of the land and looked repeatedly at the slim silver tablet he held in both hands. Then he muttered something indistinct. Jim's forefinger promptly described the hilly boundaries to the north and east. John Deere Cap nodded and made some notes. Then he lifted the tablet, plonked his elastic-sided boot against the broad base of the green sign informing the world that the island opposite him—Ava's Island—was state forest, and began taking photos. Kerry clenched her fists around sharp stalks of gritty lantana and wished John Deere Cap dead on the spot. Wished both the dugais dead.

If they'd seen her the men would have puffed up with the word *trespass* in their mouths, but her Old People had Law for trespassers before any dugai ever trod these river flats. And if intruders didn't heed a fair warning you buried them with their jinung sticking out of the good red earth. Couldn't make it much simpler than that. If Kerry had a machete she'd send a message too, cut off that dugai foot defiling Granny's land. She'd hack it off and chuck it to The Doctor for her afternoon tea. Shove the rest of John Deere Cap back in the ute so his flowing blood couldn't meet this country's spirit, and fuck both of the men off, onetime. Peering through the delicate blossom of crofton weeds, Donny made a face at her: *What the hell? Why are we hiding?* Kerry put an urgent finger to her lips. *Keep quiet, lad. Not a peep.*

She caught a phrase from John Deere Cap: "the position on rezoning." Jim propped his hands on his hips and smiled, real happy way. He looked like it was the kind of phrase he was very fond of.

Buckley licked his lips and Kerry suddenly wondered what had become of Russ, the giant cane toad that used to inhabit Pretty Mary's outdoor dunny.

Never mind bloody toads. She could sense a catastrophe unfolding in front of her, and her throat grew tight with unscreamed objections. What did these mongrels want near her Granny's land that needed words like *rezoning* and *development*? There were no happy answers to that. Kerry's fear caught, high in her gullet, and she had to hold her hands hard against her mouth to stifle a cough of terror.

On the back of the ute, the pigger bitch gave a high, impatient bark, and was ignored.

"Well, new business is what we're all about in Durrongo," Jim encouraged, walking the buyer farther around the river bend towards the scenic spot where Mount Monk became clearly visible in the distance. "Great spot for a B&B, quiet getaway . . ."

"And they're asking, what, a million?" the man asked, as if he didn't already know. Wiping sweat off his brow with a freckled forearm, Jim looked carefully at John Deere Cap.

"Without the DA, one point two. Assuming the DA goes through—and it will—you'd be talking closer to two mill," Jim said easily. "That's fully fenced, remember. But you'll need to go through my associate, of course."

"Not with the fences my client wants," the man said with a wry smile, but didn't elaborate.

Black spots swam in dizzying constellations before Kerry's eyes. Was her bag safe? Was the island? Was anything? By the time they had given the pig dog a few hard blokey claps on her ribs, pulled roughly at her ears, and climbed back into the ute, the visitor was adding to his copious notes. Jim started the engine, ran the air-con. Gotta keep the buyers happy, Kerry thought sourly. Go on, then, git. But Jim wasn't quite done. He opened his door.

"Just gotta take a leak," he said. "Won't be a sec." Kerry watched in disbelief as Buckley walked past their hiding spot, unzipped himself and pissed a long yellow ugly stream into the middle of the translucent river. As he pissed he shot inquisitive glances about him, left and right, searching for where the Harley rider was. He pissed for what seemed like minutes. The stench drifted to where Kerry was crouching in anguish. Oh Jesus. Let a branch fall and split his ignorant skull, right here, right now, she prayed. This country's fed you, watered you, and this is how you repay it? Granny Ava! Grandad Joe! Are you watching? She met Donny's horrified gaze and had to stretch out a hand to stop him from leaping up and shoving the mayor of Patterson off the bank into the widening circle of his own disgusting piss. But she couldn't let Donny intervene; she was paralyzed by her warrants.

Clearly Granny and Grandad weren't watching, for when Jim Buckley was zipped back up, he had no reason—no limb-split skull, no vengeful mundoolun sinking its fangs in his leg, not even a marauding horsefly—to stop him strolling back over to the Harley. Helpless, Kerry could only watch as the mayor casually lifted the blue backpack off the handlebar and in the same smooth movement eased it silently into the back of his ute. John Deere Cap was still deep in calculations on his tablet. The pig dog sniffed at the bag once before turning her back on it, lofty with disinterest.

"Sorry about that, but better out than in!" Buckley joked, and accelerated away with a final curious glance at the Harley. The red dust kicked up by the LandCruiser filled the clearing.

Swearing, Kerry sprinted out, dragged on her jeans, and jumped onto the bike, telling Donny to wait for her, she'd be back. With her helmet on and tinted visor down, she could catch Buckley and steal the bag right fucking back, lift it out of the tray and then outrun him. She'd show Mr. Mayor who was the boss thief around these parts, truesgod. Kerry raised her weight high, then sank to kick the bike over, but as she did, the sole of her wet bare foot slid impotently off the kickstarter, the metal bar raking hard against her ankle. She roared in agony as she hauled her right boot on over the fast-reddening scrape. But even with the boot on, kick as she might, the bike simply refused to start. She tried again and again, kicking until the engine flooded, and she fell away in disgust. When she pulled her boot off she discovered a line of red drops had oozed their way along her ankle and begun running to meet each other in a fat red clump at the back of her heel.

Exhausted, Kerry fell onto her hands in the dirt, staring in disbelief at the grass. Her precious stash, whisked away in an instant. The Lord giveth and the Lord taketh away, blessed be the name of the Lord. For white is right, and possession is nine-tenths of the law, they reckon, and a great vertiginous gulf now yawned between her and the blue bag. Jim Buckley didn't just own the mayoralty and the only real estate office in Patterson. He owned the cops and the local magistrates. He owned the town of Patterson, or he thought he did, and when an old dugai in moleskins and a blue shirt whose great-great-grandfather had been the second white man to ford the Caledonian River in 1859 thought he owned something, then by and large that old white man generally did. Oh, she'd fight him for it. She wouldn't give up, no way José, but it was going to take a mighty fucking effort to get the bag back once Jim Buckley unzipped it and looked inside. Kerry didn't much like her chances of getting to it before Jiminy Cricket went laughing all the way to the bank.

It was two minutes before Kerry staggered to her feet, enraged with the unfairness of the world. Ignoring her burning elbow, and her ankle, and Donny's rapid-fire interrogation, she watched the red cloud of dust sinking along Settlement Road. The LandCruiser had disappeared, but the dust particles lingered before they fell, slow and weightless, turning the grass beside the track to ochre, and changing the Harley from sleek black to a dirty, speckled roan.

One point two mill.

Assuming the DA goes through—and it will.

Great spot for a B&B.

Kerry stumbled to the river's edge with strength she didn't have and kneeled on the ground in the shade of the hoop pine. Help me, she prayed across the river to the graves of her ancestors.

Help me.

Chapter Three

When Kerry got back, full-to-busting with the indignity of Jim Buckley ripping her off in broad daylight, Mum and Pop were already home from the hospital. A bad sign, she thought, chaining the Harley to the Hills hoist just in case Ken or any of the local kids got any silly fucking ideas. Cos if the quacks can do anything for you, it takes forever, not a half day and then home in time for *The Bold and the Beautiful*. They'd wanted to keep Pop in, Ken reported, but Pretty Mary had kicked and screamed until they agreed to let her take her father-in-law home to die. Pop was already asleep in front of the muted TV. Clear tubes ran from his nostrils to an upright oxygen tank on the lino, still littered with yesterday's betting slips. His battered old body needed a sheet over it even in December, Kerry saw, because the weight had fallen off him since last year. His cheekbones stuck out, horribly prominent; his frail arms were like charred sticks after a bushfire ripped through.

She went cautiously to his side, afraid of waking him—afraid, really, that he wouldn't ever wake again. Pop looked like Auschwitz, or Rwanda. Last Christmas he'd hauled himself up, with much ordinary pensioner complaint, and gone outside to the punching bag. Put up his dukes and shown the jahjams what a former Silver Gloves champion looked like. Now he was reduced to this pitiful remnant, and Kerry realized what staying away all year had cost her. You wouldn't call them close—Pop had little time for females and none at all for queers—but he was still the only grandfather she had ever had. When he went, a huge slice of her childhood would be carved off and fall into the void. Kerry stood and looked down at the old relic, put a hand on his arm, unsure of everything she felt. Sadness, yes. But relief too, and something like fear. Who would they be, the Salters, without Pop around? Who would take his place?

"Took you long enough to show ya face," Pretty Mary greeted her daughter acidly from the kitchen table. "Did ya suddenly remember that old highway to hell goes both ways, did ya?"

"Yeah, I love you too, Mum." Kerry grinned. "Nothing like being overwhelmed with fucking love 'n affection after a year, is there?"

"Ya after affection ya might want to show ya face round here a bit more often, my girl."

Prone on the lounge with a longneck, Ken guffawed. He was at the stage where he wanted to be the jolly green giant. A couple more tallies and he'd begin to slur, telling incomprehensible yarns, and then getting dirty over any imagined or actual slight. But he wasn't quite there yet.

Kerry knew from long experience that there was no winning an argument with her mother. To Pretty Mary she was and always would be the Great Abandoner. Shame enough to turn out a dyke, but her far greater sin was the empty hole she'd left behind her in the family. Even in the terrible dark shadow cast by Donna's disappearance, Kerry had still up and left to live among whitefellas and city people. Sharper than a serpent's tooth, blah blah de-fucken-blah.

"I've had a lot on my plate too, ya know. How is he? What'd the doctors say?" she asked, kissing her mother's lined cheek and taking her empty coffee cup from her. Pretty Mary half rose and checked that Pop was indeed fast asleep. Then sank back down and wearily straightened her tarot deck.

As the kettle hissed in her ear, Kerry heard the news she had expected.

"How is he? He's *dying*. The hospital give us morphine today. To inject him with."

For a moment Kerry thought her mother was talking about killing the old man. Putting him down gently. Her second thought,
hard on the heels of the first, was: Just as well Ken's drug of choice
isn't morphine. If the hospital had prescribed malt whisky to ease
Pop's last days they would have been in trouble.

"How long?"

"Oh, they never know. A week. Two if he's unlucky, Dr. Carlton
reckons." Pretty Mary shook her head and stared out at the leopard
tree. Two inches of pure white regrowth showed along the center
parting in her auburn hair. One of the many tiny revelations that
come with death, thought Kerry: the small slow disintegrations of
what is normal.

"I drew The Tower four times yesterday. He ain't gonna see
Christmas."

"So that's it, then," Kerry said, shaken even though Ken had been
blunt enough on the phone last night. Soon she would have no
grandfather, no sister, no partner.

"Is the morphine working?"

"It knocks him out," Pretty Mary conceded. "But he's gone back
such a long way. Rivertown mish and all the stations. Granny Ruth
and Dad Charlie and even old Granny Ava all bin visiting him. He
thinks I'm Donna, sometimes." Her eyes filled and she looked away.
"God, it's not easy, bub, I tell ya. I wish Granny Ruth was ere ta
help . . ."

Kerry felt a lump in her throat that didn't want to be swallowed.
Pretty Mary's face crumpled into her hanky.

"Not bloody easy when he wants his winnings from a bet he
never put on, for a horse that was never foaled, in a race that wasn't
run, either," Ken added, sitting up suddenly on the lounge. He flung
himself about in imitation of a demented, bedridden Pop. *Where's
my bloody winnings you pack of thieving bloody black mongrels?*

Pretty Mary and Kerry began to crack up.

"He sits there watching them races, and whatever bin cross that

line first, *Oh! Oh! My horse won—quick, Ken, quick—where that slip?*"
Ken was choking with laughter. "*It was right ere in me hand, boy!*"

Pretty Mary flapped at Ken, trying to shush him, but it was no
good. Her shoulders were quaking.

"He ain't lost a single bet since the Melbourne Cup!" Ken roared.

"He genius punter or what!" Pretty Mary cried, giving in.

"Pop reckon 'e proper millionaire now!" Ken howled, tears
streaming.

Kerry leaned forward onto the table, quivering with the effort to
hold in the laughter. Each time one of them found some composure
a loud snort from someone would set everybody going again. She
was gulping for air, having all sorts of trouble breathing. And then, of
course, Pretty Mary's laughter turned to torrential tears, and Kerry
was somehow all of a sudden squatting down beside her. She rubbed
her mother's narrow back awkwardly.

It wasn't meant to be this way. Mum was the rock, the backbone,
the shock absorber for them all. The bad-alcoholic-turned-teetotaller,
never flummoxed by disaster because there was always a precedent
somewhere in her vast memory bank from her drinking days. Someone, somewhere, had always been through it before, whatever *it* was.
And when you lose a kid, she was fond of saying at least once a week,
you know nothing can ever be any harder. You know the world has
chucked what it's got to chuck at you when you've lost your little girl.

But now Pop was dying slow and hard, and they had no precedent for that. It was a time for plain unvarnished sorrow, and for
remembering, and for crying out to the world that Donna should
have been there to say goodbye to her grandfather too. Her absence
was a sorrow doubled, and so Pretty Mary cried in Kerry's arms
twice over while Kerry looked past her mother's head at the gleaming horses on the television, going round and round forever in that
distant, greener world. Was this who they would be without Pop
around? she asked herself, shuddering. Was this who she would have
to become? Her mother's keeper?

"Here we go. This is the three-bedder plus study I was telling you about," Martina announced, pulling up in front of an ugly brick bungalow on the undesirable southern edge of Patterson. "Brick, very low maintenance. You'll have no problem at all renting it out on this street—"

She pointed at the nicest of the neighboring houses, expertly directing attention away from the rusting gutters of the bungalow, and from the dead-end road that was legendary for Friday night burnouts. The clients, three sisters from Ballina with middle-class aspirations and a deposit, looked dubiously at the rusting mesh fence and the thin bottlebrush trees in the front yard.

"Come inside!" encouraged Martina, striding up the driveway and not batting an eyelid as she stepped over a six-foot brown snake that chose that very moment to slither over the cracked concrete and into the long grass next door. "The carpet's dated, but the floorboards would polish up beautifully. And the bathroom isn't too—"

She gave absolutely nothing away. Her patter didn't waver, her gaze didn't shift towards the long grass, nothing. The snake had never existed. There was no such thing on the planet as a brown snake. Mesmerized, the women followed her inside.

Pretty Mary had finished crying. She straightened up and retrieved a hanky from the pocket of her homemade dress. She blew her nose hard before homing in on Kerry. "We was hoping you mighta made it down for Pop's birthday. For a change. In the circumstances."

And heeeeere comes the guilt trip. The Pretty Mary Special, hello, old friend, long time no see, just not long e-fucken-nough. Out the back door Kerry caught the late afternoon sun glinting off the perfect curves of the Softail. Her mother was right. That old highway to hell *was* a two-way street. She could chuck her leg over and gun it back to Queensland, warrants or no warrants. Be home in just under three hours, easy. But no. She had her blue backpack to retrieve from Jim Cunting Buckley first.

"I'm such a bloody bitch of a daughter. I don't know what I was thinking, going to see Allie at court," she agreed sarcastically. Then, to divert her mother's attention: "Where's Black Superman? I thought he was flying up." Black Superman was her best ally. He'd listen to her about Allie, and have good advice on the kleptomaniac mayor too.

"Here by tea, he said," Ken answered. "He took them jahjams to Sandy Beach. Hire car. Must be nice to have that big gubment dollar, eh."

"Well, there ya go, the three of us all be here tonight, then," Kerry reassured Pretty Mary, careful not to make the unforgivable mistake of saying that all of them would be here. The phrases *all of us* and *everyone* had been instantly banished in Grade Nine. A small constellation of friends and rellos circled constantly about the shack—and by the sound of Troy Cassar-Daley blasting from the caravan, cousin Chris was back with them again—but the absence of Donna Zoe Salter must never, never be allowed to be far from anyone's mind, or there was hell to pay. Lest we forget, insisted the gold writing beneath Donna's fridge photo, when forgetting was all Kerry ever dreamed of.

"You lay off ya brother!" Pretty Mary rounded on Ken. "He helps me out plenty without making a big song and dance about it. And he's got them kids to worry about now too, poor little buggers."

"Never said he didn't." Ken was implacable, reaching for a handful of Homebrand salted peanuts. "Just said it must be sweet to have bungoo to chuck around, that's all. Trip to Bali last year, gym membership. Hire car whenever ya want."

Must be sweet to sit on your mooya getting free rent too, thought Kerry in silent amusement. Ken was forever resenting Black Superman, the miracle of his education, his state government job, his

fly-in-fly-out relationship with Mum and Pop. The way he got to
be the good guy with the presents and the bungoo. Ken's own ad-
vantages in life—his status as oldest son, the free rent, Mum's endless
help with Donny, his sickness benefit for the acquired brain injury
that meant he never had to talk to a job provider again—all these
were magically rendered invisible by Black Superman's govvie job.
To Ken, his younger brother was and would forever be the Spoilt
One, the one who had it good and didn't even realize how lucky his
black fork was.

"How *is* Allie?" Pretty Mary asked severely as her phone began
buzzing and spinning on the table in front of her. "Ken told me she
went and got herself blooming locked up again. She's a one-woman
crime wave, that girl, truesgod!"

"She's 'right," Kerry hedged. "Her cuz Rihanne's in B block with
her, so she's all good. Well, not *all good*," she added, catching Ken's
expression. "But she's getting on with it."

"Christmas inside," said Ken, shaking his head and crunching
peanuts. "That's the pits, that is."

Kerry agreed, trying not to think of the many empty Christ-
mases ahead. In the week after Allie's arrest, Kerry had fantasized
about getting herself locked up too, but there was no guarantee
with her warrants she wouldn't be shanghaied to New South Wales,
and then where would she be? And just as well she hadn't martyred
herself. Allie's phone call had been lacerating. *I don't wanna hear any
more fucken sob stories. All bets are off. Move on.*

Kerry stared at the peanut shells on the sink, blanking out.

"Maybe now you'll think about changing ya wild ways, and I'll
tell ya why," Pretty Mary lectured as she pressed the buzzing phone
to her chest. "Breaking the law's not all some big joke, my girl. Steal
the eyes out of a blind cockie's head, you lot would." She put the
phone to her ear. "Durrigan the Wise, hello. Yes, oh that's right, darling. I remember you, love, two moons in Aquarius. We do the Palm
Valley night market, and Patto—not the farmers' market—and Lis-

more every fourth Sunday. Otherwise by appointment. Okay, lovely. See you then."

"I did change my ways," Kerry retorted, coming to life and putting fresh coffees on the table. "That's why I'm down here and not in Brisbane Women's." She shook her head, wondering in what possible universe her mother might not have reams of useless, generic free advice to dish out. Every day, every waking hour, never telling you when you'd done right, only where you were going wrong, and when to pull your socks up quick smart. The only person she ever refused to judge was Pop, ironically enough, since if anybody in the history of the Salter clan ever needed judging it was the old one-eyed bastard dying in the next room.

"I bin hunting this customer mob away with boondies lately," Pretty Mary announced with satisfaction as she added an appointment to the Koori Knockout calendar on the wall. "Just as well too. Pop's funeral insurance ain't gonna stretch far."

"Centrelink should cough up towards that," Kerry told her, wondering if Ken had gotten in their mother's ear about his suspicion she was in on an armed rob. Nah. He'd be keeping valuable information like that close to his chest, where it would do him, Kenneth Edward Salter, the most possible good. She ground her teeth at the stabbing memory of Jim Buckley lifting her bag into his ute tray. She'd get the fucking thing back if she had to waltz into council chambers and strangle him with the shoulder straps.

"Is this Pop?" she asked, turning her attention to the tarot. The cards were laid out on the table as though for a private reading, but Pretty Mary wore no purple veil with silver moon and stars; no long dark wig or red velvet cloak or kohl eyeliner. Today she was the Tarot Reader au naturel, a stringy brown pensioner with her feet in grubby two-dollar thongs and a joint stuck behind her right ear. She wore the same homemade orange dress Kerry had last seen her in on the previous Boxing Day, giving the illusion that she hadn't changed her clothes in almost a year.

"Nah, it's Aunty Val," she said, still focused on the calendar. She rubbed the dying pen quickly between her palms and then shook it, trying to restore it to life. Kerry rolled her eyes. Who the hell among her one billion rellos was Aunty Val?

"Aunty Val there, la. Savannah's mum," said Pretty Mary. She flicked five fingertips impatiently towards the old Hanlon place next door, as though her daughter was simple, running on copper wire instead of fiber optic. Kerry's face hardened. Oh, them. The bogans with the Aussie flag on the gate, the rebel flag of slavery on their F100. Whitefellas. Red sunburn over ugly old tats. Blue eyes like boiled fish staring blind up at a dead sky. Dumb to everything not them or theirs. But normal too. Super, super normal. Whitefellas were everywhere in the shire, everywhere she went. This wasn't Logan, this was Durrongo, where dark skins were few and far between and *whitenormalsavages* ruled.

"Oh, the White Pride Brigade," Kerry said in contempt. "For fuck's sake, Mum."

Pop let out a low groan, coming back to consciousness as his morphine level dropped. Pretty Mary checked her phone. Half an hour to go. The hospital had been very clear about how much to inject and when.

"Five minutes yet, Pop," she ordered. "Turn that TV up, eh, Kenny."

Bored, Ken flicked between channels so fast that Kerry's head began to spin, until he finally settled on a nature program. The sound of whale song prompted Donny to come inside from the veranda, where he had been observing Elvis plotting a fresh attack on the hen coop. Kerry glanced at her nephew.

"Wanna watch Uncle David, my neph?" Kerry urged. Come close. Be part of the family for once.

"Yeah," teased Ken. "Check it out. They reckon there's jobs in whaling."

Donny didn't answer, but to Kerry's pleasure and surprise he plonked down, as far from Ken as he could manage. David Attenborough began explaining the impact of past whaling on humpback numbers with the enthusiasm of someone a quarter his age.

"The industry expanded so rapidly because the worth of a whale carcass in the late nineteenth century was the equivalent, in today's money, of a quarter of a million dollars. The meat, the oil, the blubber, all was hugely valuable. The ambergris, or intestinal slurry," Attenborough went on pleasantly as Kerry made a face, "was used in the manufacture of perfume, and could make a millionaire of a seaman in a day. The rendered whale oil found its way into lamps all over the globe, and the butchered meat—"

Donny blanched, yet he couldn't look away. Whale was his personal totem, and so he was obliged to discover everything he could about the animal, no matter how disgusting or distressing he found it. If Granny Ava were still alive he might have learned to call them in off some coastal headland, Kerry reflected. Mighta been taught them special songs, and all them special whale ways, but Uncle Richard in Lismore had only passed on the fact of the totem, and the lingo name for the animal. It was up to Donny what he did with that in the twenty-first century. Uncle Richard would know more, though, Kerry suddenly realized. He'd be the one to ask for help. Maybe with Uncle Richard's intervention that whale business would be strong enough to drag Donny off his computer and into the world. She'd have a think about that, once she'd gotten her backpack back.

"If they're White Pride someone musta forgot to tell Savannah," Ken boasted, heading past Donny into the kitchen and replacing his longneck with a fresh stubby. "She keeps coming over ere like I've got something to give her. I reckon I might too." He collapsed back onto the center of the lounge with a grin, arms and legs spread wide to assert his sovereignty. King Kenny, monarch of all he surveyed. A scattering of peanut shells bounced on the brown velour as he did so, and he made a half-hearted show of gathering them up, ignoring those that fell into the cracks between the cushions or onto the floor.

Kerry blew a loud raspberry.

"What's that—the clap? Oh yeah, baby, give me some of that hot, sweaty STI action!" she said, moaning and writhing in mock ecstasy from the far side of the kitchen table. Or maybe he fancied giving Savannah a smack in the chops—but she didn't say that part. Nobody knew that she'd run into Ken's ex-before-last at Beenleigh Cash Converters a couple of years back. Turned out hell hath no fury like a Kiwi chick with a missing incisor and no Medicare.

"Ya wanna frang it before ya bang it, Condoman," Pretty Mary advised. "I ain't changing no more blooming nappies, I give ya the drum."

"Clean as a whistle, me," said Ken indignantly to Kerry, before adding with a leer, "and raring to go, what's more."

"Oh, nigga, please!" Kerry objected in disgust.

"Savannah's got more bloody sense than to get back with you," snorted Pretty Mary. She opened a fresh packet of peanuts and began adding shells to her ashtray. "And don't you be so bloody racist, dort. Aunty Val let me bathe Pop in their shower for a month when ours buggered up. You know she's got the big C too, had both her susu off in August and not long finished her radiation. They got it all. I knew they would; there was nothing in the cards."

"Next door fly the bloody butcher's rag on their gate and I'm the racist. Work that one out," Kerry said, with a glance at Pop, tossing and moaning in real pain now.

"They not really racist; they nice enough. S'not their fault they got no culture," Pretty Mary said, magnanimous towards whitefellas as she had never been towards her daughter. "Oh, good on you, son." Small miracles. Ken had gotten up and was moistening Pop's lips with a sliver of ice dipped in beer.

"Everyone on the planet's got a culture, Mum, even if it's *The Footy Show* and Southern Cross tats—it's still a *culture*. Just a shit one. And anyway, why do that mob any favors now?"

"Better now than next month," her mother muttered, glancing

across to fully meet her daughter's eye for the first time since Kerry
had walked inside. Kerry was startled at the pain she saw there. Better before there was a funeral to organize and serious grieving to be
done, her mother meant. And the tarot would be a solace too. Pretty
Mary always thought pretty highly of herself in front of the cards,
seeing the flux and flow of the universe beneath her fingertips. Feeling like there was some plan to it all.

"Whatever. It's—" She came to a screaming halt, having almost
said, *It's your funeral.*

"Turn that thing back to the blooming horses!" erupted Pretty
Mary in sudden fury as Uncle David Attenborough squatted, smiling and whispering now, beside a family of bush stone-curlews.
Ken and Kerry stared, frozen, at the screen. Donny hastily leaped
for the remote and hit the off button—just too late to prevent the
bird's weird call entering the house. Pretty Mary let out a horrified whimper. Kerry felt her bladder contract. Pop groaned again,
louder this time, and Ken glared at Donny like he had just invited
the Grim Reaper inside and offered to sharpen his scythe for him.
The kid stood with the remote in his hand, looking like a rabbit in
a shooter's spotlight.

"It's not his fault!" Kerry exclaimed to the gravely silent room.
But Ken gave no indication that she had even spoken. He sat utterly motionless, his arms spread to their full gigantic width over
the back of the lounge. His blue eyes glittered at Donny in rage.
After an unbearable seesawing moment, where they all waited to
see if Ken would storm to his feet and start lashing out, he finally shook his head where he sat, and everyone breathed out a
little. Kerry hated herself for breathing again. Ya weak as piss, she
told herself. Stand up to him, the great overgrown bullying prick.
There's not all that much more he can do to ya that he hasn't already done.

"Nice one, ya fucking moron," Ken snarled. "Hope ya happy
now. Fuck off outta my sight."

"I didn't know he was gonna . . ." the boy said weakly, before pushing the remote aside and trailing down the hall to his room. The silhouette he made as he walked the corridor was that of a stick man.

"Yeah, you didn't know, Donny!" Kerry called bravely to his back. "It's not your fault, bub!"

"*It's not your fault, bub*," Ken mimicked sarcastically. "Useless cunt." Whether he meant her or Donny, or both of them put together, was left unspoken.

Kerry looked straight ahead at the TV, sick in her guts just like when she was a kid. *Hope ya happy now*, when happy was the last thing Donny was. Oh Jesus. She had to get out of this poxy dead hole. A week or two, her mother said Pop might last. A few extra days to organize the funeral, at the outside another few to see Mum back on her feet. Pretty Mary would be lonely with the old fella gone, but there was always the barrel-chested prick in front of her to be placated and fed, and his victim in the back bedroom. Cousin Chris coming and going with his girlfriend and their little baby girl. Pretty Mary would get over it. The tarot will pick right up without the stress of nursing Pop, Kerry told her conscience, and I'll be home free by the middle of January. Three weeks, absolute max.

Kerry got to her feet, grabbed Pretty Mary's lighter, and went to spark up a spliff in the backyard. She leaned against the chook shed and gazed at the shadows lengthening to long fingers in the bull paddock. If Allie could do five years cold inside BWCC, and if Pretty Mary could happily spend a lifetime in Durrongo, then she could surely put up with Ken's bullshit for a few more weeks. If, if, if. Fingers crossed, on all three counts.

––––––––

Kerry's mobile rang. It was Rocky, fresh out of Numinbah, speeding off her dial, and wanting to con her into a job. Kerry shot a sideways glance at the Harley, took a deep breath. Feel the fear, girlfriend, and say, *Fuck to the no, no fucking way*.

"Nah, not interested. Plus I'm down New South Wales anyway, bunji."

"Yeah, I know. But we got a fucking awesome score, sis. This electrician that me sister's rooting told us about this safe in Sunnybank, Chinaman house. No dogs, one alarm. Thirty grand minimum, between the three of us. And Peanut's got *dry ice*."

"Whaddya mean, ya got dry ice?"

Rocky explained her fail-proof plan. The sides of Kerry's mouth twitched. Rocky had really gone round the corner this time.

"Like I said. Not interested, sorry."

"But we gotta . . ."

"*Sister*—I said no."

Kerry was about to explain why dry ice was a bad idea, when Rocky hung up. Kerry shook her head, laughing uproariously. Dry ice. Yeah, okay, dickheads. That's gonna end well.

Four thousand dollars richer than she had been at breakfast, Martina shook hands with the Marsdens and assured them that waiving the prescribed cooling-off period was definitely a smart move under the circumstances. She pointed Jasmine Marsden in the direction of the Patterson hardware shop, congratulated her yet again on her foresight and energy, then merrily sent the young couple out the door and off into the Divorce Zone. But then you just never knew. Hubby Ryan was a tradie. He might actually be able to do something with the shotgun shack that Martina had glimpsed in her single lightning visit to Durrongo since she arrived. And if the usual thing happened, if Jasmine appeared in the doorway in a couple of years on the verge of tears, wanting to take any reasonable offer to get the hell out fast, it would be just one more commission in the great roundabout that was real estate. Death, divorce, promotions, or lotto wins. All of life's vagaries had one common denominator: fresh listings. A smart realtor could flog off a property at both ends of a marriage and still come out friendly with both husband and wife. Martina smirked down at the countersigned contract on her desk. There were days she wondered if she wasn't simply a very highly paid psychologist.

As she updated her files, and noticed a text from Jim requesting to meet ASAP to discuss the riverfront development, Martina was restless. She was four grand closer to her own agency but still a million miles from civilization. And she was never going to feel at ease in Patterson—another six weeks would feel more like six years. At Newport she and Will could have hit Antonelli's for a slap-up celebration dinner, maybe gone on to the casino or a yacht party where someone would surely have had some speed or coke. Lived a little. Patterson held nothing beyond its two hotels and a passable Thai restaurant, and there's only so much Asian takeaway one woman can eat, Martina told herself. The idea of coke nagged at her, but she was hardly about to go and buy drugs from a toothless bikie at the Top Pub. She gazed out at the street in frustration. The Sugarloaf Bakery (leasehold: $2,400 per calendar month) nestled between Mickelo's Fruit Barn (freehold: $400K give or take) and the Patterson branch of the Bendigo Bank. "It's like being on *Survivor*," she muttered darkly under her breath.

"Pardon?" asked Kylie, the office manager, halfway out the door to collect her granddaughters from netball practice.

"Oh, nothing. Just missing the big smoke." Martina sighed loudly. "And my so-called partner, who can't be bothered to get on a plane until Boxing Day. Serve him right if I get a roving eye."

"Touch footy finals this Saturday," Kylie offered. "Them Grafton boys are a bunch of hot spunks!"

"Fifty shades of mud," said Martina doubtfully. She hadn't stepped outside her room at the Scrub Turkey Motel since she arrived in Patterson, except to go to work and to distant Byron, far enough away to feel like she was in another, shinier world. "I'll bear it in mind."

Boyfriend. She needed a new *boyfriend*; that was the problem. It was weeks since she'd had anything approaching good sex. And eligible men were as thin on the ground in Patterson as talking dogs. Oh, the offers were there, there was never any shortage of *offers*. She had been confidentially informed by Kylie within forty-eight hours of hitting town that, direct quote, all the boys in the office want to chuck one in ya, unquote. Her skin had crawled. God save me from rural realtors. No, that hitchhiker in the hat was the first bloke she'd noticed having any kind of style in Durrongo, the first man she'd seen without either a ragged Bintang tank top or a non-ironic Akubra. God, was she reduced to cruising nameless hitchhikers now? That was a truly depressing thought. She glanced up at the calendar. All she had to do, really, was flog off the remaining shacks in Durrongo, seal the deal on the Patto petrol station, and then warm Jim's seat until it was time to piss off back to Sydney after Christmas.

With Kylie gone, Martina was alone in the building. It was six forty. The shutters were down on the shopfronts, and a few of the cars driving past on Nunne Street had their lights on. She got up and lowered the office blinds. Then she opened her phone and began to swipe left.

Chapter Four

Kerry woke in the top bunk bed. She lay staring at the ceiling two feet from her face. The world outside was dim and cool; the house was unusually silent. Not even the roosters were awake yet. It had been a night of tossing and turning, hearing muffled cries from wildlife in the creek and the scrub beyond. Nightmares of childhood and the BWCC had pressed in on her, locked doors and shaven-headed white men with guns. Now, sleep-deprived, she could hear Donny's steady breathing in the bunk below, and the very sound of him put her tired nerves on edge. Oh sweet Lord, give me coffee, give me yarndi, give me some fucking *space*. She could have happily put a fist through the fibro beside her and not even blinked. But this would be her life from now on. Waking up in single beds, or alone in double beds, with no gorgeous Allie naked beside her. And every bastard in the world always wanting something, taking from her like Jim Buckley had taken, waltzing into her orbit and helping himself to whatever took his fancy, just like whitefellas had always done from the year dot. Well. She was gonna do something about old Jiminy Cricket just the minute she figured out how to not get caught.

Donny began a light, erratic snoring, and Kerry gritted her teeth. She bunched her right hand into a solid mass, drew it back ready to smash the fucken—

She let her arm fall back onto the bed.

Waking up wanting to punch holes in the wall is not a good

sign, she told herself, breathing deeply. Time to take your medicine, girlfriend. She swung her bony legs out and down, slid noiselessly onto the cracked gray lino of adolescence. Three minutes later she jogged up the grassy strip at the center of the gravel drive, Donny's yellow Nikes on her feet.

Out on the road in the dim light, Kerry ran straight over the tarry mark that was all that remained of yesterday's brown snake. She ran strongly, knees aligned, head up, elbows tucked, the way the coaches all said. It came naturally to her. When other kids had sweated and whinged about the cross-country course, she had been the one looking for the finish line, powering up heartbreak hill, loving every minute. Genetically gifted, the coaches all agreed. Black, skinny, driven, she was a trainer's wet dream. Had they realized at all that running was a bulwark against the taunts slung about so casually at Patto High? *Nigger, nigger, pull the trigger.* Kerry would sneer at the white faces mouthing the words—*Abo, black bitch, boong*—and picture their owners wheezing on the edge of the track as she floated past triumphant, her giant banner reading: *Whatever, maggots.* And her indifference—part pretense, part real—meant the insults quickly found their targets elsewhere, in the small handful of other Goories who usually decided to fight back, and who were quickly expelled for expecting a bit of common decency in their lives. The black kids of Patterson High who were there one day and gone the next had drifted off to Brisbane or Sydney or the Gold Coast. You heard their names around the district for a few years, then nothing much more. Locked up, knocked up, or finished up was her guess. Kerry had met girls in BWCC who knew the whereabouts of some. Not that she was looking. Durrongo was best left on the back burner, it and all that had happened there.

After ten minutes of jogging she upped the pace, arms pumping and her upper legs beginning to feel the burn. She ran past a familiar wooden cottage with a *For Sale* sign plastered hopefully on its rotting veranda, and then saw the triple peak of Mount Monk looming in front of her. She would run to its base, no more than four kays, and look up at the creased sides of the rock cliffs she knew so well. It marked you as a true local, the feeling of comfort you got when you saw that familiar outline against the sky and something nameless in you was fulfilled by it. Pop used to love to look at the mountain from the veranda or the paddock. He would examine it in all kinds of light, talk to it, ask it questions and take guidance from it, somehow. It was a kind of old friend, he used to say, for all that his family came from somewhere unknown beyond Rivertown, and he was hardly Bundjalung at all. The mountain had never steered him wrong yet.

As a kid Kerry had noticed that some old white farmers liked to talk about Mount Monk in a hopelessly overfamiliar way. They seemed to need that edge of faint contempt in their speech where nature was concerned. The mountain had always been there on the outer edge of their consciousness, and so they considered it held no mysteries. Pop felt different. He was adamant that a mountain could never be really fully known, any more than a person could be. Oh, when dugais asked him in the right way he might amuse himself, spin them some bullshit about the snake that travelled from the coast and made the mountain, or how it was a black woman on her back or a dingo's skull turned to stone in the Dreaming. Kerry had heard these various stories. She made a point of never asking, though. Asking questions was the worst way to find something out, where Pop was concerned.

One Saturday, she remembered as she ran around a bend that brought the mountain into full view, the family had been shorter than usual of both money and tucker. Tempers were fraying. Pretty Mary was cultivating a migraine and intent on sharing the misery around. *Come,* said Pop, picking up his round tin of tobacco and his Tally-Ho papers. Not for her company, Kerry surmised, and not to further her education either, but to help him carry the catch while the boys were off at footy in Ballina. Nudging thirteen, she must have been. Scrap of a kid, a brown tomboy still looking much like her brothers. After a half hour of fruitless searching through Scruffy Mc-Carthy's back paddocks, Kerry heard the shot. Pop cooeed, Akubra pushed back and the .22 hanging loose in his right hand. A wallaby kicking and seeping red a few steps away. Pop went over and shot it in the head, no mucking about. Kerry hung back from the peppery smell of the gunpowder and the blood mixed together. The awful wonder of the rifle, delivering death to anything Pop chose. She felt a bit sick from it. Why had he even brought her? He never had before; hunting meat was men's work, not that of a girl, a lesser being.

He glanced at where she stood hesitating.

"C'mere. I won't shoot ya."

She stepped closer. Not because she wanted to. The animal lay with its body slack, one ragged bullet hole in the neck and the *coup de grâce* smaller and neater in the head. Flies already buzzing. The single visible eye had glazed over and the mouth was slightly open, showing a row of tiny snow-white teeth. Her stomach made a noise. *I'm sorry*, she told the animal silently, knowing full well that it had to die in order for them to eat. With dinner secure, Pop was happy. He turned Kerry by the shoulder to face the mountain and flapped a hand at the ground. They sat side by side, flicking flies away while he rolled a smoke. In the distance Kerry noticed the rest of the wallaby family on the slope of the mountain, standing upright with their ears pricked in her direction. When she asked Pop if they were going after another one, he said no, no need to be greedy, and anyway he thought he had some work coming later that week from young Matt Nunne. Castrating and branding calves.

It was healthy pasture they sat on. Thick grass. A scatter of thistles. Here and there a eucalyptus sucker trying to claim back the open ground. McCarthy was a good farmer, Pop said. He knew about overgrazing and so this paddock was empty other than for a few dry cows mooching around the creek. The paspalum blades they had walked over were mostly intact, green leaves with near-invisible lines of teeny tiny veins running the length of them, delivering food and water, same as veins did for a person. Or a wallaby. But just here where they had stopped was an obviously nibbled clump, freshly nipped in the last hour or two, likely by the animal Pop had just shot. The grass that had been grown for McCarthy's cows lay undigested in the stomach of the jiraman her family would consume that night. It goes on and on and on in a dizzying loop, Kerry thought. It never ends. The beginnings that are endings that are beginnings again. Was that what Granny Ruth had meant when she said: *Everything is connected up, bub, always, whether you can see it or not.*

Pop squinted at her.

"High school soon."

She nodded, shifting uneasily under his one good eye. Pop liked to yarn with adults. To kids he generally doled out either orders or the strap, not conversation.

"Lotta new whitefellas there. Steer clear of em, ya hear? They're savages. And don't be like ya slut of a sister either, putting herself around."

"Yes, Pop."

Kerry stared at the blades of grass. Probably a better sister would resent Pop's description, but it was true. Donna was well on her way to being the town bike. That wasn't for Kerry. The contempt from Pretty Mary would kill her, for a start. And what was so great about boys, anyway? But Donna was all mouth, all the time. You couldn't tell her anything. Ken survived because of basketball and footy. Black Superman, well, he went his own way, had his own battles to fight, different again that fella. Pop could tell she was only half listening. He batted her upper arm and changed tack.

"That hill there, la. What's 'e look like?"

Kerry tilted her head. The question the whitefellas always wanted answered, the loud ones at the pub with the gammon laughter, the ones Pretty Mary called her friends, and brought home to sleep it off, and whose faces changed the instant her mother turned to the door. If Kerry was honest: wallaby ears sticking up out of the earth. Or a giant frog's eyes peering down on them. She shrugged. It didn't look like any monk, that was for sure.

"Doob lying on her back?" she muttered. Pop grunted. Something had pleased him, but what, Kerry couldn't have told.

"Some say that. Grandad Chinky Joe for one. When I was just a young fella, a year or two more'n you are now, Sergeant Buckley, that's Jim's old grandad, 'e chased me up that hill on his horse." The rifle lay quiet in the grass beside Pop as he yarned. "I runned away from Rivertown mish again, see, needed to get away from Father O. Made it up here and made for the scrub there, la—plenty of places to hide on the sunset side. But Sergeant Buckley, he knew that mountain pretty good for a dugai. He caught me and brung me back to town. Give me a proper flogging out front of the old Patto cop shop too. Main Street. Wanted to bash the black outta me, 'e said."

Pop shook his head.

"By Christ, 'e was a hard man, Bob Buckley." That was something, coming from him. Pop paused, remembering.

"Father O come up from Rivertown to fetch me, and he stood there alongside half the town, watching it, with a big fucken smirk on his face, the mongrel. Nothing ya could do. Black man had no rights them days."

"That's dugais for ya." It didn't make any sense to Kerry. If you were black, you were black. How could you become white from a flogging? If floggings made you white, then Donna and Ken would be albinos. Not her, though, and not Black Superman. She was too little for Pop to want to hurt. And she was nobody's fool either. She prided herself on being able to read the signals, knowing when behind the chicken coop or on the other side of the creek was the safest place to be. She could count the times she'd been hit by Pop on both hands. And Black Superman had something mysterious in his eye that made Pop pull up with him too, so maybe it was to do with color after all; the two of them were much darker than Ken and Donna. It was all very confusing.

Then Pop did yet another puzzling thing. He raised his right arm towards the mountain, as though saluting it, and slowly closed his fist against the afternoon light. He leaned in towards Kerry, putting his head closer to hers than she could ever remember him doing, so that their shoulders met and she was looking directly along the length of his extended arm. The three dark bumps of his knuckles protruded against the blue horizon. As he lowered them she saw that they exactly mirrored the peaks of the mountain behind them. A carbon copy.

"See it?"

Kerry nodded.

"Maybe it was a dog to begin with, or a doob, for that matter. But make no mistake. That mountain's a *fist* now, girl," Pop told her, letting his arm drop. He looked at her in anguish. "It's a gunjibal's fist waiting for us mob to step outta line, waiting to smash us down. We livin' in the whiteman's world now. You remember that."

Pop ground his smoke out against the sole of his boot and stood up, rifle in hand. He looked down at Kerry and something in his expression, some glint of long-buried rage, made her flinch away. She pushed down a sudden idea of his rifle swinging around to meet her fragile skull. Another bleeding hole. Another body on the ground. Stupid. A flogging with the strap, yeah—or maybe the cricket bat for cheeky Donna, bad Donna—but Pop would never have used a rifle on his own son's children.

"Ere." He passed the weapon over, as if to prove her right. Stooped and gutted the wallaby with a few fast slashes of his knife, tossed the entrails into the thick scrub, then slung the carcass over his shoulder. Set off home with blood spatter trailing down his back, and Kerry picking her way cautiously in his wake between grass tussocks and cow pats. She kept the safety on and the weapon pointed at the ground, all the way. Mum's headache cleared up fast when she

saw the wallaby; Ken had got Man of the Match in the win against
Grafton. The stew that night tasted fucking marvelous.

––––––––––––

Kerry rested her hands on her hips as she walked in a sweaty circle
on the cracked and potholed surface of Mount Monk Road. Then
she simply stood, rocking back and forth as she sucked the oxygen
in. Dawn had broken now, and the faint edge of night cool was
all gone in an instant, the heat of the day now only minutes away.
It was December she was pulling into her lungs and no mistake,
and running in it was like running in a rainforest. Three bloody
kay and her ribs were on fire. Too much Harley, not enough foot
Falcon, that was abundantly clear. The legs that fed into Donny's
Nikes were the same bony stalks they'd always been, but skinny's
not the same thing as fit. She tightened her ponytail and wished
she'd plaited her hair before setting out.

   The mountain looming in front of her was different to the dim
silhouette she'd seen from Pretty Mary's front gate. It had turned
khaki, treetops appearing out of the lightless murk, and the sky gone
all pink and gray behind it. Sailor take warning, but nah, this was just
dawn pastels, nothing to worry about. Kookaburras gone quiet now,
and the crows and magpies having their turn at it. The first Coolan-
gatta plane leaving for Sydney was high overhead, a bunch of suits
yawning on their way south to screw the workers that little bit more.
To them that hath, shall be given. From them that hath backpacks,
shall be taken away. And then something wholly strange, a thudding behind her, *thud thud thud* exactly like her own feet a minute
ago. Kerry tensed, instantly aware of being winded and three kays
from home, with only one or two decrepit houses within sprinting
distance. In Durrongo, nobody can hear you scream. Cos they all
too busy screaming themselves, Ken reckoned. She looked down for
rocks to throw in an attacker's face. Go down swinging, always.

   Before she could think or do anything else, though, a moving figure two fence posts away turned into a man running, a vaguely familiar face pale beneath brown curls.

Thirty-something. High cheekbones, fit like a fox. Out running on the same bloody middle-of-nowhere-shit-all-ever-happens-here road as her. And grinning at Kerry as if she was the one person on Earth he had always wanted to meet.

This white man in front of her wasn't full-blood *whitenormal-savage*. Proper dark brown eyes like her own. Color a bit like Donny, that yellow, some sort of wog. Definitely a major spunk.

Turn-up for the books.

"Hey there." The man smiled, slowing down to check her out. He looked to have run a long way already; his jaw and forehead glistened with sweat. Curve of sweet, sweet muscle from shoulder to wrist. A loose white tank top showed as much as it covered. This fella was built for action and speed, all sinewy around the joints like a serious athlete, big in the thighs and shoulders where he needed explosive muscle. A League player? Or a pro cyclist, except here he was on foot in the middle of nowhere.

"Hello," Kerry said uncertainly, rocked by the bizarre tableau. Scrub-covered mountain. Grazing Herefords. Hot, spunky dude chatting her up. What the actual . . .

The man used his tank top to wipe his forehead and Kerry glimpsed the hard ridges of his six-pack underneath it, as she was meant to. When he let the shirt drop he looked straight at her, shameless, his eyes bright with unspoken suggestion. It was a look she knew well: *I'm up for it if you are.* Since she was fourteen, most men had looked at her with either hopeless longing or with anger, but this look was different—it was a bold invitation given without begging or expectation.

If I was remotely interested in white blokes, Kerry theorized, *you might be the kind of white bloke I could get interested in.*

"Coming this way? I'm going as far as the bridge."

Kerry suppressed a grin at his barefaced cheek.

"Nah, I've had it," Kerry said dismissively, but couldn't deny she was burbling-jumping-fizzing on the inside. She used to enjoy this game, before Allie. They didn't need to speak another word, could be fucking like bunnies in three minutes. She half turned away, grabbed a toe and held it up behind her to stretch the quad. Faced home. Swapped legs and didn't make eye contact. Wrong team, pal. And she still held a torch for Allie, anyways, breakup or no breakup.

"Pretty warm now the sun's over the hill." Major Spunk was jogging on the spot. Keep that blood pumping.

"Yeah. Too hot for this black duck; I'm done."

Kerry found that she was pleased to be wearing her best pair of shorts, and to have left Allie's silver ring on the windowsill at home. Ah, knock it off.

"Tomorrow, then. Same bat time, same bat channel." Still happy smiling, good white teeth, teeth from money. Nobody in my family never had no teeth like that.

"I doubt it. But never know ya luck in the big city." Over beside the mountain, a Hereford let out a solemn bellow.

He grinned. "Lucky's my middle name."

"Maybe so, but luck comes in two flavors, last I heard."

Kerry bent and put her palms on her insteps, feeling the slow burning ache up her legs as her hamstrings lengthened. "Got a first one?"

The man laughed.

"Steve. Steve Abarco. And you're Kerry Salter."

Kerry straightened like a flick-knife.

"You don't remember me, do you?"

The memory made her gasp. Arco back then, not Steve. From a teenage time when dignity was in such short supply it had to be scraped from a nickname here, a smile withheld there. He was right. She hadn't recognized him.

"Oh God! You've, ah . . ." Her fingers sketched inarticulate circles in the air. He laughed.

"Filled out, yeah. And lost the Afro. Remember a string bean behind you in Maths One?"

Filled out nicely at that. Those arms. The tantalizing glimpse of a six-pack. Yes. Think about that.

"I do recall a certain annoying string bean, actually. Weren't you a high jumper or something?"

"Good memory. Well, that high jumper found the door to the gym about ten years ago. Mixed martial arts these days." Steve joke-flexed his right biceps and Kerry's stomach flipped. "How the hell are ya? Still in Durrongo, I see. Any kids?"

Kerry laughed. He thought she'd stayed here all this godforsaken time.

"Nah, I got out while the going was good. I'm just visiting from Brissie. And no kids. You?"

"I moved back to Patto a couple months ago to start a business. My little girl's five, but she lives with her mum at Burleigh." Steve Abarco stood there grinning at her with no woman and no plan to stop grinning any time soon. Kerry thought of Allie, three and a half hours' distance and a world away. Locked behind razor wire for the next five years.

All bets are off. Move on.

"Look, I seriously do have to go. My Pop's dying of cancer and I'm just in town to . . . well, you know."

"Shit, I'm sorry—"

Kerry gifted Steve a quick smile as he blurted more apologies, but she didn't wait, was off up the road, really hammering the tarmac now for all it was worth. A pair of wood ducks startled from the creek as she sped past. A family of plovers screamed at her, their incoherent gabble warning of great pain and danger ahead. Her shins ached as she pushed through the air that was obstinately keeping her from home. Oh, she remembered Steve Abarco, alright. The only white kid who had ever had the balls to front the arseholes over *boong, nigger, darkie.* Or *poofter* and *retard,* for that matter. A few of em sucking piss in a group out the back of the Grade Nine disco, three-quarters charged on disgusting Passion Pop and the thrill of turning fourteen. Could have kissed him that night, but he never knew and she never said. And then he left soon after, vanishing just like . . .

. . . but nonono. She wouldn't think about that. That was the last thing she was gonna think about. Fuck you, Arco. That was nearly twenty years ago.

She would get in the shower. Put a hand flat on either side of the cubicle and stick her head beneath the fast-streaming jet and let the beautiful cold water wash them memories away, yeah. Definitely. Wash it away, wash it away, wash it all the fuck away.

———

Fifteen minutes later Kerry stood dripping in the kitchen with a brand-new plan. She had to leave a note, but in her hurry the damp writing pad tore beneath the failing ballpoint. *Christ*. She scrunched the paper angrily and hurled it behind her, sending the orange cat fleeing beneath the sleeping house. She found a blunt pencil stub and began again.

Gotta go home. Back for Xmas. xxx K

The shower had failed to calm her and now she had only one idea: escape. Escape from the hideous images, the shifting, blurring pictures that had piled one upon the other, keeping her from sleep. The harp of Donny's rib cage at the river. Buckley driving off with her future in the tray of his ute. Ken slurring insults at the world, his arms spread wide on the lounge. Pop lying in the next room with barely a breath left in him. And now, suddenly the horror of ghosts running up out of nowhere and grabbing at her with their ghostly white fingers and their six-pack abs and their memories of that long-ago time when Pretty Mary sobbed and Pop raged and— No! Fuck Durrongo. She could wheel the bike up to the road, be gone long before Pretty Mary woke to insist, with her raised voice and her terrible, wounded eyes, that Kerry stay and suffer here with the rest of the family.

Kerry crept barefoot across the kitchen and slid the note beneath a jar of vegemite. To her horror, the overhead fan belting at the hot sludge of air in the room made the edges of the paper flap loudly on the laminex—*shuttup shuttup shuttup!*—until she hastily weighted it down with peanut paste as well. Homebrand junk, more sugar and salt than peanuts. Ah fuck, who cares about peanut paste; grab your stuff and get! Her panic fed upon itself; the idea of staying another fortnight now seemed unbearable. Her petrol tank was full and she had a twenty-dollar note stuffed in her bra. One minute to wheel the bike up to the road; kick it over and be at the highway in another two; then gun the motherfucker hard all the way to the border, home by ten o'clock opening to suck cheap piss with Allie's family until the memories finally went blank. And let the fucking gunjies catch me if they think they're good enough.

In the bedroom, her mother coughed a smoker's cough. Kerry froze, deer in the headlights job, then sprang into action.

She oh-so-quietly picked up her heavy boots. See ya, Pop, she murmured guiltily over her shoulder, see ya on the other side, Old Man. See ya, Pop, see ya, Donny, see ya, Orange Cat, yeah, even you Elvis, ya fucken half-tailed moron. She bent to pat the dog one final time, then slowed, paralyzed by a sudden wave of shame. Ya might never. He might be gone by the time you. And so she crept over to the narrow cot where Pop lay asleep with a betting slip still clutched tight in the dark claw of his hand. Went with her eyes moist, and bent over, and real quickway kissed his dead-straight hair that only Ken had inherited, only . . .

Only . . .

Christ Almighty, no.

Nothing there.

Oh, fuck me no, no, no.

Kerry dropped her boots and let out an indistinct cry. He was gone. Pain rippled through her, hollowing out her arms and legs. Oh no. Oh Christ. For a mad moment she looked around, as though the corners of the room might reveal some answer.

"Kerry? That you, bub?"

No movement. No breath of life. Not much warmth left to Pop's cheek, his forehead, his arm, in stinking December. So he must have been already dead when she left to go running; she had probably bumped into his ghost on her way out the back door. Thank God his eyes were shut and she didn't have to do that thing. His body was exactly the same, lying there. Pop and not Pop at once. Bring smoke, bring earth, bring song, she thought. All that, it was a cliché, she knew; yeah, bring all them things, bring the mob to remember and laugh and to cry, but don't make out like it's for him, for this, this container. He's gorn. Ring all them bells.

"Kerry? How's about a cuppa tea, love?" Followed by more coughing as Pretty Mary tried to dislodge a lung.

Pick me up, said Kerry's boots from the floor. *Put me on and then just walk down them back stairs. You'll be free as a bird. Nothing to it.*

Kerry swayed lightly on the balls of her feet, torn. Pretend she'd seen nothing and heard likewise? Make a bolt for the stairs? Or stay with Pretty Mary in this hardest of hard hours? Standing there beside the body, she had the astounding thought that of all the billions of people on the planet, only she, Kerry Salter, knew that Pop was dead. Of all those billions, she alone held that singular nugget of information. It wouldn't last; only seconds, and the family would begin to learn what she knew. But while it lasted it was very strange. Her particular burden.

Pretty Mary's bed creaked. Kerry heard the repeated clicking of an empty lighter.

"Yeah, hang on, old girl, it's coming!" Kerry called out in panic, not knowing what else to do or say to keep her mother in the other room a few minutes longer and to thereby preserve her innocence.

So. The decision was made. Now she had to stay. She put her boots back behind the lounge and wondered what the hell to do. Would it make a single iota of difference whether Pretty Mary had a cup of tea in her hand when she got the news?

Racing.com was still on as it had been on all night: muted, showing recorded footage. Today's races wouldn't start for hours, but there were talking heads looking serious, and ads for stallion services. Statistics flashing up. What yesterday's winners had paid. Kerry looked at the betting slip Pop still clutched grimly in his left hand and slid it out. Like taking candy from a baby. Race twelve, Warwick. Belle of the Ball had placed fourth and Pop had blown five bucks. Oh, darling. Save that last dance for me.

"Just not your lucky day, Pop," Kerry told him, folding the betting slip—suddenly heavy with significance, the last bet he ever made—together with her own redundant note, and shoving both deep in her jeans pocket. She looked at the clock on the wall. Six forty-five. In exactly one week it would be Christmas.

Chapter Five

A raucous wolf whistle filled the air, and Kerry stiffened in her stride. She didn't look across the road to the pub. Wouldn't give them arseholes the satisfaction. Next to her, Black Superman spun on his heel, shaded his eyes, and then blew an extravagant kiss to the invisible observer, jerking his hand upwards only at the very last moment into two savagely upright fingers. Loud laughter erupted from the Droughtmaster Bar.

Entering the corner store, Kerry glanced up automatically. No cameras. Durrongo really was in a time warp. Behind the counter, Kath, who was fifty-eight and morbidly obese, raised her eyebrows.

"I remember when I used to get whistles, love. You'll miss it."

"*Excuse me.* He was whistling at me, darling." Black Superman drew himself up. Kath grinned, opened her mouth, then discovered she had nothing to say and shut it again.

"And our Pop died four days ago—ya think I need some random dickhead telling me how much he likes my tits?" Kerry said as she went to the fridge.

"Oh, sorry, darl. I heard. It won't be the same without him. Never go down the pub without seeing him having his bets on."

"Thanks." Kerry pulled a twenty out of her bra for two loaves of bread and four liters of real milk to replace Pretty Mary's Sunshine powder. It was already not the same. Pop's cot had been collected by the hospital, and the gap in the lounge was filled with Brandon and Lub Lub's toys and kiddy mattresses. Racing.com was a thing of the past; the TV was welded, now, to the cartoon channel, or the reality shows Ken loved to hate. And the smell of an old man slowly decaying had been chased out by the determined puffing away of Pretty Mary, Aunty Val, Savannah, and Black Superman, who were trying to outdo each other in their race to exhaust the world's supply of tobacco.

"Mum's durries," Black Superman reminded Kerry, dragging two fifties out of his wallet and thrusting them at her. "Get the old bag an extra pack. And the paper, for the notice."

"When's the funeral, hon? I'd like to try and get there." Kath attempted to hand the change from the hundred back to Kerry. Black Superman promptly knocked his sister's forearm aside.

"I'll have that. Two thirty today at St. Michael's," he said cheerfully. "All *very* welcome to come and make sure the old bastard's really dead before we spark him up."

Kath was rendered speechless for the second time in a minute.

"Shut up, *fuckwit.*" Kerry shoved him hard towards the door as she grabbed the free local paper off its metal rack, adding over her shoulder, "You're welcome to come, Kath. Wake's at the pub."

"Oooh, forgot, mustn't speak ill of the dead," Black Superman cried, stumbling as Kerry pushed him down the low stairs at the front of the shop.

"Do you have to be such an *Attention. Seeking. Queen?*" Kerry lectured loudly, handing him the bread. "Some people have to live here, y'know."

Black Superman hooted with laughter and allowed his voice to drop an octave.

"Can't help meself, honey. I set foot back in the shire and I'm fifteen again. Anyway, it'll give Kath something to talk about down the razzle Friday night."

"He was our grandfather," Kerry pointed out acidly. "For all his faults, he was still an Elder. We wouldn't even have a house if it weren't for him."

"He wasn't an Elder's arsehole," Black Superman retorted. "Flogging me unconscious for coming out. I'll never forget that, and I'm certainly not gonna fucken forgive it either. The miserable homophobic prick can rot in hell, girlfriend."

Kerry twisted her mouth. There were things you could let go of in life, and things you couldn't. Black Superman drew the bar higher than most.

"Why even come back, then?" she asked shortly.

"Like I said. To make sure the old prick goes in the oven. And to see you, my darling tidda girl."

––––––––––

"Susu," Kerry said five minutes later. She plonked two heavy plastic bottles on Pretty Mary's kitchen bench, where they immediately made watery milk rings. "Bread." The loaves thudded beside the Norco bottles. "And the paper and ya smokes."

"Ooh, Rothmans, my little angels!" Pretty Mary answered approvingly, arms deep in washing-up water and eyes fixed sideways on the tobacco. "Light us one, will ya, bub? And can ya make sure them cups is all ready for the pub?" The phone rang for the thousandth time that morning as Kerry placed a lit fag carefully between her mother's pursed lips, and Black Superman swooped down to confiscate the kids' laptops and lock them in the hire car.

"No lappies before ten o'clock!" he told them.

In the wake of this sudden loss, six-year-old Lub Lub sooked loudly for her Sydney gran. Her older brother, Brandon, arced up, swearing and hurling the remote towards the plasma TV. Ken leaped to his feet, knocking over a kitchen chair, and grabbed the lad's arm, lifting him clear off the ground for all that he was a chubby forty-five kilos. Ken grabbed the remote and turned the TV off.

"Knock your bullshit off!" he growled, shoving Brandon onto the lounge and holding Pretty Mary's mobile to his ear with his shoulder. "I can't hear meself think."

"Uncle Donny's allowed on his computer!" Brandon protested fiercely. "It's not fair!"

"Uncle Donny's seventeen," said Black Superman, returning to the house and lifting the bawling Lub Lub onto his hip. He put himself between Brandon and Ken. "When you're seventeen you can do what ya like too."

"I fucken hate it here!" Brandon snarled at both men. "I'm going back to live with my Nan, ya faggots!"

"Shut them fucken jahjams up, will ya?" Ken roared. "I can't hear Uncle Richard!"

Lub Lub cried louder, lurching on Black Superman's hip like a sailor clinging to a mast in a cyclone. Black Superman was unperturbed.

"Ya Nan's real crook, bud, so ya stuck with me. And I told yez." He took Brandon's shoulder, voice stern. "No computer till ten o'clock. Go outside. Go climb a tree."

Brandon looked at Black Superman like he had two heads.

"What for? I'm an eel. Eels don't climb trees."

"He gotcha there, son," Pretty Mary smiled through grief-swollen eyes, drying her hands on a tea towel.

"Eels don't use iPads either," Kerry pointed out. "Or watch TV. Or go to Maccas . . ." This provoked a fresh scowl from Brandon, who pushed savagely free of Black Superman and stomped to the back door. Elvis saw him and went to hide beneath the house.

"What for? Jesus, call yourselves Koories? For bird eggs, for honey, for the bloody exercise. Go on, git! The internet won't disappear just because you aren't online for a couple of hours." Black Superman hunted both kids outside. "These jahjams, make ya weak! I'm gonna go shower before I strangle em on their own guts. Can ya watch Lub Lub?"

Kerry nodded and pushed her chair back.

The kids went outside, but that was exactly where their compliance ended. When Kerry looked into the yard, they were using fragments of a broken brake light to scratch their names into the pale trunk of the leopard tree. Brandon had carved *BRANDON EEL MAN RULES* and was underlining it three times for emphasis.

"Don't even think about going near that bike, eh, cobber?" she told him as Brandon wandered idly towards the clothesline. There had been stern words about the Harley when Black Superman first arrived, but Kerry had no faith in his warnings. His foster grannies had long been trained into deafness. Their first language was one of raised voices and closed fists.

"Don't call me copper!" Brandon spat, turning away and hurling the broken brake light loudly at the chook shed. A cacophony of squawking ensued.

"Cobber, not copper. It's an old whitefella word. It means mate," Kerry explained.

The kid kicked at the dirt and was silent.

Poor little bugger didn't know her from Adam. Brandon and his sister were rellos in a distant complicated way, but the kids, Sydney born and bred, hardly knew Durrongo existed until a month ago. Of course he'd be suss of some random aunty bossing him around. He'd be wondering what her agenda was, how long it would take her to promise him the world and then deliver considerably less than fuck all. Or maybe bash him, or start in on his sister. Or (d) all of the above.

"You ever set a chook shed off?" she continued, knowing the answer. Keeping chickens required land and stability, not the overwhelming features of his life until Black Superman stepped in last year just before Department of Childstealers did. Brandon shrugged. Kerry went down to the shed and launched into her best cock-a-doodle-doo. Beneath the stairs, Elvis tilted his head. Kerry crowed again.

"You try!" she urged. Sulky at first, Brandon gradually got into it.

"COCK-A-DOODLE-DOOOOOOOOOOOOOOO!!" crowed Kerry, arms flapping.

"COCK-A-DOODLE-DOOOOOOON'T!" countered Brandon, top note.

Elvis emerged. He began to bark and run in circles. Lub Lub appeared and joined in.

"Louder!" said Kerry, doubting if Brandon had ever in his entire life been urged to make more noise. Pretty Mary's young roosters soon grew excited and began to sound off as well, until the chorus of crowing and barking reached such a pitch that an urgent tinny banging came from inside Pop's caravan.

"Can youse fucken keep it down a bit?" yelled the caravan.

Chris had been fast asleep, Kerry suddenly realized, after working a late shift at the Top Pub. Whoops.

"Sorry, cuz!" she called, grimacing at Brandon. He grinned at her and Kerry ruffled his hair.

"You done that, bub," she told him, gesturing to the roosters. "That's down to you. You're the boss chook whisperer."

"Pop's spinning in his grave with all ya racket," called Pretty Mary from the loo. "Give it a blooming rest, will ya?"

"Can we go play next door, Aunty?" Lub Lub asked. Kerry looked towards the pack of feral white kids on the neighbor's back patio.

"You know them jahjams?" Kerry was doubtful.

"Yeah, they're our friends." Lub Lub's dark face shone with innocent joy. Six was still too young to notice skin color very much, or to notice others noticing hers. Brandon had spied Dr. No and the others frolicking in Aunty Val's blow-up pool, and was halfway to the gate. His own man at eleven, already making his own rules, and why not, when he'd raised himself and his sister in a world of angry faces and stony hearts. Kerry narrowed her eyes. Death penalty for ice dealers. One warning. Then a spear through the fucking carotid artery.

"If they say yes, it'll only be for a little while, bub, cos of the funeral. Hang on."

She slid on her mother's thongs and headed next door with her hackles up. You never knew what to expect. That flag on the Ford might mean folded arms and murderous eyes, or it might mean genial morons as pleasant as the day is long.

———————

"How do I look, Kyles?" Jim asked, preening in the mirror at Patterson Real Estate. He picked up his suit jacket and squinted at the sun-baked town outside. Summer funerals were godawful affairs, and those at St. Michael's were hotter than most. But when old-timers shuffled off, even black ones, you had to show your face, and in this particular case, doubly so.

"You look like a fifty-nine-year-old politician, Jim," Kylie answered. "Hard to believe, I know."

"Just like a real boy," Martina teased from her office. She was more interested in realestate.com.au than in Jim's visit to retrieve his jacket. Houses in Rose Bay were trending up sharply. She exhaled. Easy money to be made on the ground in Sydney, and here she was, stuck at the arse end of hell. Jim picked up his car keys.

"I'll be back at council by four," he told Kylie. "Did those docs come through from the department?" Jim was sweating, not because it was Christmas in a few days but because he had a cool two hundred grand riding on the sale of Lot 14, Settlement Road.

"They hadn't five minutes ago."

"Text me. And Martina, we need to sit down and go through those transfer details, ASAP. It's got to go through first time, with all this NIMBY bullshit starting. Can you be at Chambers at four?"

Martina stretched and smiled, as though Jim had all the time in the world. Endless weeks in which to sign dodgy transfers to make it look like she, not he, was flogging Settlement Road to a state government–backed consortium. Due to some strategic delays, plus the absolutely sweet bonus of a Greens-led groundswell against the project, Jim was now well and truly under the hammer. Martina knew he was in for a killing—provided ICAC didn't find out he was still trading while sitting in the mayor's seat. Poor foolish Jim, thinking he could use her as the fall guy.

"Yeah. We need to talk about that, actually," she said, smiling at him through her open door with cold commercial eyes. *Fool me once, shame on you. Fool me twice, shame on me.* Jim paused, Cruiser keys in his hand, and his world tilted on its axis by precisely one degree. Had he underestimated this smart Sydney bitch?

"What's to talk about?" he snapped, walking closer. "I told you the deal. Five listings you wouldn't otherwise have. Money for jam."

"Yeah," Martina said. "Five shotgun shacks in outer Bumfuck. Sorry, Jim, I just can't get too excited about the deal . . ." She paused and counted to three before adding, "as it stands."

Kylie goggled. Nobody ever spoke to Jim this way. Even the cops deferred to him. Magistrates. Business people went out of their way to lick his substantial arse. Martina clearly didn't know what she was starting. Jim strode to Martina's office and closed her door firmly from the inside.

"I don't know what you think you're doing," he growled. "But don't try and play a player, honey, cos you'll live to regret it."

Martina gave not the tiniest sign of feeling intimidated. You have no fucking idea who you're dealing with, pal, she thought. She suppressed the urge to rip Jim a new one. Instead, she gave the faux-relaxed shrug she had observed in Will and decided to adopt—that icy English cool. More productive in the long run.

"Settlement Road is a sweet listing, Jim. And I'm helping you out. Thirty percent cut sounds about right to me."

"Thirty percent!" Jim's face was beetroot red. "Are you fucking insane?!"

"That's my negotiation point, Jim. I'm all ears if you change your mind." Martina made a note in her diary and turned serenely back to her computer screen, dismissing him. Jim had the strange and distinctly unpleasant sensation that he had been outwitted by a female. It didn't make any sense to him at all.

"Are you a dyke, are you?" he snarled. Martina laughed. Did this vain little cocksucker really think she would put herself in the line of prosecution for so little while he waltzed off with over two hundred grand? She was used to being underestimated by men, but for fuck's sake. It was time to let him know how things really stood. She swivelled to face him again.

"Me? No. But several of my good friends at ICAC are."

Jim's mouth made some unfamiliar shapes.

"You really are a piece of fucking work, aren't you?" he finally spat, rage mingling with a horrified new-found respect. Martina tilted her head back at her screen.

"Well, I'd say at least thirty percent of me is," she agreed.

Jim flung her door open and stalked outside. As he slammed the sliding door to the street, a blast of hot December afternoon hit Kylie, sending her reeling.

"It's like a pizza oven out there," she observed, dying to ask Martina what the story was and suss out who was winning the fight.

"Whose funeral is it?" Martina called from her desk. "Must be important to get buggerlugs into a suit." Jim never wore anything but moleskins, elastic-sided boots, and blue cockie's shirts. The country uniform made the farmers feel relaxed and the city people feel like they were in valuable communion with some kind of deeply authentic Australia. People are so very fucking stupid, Martina reflected.

"It's at St. Michael's. I think one of the Aboriginal Elders died."

"Seriously?"

"Forgot my coffee," said Jim, returning just long enough to snatch up his World's Best Dad travel cup with a glare at Martina. "This fucking heat's trying to kill me. Kyles, get some iced coffee in, will ya!"

"Will do. And whose funeral is it?"

"Old Owen Addison. Remember Kenny Salter, that blackfella who coached the under-fourteens a while back? His grandad. Apparently the tribe used to squat out on Settlement Road for years, so I'd better show me face before they slap a land rights claim over it."

"Fuck me sideways," swore Martina at her screen.

"What?" Kylie asked.

"Average house auction clearance on the North Shore: *eighty-nine percent!*" she told Kylie as she got up and slammed her office door shut. She returned to her desk and sat staring at her Sydney to Hobart desk calendar. Coming to a strange agency in Patterson was without question one of her worst decisions of recent times. And why hadn't Will returned her texts from last night? She sat stewing for several minutes, then went and rinsed her face in the bathroom and reapplied her makeup. She might be a lot of things—she *was* a lot of things—but she was no quitter. And now, on the way back to her office, she could see two window shoppers hovering on the footpath. He had Calvin Klein sunnies and a bemused expression. The wife was doing the talking, though, and that diamond ring was a full carat.

"Watch and learn, grasshopper," Martina said to Kylie, heading outside with her hand extended.

"Martina Rossi. Looking to invest? Great. Now, I expect you probably already know," she told them, carefully standing to block their line of sight to an invalid pensioner heading inside the grog shop on his motorized scooter, "that this area's really changing. Byron Shire buyers are *definitely* coming to Patterson these days. Hey—great ring!"

————————

Ken was nursing his fourth UDL of the day when the XD pulled in late at St. Michael's. He was a long way past driving, but not too far gone to register that the crowd was on the small side. The realization fanned the embers of his resentment into a roaring blaze. "Every cunt's right there when they want something," he slurred to Pretty Mary as she reapplied her lipstick, "but they can't be arsed turning up for his funeral, can they? Pack of mongrel dogs."

"Settle down, son," she urged. "It's too close to Christmas for a lot of people. And the heat would kill a horse." She patted at her sweating neck with a hanky. "Look, Uncle Richard mob ere." Pretty Mary was faint from lack of sleep and the heat, but she kept it to herself. "Pass me them tissues, Donny." She stashed the box inside her handbag and opened the car door. "And grab them gum leaves and the didge outta the boot too, bub." She wiped her eyes and redoubled her determination to do things just right.

Kerry was already waiting outside the church. Like Ken, she'd been surprised to see several vacant parking spaces on the street. Pop had been one of ten central figures to set up the Patterson Aboriginal Co-op in the eighties. "You'd think more mob would make an effort," she told Donny, who simply shrugged. Donny had very low expectations of the world.

"Chill, bruz," Black Superman reassured Ken, walking him towards the church. "Them ones that matter are all here, 'cept for sissy of course. So fuck the rest of em, eh?"

Ken's complaints stopped, but his bad mood hung over the family as they made their way through the crowd. Donny kept to the rear, well away from his father's derision, and when they got inside the high-ceilinged church, he hung back while Pretty Mary argued with Ken.

"No bloody way! I'm the oldest, it's my responsibility," spat Ken. "I spent all last night on the fucken eulogy!" He thrust an illegible page of scrawl at his mother as proof. Always big, Ken seemed to double in size when rage took hold of him, as though his anger had physical mass and bulk to it.

"I know, but I want you with me, Kenny Koala," Pretty Mary lied, the church swirling around her. "I need my eldest son beside me on a day like today." As though to illustrate the point further, she lurched down the aisle and sank, exhausted, into the front pew. Ken remained on his feet, arms folded and jaw set.

"Ya think I can't do it? Gotta get a little gay boy from the city to talk for us mob!"

"It's not about you and him," Kerry interjected. "It's about Pop. And Mum. Look at her! She's crook!"

"You keep ya nose out of it," Ken slurred, shaking the last drops from his UDL into his mouth. "Show up after ten years and start telling us mob what to fucken do . . ." He crumpled the can and threw it twenty meters into a metal rubbish bin in the foyer, the loud clang attracting the attention of the small crowd.

"Three pointer," Ken crowed. "Still got it!"

Black Superman narrowed his eyes and made a low warning sound, somewhere between a growl and an exhalation.

"Kenny, please! I can't take much more of this." Pretty Mary's voice rose to a tearful quaver. Aunty Val went over, two of Savannah's curly blond jahjams clustered about her legs like day-old chicks. The normally snotty urchins had been scrubbed and shampooed and plaited within an inch of their lives. Hmmph, thought Kerry, nodding a tight hello. That shows some respect, at least. When Val sat down and put a fat white arm around Pretty Mary's shoulders, tears began to trickle down her mother's cheeks. Pretty Mary dabbed at her face some more and leaned into Val's shoulder, shuddering with grief.

"That's it, darl," said Aunty Val, who was cagey enough not to tackle the problem of Ken head on. "Don't hold it in, that won't do anyone any good. Have a good cry, love." She put both plump arms around Pretty Mary and held her tight. To Kerry's shock, her mother began to cry loudly and wetly against Val's prosthetic breasts.

"Mum needs ya next to her, bruz," Black Superman said in a hard voice. "And Pop woulda wanted us to look after her today, of all days."

"Christ all-fucking-mighty. Have it your way, then," Ken said, with a glare at the crowd for general consumption. "Ya always do." He folded his scrawled page one-handed and stuffed it back in his pocket. Donny, who had been hovering cautiously on the other side of the church, slid in at the end of the pew next to Kerry, pleased to be separated from Ken by his aunty, both neighbors, and a three- and five-year-old in pink satin flower-girl's dresses.

Black Superman's charcoal suit put those of the undertakers to shame. Clean-shaven and somber, he murmured in the ears of those who wanted tactful murmurs. He joked with those who needed to laugh. He made sure oversized egos were flattered and that myriad minor community fissures stayed underground. And mostly, it worked. After Chris played his didge low and sad to bring the casket inside for the smoking, Black Superman gave an improvised address, which most present took to be the eulogy. Then he invited up Uncle Richard, a local legend whose offspring and hangers-on made up a good quarter of the crowd.

Uncle Richard faced the congregation, his handsome face lopsided now from Bell's palsy, and told yarns he'd heard about Pop growing up near Rivertown, a long way to the south. He spoke about Pop's service to the local community, and followed with a pointed suggestion that Black Superman could do worse than work for his mob closer to home, like his Pop had. Just as Kerry was interpreting this as a rebuke, Uncle Richard floored her by observing that Black Superman had the same guts as his grandfather, and the same intelligence to know just what the Goorie community needed and how to get it. Kerry nearly fell off her chair. An openly gay man was being anointed as Pop's successor in a dusty country town run by corrupt rednecks. She looked around and saw some old people nodding in enthusiastic agreement. It's 2018 and Patterson finally gets over a bit of its homophobia, she thought warily. Wonders would never bloody cease.

Forced to sit and watch Uncle Richard bestow this status on his younger brother, Ken looked daggers. He sighed loudly and jiggled his right foot on the white-tiled floor. Waves of aggravation came off him. Don't blow, Kerry silently prayed. Mum can't cope with much more.

"And I'm not forgetting all you've done for our family, Kenny,"

Uncle Richard added from the podium, turning to face Ken square on. "We all know you were there for your pop, just like you'll be there for your mum and everyone else, nephew. Sometimes the hardest and most important jobs are the ones done behind closed doors, the work that nobody else sees. That's the real Goorie culture, that is. Respect you for it, my nephew."

Shrewd old bugger, thought Kerry. Ken nodded, mollified just enough to sit and swallow the insult of Black Superman's elevation.

A battered old boxing mate got up then and waxed lyrical about Pop's Silver Gloves glory, the actual gloves sitting right there in pride of place on top of the coffin above a replica of King Bobby Saltwater's precious kingplate, which had long been lost to history. The replica was only brought out by Pretty Mary for special occasions, in this case over the objections of Black Superman, who had argued that not being a King Bobby descendant, Pop didn't deserve the honor. The boxing mate lionized Pop, repeating the words *warrior* and *fighter* ad nauseam, to general approval. Then, doing her best to ignore Ken's agitation, Kerry got up and read a poem about absent friends and those who'd gone before, which made Pretty Mary sob and cry out for both Donna and Pop in the same breath.

Ken's foot-tapping grew more compulsive during the reading of the poem. He drummed his fingers silently on the end of the pew too, until, as Kerry returned to her seat, relieved that the program was nearly done and she would soon be able to escape, he rocketed to his feet and brushed Black Superman aside to get to the podium. It had been an age since Ken had binned the UDL can. Didn't your body process one alcoholic drink per hour? Kerry prayed that he had sobered just enough to fake it. Prayed that he might not slur or stagger sideways or say anything too outrageous to those white townsfolk who had shown up at Pop's funeral for mysterious reasons of their own. And to her huge relief, up on the podium Ken came across not as charged up but wobbly with grief. He talked of how hard it had been to lose Donna back in '99, but how they had all

managed to pull together through the horror. About Pop's popu-
larity as a one-term Aboriginal and Torres Strait Islander Commission (ATSIC) commissioner, and how his teenage boxing had kept
his family mostly free of the Rivertown mission, buying them the
chance to eventually come north to Durrongo, where the grip of
the church and the Welfare was slightly less tyrannical.

He told of a middle-aged Pop outwitting a state minister for
housing with free booze and strippers, an outwitting that had meant,
in the end, another black house purchased for the co-op. In the second row, Jim Buckley, who belonged to the same political party as
the member in question, grinned as widely as anyone at this yarn.
Kerry noticed Buckley discreetly checking the time on his phone,
and shot laser death-rays from her eyes. *Peeyow. Peeyow.* Time to go
rip someone else off, must be. Time for another dodgy deal. Kerry
fought back an impulse to run from the church immediately and
ride straight out to Jim's acreage mansion on the river. Break in and
ransack the joint, till she was holding her backpack in her own black
mitts once again. But it was probably already too late, she thought
in silent fury. Buckley would have opened it in the past few days for
sure, and her precious swag would be history.

On the podium, Ken reflected on the time Pop had bought a flash
Chevrolet with a windfall from Jupiter's Casino, only to have the car
break down the very next week a hundred kays outside Coffs.

"Pop was so wild at being taken for a mug by that car dealer, he
just got out and walked away on the spot!" Ken told the assembled
crowd. "It was easy come, easy go with him. He was a real traditional
blackfella like that . . . yeah, yeah, yeah." Ken waved Black Superman's entreaties away breezily. He wasn't finished yet by a long shot.
He was the oldest. He owned the story of Pop's life, nobody else.
Black Superman could kiss his date, the little faggot.

"And look, Pop had his faults. But I don't think anybody here's
in a position to cast the first stone; we ain't none of us perfect," Ken
went on. "He had a temper on him. I know more than one white-

fella regretted running his mouth to Pop. You didn't want to cross him unless you could knuckle on, that's for sure. But you know, he was always there, at the head of the family. And you know what else? He learned how to fight from the mish mob down in Rivertown, and from our deadly Elders here too. Them Elders who came before us, who had to really fight the dugai who wanted them gone so they could steal our land."

Here Ken glared at the scattering of white faces in the pews. He spied Jim Buckley and gave him a particularly ferocious scowl. Although a few ancient aunties looked disapproving, plenty of the Goorie men and women nodded vigorously, giving Ken fresh impetus.

"Pop grew up doing it hard, on and off the mish! He copped some savage floggings in his time, you better believe it. And he fell in love with this ere country when his son Charlie married a Durrongo girl. Ava's Island's where he wanted to be put, and Ava's Island's where he's going to be."

More nodding, and several cries of loud agreement from the crowd. Jim Buckley narrowed his eyes at the mention of Ava's Island. Ken's eyebrows drew down low. He leaned forward. His voice changed from grieving-but-genial to something close to apocalyptic. He loomed over the crowd like a thundercloud about to burst. One or two white people shivered.

"And because he was a *leader*. And because he came from a line of *fighters*. Fighters the same breed as Grandad Chinky Joe and Granny Ava and Granny Ruth. That's why this—"

And here Ken produced that morning's copy of the *Patterson Herald* from beneath his coat. He held it aloft, his arm trembling. Kerry suddenly saw that Ken was shaking, not with alcohol or with sorrow but with sheer unadulterated rage. With his free hand, he began to thump the podium, hard.

"—this, this *bullshit* isn't about to happen (thump). It says here council wants to sell off a hundred acres on Settlement Road and let a joint consortium build a *correctional facility* on the bend there right near Ava's Island. Yeah, I can see you sitting there, Jim Buckley, yeah, that's right (thump)! Well, I fucken got news for you, pal!" Ken hurled the newspaper towards Buckley in violent disgust. His aim was off and it scattered, instead, over the top of the coffin, ending up on the floor. Buckley flinched as the crowd gasped.

Ken pointed directly at Jim Buckley with his right index finger. If looks could kill, thought Kerry, amazed at how far Ken would actually go. In a church. At their grandfather's funeral.

"I'm here to tell you, Jim Buckley, that over my dead Bundjalung body will our land ever see a jail on it. That's a sacred site, right there (thump). Our grandmothers are buried there (thump), our great-grandfather is buried there (thump), and our Pop's gonna be buried there too (an extra loud thump)! So I suggest that anyone who thinks otherwise had better stand up and clear off, right fucking now. Keep ya stinking jails off our land! You want a fight? I'll give ya a fight alright, a fight you'll never bloody forget!"

Ken reached down and seized the replica kingplate from the top of Pop's coffin. He glared at the assembly and raised it high as he let out an enraged yell.

The blackfellas in the church cheered loud and long. A show, a bit of excitement for once in the sleepy country town that was Patterson! This was a lot more like it! Pretty Mary cried out in wild agreement and waved her sodden hanky enthusiastically in the air, unfortunately seeming to signal surrender, but everyone knew what she meant. Sitting immediately behind her, Jim Buckley was trapped. He couldn't stand and leave as Ken had challenged him to. He couldn't argue back—it was a *funeral*, for Christ's sake, despite all the unbelievable carryings-on around him. He had to sit tight, retain the dignity of the mayor's office, and hold fast to the comforting thought that Ava's Island might well be protected state forest, but the land on the riverbank opposite was freehold for kilometers on either side. Kenny Salter could threaten him with grandmothers and sacred fucking sites till the cows came home. He hadn't a leg to stand on.

At the precise minute the loud cheering was beginning to fade, Black Superman stepped up to Ken's side. He made a brief power salute in solidarity, then dropped his arm around Ken's shoulders and skillfully relieved him of the kingplate with the other. Ken somehow found himself offstage and delivered into the practiced custody of the undertakers. Kerry collected the scattered pages of the *Herald* as Black Superman urgently signalled for the final song. Then Chris began to drone on his didge once again and the coffin bearers stood, ready to carry Pop out. They were four when they should have been six—Ken was outside with Uncle Richard in the rose garden—and Black Superman bit his bottom lip. He frowned, deep in thought, before tapping both Donny and Val's husband, Neil, on the shoulder to take their vacant places. Donny looked in terror at Kerry. "*You can do it*," she whispered fiercely. And so, with his narrow wrists and bony shoulders, Donny took his place among five grown men and bravely helped carry the weight of his great-grandfather away.

Black Superman and Kerry stood at the front door as the crowd thinned and drifted towards the car park. Ken had been whisked off to the wake, away from further troublesome speechifying. Mayor Buckley had glad-handed a few voters and deflected their pointed questions. Understandable emotion, he said. Difficult time for the family. All the proper processes sure to be followed. Then he signed the guest book and, with a tight-lipped nod towards Black Superman, fled down the rear stairs and back to council chambers as fast as his LandCruiser could take him. Only a sprinkling of mourners remained chin-wagging in the foyer, where the Christmas tree had been tactfully pushed to the back corner, lest it shed too festive an air on the afternoon's proceedings. Uncle Richard came to the door alongside his wife, Trish, the beloved couple trailing jahjams like the Pied Piper. Uncle Richard smiled ruefully at Kerry and Black Superman.

"You know I can't stay here, Uncle, eh, my job's in Sydney . . ." Black Superman said, hugging the old man tight. Like most of the rellos, Uncle Richard was long and lanky with a medium-brown complexion. Tall, dark, and *oh so handsome*, as the Salter men liked to chant, or at least he had been, before the palsy dropped one half of his face a good two inches below the other. But Uncle Richard's brown eyes had remained deep wells of kindness, beneath a fringe of silver curls.

"Yeah, I know ya not ready, neph. But it's important to let everybody know where we stand, eh. You too, bub," he added to Kerry. "You mob need anything, need any help at all, you let me know, alright? This country's crying out for you young ones to come home." He opened his arms to her and Kerry fell into them tearfully, wishing—not for the first time—that his branch of the family had been in Patto during Pretty Mary's drinking days. Lismore was a long enough drive on winding country back roads to feel like another planet at times. When Uncle Richard and his entourage walked outside, Kerry saw him sling an arm around her cousin's shoulder, and her throat caught fire with jealous longing.

I wish you were my dad. I wish that arm was for me.

"Never a dull moment with Kenny fucken Koala around," Black Superman murmured, smiling and waving polite acknowledgment of some scandalized aunties from Kyogle.

"Come and see us before you leave, bub," one aunty ordered. Black Superman promised he would.

"Christ, what a shamejob," Kerry muttered, glad that she was too dark to blush. She paused, still gobsmacked at the idea of a jail plonked on Aunty Ava's river bend. "Not that that greedy cunt Buckley hasn't got it coming. Of all his stupid ideas, this one just about takes the cake."

"I can't see it getting up," Black Superman replied. "It'd take millions."

"Didn't you read the paper? Chinese consortium's behind it," Kerry told him glumly. "Plus the state government." You didn't have to love white people to be a realist. What dugais wanted, they usually got.

"Sorry for your loss, sis. Uncle Owen got me my apprenticeship back in the day, when I was headed down a real bad track," a nuggetty Githabul man told Kerry, kissing her cheek and adding to the collective germ count there. "I'll always be grateful to him for that."

"Aw, thanks, brother. Pop was real proud of you, eh."

The plumber clasped hands blackfella style with Black Superman and headed off, crossing paths as he did so with a familiar figure on the far side of the foyer.

"Oh no. You have got to be bloody kidding," said Kerry, recognizing the back of a head of light-brown curls. Black Superman drew himself up and straightened his already immaculate jacket.

"Well, well, well," he murmured in his sister's ear. "I spy with my *littlest* eye a very hot tin of meat indeed."

Kerry put her hands on her hips.

"At Pop's *funeral*? Just how big of a slut are you?"

Black Superman ignored her disdain as puritanical and irrelevant. "Sex and death, baby. That's what it's all about. And keep right on rolling them eyes too. Ya might find the keys to the city back there."

"He's straight," Kerry told her brother witheringly. "He's white. And unless he's completely out of his head, Ken's little performance will have him running for the hills. Nobody's that womba."

"They all straight till they ain't, baby," Black Superman was insouciant. "And how do you know, anyway? Been there?"

Because it took that hot tin of meat less than thirty seconds to crack on to me the other day, Kerry thought. By, um, smiling and asking me if I remembered him. She wondered suddenly if it had all been in her head. Maybe Steve was just being friendly. Maybe she had tickets on herself.

"He went to Patto High," Kerry said as Steve headed in their direction, wearing a black polo shirt filled with muscle in all the right places.

Black Superman narrowed his eyes at her. Kerry sported a silver cross beneath her silky cream shirt and two silver rings on her right hand. With her slimline black trousers and heavy biker boots, and her dark hair gleaming halfway down her back, she could very easily get in the way of his newest attraction.

"Well, I seen him first!" Black Superman hissed into her ear, then turned back and adjusted his tie. "And you're a *dyke*!"

"You're a *parent*!" she snapped indignantly. "Think I'm babysitting for ya while ya try and root straight white boys, think again, man-whore!"

"What do you care? Jelly?" Black Superman's nostrils flared.

"Steve! Didn't expect to see you here." Kerry flashed him a smile, desperately hoping that *man-whore* hadn't carried the width of the foyer.

"Very sorry for your loss," Steve said, shaking hands with Black Superman with just the right degree of friendly seriousness. Then, murmuring the same words, he leaned in and kissed Kerry. Ridiculously, her thighs trembled as his lips came oh so very close to her mouth. Right there. In church. In public. Clearly, she was losing her mind.

"Thanks for coming," answered Black Superman formally, as though the words *a hot tin of meat* had never been uttered. "Steve, isn't it? Did you know Pop, then?"

Steve explained that he had done a bit of boxing with the old bloke as a kid and never forgotten him. He'd been looking for something at thirteen and like a lot of boys went to the boxing ring to find it. Black Superman nodded knowingly and invited him to the wake.

"For sure. I might need a lift, though." Steve turned to Kerry. "Did you bring a car?"

His eyes met hers and none of it—not one tiny little bit—had been in her head. Look away, she told herself, look away right now, and think about something else. Forget about those soft lips, those shoulders, ignore his narrow man hips in blue jeans and how you'd like to undo that worn leather belt and then start slipping those silver buttons through their denim holes, drawing them jeans down lower and lower still . . . Forget how his arm looked when he flexed it; how much you wanted him to reach for you then, and draw you in till your mouth was on his and your tongues began to oh-so-gently meet each other, and then have his hands slide up your neck to the back of your head and hold you perfectly still with both hands and then you'd kiss until—

"Oh, I'm sure we can rustle you up a lift," Black Superman said matter-of-factly, beckoning Uncle Neil back inside so that a ride could be organized. "Damn shame Allie couldn't be here with you, hey?" he asked Kerry in a loud, clear voice. Kerry decided to poison Black Superman before sundown.

"Who's Allie?" Steve asked as Black Superman turned away.

"Ah. No car here. I ride a bike," she said. One question at a time. And who *was* Allie, anyway? The love of her life, who had unceremoniously dumped her in a thirty-second phone call from BWCC. She nodded at the bike parked on the front lawn, at the epicenter of a group of admirers. Kerry had never in her life been so pleased to ride a Harley.

"Ah, the Softail. That explains the boots. Well, who needs a car?" Steve grinned.

"Sorry. No spare helmet," Kerry said, pretending a massive indifference as to whether or not this fine-looking specimen was pressed hard up against her on the back of the bike in the next five minutes. Hands slung low around her waist. Only two thin layers of denim separating the riders as they hurtled down the highway. Steve laughed an easy laugh.

"I've ridden all around South America," he said. "If I'd worried about helmets I'd still be the dumb gringo waiting at Mexico City central station."

Steve pushed his fists into the pockets of his snug jeans. His wide shoulders curved forward just a little as he leaned in closer. Kerry could smell his aftershave, could glimpse beneath his shirt collar where the deep furrow of tanned neck muscle met his shoulder. Could almost feel that muscle beneath her fingers, imagine it meeting her mouth as she melted into him.

"Or don't you want to ride with me?" he asked, nudging her shoulder and smiling, as though the question was ridiculous and the matter already settled.

Kerry felt everything slipping sideways. She was sand beneath an outgoing tide. Nobody but Allie was allowed on her bike. And she had warrants, the kind that would see her slapped in prison with no prospect of bail if the cops caught up with her. It would be an act of pure insanity to risk riding down the highway carrying a helmetless Steve Abarco, no matter how gorgeous those brown eyes locked on to hers might be, or what they might be promising about the night to come.

Fuck it all to hell, Allie. Fuck it all to hell. Who knocks off TAB shops with cop cars next door?

"Did you need me?" Uncle Neil asked Black Superman, arriving with a memorial booklet in one hand and his car keys jingling in the other.

"It's not that I don't want to," Kerry croaked hopelessly at Steve. "I just can't."

She bolted to the front lawn, yanked her helmet on, and blasted away. *Who's Allie?* She heard the question echo all the way down the highway. *Who's Allie?* as she gunned it hard in the right-hand lane. *Who's Allie?* My ex, the stab of the dumping still bitter to recall. *Who's Allie?* The idiot who let herself be identified during the hold-up; the staunch one who didn't dog me to the gunjies even though I copped the swag. The one with *here for a good time not a long time* tattooed on her arm and *Thug Life* Tupac-style on her belly in red, black, and gold. The womba one who thinks I shoulda got arrested with her, and who dumped me when I ran. There were a thousand answers to Steve's question, and not one of them was a cure for the heartbreak tearing her apart.

After twenty minutes, Kerry dropped into third and turned left onto Main Street. Allie might be a Pandora's box too painful to contemplate, but at least Kerry knew who she herself was: a Salter and a blackfella, and a woman too fucking smart to fall for the first handsome dugai who smiled at her. So, when she discovered herself a fly suspended in a sticky web, the general store on her left, the pub and the wake and all its attendant dangers looming on her right, she took a very deep breath, dropped her wrist, and with a wild roar of anguish kept on riding towards the T-junction, and Mount Monk, and home.

Chapter Six

Pretty Mary paused in her wrapping of the Christmas presents.

"I keep telling ya there's not gonna be any prison, bub. Why would they put a prison on our beautiful river?"

"Same reason they do anything. Shit for brains was on the news the other day, saying how there's jobs in locking up criminal blacks. He's got a fucking nerve. If I'd had me phone to film him at the river that day it'd be a different story. Coulda sent it to ICAC . . ."

"Lotta cash in nigger farming," Ken chimed in, washing down his antidepressant with a slug of coffee. He and Kerry had found common ground lately through a shared loathing of the mayor. Kerry had even contemplated asking him for help retrieving her backpack.

"Oh, don't, bub, please. I hate that word." Pretty Mary looked raw and weary, as she had all week. Her blood was tired; her bones were tired. Her *hair* was tired. She picked up a few *Watchtower*s off the floor and stacked them with the others on the kitchen table, trying to neaten the pile with both hands, only to have it slump into disorder again the instant she stopped.

"Me too. But not as much as I hate that prick," Kerry told her. To her fury, Pretty Mary shook her head.

"The cards don't lie, my girl."

Kerry swore energetically under her breath as she stomped downstairs to wash the bike. Nothing, absolutely nothing, would convince her mother that the threat was real. According to Black Superman, lofty with the three units of psychology he'd done at teachers' college a decade ago, it was a classic case of denial. Same as the crippling gut ache their mother had suffered since the funeral. "It's just stress and grief playing out, and it takes time, that's all," he told Kerry from where he sat on the back stairs.

"Time's exactly what we ain't got," Ken said, leaning out the kitchen window, blowing out a white cloud, for he had taken up smoking again after being appeased at the wake with durries as well as grog. "We gotta act, bruz, not just bloody talk, talk, talk." Action was his new catchcry; Ken's self-image had shifted from Retired-Footy-Hero-cum-Sex-God to Activist and Culture Man. So far his activism had consisted of vague threats of revolution down the pub and of dragging an ancient land rights shirt from the bottom of the hall cupboard.

"Oppressed peoples must be the agents of their own liberation," Ken quoted, then turned to Pretty Mary in the kitchen. "Mum, you gonna heat up them party pies or what? Me stomach thinks me throat's cut."

Kerry soaped her bike wheels, seeing the white bubbles on her sponge turn into a stream of red suds dribbling over the ground beneath the house and onto the lawn. The red dust had begun life deep in the volcano to the east. Then with the big eruption millions of years ago it had been pushed sky-high to form the Great Dividing Range. Which then eroded over thousands of centuries to end up in the clearing opposite Ava's Island. Now the dirt was entering another incarnation, destined to spend a decade or three in the backyard at Durrongo before washing down to Stockman's Creek and, eventually, out to sea on the far side of Patto. Human lives are nothing compared to the land. We are so tiny, so insignificant, Kerry thought, mesmerized by the red bubbles. And yet at the same time, our lives matter too.

She looked up. What was Ken mansplaining now?

"Good point," said Black Superman. "I know a barrister through work. I'll find out if there's an injunction or anything we can bring against it. Get on to the Land Council too."

"Land Council's flat-out with native title," Ken said dismissively. "They won't give a shit, anyway, not with Warren running the show."

"Tell yer QC mate we're making pipe bombs," said Kerry, polishing her petrol tank with a chamois. "And some of them IEDs, or whatever they call em. Invade my Granny's fucking land, good go." She drifted off into a fantasy of the entire family standing in the middle of Settlement Road. Buckley faced them, revving his LandCruiser from a hundred meters away, his pigger bitch growling in the cabin beside him. A shotgun pointed across the dash; they could see its two deathly eyes looking straight at them. Kerry, in the center of the Salter mob, took her hands off her hips and taunted Buckley, showing him two emphatic middle fingers. Cross this line, motherfucka, and see what ya get. And as the mayor drove forward onto the IED—KABOOM! Bits of Establishment blown sky-high from arsehole to breakfast time.

"Molotov cocktails too," added Ken, sending off a text in the hope of winning a new washing machine he could flog on eBay.

"Ah, Molotov cocktail so last century, bruz," Kerry told him scornfully. "Get with the program!"

Inside the house, Pretty Mary burst into song. The loud strains of "What a Friend We Have in Jesus" radiated from every open window, chastising her children for their apostasy and faithlessness.

"Natural born Christian," said Ken, shaking his head.

"I better grab them little street rats," said Black Superman, heaving himself off the stairs. "Aunty Val'll have em fulla red cordial."

"I'll go," offered Ken, heading next door. Kerry frowned suspiciously, wondering aloud if Val had grog on offer. Black Superman snorted and gave her a pitying glance. Ken was sniffing next door for a scrape, he told her. Ken and Savannah had hooked up again over the Black & Gold sausage rolls at the wake. Hadn't she noticed what a good mood he'd been in since the funeral?

Kerry groaned. It wasn't just the antidepressants kicking in, then. She could see it now, Pretty Mary's next grandchild, plonked on Aunty Val's hip with a rebel flag waving in its little white hand.

"You're just bloody racist," Black Superman laughed.

"I wish Ken fucking was," she retorted. "If he's gonna make more fairskin kids they could at least be bloody Black."

"You saying Donny's not Black?"

"Course he's Black. But we growed him up, not a pack of dopey fucken bogans listening to Alan Jones and voting for One Notion."

Black Superman grinned and went inside to tell Pretty Mary to hide the presents. There was no arguing with Kerry about dugais. Of the four Salter kids, she was the only one who had never gone with a whitefella, never even looked like she might. They're so full of themselves, she would always say with a curled lip. Look at em. The *whitenormalsavages*, could ya even wanna.

———————

Christmas passed with the usual quota of street brawls, fierce hangovers, and car accidents up and down the Far North Coast. Ken punched out the wrong redneck and got himself barred from the pub for a month. New Year's exploded in a brief scattering of fireworks over the Patto showground, and as January creaked on, Pretty Mary retrieved the Tarot Teepee from the back shed, despite the persistent pain in her stomach.

After Black Superman took the kids home to Sydney, Kerry and Donny went to the river daily. Kerry was determined to swim with him there, and fish, and yarn her nephew real good ways, never understanding the cruelty in what she was doing. She drew the lad out of his room, took him from his safe fantasy world on the computer, and handed the river to him on a plate, in all its complex glory, its dangers and beauty and wholeness. She drew Nature Boy out of long hibernation, poked and prodded him to life, blinking and yawning, and hurled him back, literally, into the stream of life. Into the river that was about to be stolen away again, as it always had been since Captain James Nunne Esq. first rode up with his troopers, one, two, three, crying, *I'll have that, and that, oh, and that too, while I'm at it.*

Kerry did this each morning, thinking she was doing Donny a service by remaining in Durrongo. Then lay sweating buckets on the veranda every afternoon, until the shade of the leopard tree shifted onto the rusting roof and the air grew cool enough to move again. She rode past Jim Buckley's mansion a half dozen times, her plans for revenge constantly stymied by its high fence and swivelling cameras. She took tarot lessons from Pretty Mary to pass the time, not believing a single word of it.

What she didn't ever do was run in the early morning past the cattle farms at the base of Mount Monk; that, or let anyone realize how often she looked out the window around dawn, hoping—and yet not hoping—to glimpse the passing figure of Steve Abarco. Instead, she focused on her nephew, and on the profoundly corrupt mysteries of the council's decision-making process, and never let herself forget the oily smile on Jim Buckley's face as she squatted in the lantana that day, watching him flog off her granny's country to a stranger in a John Deere cap.

───────

"What about Jiminy Cricket, then?" she asked her mother, expertly twisting the end of a newly rolled spliff. Pretty Mary sweated on the veranda in a pink tank top, stripping her weaving grasses and worrying about the power bill. Elvis hovered near the foot of the back stairs, waiting to relive his golden age when he was fast enough to nab a pullet before Pretty Mary's wrath fell on his head. Elvis had slowed with age, but then so had Pretty Mary. This question of speed was a constant equation in his doggy mind. While Elvis waited patiently for the exact moment, he raised a hind leg against the passionfruit vine growing on the sunny side of the back shed. Kerry made a face and thrust aside the unwashed purple fruit she had collected earlier.

"'E got brain damage from that accident, poor fella," Pretty Mary mused, getting ready to throw her weaving water on Elvis if he got just one step closer to her speckled favorite.

"What?!" Kerry spat out coffee from where she sat cross-legged on the bare wooden boards. "Since when?"

"Since his accident." Her mother seemed unnaturally calm about it. "When Matty Nunne first bred him—"

"Matty Nunne bred him? What? Buckley?"

"Jim? No!" Pretty Mary screwed up her face. "Which way! When Matt Nunne had Elvis as a pup, and he run under the tractor. That's how come we ended up with him; damaged goods, see . . ." Both women laughed, and Kerry was pleased for her mistake. Laughter had been in short supply since the hearse drove out of the church gates. Having Pop on top of the kitchen cupboard in a gray plastic container put a bit of a dampener on things. "Mind you . . ." Pretty Mary reconsidered, measuring grass stalks as she drew them out of the soaking basin. She sighed at their inadequacy. "I do wonder about Jim . . ."

"Buckley's not brain damaged, he's just plain evil, the dirty thieving dog." Kerry remembered another agenda item. "Whaddya want for your birthday, Mum? How about a run over to Westville, go see Aunty Tall Mary mob?" Pretty Mary had been partly raised on the Westville mission with Aunty Tall Mary, the mother of Doris and Helen; they were classed as family.

"Oh, no, bub, just leave it." Pretty Mary winced. By a hideous coincidence, her birthday fell in the same week as Donna's. The coming month of March was purely something to survive.

"Mum." Kerry wasn't giving up.

"I hear Doris is back on the ice too. She's buggered off from rehab and gorn proper silly," Pretty Mary added, clinching her refusal. "And Jamey boy bin go hospital, for his epilepsy, and you know Uncle Tony in Kyogle, well, his oldest daughter, Sjaan, the one with the twins? Well, you remember how she got that good job with the *Koori Mail*—"

"Shit, that's no good 'bout Doris. But you're not gonna get away with doing nothing," Kerry told her, interrupting what threatened to become a three-hour gossip sesh about the doings of the Kyogle and Westville and Toowoomba mobs. "It's a big deal making it to sixty-five, hey Ken?" she called inside. "And sissy woulda been, what, thirty-five too."

"She is thirty-five!" said Pretty Mary vehemently. She had never let go the scant thread of hope that her daughter wasn't lying in a shallow bush grave.

"Bloody oath," Ken agreed, reaching into the workings of the busted loo, hauling the wire up, and holding it high to flush the cistern. He wandered out, wiping his hands on his shorts. "Let's get a keg and a pig on a spit and get the old joint hopping again. Speaking of joint—" He gestured to Kerry, and she handed over her spliff of homegrown bush. Ken drew back hard and shortened it by an inch.

"We'll see," Pretty Mary said insincerely, accepting the joint off Ken before turning to Kerry. "Listen. I wanna go over to the coast, bub," she said. "These reeds is too short. I dreamed last night we went and got some nice long ones from Sandy Beach. Look—" Pretty Mary lifted an asymmetrical basket and handed it to Kerry. There was no denying the shape was off. Mum could spin a good yarn with the tarot and come home three hundred bucks to the good, but turning a profit off wonky fruit bowls was a different story.

"Sandy Beach? It'll take a full tank." Kerry was dubious.

"I'll take the bike for a run," offered Ken, grinning broadly.

"No, ya fucking won't," Kerry said, dropping her eyelids and making a mental note to hide her keys. "What's wrong with plain river reeds, Mum?"

No, Pretty Mary insisted, growing peevish. Was Kerry deaf? She'd had a *dream*. A trip to Sandy Beach was required, and the trip needed to happen while the moon was still waxing too. Kerry swore quietly at the chickens. Since the funeral, Pretty Mary was increasingly anxious about making decisions if her dreams, or the cards, or the myriad signs from the birds and animals were against it. It was a wonder she ever left the veranda.

"The Harley's nearly as thirsty as the car," Kerry said, remembering that her mother was still waiting on funeral money. A trip to the coast might be just the ticket to get her across the threshold of Sphincterlink. "We may as well take the Falcon, eh. Make a real go of it and clean up at the Channon next week."

"I was gonna fix them brakes tomorrow too," Ken said, inspired by the yarndi to start putting his life in order. He was a man with plans, big plans.

"Aw, deadly!" Kerry said, pretending to believe in him. "You got them parts?"

"Not till I get paid Friday," Ken told her, no shame. "Wanna sling us a hundred in the meantime?"

Kerry snorted. Ever since Ken had assumed control of Pop's Ubet account he was biting hard for gambling price, morning, noon, and night.

"Do I look like an ATM, brother? Hit Chris up; he's working," she suggested, and Ken went back inside in disgust. Pretty Mary cackled. Gotta get Mum some hair dye on payday, Kerry thought. That regrowth's bloody shocking.

"Now, what about your birthday, Mum?"

"Oh, we'll see," her mother muttered, hoping the idea would be dropped. "So long as I get me grasses."

"We'll go soon," Kerry promised her, turning the wonky basket in her hands. The lomandra fibers felt good. Strong. Natural. Perhaps she should take up weaving. Get all cultural and that.

"What's the lingo again?" she asked her mother, putting the basket down.

"Dhili," Pretty Mary said wistfully. "Granny Ava always used to say, 'Yan bulloon, granddaughter, go river, and fetch me punyarra dhili, pretty ones.'"

"Aw, solid," Kerry said. Granny Ava was the link: the last heathen of the family to speak the lingo fluently, before the Church waltzed in and jammed the Lord's Prayer in Granny Ruth's twelve-year-old mouth instead.

"Granny only sat still if she had something in her hands," Pretty Mary went on. "We'd be under her tree for hours, jalum bira, and weaving our dhili." A picture entered Kerry's head of herself and Pretty Mary sat on the veranda in a few years. The fuzzy white caterpillar at the center of her mum's scalp had grown out, making her entire head snowy white. Kerry's dark curls reached to her waist. Ken had fucked off somewhere, rehab with any luck, and she and her mother had built themselves a castle of woven-grass baskets, were working away inside it like two old spider women. They didn't leave home much; instead rich white people came to them, proffering copious hundred-dollar bills for their precious work. They were renowned far and wide as the famous hermit weavers of Durrongo—

Jesus wept, Kerry thought in sudden horror, I'm turning into a fucking old-age pensioner. She leaped to her feet and hurled the butt of the spliff down to the gravel, where it sent up a tiny smoke signal. SOS! I'm trapped here, turning into my mother, attention all ships at sea. Action, Kerry thought, bracing her hands on the railing and channelling Ken. Girl, ya gotta bloody take *action*. Either go back to Trinder Park onetime, or stay and do something, anything, to stop Jim Buckley. Or you'll wake up before you know it with a big ugly prison plonked fair and square on Granny's river bend. But how to organize a campaign with nothing in the fridge or the bank or the petrol tank?

"We can get your dhili tomorrow, and then go see Centrelink, find out about that funeral pay, eh?" Kerry said. She clapped her hands down hard onto the railing.

Pretty Mary's expression shifted rapidly during the course of this last sentence, from joyous to pained. "Centrelink," she said sourly.

"I don't wanna go see them mob. Standover merchants! On the phone for nearly two blooming hours and then it cuts out! Now I got no pay 'n no credit! Person could starve to death for all they care!"

"I know, Mum," Kerry reassured her, "but it's thousands ya get for funerals, biggest bungoo." Personally, she thought Ken had it all over Centrelink in the standover department, but Pretty Mary flew into a rage if Kerry dared criticize him lately. For all Uncle Richard's pronouncements at the funeral, all his praising up of Black Superman as the heir apparent, inside Pretty Mary's four walls Ken was very clearly the new boss.

The day before flying south Black Superman had handed Kerry an envelope with six hundred dollars in it. "Make sure Mum gets the benefit," he told her, "and not the bloody TAB. I'll send the same next month."

"Shit, I'll be long gone by then, bruz." Kerry recoiled. Black Superman had just nodded and pressed her hand down onto the envelope. That had been a fortnight ago, and the bungoo had quickly dwindled to a single blue ten left in her wallet. One rates bill, two tanks of juice, one overnight trip to retrieve some clothes from Trinder Park, and the odd six-pack to keep Ken happy.

"I'll talk for you at Centrelink, if you want," Kerry offered. Pretty Mary remained subdued, her earlier laughter wiped away.

"I still got this bad pain," she muttered, holding her belly. "I can't be going Centrelink with this pain."

"Well, you wanna go to the doctor?" Kerry asked impatiently.

"I just want some decent grasses," Pretty Mary erupted. "Not a birthday party, not Centrelink, not doctor! Grasses! How do you lot expect me to go bury Pop in a plastic blooming can, like an old bitta rubbish! Like he was nobody! I just want to do right by him! I promised ya father when I married him that I'd always do right by Pop and that's what I'm gonna do, by jingo!"

"Okay, okay, keep ya hair on. We'll go get em tomorrow. And

maybe we can do Patto market this weekend. I'm down to the bones of me arse." Kerry stomped her way inside to sweep the kitchen out and start dinner. No wonder the culture taught you to respect your Elders and treat them well no matter what bullshit they served up. There'd be the biggest bloody spate of mass murders if it didn't.

"Shout us a six-pack, sis," Ken said automatically, looking up from the lounge where he was texting an entry to win a brand-new Toyota Yaris. "Pay ya back Friday."

"Kingilawanna! Finished! I got *nothing*!" Kerry told him, throwing her hands up in annoyance. "Mum's drained me for petrol price. You heard her."

"Ya had big bungoo in ya hand Monday," Ken argued.

"Paid the rates, didn't I, Einstein?" Kerry raised her voice. "And went and got dog food and groceries and juhm since then. Never mind what's in my hand, brother, how about *you* chuck some bungoo *this* way. And how do you fucking know what I've got in me hand *anyway*? Fuck me!"

For the first time in years she simply ignored Ken's outrage, and reached for the broom.

———

"You mob ready or what?" Pretty Mary called from the Falcon, noticing with displeasure that the lawn was now high enough to cover the rusted base of the chicken coop.

"Hold ya horses!" Kerry yelled as she maneuvered Donny's heavy wooden tallboy back into position. She'd grabbed her wallet from beneath it.

"Last chance for a trip to the coast," she told Ken on her way through, knowing he wouldn't take her up on the offer. He was shaved and showered and waiting for Savannah. They were having lunch at the pub now that his ban was finally lifted.

"Definitely no need for you lot to hurry home," he grinned.

"*Whatever*. Just keep them fucking rugrats of hers away from my bike." Kerry ran down the stairs, scooped up an unsuspecting Elvis, and chucked him through the back window onto Donny's lap. Donny hollered. Elvis trampled on the lad's privates as he did ecstatic laps of the back seat, spraying dog spittle far and wide.

"Aunty *Kerry*!" Donny wailed, shoving Elvis off and bending forward in agony.

"Why shouldn't the El-Dog have some fun too?" Kerry grinned, hopping into the driver's seat and sliding her wallet beneath it. She steered towards the coast while Pretty Mary cranked up the volume on the CD player. Only two of the car's four speakers worked, but it was enough to hear Uncle Archie singing over the top of Elvis barking. *Sensual Being* was finishing for the second time as they pulled in at the Sandy Beach lagoon. The water rippled under a light breeze, shining brilliant sapphire blue, and there were a couple of smoking-hot chicks on stand-up paddleboards. Kerry eyed them with great interest. A Goorie wouldn't be dead for quids.

"Look at them lovely big dhili," beamed Pretty Mary, taking her scissors out of her handbag. She smiled, thought Kerry, realizing in astonishment how long it had been since she'd seen her mother looking really happy.

"I'm going in," she said, ripping her shirt off and straightaway feeling her skin heat up beneath the blinding summer sun. "Coming?"

"Yeeaaaggghh!" screamed Donny, running with his arms raised along the water's edge, where fine white sand bore the tracks of a dozen different bird species. Elvis ran barking beside him all the way. In revenge for being trampled, Donny tossed him into the lake. Elvis began struggling towards the sandy edge, only his head visible. Pretty Mary tutted from the passenger seat.

"Watch he don't drown, Donny!" she called fearfully. "You know he womba."

"Elvis … has left … the shoreline," Donny turned and announced, being Uncle David Attenborough. He had the Pommy voice down real good, complete with breathy pauses. "But soon . . . the canine . . . will be making his way . . . back to the vehicle . . . where he will endeavor to urinate . . . upon the clothing . . . and the possessions . . . of his entire clan."

Kerry cackled loudly and fell backwards into the lagoon, letting the sweet balm of fresh water flow over her hair and into her ears and up her nose. Donny was talking, joking, even eating a bit, lately. Mum had *smiled*. Ken was two hours away in Durrongo with someone else to annoy, and everything felt like it might—by some miracle—actually work out okay.

Chapter Seven

Three days later Kerry pulled up outside the Patto market. She loved the markets. From when she was young they had been an astonishing oasis in the rank shithole that was Durrongo Shire, where the goss about who was doing what sexual favors for whose husband or father or boyfriend was what passed for entertainment. Before the markets, one particularly dismal Sunday afternoon had lasted for about fifty or sixty years. With the rest of the town at the footy, Kerry had wandered the empty streets. The most interesting thing to look at—the only change she could discern in Patto from the previous Sunday—was a stray cat in a gutter, surrounded by brown autumn leaves. The poor thing was properly finished up—kaput, finito—its dark fur ragged and its dead eyes beginning to pucker. When she poked it with her toe it was as stiff as a bit of wood. To eleven-year-old Kerry, the dead cat came to stand for Patto and all that her life there was ever likely to be. Then the wonder of the markets had arrived, and the thrill of discovering people who talked about things other than the pub and the footy and the rain gauge had never quite gone away. But the markets would have a job to work their charm on her today. Allie's sister had rung two hours ago to ask her to collect her remaining gear from Trinder Park; her bedroom had just been given to a homeless Elder, and oh, by the way, love had blossomed in B block. Allie had a new partner, a Wakka Wakka sistergirl from Morayfield, and there was a brand-new fist-shaped hole in the wall beside Kerry's pillow.

Kerry pocketed her phone and went in. Go left at the ginger beer stall, Ken had said, and it's on the slope just below the German-sausage wagon. When she heard *German sausage*, Kerry's mouth had begun to water. As starving kids they had stood in front of the wagon with its sizzling pans, wishing they had the bungoo to do more than drool. Sometimes the wagon owner would sling them a burnt snag for free; occasionally tourists would take pity and offer to shout. Black Superman was too proud, and Kerry far too wary, but Donna would gammon light up every time, saying, *Ooh, yes, please,* even to the disgusting white men whose eyes slid all over you like you were naked. *Who cares,* Donna would laugh as she distributed the bounty. *For German sausages they can look all they want.* A few years later, Kerry realized that the shit talk at school about Donna's six-pack head jobs might have been true, after all.

She felt the coins in her jeans pocket as she made her way miserably around the footy oval at the center of the market. She'd rather starve than have to talk to them ones again, the dirty white dogs. Even the sight of them made her sick. And fuck Allie too! Doing dumbarse crime and getting pinched. Hooking up with a shiny new fuckbuddy after, what, three months? So much for undying love, yeah right. It was time she changed the wallpaper on her phone. Made it a picture of the Hog, or maybe Donny.

It was true, of course, that Kerry was one tiny slip, one RBT or traffic check, away from the lockup herself, but that was theory, not fact. And the longer she stayed over the border the less worried she was. The New South Wales gunjies pretty much stuck to Byron and Lismore and Casino, the bigger towns where they could fish more easily to meet their monthly ticket quotas. Places like Durrongo were almost expected to police themselves. And because Ken had laid down the law at the pub—*No fucken ice in my town, boys*—Durrongo mostly did. A bit of small-time pot dealing and half a dozen girlfriends nursing black eyes and busted arms didn't rate as a reason for the authorities to raise a sweat. Luke Chin drank at the

Durrongo pub on Thursday nights, but he didn't often come by in uniform. Some things didn't change in a hurry.

"Don't smile, ya face'll crack," Ken told Kerry as he adjusted the ropes on the fake deerskin of the Tarot Teepee. He propped a red and gold sign reading *Know Your Future—Durrigan the Wise—Tarot Readings and Dream Interpretation* on the grass. Then he saw that his sister's eyes were red and swollen.

"What's your problem?"

"Allie's already rooting some chick inside," Kerry spat, going inside to swap her jeans for Pretty Mary's black and purple costume. She slid it over her head and grimaced. She could cope with the extravagant flowing sleeves and even the garish sequins, but the outfit was far too low-cut for her liking; she tried in vain to pull it up, to cover the paler brown skin at the top of her susu. Pretty Mary ignored Kerry's protests and draped a large crystal pendant around her neck to join the silver cross already hanging there. Her daughter's first lesson would be that a surprisingly large chunk of Durrigan's custom came from very straight-edged blokes. Bit of tit never went astray where men were concerned, any moron knew that.

"Maybe ya shoulda busted her out," Ken advised from outside the tent. "Like that mad cunt with the chopper at Long Bay."

"No doubt. Apparently I abandoned her, when she's the fucking genius that went and got herself locked up. I'm over it."

"Stand still for once in yer life," said Pretty Mary, carefully tying a chain of fake gold coins across Kerry's forehead. Kerry screwed her nose up at her reflection in the side-view mirror taken off Ken's spare XD and hung on a bit of fencing wire from the center pole. *Things in the mirror may be shittier than they appear.* She ripped the fake coins off. Pretty Mary pursed her lips and tried a black lacy veil, which covered Kerry's forehead, mouth, and chin, rendering her mysterious.

"I look like a Muslim," Kerry said doubtfully. As if she didn't cop enough shit for being a blackfella. It was better than the gammon coins though, so she left it.

"Keys," Ken said, sticking his hand through the teepee flap. Kerry had bribed him into putting the tent up with the promise of riding the Harley home.

"Don't prang it. Or go off on any adventures with Sav. And for Christ's sake don't get fucken caught," Kerry instructed.

"See ya in a couple of weeks!" Ken teased, jingling the keys in triumph. After backing two winners last night he had a pocketful of cash and every intention of blowing it in Byron.

"Not if ya wanna keep ya junk intact, ya won't," Kerry muttered, already regretting the deal. Ken waltzed off, all hail-fellow-well-met to the other stallholders getting their floats ready for the evening. They were singing their usual song of woe about the market management, but Ken was in the good mood he'd been in for weeks. Nothing like a regular root to turn him into the jolly green giant. Back at the teepee, Kerry grinned. Her brother'd be a lot less jolly once he realized she'd drained the fuel tank close to empty. Ken was cuntstruck, and she wasn't taking any chances on the Harley leaving the shire.

Martina smiled when the hitchhiker's face appeared in her open passenger window. He hadn't had his thumb out this time, but she had plunged to a halt beside him anyway. He hopped in next to her, and she adjusted her Jackie O sunglasses for a better look.

"I'm Martina. Don't I know you?" she asked with a smile that managed to be friendly and predatory at the same time. "Or do you just have one of those faces?"

"Steve. One of those faces, I'd say. We were locals once, but we moved up the Goldie years ago. You?"

"Sydney, mostly. I miss it, the beach especially. You look like you surf," Martina flirted. "I mean, look at those arms. Surfer arms!"

Steve smiled and told her he had always moved around too much to learn to surf. Waxing lyrical about the Coogee break, Martina pulled her T-shirt off her shoulder to show her bikini, one she'd ordered especially from the US. No reaction. Martina grew a bit sniffy and an awkward silence fell.

"So I'm opening up a gym in the industrial estate," Steve finally offered. "Patto Gym, for all your fitness requirements."

"Personal training?" Martina asked, slowing down as they entered the enormous roundabout on the outskirts of Patto. "In Sydney I have PT four times a week. Agonizing, but worth it." Personal training wasn't the main game, he told her. His was going to be a fighting gym, MMA. Lots of free weights, and a round boxing ring.

"Those guys who fight in the cages?" Martina breathed.

"Girls too," he told her. "But there'll be ordinary cardio group sessions for people like—well, for people who don't want to get hurt."

Martina arched her eyebrows. *Oh hello.* This guy thought she was some kind of wimp. A pampered princess in her flash red princess car. That was pretty funny. She shifted down into second, making the engine growl as she whipped around the curve past the servo.

"You think I couldn't fight if I had to?" she asked. "Or is it that I'm too old?"

"No, not at all. But being realistic, it is a pretty tough game," he said, delicately maneuvering. "The Kiwi girls on the Goldie don't take any prisoners. But hey, if you want to train . . ."

A pretty tough game. The phrase rankled Martina; in fact, it really gave her the shits. If he wasn't interested in her romantically, the least he could do was pay her a little bit of fucking respect.

"Train, but not fight?" she asked pointedly.

"Either way. I fight for a living, kind of. But why get in a cage when you don't have to?" Steve's calm logic only made things worse.

"I didn't always have a Mazda6, honey," Martina told him, flushing with anger, and shifting down again, this time to hug the tight bend near the footy club. The tires gave a squeal. "I might look all North Shore or whatever, but what you clearly don't realize—"

The lights up ahead were turning orange. Her passenger grabbed the door handle.

"I'm sure you didn't. I'm sorry if I offended you. Look—" He grinned at her, baring his perfect white teeth. Martina shrugged a very Mediterranean shrug. Steve slid his teeth out onto the palm of his hand, and Martina blanched. The false teeth sat there between them, looking nasty, the gums an awful plastic pink. When he put them back in he wasn't grinning.

"What doesn't kill us means craniofacial surgeries and metal rods pinning our limbs," he said bluntly.

He undid his seat belt.

"I won my last four fights," he went on. "But that didn't bring my teeth back. I run fifty clicks a week and do three hundred sit-ups a day. If all that sounds like fun to you, the gym'll be open next week. Just here's fine, thanks."

Stony-faced, Martina pulled over. Steve made his escape through the crowd streaming into the market.

———

Kerry folded a fifty-dollar bill into her wallet, where four more David Unaipons already sat gazing thoughtfully up at her from among the coin. There ya go, Uncle, Kerry told it. Sit tight and don't be going walkabout on me. She grinned. Why even knock over TABs when gullible white people fell over themselves to hurl bungoo at you?

"Nothing to it, eh," she crowed. Pretty Mary looked up from the shadowy rear of the tent.

"Don't go getting cocky, girl," she lectured. "Don't take the cards lightly, or it'll come back on ya. And go easy on the tall handsome strangers too." Kerry had begun the day green and nervous, especially after discovering imminent pregnancies in her first two readings. She'd saved face by concluding that the babies could belong to sisters or nieces of the lesbian couples on the other side of the table. They were delighted to be persuaded, luckily. The cards don't lie, she parroted Pretty Mary, whenever she scented scepticism. Nobody was paying her to prevaricate.

"You wanna jump in yet?" she asked Pretty Mary. Pretty Mary declined, but when the Two of Cups turned up again in Kerry's fifth reading, a lightbulb went off in her mother's head.

"It's because I'm here!" she declared. "Of course you're gonna be drawing the Cups sitting next to me, cos you're my child." She gazed at Kerry in dismay. There was at least another full day before Kerry flew solo in the Tarot Teepee.

"Hows about I grab us a feed," offered Kerry, whose stomach had been growling shamefully all afternoon. *Quit while you're ahead* was one of her favorite mottos, along with *If it ain't broke, don't fix it.*

"I'll go jull first," Pretty Mary agreed, rushing out through the tent flap and slamming straight into a handsome young fella who clutched her by the upper arms to stop her toppling. "Oops, sorry, bub," she apologized, pushing her foot back into a dislodged sandal. She peered at him, her bladder full to bursting. Hadn't this lad been at Pop's funeral? Who owned him? Her curiosity battled with the urgent call of nature.

"Give it a whirl, darl, let Durrigan tell you what's in your future," she suggested, gesturing to the teepee as she raced away. Steve grinned and ducked inside to find a horrified Kerry shuffling the tarot deck and looking anywhere but at him in his Parramatta shorts and red muscle shirt.

"Welcome, stranger. Have a seat," she said from beneath her veil, unsure whether Steve could recognize her simply from her eyes and hands. Oh, yeah, and the tops of her tits. Steve sat down opposite her in the dim light. Only a small, square table separated them. Kerry shuffled the cards and began to lay them out.

"Did you want the fifteen- or the thirty-minute reading?" Kerry asked, almost dropping the deck. Steve didn't answer. Instead, he plucked a random card off the table, examined it closely, and then turned it around so Kerry could see it too.

"You begin by formulating a question," she started, but Steve interrupted her patter. His eyes glowed with mischief.

"The Fool?" he queried.

"New beginnings and innocence," Kerry replied warily, wondering if her cover was blown. Surely he wouldn't be giving her that look otherwise? Or was he some giant slut who looked at all women like that, trying it on for young and old? It was an unpleasant thought, but Kerry was nothing if not a realist.

"Particularly to do with career, but it can also be things like housing. Sometimes family stuff. Really, though, we need to formulate a question before—"

Steve was looking from the card to her and back again.

"New beginnings," he echoed, leaning back. "I like the sound of that."

"It's, ah, twenty-five dollars for the fifteen-minute reading. Or fifty for the half hour . . ." Kerry went on, wondering when Pretty Mary would be back. She didn't know how long she could keep pretending not to notice Steve's barely clothed body, a meter away. His hands were right there, almost touching her own when she straightened the tablecloth or laid the cards out.

"Better make it the fifteen. Because I see you having a drink with me in the very near future." He smiled. "Before you zoom off on your Harley again."

Behind the veil, Kerry was grinning too. Cheeky bugger. She put her hand out for the card he held and expertly shuffled the pack.

"Let's see what Spirit has to say about that, shall we?" she answered.

———

"Lotta mustard, please, mate," Steve told the sweating German-sausage man when they finally reached the top of the queue.

"Make mine plain," Kerry said, fossicking for her wallet. Steve interrupted her with an electrifying touch on her forearm.

"My shout," he said. "C'mon."

"Nuh-uh, I ordered three," she told him, brandishing one of the fifties she had earned that afternoon. *But, um, you can leave your hand right there. For just as long as you like, bunji.*

"Ah, knock off, it's all good," Steve insisted, with a quizzical expression. He let his fingertips linger, and Kerry put her wallet away much slower than normal. *You would be incredibly welcome,* she said in her secret inner voice, *to run that hand wherever the hell you please.* When the sausage man handed the kai over, Kerry passed two wieners to a pair of skinny white kids who had been watching the queue the whole time. She nodded at the older one and kept on walking. Steve glanced behind as they walked and saw the kids hoeing into the snags like there was no tomorrow.

They found a spot below the huge camphor laurels and folded onto the grass. On the oval in front of them, two snooty-looking camels were being led about with worried punters on them. Punters who had only just realized how high off the ground a camel's hump was, and what odd predicaments they had asked—nay, *paid*—to be in. Kerry twisted her silver necklace obsessively and hoped that she looked cooler than she felt.

Her body was on high alert, every nerve rattled. Had she been a fire engine, her sirens would have been screaming, her red and blue lights flashing for all the world to see. But she wasn't a fire engine. She was a going-on-thirty-four-year-old Goorie doob being doggedly pursued by a spunky stranger, and the only visible sign of it was the shit-eating grin she couldn't seem to wipe off her dial. And someone had forgotten to remind her junoo that she preferred fucking girls. Every last molecule of her was itching to get closer to Steve. It felt like the gap between them was filled with something other than ordinary air. Something more liquid and far more enticing drifted between them. It wouldn't have surprised Kerry in the slightest if fireworks or laser beams had exploded when Steve playfully pushed her, teasing her with the idea that she herself had wanted all three snags.

"How'd you know those kids weren't buying?" he asked her, abashed that he hadn't spotted their transparent poverty.

"Cos I used to be them," Kerry said, holding three-quarters of a hot dog up and away in demonstration. "We'd stand out front of the van, dribbling, while all the whitefellas fed their faces. It was torture."

"Good time to make up for it now, then." Steve buried his face in hot relish and mustard. When he looked up, a bit of tomato sauce was smeared on his chin. Kerry smiled faintly and looked at the camphor laurel leaves littering the lush green lawn. After seeing her lash out like that with a fifty, Steve probably thought she ate hot dogs with gay abandon these days, handed em around like lollies. Probably assumed that there was always a David Unaipon stashed in her back pocket. Or enough on her cash card to buy an eight-dollar feed any time she wanted. Some people lived that way, she knew. But the crew in Trinder mostly ate bread and chips when they ate at all. Meat was strictly for pay week, same as shop-bought grog and smokes were. Off-pay week was hungry week, sniffing around friends' and rellos' houses for someone who'd scored a food parcel or a job, or had a win at bingo. She looked down into her lap. It was a shamejob to go explaining how blackfellas lived. Even if dugais believed you, they were full of useless fucking genius suggestions on how to climb out of poverty. Like it was simple. Like it didn't suit the powers that be to keep poor people scrabbling in the shit, keep their attention off the rich world's sparkling goodies in case they got any bright ideas about grabbing some for themselves.

"I used to shoplift food when I was fifteen, sixteen," Steve said matter-of-factly.

"Yeah, for thrills." Kerry sniffed at the idea of white kids thinking they were all badass and shit.

"Nah, cos we needed the bloody tucker! Mum thought we were down the beach, but me and my brother'd be up the Burleigh Four Square stashing bacon down our daks."

Kerry's eyes widened.

"Ever had a greasy, cold packet of bacon in yer undies?" Steve screwed his face up. "No joke, let me tell ya! But frozen burger patties were the worst!"

Kerry burst out laughing.

"It taught us how to wash up, anyway," he added. "We'd pinch the stuff, go home, cook it, eat it, and then get rid of the evidence before Mum got home from her shift."

"I woulda picked you for rich," Kerry said.

Steve gaped like she was off her dial. "Yeah. Course. Rich people always hitch everywhere."

"I thought you were a greenie. And you said you're starting a business . . . plus look at your shoes!" Expensive runners. Perfect teeth. Steve's brow was still crinkling at her. She shoved his shoulder in turn. "What? Don't look at me like that!"

"My sponsor gives me the shoes, and the gym's basically a massive debt, so far. You've got a bit of catching up to do, girl," Steve said, reaching to pick up Kerry's mobile, which had fallen onto the grass. "Listen, before you run off on me again, I'm gonna call my phone with yours. You'll have my number then, and I'll have yours."

"Gimme that!" Kerry cried, snatching at the phone. Steve rolled sideways, easily avoiding her lunge, and then lay on his back in the sunshine, dialling and laughing. His shorts pocket began to trill with the sound of an old-fashioned handset.

"You cheeky bugger!" Kerry was surprised at how easily he had out-wrestled her. She had grown up fighting Ken and Black Superman, and knew a few moves. Steve teased her, then, holding her phone at arm's length as she clambered about trying to retrieve it. In the struggle Kerry somehow ended up astride him. Both her hands were planted flat on his chest, and her mobile sat there too, safely beneath her right palm, but Steve held both her wrists in a clamp grip. It was a stalemate.

"Give up, whiteboy?" she panted, trying to bluff him.

"*No pasarán*," he told her, rocking his hips sideways to make her wobble on top of him. "No surrender." She dug her knees into his ribs and leaned more of her weight forward onto her palms. Her hair fell forward so that she was looking at him through a curtain of dark curls.

Their eyes locked. Both of them forgot about the phone as they suddenly realized where they were. Kerry was sitting on top of a grown man she hardly knew, and their sweating thighs were separated by little more than his flimsy nylon footy shorts. Kerry shifted her weight, shamefully aware of the heat of Steve's hips and the fact of his groin directly below her own. Her body thrummed inside with this awareness; a long unconscious groan slipped from her. Steve heard, and a slow smile spread across his face.

"Have dinner with me tomorrow night and I'll surrender the contraband," he bargained. Kerry tested the strength of his grip on her wrists and what she discovered sent a deep shiver of anticipation down the entire length of her body. Beneath the purple costume her nipples began to grow taut.

"Did you want to maybe get a room," suggested a man walking past with a burbling toddler on his shoulders, "or start charging for pay-per-view?"

"Thanks for the tip," Steve shot back. He peered up at Kerry. Her hair spiralled wildly in all directions now, and the crystal pendant hung skewiff against her cleavage, rising and falling with her deep breaths.

"Well, what do ya reckon?"

"I'm doing the night markets tomorrow." Kerry shut her eyes. Steve had the most amazing shoulders. She could feel his ridged six-pack against her lower arms, and she was hornier than she could remember being since high school. But this had gone way beyond flirting and was fast turning into something else. What was going on? After all these years, a white man, *really*?

"And besides . . ." she began awkwardly. Steve was hard underneath her, and his hips were still rocking gently from side to side. She closed her fingers around her phone.

"Look at me," Steve said, releasing her wrists. He ran his hands up her trembling arms to her head and very gently pulled her down. Kerry's last fragments of resistance shattered. Their lips met, tentatively at first, and then they were kissing long and deep, ignoring the catcalls and whistles of passersby. Kissing Steve, Kerry had the odd sensation that the time that had passed since the Grade Nine disco, since that night when she wanted to kiss him and hadn't, those nineteen years hadn't really changed anything at all. They had barely even happened. There had been a strange and tremendous pause in things, until now, that was all; and as they lay together on the grass and kissed, the huge and immobile hands of time were creaking terribly slowly into gear again, and life was starting up afresh after that long but meaningless hiatus.

"So will you come quietly," Steve teased when they finally broke apart, "or are you going to put up a fight?"

Kerry closed her eyes again. By touch alone, she used her index finger to trace the rectangular edges of her phone until she found the off button. She pushed it, hard. With a soft gurgle, the phone shut down to a blank, anonymous screen. Then she opened her eyes, which were soft and dark with longing for more kissing, for more Steve. For new beginnings.

She didn't answer him in words. Instead she played for time, reached out to toy with the flap of his nylon shorts, running her finger gently beneath its lowest edge where it met his upper thigh. Then she brought her finger out, this time using it to trace the Parramatta Eels logo, and now it was Steve's turn to moan with longing. He was rising to kiss her again at the same moment that Kerry leaned forward, slid her hand down low between their hot, close bellies and she found his erection. Steve's cock leaped at her touch, and just like that, she had gone so far that the idea of stopping became impossible. Kerry knew she would fuck this stranger no matter how wrong it was.

"Yes," she said.

Chapter Eight

Steaming February inched towards humid March. Kerry gave up arguing when Pretty Mary—never a huge Allie fan—referred to Steve as "your Mulaga." At their first meeting, Ken had looked daggers at Steve but by the end of the day had settled into a shallow, easy blokiness around him. To see them fixing the XD brakes together you'd have thought they were mates from the womb, Kerry mused, for all that Steve was a pure merino. He had learned a bit from the Murri and Thai fighters he'd trained alongside for years on the coast. Had the brains to just shuttup and listen when anything Black came up. That was a plus. And he had the rare knack, too, of deferring to Ken's alpha bullshit without becoming lesser or losing his inner balance. There was something about him that reminded Kerry curiously of Uncle Richard. A solid way of knowing who he was in the world and accepting it, neither shame of being born a whitefella nor silly about it. Whenever Kerry put casual, mocking shit on Steve for being a dugai and a colonizer he would flummox her by agreeing. Then add, *The Poms dispossessed my mob too, of course, and plonked us here on someone else's country. To enjoy the fruits of our genocide,* Kerry quickly pointed out. *It's called the Caledonian River, pal, not the Albion.* And once more he just said, *You're absolutely right, your mob's loss was my mob's gain,* then pulled her closer for more distracting kisses.

Pretty Mary joked that the Salter family had two whitefellas in it now: Elvis and Steve. I wouldn't go that bloody far, Kerry retorted. There was a big difference between having a bit of fun and outright owning a dugai. Let alone—perish the thought—being owned by one. No, Steve was strictly kept around for a laugh and she wasn't about to let him forget it. When he had suggested dinner in Byron on Valentine's Day, Kerry told him to buy hot chooks that the whole family could enjoy. Everyone except Donny, that was. Her nephew was still refusing anything other than lollies and two-minute noodles.

———

A week before the council was due to meet, a pow-wow was called. Pop's plastic urn had been on top of the cupboard for weeks and a decision had to be made: would they take him to the river early? At least a year rightly should have passed before he was put back in the earth.

"I know, I *know*, but this is the whiteman world we're living in," argued Black Superman on FaceTime. "Better that he goes onto country now, cos if that jail gets built, there's no telling if we'll ever see Granny's island again without being locked up next to it—"

"The jail's not gonna be built," said Ken implacably, as if that was an end to it. His word the law. You wish, thought Kerry. Snap back to reality, brother, it's been waiting for you a while.

"I need more time to think," complained Pretty Mary, sorting the washing faster and faster in an effort to quell her nerves. "Spirit don't like it. And I can't be put on the spot like this!" A tower of threadbare towels wobbled in front of her.

"Well, don't think too bloody hard," said Ken, scrubbing at his stubbled face with both palms, "or a piece of goonah might fall out ya ear."

"I reckon we do it now," said Kerry with a stroke of sudden genius. "Cos maybe this is *why* the cards are saying no. Maybe it'll help stop the jail." In truth, Kerry simply wanted to get the whole damn business sorted. Draw a line under the old man's death and move on.

Maybe then Pretty Mary's guts would stop paining her. Maybe then the sobbing from the next bedroom would ease off, and she could think clearly about retrieving her backpack and making tracks away from Durrongo, where she seemed to have somehow gotten hopelessly mired for the second time in her life.

"Hmm . . ." Pretty Mary's resistance was weakening, and when Black Superman promised to fly home for the ceremony, it crumbled altogether. The prospect of seeing her favorite child overrode Pretty Mary's guilt about protocol.

But in the end Black Superman had to attend by FaceTime after a massive storm cell cancelled every flight out of Sydney. Aunty Tall Mary and Uncle Richard likewise sent their apologies from the big Treaty meeting in Canberra. Pretty Mary moaned and wept, but there was no alternative. It was better that most of the family put Pop to rest than none of them at all.

―――――――

"Slow down!" screeched Donny as Ken took the gravelled turn into Settlement Road at speed, sending Kerry sliding into Steve's lap. In the front, Pretty Mary clutched Pop in his beautifully woven basket and prayed aloud. Ken whooped, and drummed on the roof with his right hand. He hadn't meant to make the car fishtail, but he was high on adrenaline and loving every seat-clutching, dot-squeezing moment. In Donny's lap, Elvis yipped as he came ever closer to flying out the window. Kerry seized his back leg as a precaution.

"Slow down, ya stupid prick!" she echoed Donny, to no avail.

"Imma give the old fella a proper send-off! Bunch of pussies!" Ken yelled as the XD straightened up. He planted his foot and hurtled down the dirt track running parallel to the river, the big crack in the windscreen giving the passengers the illusion that they were watching an action movie on multiple screens.

"What's going on? Youse there yet?" Black Superman crackled, his face blurring to a smeary brown jigsaw as the reception on Pretty Mary's iPhone faded in and out.

"Ken's driving like a maniac!" Kerry told him. "Cos, you know, we all immortal, us mob."

"Hail Mary, full of grace, blessed art thou among women—"

Ken was still laughing when Accadacca came on the radio. "Aw, deadly!" He turned the dial as far as it would go.

"*Jailbreak!*" he sang, becoming Malcolm Young. "*Jaaaaiiiilllbreak!*"

"Will you take it easy, for fuck's sake!" Kerry insisted, hauling herself up out of Steve's lap. "We nearly lost Elvis that time!"

Steve held the phone out the window in a futile search for better reception.

Ken was speeding into the final left-hand turn when, appearing to finally hear their pleas, he hit the skids hard. But they didn't have long to feel relieved. The Falcon slewed around the bend in a shower of red dirt and shuddered as it came to a long, sliding halt. With the car at a standstill, and dust blowing in all directions, everyone gaped. The Falcon's faded blue bonnet had stopped hard up against a brand-new weldmesh fence blocking the width of the entire road. There were no workmen in fluoro vests. No orange witches caps. No road-working equipment. Just the river glinting in the distance, and the silver barrier of the fence, right there smack bang in front of them. Wired to the fence was a red and white Patterson Real Estate sign. *For Sale.*

And plastered across it was a large diagonal sticker that read: *Under Contract.*

Half a minute passed before anyone could talk, and then they all spoke at once.

"Be fucked," said Donny.

"I'll sing that fucken dog!" erupted Ken. "He wants a bullet in the brain, truesgod."

"No, it can't be right," Pretty Mary protested, waving her hanky hard against the sign. "Can't be right . . ."

"I'm gonna fucken kill Buckley," threatened Kerry, punching the back of Ken's seat over and over, until Steve grabbed her arm. He held her and she burst into hot tears. Donny sat stunned, looking as though their trip to lay Pop to rest had been hijacked by little green aliens.

Pretty Mary stumbled out, gray-faced, onto the gravel. Donny unfolded his skinny legs and went to stand with ten fingers latched through the diamond mesh of the fence, gazing dumbly at the promised land beyond. Ken thrashed around the scrub, discovering that the weldmesh fence stretched to the riverbank in one direction and deep into thick bush on the other, where the XD had no hope of going. The fence was seven feet high and its posts were concreted into the ground: there was no way Pretty Mary, or probably even Ken, could get over it so they could scatter Pop's remains as a family. He joined the others, who stood in a mute semicircle, facing the terrible sign.

"Knock the cunt of a thing down," offered Donny with a hard kick at the real estate sign to demonstrate his seriousness. "We can just drive straight through it, eh." Kerry looked at the boy in surprise. His father glanced sideways at him, nodding. The shitheap XD was already old and scratched up; the weldmesh would probably come away from the uprights if they had any kind of speed up at all. Donny was on the money.

"We have to get there," urged Pretty Mary. "I promised Pop I'd put him at the river with Granny and Grandad and your father. I *promised*." So breaking the law's okay sometimes, is it, Kerry thought with a sharp flash of resentment.

"Or could we get a tinnie, come up the river . . ." Steve mused.

"Show them dogs a thing or two." Ken nodded, but he was agreeing with Donny, not Steve. "Why should we have to sneak onto our own land to keep a pack of Captain Cook cunts happy? I should set fire to the whole bloody lot." Ken angrily lit a durrie, then with a wide-flung arm described an arc at the bush they stood in—five hundred acres of state forest surrounded the dozen freehold

acreage blocks that fronted the river. Kerry heaved a great sigh. Little
wonder that her older brother had done not one or two but three
stints in Grafton jail. Ken was the smartest fucking moron around,
truesgod.

"You mob all blind or what?" she asked, pointing with her lips
to the security camera stuck high in a gum tree five meters above
the fence. Ken swore, put his smoke in his mouth and then jerked
two fingers at the tree. Steve stared at the camera for a long minute.
The group sagged. Then Elvis trotted over and casually lifted his leg
against the fence. A pungent yellow stream formed a puddle beneath
it, and everyone cheered.

Kerry looked behind her. Pretty Mary was back in the car, rocking back and forth, keening, with Pop's woven basket clutched to
her chest. Ken said, "Ah fuck this fer a joke," and returned to the XD
as well. He started up the engine with a loud, clattering roar.

"Wait, Kenny!" cried Pretty Mary, who had dropped the basket
in fright, spilling a few grains of Pop's ashes onto the rusted car floor.
Pop didn't belong on the road for workmen to drive their machin-
ery over; it was the riverbank itself they needed to reach, that hal-
lowed ground where Grandad Chinky Joe had sung his songs, and
where Granny Ava had plunged into the river, saved her own life to
give it to all the clan.

"I'm gonna show these dugais who they fucking with," Ken told
his mother, revving the engine harder. He stuck his head out the
window and gave the security camera an earful of abuse.

"Just WAIT!" Pretty Mary ordered him in distress. "Wait, son, till
I get this—him—this up off the . . . ow, Christ!" She gestured at the
spilt ash. A drop of blood hovered from her index finger, about to
fall and christen the basket.

"Put ya seat belt on," Ken said.

Kerry ran to Pretty Mary's open door, yelling at Ken that they
needed to come back at night when they couldn't be identified. He
ignored her and put the car in gear.

As Ken began a wild zigzagging in reverse, Pretty Mary still groping at the car floor with her good hand, Steve came swiftly and unexpectedly from behind everyone. He sprinted straight at the shining silver panels of mesh. In his right hand he held a thin dead eucalyptus branch. Kerry had only enough time to wonder if he was going to somehow pole vault over the fence, and to decide that the branch was far too slight for that, when Steve hurled his lance at the camera with deadly accuracy. It landed square in the center of the lens with a satisfyingly loud smash, followed by several moments of tinkling glass. As an angry electronic buzz issued from the camera, the spear stayed jammed in the middle of the broken lens, poking out at the world like a great, long, white tongue.

"Bugger me roan," Kerry exclaimed in astonishment.

"Not just high jump," Steve panted. "Javelin too."

Donny burst into laughter at the spear stuck fast in the camera, the funniest thing he'd seen in ages. The XD roared, as Pretty Mary yanked her seat belt on.

"Love ya work!" murmured Kerry in approval. Ken planted his foot and plowed through the fence.

The car continued forward with a hideous shriek as the diamond mesh caught against the bonnet and sides, and tore away from the posts. Then, from the far side, Ken leaned on his horn to announce victory.

Cheering, Kerry, Steve, and Donny all galloped through the gaping, ragged hole, AFL players bursting into a game, to pile into the car and take Pop down to the ancestors.

"Close the gap!" laughed Kerry, scrambling into the back seat with a yipping Elvis.

Ken squinted in the rear-view mirror at Steve.

"You sure you're white, brah?" Ken asked.

"Full-blood Scot, me. Irn-Bru running in me veins," Steve answered, one arm around a beaming Kerry and the other clutching Elvis's collar. "Except for a little bit of Spanish."

Pretty Mary smiled skeptically.

"Spanish, yeah, right," muttered Kerry. "Musta been more Spaniards in Australia than there was in Spain, back in the day."

"But don't hold my color against me," Steve said, not understanding.

"Wouldn't dream of it, brah," Ken answered, before adding drily, "Ya might spear me."

"You always wanted a full-blood man, eh, Kerry?" Pretty Mary asked, having a sly dig as she got out to light the fire for Pop's ceremony in the clearing by the river.

"Oi," said Ken sharply, hating the word that had dogged him and his only-just-dark-enough skin all his life.

"We was all full of blood, last time I looked," Kerry said, before adding, "We swimming Pop over to the island or what?"

"Not on ya life," answered Pretty Mary, aghast, passing the woven basket to her son. "Kenny'll have to do it. Put him there under the pine, son. I'll sing him from this side . . ."

Pretty Mary blew hard into her metal bucket. Everyone walked through the clouds of billowing eucalyptus smoke so that Pretty Mary could paint an ochre crucifix on the nearest boulder, and cry, and sing Pop back into the ground.

An hour later, when the ashes had been scattered and Ken had swum back over to the clearing, he surprised everyone by upending a full UDL over a boulder in Pop's honor. When Kerry asked why he'd used the entire can, Ken shook the last drops onto the summer-dry earth, where ants and flies were already swarming to the sugar.

"Rest in power, Old Man." He gestured to the island. "Go well." Then he turned to Kerry and began to laugh at her question, real silly way.

"What's so funny?" she asked, grinning along without knowing why.

"Don't you remember, sis?" Ken crumpled the empty UDL can in his fist. "That ad?"

"What ad?"

"Things go better with Coke."

"Aw good go, you're bloody womba you are." Kerry curled her lip but had to laugh too, slipping her hand into Steve's.

A few steps away, Pretty Mary was still weeping into the current of the river. The next time it floods, Kerry mused, a little bit of Pop will be washed into the slipstream and start a long, slow journey down to the ocean. Ah well, it's only right. He might not have known exactly where he was from, buggered up by missionary like so many others, but he knew he was a saltwater man, at least. And the borrogura calls us all back in the end, that great mother lode. The moon pulls the ocean and the ocean pulls us and everything is always pulling at everything else whether we know it or not, just like Grandad Chinky Joe insisted to the very end. The dugai can flap their jangs as much as they like, Pretty Mary had reported him saying, but us mob got the law of the land, granddaughter, and that's that. We's in everything: the jagun, the trees, the animals, the bulloon. It's all us, and we's it too. And don't ever let the dugai tell ya different. They savages, remember.

"Coming in?" Kerry asked, stripping down to her sports bra.

"Bloody oath," said Steve, ripping his tank top off. Kerry stood transfixed. Those sweet, sweet abs. The way his rib cage showed just a tiny little bit, high up above the planes of muscle sloping below and around them. Oh yeah, baby. But Kerry's enjoyment was short-lived.

"Eeyah, knock orf!" Pretty Mary erupted from the water's edge. "No swimming, you moogle lot! The Doctor's in there, you'll be shark goonah by this time tomorra!"

Kerry heaved a great sigh. Jesus Christ. Here we go again. Signs and fucking wonders, at every turn.

"Mum. We swim here *all the time.*"

"C'mon, lad," said Ken to his son, yanking his T-shirt off over his head. "Us mens is right." He dived in, surfacing to taunt Kerry with loud pronouncements on the refreshing qualities of the water and the benefits of being a wardham. But Donny sat on the bank and dangled his skinny ankles in the current. He was shame to undress in front of Steve.

"Don't Mum me." Pretty Mary stubbornly kept on at Kerry. "They bin promised that minya and they never got it. You stay outta there, my girl. And Steve, you specially. Ya stay on dry ground if yer know what's good for ya."

Steve looked at Pretty Mary in bewilderment, until she explained that being of the shark totem, Ken could safely swim in the river, and his protection would likely extend to his son. She and Kerry, on the other hand, risked being ripped limb from limb. And that went triple for Steve, a whitefella with no protection at all. They had to stay out of the water, she insisted fiercely. A debt of blood is the most serious debt going, and has no time limit.

Steve groaned. Being eaten by a shark seemed preferable to dying of heatstroke.

"I thought you swam here all the time?" he muttered unhappily to Kerry.

"I do. And I reckon it's a load of horseshit, cos the last time The Doctor got spotted this far upriver was the 2014 floods. But ya can't tell Mum, eh."

"Mmmm, lubbly and cold here, almost *too* cold," Ken taunted from mid-river before duck-diving to the bottom to search for Granny Ava's long-lost kingplate.

"Oh, GET FUCKED, BRO!" Kerry yelled, sprinting to leap and bomb off the highest boulder. She exploded through the surface of the water just as Ken's glistening silver mullet reemerged, swamping him and making him choke on a mouthful of river water. Kerry's laughter rang over the island like a bell.

"You'll be sorry!" Pretty Mary lectured over Ken's spluttering. Shaking her head at her children, she went and sat in the shade to cheerfully prophesy more disaster. In a move that made Kerry stare, Steve leaned over the rocks to soak his tank top. Then he squeezed the excess over his head, put the tank top back on over his sculptured body, and went to sit and yarn with Pretty Mary.

"Pussy," accused Ken with a last spluttering cough. He shook his hair wildly to make spray fly in all directions. Elvis ran up and down the riverbank, barking orders.

"And here's me thinking you was all about culture, bruz," Kerry said to Ken. She nodded at Steve. "That's respect, that is."

"He don't believe it, but," Ken mocked. "He's just making out. Cos of you."

"Well, good. Least he makes a fucking effort. I don't see Savannah here," Kerry said, rolling onto her back and ignoring Ken's tedious need to be better than every other male around. A better pub fighter. A better culture man. Or just a better fucking idiot. But even Ken's dickheadery wasn't going to spoil this swim for her. The water was too glorious; their triumph in busting through Buckley's fence was too perfect.

She gazed at the shining river bend. No houses. No noise, other than Elvis. No whitefellas. This was the Australia she yearned for, the green sanctuary of the island with its palms and figs and wattles. The hoop pine proud in its place casting its deep shadow. She was suddenly overwhelmed by a longing that they could turn back time; set up camp and live together on the island, fish and yarn and laugh themselves silly over nothing like they had in her youth. But no good. Ken would be whinging after the first night, wondering who won the seventh at Wangaratta. Donny would simply lie down and die without his computer, and even she liked the comforts of home, truth be told. They were soft, her generation, soft and spoiled. At seventeen she'd thought she was shit hot after them first sneaks in Coolie, running amok in Burleigh and Surfers. Surviving her first stretch in BWCC the year after, but nah, gammon. She woke up to that thug life bullshit real fast.

Tough wasn't scraping by on petty crime or winning street fights or even going to the lockup. Tough was not relying on the white man for *anything*. Like Granny Ava and Grandad Joe, dodging the mish life to live on what they grew and hunted and earned. Slaving as a stockman and a domestic, yeah, but managing by a minor miracle to do it for wages, not under the whip hand of a god-bothering priest or mission boss. Tough was Granny Ava, big belly full to busting with the only child she ever got to keep. Shot in the back and swimming a freezing river with only a chain around her neck for protection. Pop too, in his own way, the old bastard. He had his faults, but he was staunch. And that's what graves are for, the realization dawned on Kerry. They distilled your family history. They took what your ancestors did and who they were and gave it to you in one place, so you could go there and think about their lives and learn the lessons you needed to learn in order to keep on going. Inspired, Kerry swam over to the island. She leaned down and touched the rich dark earth of the riverbank with her right palm. Her fingers were the exact color of the soil, and they blended into it as though they were raised tracks made by some mysterious passing creature. The months to come would need the strength of Granny Ava and Grandad Chinky Joe, and then some, if the river bend was to be protected. *I promise you both*, Kerry said silently. *I promise to try and save it.*

"My daughter should be here," exclaimed Pretty Mary sorrow-fully, not expecting any answer since there was none to be had. She bent to wash her face and hands in the current, then stood with river water streaming down her arms and cheeks. The wet rocks beneath her glistened black and shining. The old lady gazed down where fish darted and shimmered as the slanting sunlight hit their scales. When she looked back up her jaw was set. She's switched, Kerry saw in surprise from the far side of the river. She's like she was years ago, before Granny Ruth died. Pretty Mary clapped her hands together loudly. Once, twice, three times. Then she put her hands to her mouth and cooeed. The intense call reverberated across the water and through the trees on the island, then died away to a deep and solemn silence. Even Elvis quieted down. Everyone waited. Then Pretty Mary—the old Pretty Mary—put her hands on her hips and turned her attention to the living. In the river, Ken and Kerry trod water, watching her.

"Listen up, youfla. Pop's at rest here now. We're done with Sorry Business. And that means we gotta step up and finish this blooming jail nonsense, ya hear?"

"Bloody oath," said Ken.

"Only what I've been telling ya for weeks," responded Kerry.

"I'm in," said Steve, sitting in the shade of the gums.

"Me too," said Donny, leaning on the car.

"Right," said Pretty Mary. "Let's get cracking, then, and go do something about it."

As Kerry climbed out, Steve offered her his strong right hand, and she clasped it willingly. He hauled her up onto the bank, then kissed the top of her head before throwing his arm around her wet shoulders.

"Definitely whipped," Ken teased him as they headed to the car, but Steve was too happy to care.

From its branch high above the clan, a kookaburra sat, watching in silence. Nobody but it saw the slender dark shape cruising slowly upriver towards Granny Ava's tree, the tip of one pointed fin just breaking the surface.

Chapter Nine

"Another hit?" Steve lifted the steaming jug off a tiny stove hidden beneath the reception desk. Kerry shook her head. Steve's coffee made her head spin, and she wanted to test out some gym equipment. It was a lifetime since she'd been a teenager pumping iron at BWCC. She quickly pushed away the thoughts of Allie that followed on from "BWCC" and plonked onto the vinyl seat of the lat pull-down machine. She grasped the chrome bar above her head. Muscle memory told Kerry exactly how her back and neck and arms would feel under the strain of the weights.

"Bit wider," Steve said, coming to stand behind her with his hands lightly on her shoulders. He placed her palms a couple of centimeters farther from the center of the bar and adjusted the peg. "Now, nice steady pull. Easy does it."

Kerry's cheeks bulged but the bar barely trembled. Steve frowned and fiddled with the weight stack.

"That's forty kay gee now," he said. "Try again." Kerry did, with the same result. She let go of the bar, puffing heavily, and rubbed at her right shoulder. When they swapped places, Steve slid the weight up and down its rail with ease. He shrugged, baffled, as Kerry failed for a third time to bring the bar down.

"Do you want to try thirty kilos?" he asked, already bending to alter the weights a second time. "Or twenty?"

"Thirty kilos is less than what Lub Lub weighs," said Kerry scornfully.

"You have to lose the ego," Steve advised with a small smile. "Start where you are and work from there."

"Okay, okay." Kerry heaved ferociously at the adjusted bar only to have it come plummeting down in a rush. She swivelled in her seat and pinned Steve with a suspicious glare.

"Might be cos I moved this?" he grinned, gleefully showing her the steel safety pin that had been locking the weights securely in place.

"Bastard," Kerry accused, abandoning the machine to chase Steve around the enormous room. He dodged and feinted like a footy champion, leaping from the sofa bed to behind the reception desk and all around the weight stations, until Kerry realized that she was never going to catch him. She stood winded in front of a poster advertising 8 a.m. Boot Camp.

"You'll keep. I'd better let ya get ready for Root Camp, anyway," she informed him loftily, heading for the ladies. Steve watched her arse rise and fall in nylon shorts as she walked away, and checked his watch: 7:19 a.m.

"I might have to join you," he said, following her in and stripping off his boxers.

"Oh, hello, sailor," she laughed, seeing that he was already hard. "This'll be quick . . ."

"Plenty of time," he assured her, stepping into the shower cubicle, where Kerry was already gleaming wet beneath the spray. He began to lather her up and down with shower gel. The white bubbles contrasted with her skin, running in narrow rivulets down her tautly muscled runner's thighs. Kerry smiled. She reached one hand down to fondle his cock, gently sliding the loose, thin skin over the hard shaft. The one clear bonus of fucking cisboys. Steve closed his eyes and sighed with pleasure.

"Turn around," he told her, running foamy hands over her breasts and down down down past her abs to the front of her thighs. He pressed in even closer. At the back of her neck where a tattooed dolphin swam beneath her hair, Steve first began to nibble and then to nip hard at her neck. Kerry braced her hands against the clear shower panels. She slowly began to bounce her hips in time with Steve's gently probing fingers. When she was moaning without knowing that she was, and when the world had shrunk to the water falling down on her and what was happening in and around her junoo, Steve slid wetly inside her from behind and began to thrust. He gripped the top of the cubicle hard with his free left hand and steadily fingered Kerry until she felt a great shuddering wave begin to surge through her—just as the first client of the morning pulled into the car park.

"Hurry up! Get out!" she urged him sixty seconds later. Steve needed to maintain the pretense that he wasn't living illegally in the gym. He snatched up his clothes, half tripping on the wet tiles, and scrambled into the men's changing room just in the nick of time. Soon customers began to stream in. Working stiffs, Kerry observed, who needed to fit the gym in at 8 a.m. so they could sell the rest of their lives to capitalist bullshit. Quite a few were soccer mums coming to perve on the instructor. *Occupational hazard,* Steve had said when he'd first shown Kerry the gym, and seemed secretly disappointed when she roared with laughter, giving zero fucks about soccer mums. Piqued, he'd asked Kerry that night about Allie for the second time. "Just an old fuckbuddy," Kerry had brushed him off, and something in her answer told Steve not to ask any more questions.

"Ya picked up my shirt so I'm stealing yours," Kerry yelled as she left.

"Bloody thieving blackfellas," he teased from the men's. "Nothing's safe from you lot!"

"Well, you will go and put it on my land, pal."

Kerry was already astride the Harley, smirking behind her visor, when a white ute followed by a flash red sports car arrived. If working a straight job meant you could afford the latest Mazda6, it had something going for it. Not enough to tempt her into an office—if such a chance even existed—but something. She kicked the Hog to life and roared away to a Centrelink appointment in Murwillumbah. It was time to give them overfed mothers a tune-up. Black Superman had put his hand in his pocket for the funeral in the end—and just as well. If it was left to the bureaucrats Pop would still be lying in the morgue with a five-thousand-dollar pawn tag on his big black toe. Kerry had a long and impressive history of professional thievery behind her, true, but stealing her grandfather's corpse from the secure cold room of the Patto Funeral Home was beyond even her.

———————

Ken and Savannah stood shoulder to shoulder blocking the front stairs of the council building. Like the rest of the protesters, Ken was holding a placard that read *NO NEW JAIL: JUSTICE REINVESTMENT NOW!* Unlike the others, he had zero commitment to the principles of nonviolent resistance informing the rally; he was considering instead what it would mean to knock Jim Buckley's teeth down his snivelling gammon white throat. Beside him, Savannah ground a smoke out on the footpath and then kicked the butt symbolically towards the council offices. Pack of elite wankers.

"Shame, police state!" yelled a dreadlocked seventy-year-old anarchist, as a cop car slowed and then drove up onto the footpath beside Ken. Three dozen pairs of angry eyes locked on to the vehicle and the men inside.

"How they hanging, Kenny?" asked Senior Sergeant Luke Chin, sticking an elbow out the window of his paddy wagon. "Not gonna give us any drama, are ya, mate?" he asked pointedly as he scoped out the assorted lunatics, blackfellas, and socialists who had been attracted by Ken's hand-lettered flyers.

"I didn't start this fight," replied Ken. "Jim Buckley did. He'd steal the eyes out of a blind cockie's head, the corrupt prick."

"Well, let's try and keep it all legal, mate," said Luke. "And I'll see ya at the pool comp Thursday."

"Ya still owe us the entry fee from last week," Ken reminded Luke, who had been skillfully avoiding paying his debts since he played with Ken in the Patto under-seventeens.

"Shout ya a pie?" Luke offered, putting the paddy wagon into first gear.

"Make it two. Steak and mushroom," Ken said. "And get us plenty of sauce too, ya cheap bastard."

Luke pretended he hadn't heard this jibe, and drove away from what passed for dissent in Patterson to park in the shadow of the Unknown Soldier, opposite the Sugarloaf Bakery. He squinted up at the statue bowing its head sorrowfully over its inverted rifle. Unlike most small country towns, Patterson hadn't had an Unknown Soldier until 1980, the year Zayan Damali took a triple dose of mushrooms at a Channon dance party and applied for a regional arts grant while still high as a kite. The bronze ANZAC he'd sculpted was exactly three millimeters broader in the nose and fuller in the lips than standard, and had been bothering white Patterson ever since. Luke grinned, winked at the Soldier, and went inside the Sugarloaf.

"Let's link arms," suggested a pregnant hippie, back at the demonstration. Everyone agreed that this would be a brilliant display of their solidarity against the prison-industrial complex, and would make a top photo in the local rag to boot. When the councillors turned up several minutes later, the protest stood as an immovable barrier. The sole beleaguered Green was allowed through with approving backslaps; the other six councillors were forced, to the sound of booing and jeers, to detour through the rear. The linked protesters weren't able to shuffle quite quickly enough to prevent their democratically elected reps getting inside, but Ken broke free. In a move reminiscent of his days with the Brisbane Bullets, he abandoned his placard to make up fifty meters in seconds. It was too late, though: the politicians had already fled inside and locked the back door. Ken stormed back around the front to stand in the public gallery with Savannah and the others. The Green did his best, but it took less than fifteen minutes for Jim Buckley's DA to pass. When Ken saw the mayor smile in triumph, his blood pressure shot through the roof.

"This ain't over, Buckley!" he bellowed, the sheer force of his outrage bringing the protesters clustering to him like iron filings to a magnet. An insistent chant began: "This ain't over." Buckley looked across at the furious mob, and at the security guard on high alert beside the door that led to the council offices. In the crowd, the dreadlocked seventy-year-old took out a Zippo lighter and idly began to roll his thumb on the sparking mechanism. The youngsters grinned and began drumming their fists on the plastic seats. Encouraged, Ken moved closer to the councillors, until only a low wooden wall and ten meters of carpet lay between him and his nemesis. Savannah, though quietly thrilled at the idea of Buckley getting his block knocked off, began reminding Ken he was on parole. Ken was deaf to her.

"Hey, Buckley? Think we don't know about your dodgy deals? You got no social license for no fucken prison!" Ken yelled. "*This ain't over!*" The chant swelled and echoed inside the room. The security guard urged the mayor to take a break. It would let the protest dissipate, Rawiri argued. Ken stared the mayor down, a vein throbbing violently in his temple. He raised his right fist high then drove it hard into his left palm, grinding it there as he glared. Ken was waiting for the tiniest grin of triumph, the slightest grimace of disdain, to propel him over the low wooden wall and start putting Buckley in intensive care.

The mayor snorted. With a slack hand he batted away the protest. For two hundred grand plus, Kenny bloody Salter could yell at him till he turned blue in the face. It was all water off a duck's back to him.

"Ah, he's all piss and vinegar. Now. Through the chair—" the mayor addressed council again.

Ken grunted.

"I'm gonna sort this clown out," he announced, putting his hands on top of the low wall and bouncing over it with surprising agility. "Once and for all."

The chant faltered as the horrified hippies realized that Ken was serious.

"Think yer above the law, donchya Buckley?" Ken bellowed, bunching his hands back into fists and readying to use them. "Well, you ain't above Bundjalung Law, pal—" And here he glanced at Rawiri, who had last year beaten Chris into second place for the job of council security guard. "And you can piss the fuck off back to Aotearoa, *mate*."

"Uh! Uh! Sir! I need you to get back behind the wall *immediately*!" Rawiri yelped, leaping to stretch his tattooed arms wide and shield the councillors from Ken, who was suddenly much closer. Rawiri was paid to be a large and angry man, but Ken was an even angrier man, and he wasn't fighting for a pay packet. With the low wooden wall breached, the scales suddenly dropped from Buckley's eyes. He remembered the brandishing of the imitation kingplate at the funeral and the crazy talk from Ken that day. And come to think of it, hadn't his old man been a bit of a nutter too? Told to keep his distance from the footy club after one blue too many in the stands?

Rawiri was shaping up to Ken when, without warning, Luke Chin was between them, proffering pies and sauce. "Here ya go, Kenny. They only had the one steak and mushy left," he bullshitted for the sake of distraction. "And I couldn't remember if ya liked chicken mornay so I got ya a plain one for the second. I didn't think you'd go for the mushy peas." Miraculously, Ken hesitated. There were pastry crumbs on Luke's uniform collar, and tantalizing pie smells from the bag Luke was thrusting under his nose. Luke edged his way around to better block Ken's access to the mayor. Without even agreeing to accept them, Ken found himself holding a hot pie in each hand.

"C'mon, Kenny," Luke urged. "That's some bloody nice tucker there. And aren't ya on parole, bud? Whaddya reckon we head outside, eh?" He clapped Ken on the back, precisely once, then let his hand fall away.

Ken wavered. His parole only had a couple of months left to run. His bung knee hurt. Rawiri was young and looked like he worked out.

"It's hard to fight the good fight from behind bars, brother," offered Zippo Man. "Let's regroup and talk about what's next."

"Yeah. Well, you'll keep, *cunt*," Ken spat at Buckley, before walking back to the protesters, pies delicately balanced on his outstretched palms.

"Meeting adjourned," Buckley said shakily, gathering up his papers and heading to the inner recesses of the building, where the faint ghost of the chant *This ain't over* could still be heard.

"Yer too bloody late," Ken accused as Kerry and Pretty Mary arrived home penniless from Bruns. "As usual." Kerry parked the XD beneath the leopard tree, instantly tense. Here we go. She scoped the scene. Black can in Ken's hand. Chris's car absent. There had been only three UDLs left in the fridge last night; Ken couldn't have bought any more unless he'd had (a) cashed-up visitors or (b) a big win. There were no visitors' cars in sight, and if he'd had a big win he'd be down the road gambling. Ergo, he was no more than three cans to the wind, practically sober. And if he was sober then she was *definitely* refusing to toe whatever bullshit line he had decided to draw today.

"Yeah, and you're ugly, as usual. Late for what?"

"The DA passed," he told her. "Plus I nearly got in a fight with that big Maori prick at council. And then Luke Chin wanted to arrest me!"

"Shit! Why didn't ya text me?" Kerry slammed the driver's door—it was the only way it would close since plowing through the weldmesh fence—and Pretty Mary startled.

"I told ya I got no credit!" Ken was enjoying the catastrophe now that he had Kerry to deflect the blame onto. She had sworn blind that she'd be back in time for the demo and would drag Donny along as well. "But, y'know. Thanks for being there, sis. Thanks for having me back, eh."

"Well, just to add to ya joys, Centrelink says there's nothing owing. Something's gone wrong with the system, looks like," Kerry said, deciding to ignore Ken's sarcasm. "That's why we took so long. You know, trying to get the bungoo together to save the island. So there's no need to act like you're some big hero and we ain't doing nothing."

"Black Superman rang," Pretty Mary added as she stumbled past Ken into the kitchen, exhausted by the stress of Centrelink. "He reckons he's found a top QC for half the price."

"Oh, yeah," Ken spat. "He forking out for it, is he?"

"He paid for the funeral," Pretty Mary said bravely, ignoring how woozy her head felt. "He's not made of money."

"Well, why bother to come up with genius fucking ideas like a QC, then, if he ain't got the bungoo?" Ken's eyes glittered, all his jealousy condensed into one livid question. "Why not bring in the army and air force while he's at it? Hey? Or get on to The Rock—he'll help a brother out!"

"How about," Kerry countered tightly, "how about we let Mum sit down and get a cuppa tea like the *old lady* she is, before we talk about it?"

"I'm sick of fucking *sitting down* and *having cups of tea*. We need to act." Ken snatched his keys out of Kerry's hand and flung himself into the Falcon. He swung the steering wheel hard and fired the engine. "If nothing changes, nothing changes. And if you'd hock your bloody bike we might actually be able to hire a QC and finally get somewhere!" he told Kerry over the roaring engine.

"You stink of rum. If the RBT pulls ya up you're cactus, mate." I should ring the cop shop and get Luke Chin over here, Kerry thought furiously. See how ya like that, *arsehole*.

"Stop it, you two," protested Pretty Mary. "Youse wanna knock orf!"

"Funny how every bastard's problems are suddenly over if I sell the only decent thing I ever owned," Kerry shouted at Ken. "How about you flog off a few of these useless old shitboxes?" She gestured contemptuously at the creaking ruins that had multiplied around the leopard tree. Every time Ken won at the TAB, he was straight on to eBay for the latest two-hundred-dollar rust bucket to bog and flog. Ya gotta spend money to make money, he'd say at least once a day, perfectly serious, gazing with terrific pride upon his dilapidated field of dreams. *Gunnagunna Motors*, Kerry had hooted. But Pretty Mary supported his vision, and Chris or Donny or even Uncle Neil could regularly be found underneath a raised bonnet, listening for Ken's instructions, bellowed from behind a missing windscreen as he revved a dodgy engine.

"Whaddya *think* I'm doing with em, ya stupid bitch!" Ken yelled back before taking off, leaving a large cloud of dust billowing behind him and chickens scattering in all directions.

"Why dya hafta stir Pop up like that?" Pretty Mary accused Kerry. "Why not just keep quiet? He don't mean half what he says."

Kerry stared at her mother.

"Pop? Whaddya mean, Pop?"

"Kenny, you know I mean Kenny. Why dya hafta stir him up for? He'll blow a gasket one day just like ya father did."

"Yeah, blame me, good on ya . . . That prick was *born* with a blown gasket." Kerry stuck her head out the back door and hurled this comment at the driveway, before wandering over to the fridge to see if Chris had picked any susu up after his shift. She put her hand on her neck below her left ear. It was years since Ken had flogged her up, but blueing with him still made her ache. Her big brother was literally a pain in the neck. And their mother was his enabler: He doesn't mean it, let it go. He'll be over it in a few minutes. He was drunk, he was tired. He. He. He. Kerry was getting pretty sick of hearing about Ken at the beginning of every sentence.

"Bub," said Pretty Mary unsteadily. "I don't feel too good."

"Then lie down," Kerry ordered, grabbing her mother's bony elbow and steering her towards the lounge.

"I think I'm on me way out," her mother said. "The Lord wants me to come home."

"No, he bloody doesn't," said Kerry as she laid Pretty Mary down with her feet up and a wet washer on her face. She wasn't losing another one, not this soon.

"Promise me something," Pretty Mary whispered, holding her head up off the maroon velveteen cushion to gaze pathetically at her daughter. "Find sissy, bub. And if she's really gone, I want ya to—"

"*You. Aren't. Dying!*" Kerry screeched. "And till you are, my promises ain't worth much. You of all people should know that by now."

There were no prizes for guessing what else Pretty Mary would ask if Kerry indulged her hypochondria: Hock the Harley. Hire Black Superman's QC. Stop the prison defiling Granny's land. Oh, and find a cure for cancer while yer at it. Kerry opened the louvre windows another crack. From where she stood, sponging Pretty Mary's forehead, she could see the bike gleaming beneath the clothesline. Twenty grand there for the taking. Or the selling. Turned out QCs were three grand a day, even at mates rates.

Unusually, the bike wasn't alone beneath the Hills hoist. The orange cat had decided to perch itself comfortably on the wide leather seat, with its striped tail wrapped snug around its front paws. The cat was looking straight ahead through the handlebars as though contemplating life on the open road. Off to sunnier climes where it wouldn't have to outwit both Elvis and the cane toads to lick the Homebrand pet food tins scattered under the house.

Still Life with Cat, Durrongo Style. And the Harley was pretty much the only thing in Durrongo that had any bloody style to it, the only part of life here that didn't scream poverty and desperation. It was the single thing that said to Kerry each morning that she had made it out of Shitsville alive, that she didn't belong forever in the godforsaken dump she'd fled at seventeen.

The cat turned and looked directly at her. *Three grand a day? Tell em they're dreaming.*

Spot on, budigan. Time to dust off the work clothes and find that backpack. Cos dickhead's right about one thing: if nothing changes, nothing changes.

PART TWO

IF YOU DON'T FIGHT, YOU LOSE

Chapter Ten

Kerry examined herself in the mirror on the cupboard door. Hair plaited. Black jeans with runners and Ken's oversize shirt. Perfect. She was any gender, any dark race.

Red rover, red rover, here I come over.

She stuck her head into the hall. Mum and Aunty Val had gone to town for a doctor's appointment and the $7.95 dinner special at the razzle. Ken and Sav were next door in front of the pre-season footy commentary. Donny was glued to Warcraft. Chris was visiting his on-again-off-again girlfriend in Mullum, trying his hardest to flick the switch back to on and be a part of his daughter's life. The coast wasn't going to get any clearer. Kerry's pulse quickened as she grabbed her keys and went to the top of the back steps, looking around before easing a black nylon balaclava over her head. As she went to add her bike helmet, she heard an unexpected giggle from the corner of the lounge room, and her heart sank like a stone in still water.

"You look funny, Aunty Kerry!" chuckled four-year-old Dr. No, appearing from behind the sofa bed with Ken's phone in his hand. *Christ. What the fuck was Dr. No doing here?*

"Hello, bub," said Kerry, trying to sound calm as she rolled the balaclava up to resemble a beanie. Her blood banged wild through her veins. *Hurry, hurry, no time to lose.*

"Uncle Ken told me to sit here and play Happy Clicks," Dr. No said, glowing with independence. "While him and Mum go shop for smokes 'n that."

Oh, did he now.

"Is that a good game, bub? Is it your best one?" Kerry sat at the kitchen table and desperately tried to distract the kid. Dr. No chattered happily about the mindless game as Kerry wondered what the hell to do. The kid must have trailed after Ken and Savannah when they came home hunting durries, and rather than backtrack the hundred meters to Val's, they had left him alone in the lounge with only Elvis standing guard. She was home, yeah, but nobody had said anything to her about keeping an eye on a four-year-old.

"Well, bub, I need to go out, so how about you run home to Poppy Neil?" Kerry suggested brightly. "Or will I take you home on the bike?"

Dr. No nodded.

"I wanna helmet too," he asserted.

"Not to just go next door, bub. Ere, come on! I'll put ya in front of me and we can make out like you're steering, hey?"

Kerry slid the balaclava off and stuffed it into her jeans pocket. She dropped Dr. No home and waved to Uncle Neil, who was working on his truck in the driveway. A man of few words, he straightened up and flung a hand at her in return, acknowledging the delivery. Kerry wheeled around and headed to Patto in the fading twilight. Jim Buckley thought he could use his cunning bloody dugai ways against her without any blowback, but it was time for Jiminy Cricket to fucking think again. Karma, thy name is woman.

———

An anonymous dark figure rode past the old Baptist Hall, which was abuzz with the Blue Light Disco, Rihanna's bass pumping from every open window. Easy does it. No need to draw any attention. Just cruising past chugga-chugga-lug like ya done a million times before. A marked cop car with its lights flashing on silent made her guts churn, but Kerry looked resolutely at the white line of the road. Sticking to the straight and narrow, officer. Nothing to see here and look la, a dozen teenage schoolgirls over thataway with crop tops and skintight leggings, all out for a good time. Pretty safe bet where the pigs'll be for the next couple of hours, Kerry told herself as she neared the showground.

She pulled up in shadow near a suitable puddle. The nearest street-light was a hundred yards away, and the moon a mere sliver. Stepped into the thicket of fragrant camphor laurels beside the showground stockyards and retrieved the balaclava, stretching the thin material between her fingers. She wavered. It would be so easy to back out. To give up and let Buckley win. Ah, don't be such a fucking gutless wonder, she told herself as she yanked the mask on for the second time that night. For the straight world, crime was a problem or an abstraction, but for people like her, crime was the solution. Not that she called it crime; she called it reparations.

Kerry crouched down to dirty the Softail. "Forgive me," she muttered, flinging handfuls of sloppy wet mud at the machine until it looked like she had bush-bashed her way into town across a plowed spud paddock. When she was done, the underside of the bike was filthy, and the small rectangle of the bike's Queensland number plate was entirely illegible. Nobody was going to get her rego number tonight. She rinsed her hands in the puddle and then stood, giving the mud a moment to dry and stick. With shaking fingers she lit the narrow joint she had stuffed into her bra that afternoon. When she'd smoked it she looked at her phone. Eight p.m. The parents of the youngest Blue Light Disco kids would be picking them up in an hour. She pitched the joint stub into the puddle and pulled on her black nylon gloves. It was high time Patto found out what happened to thieving bastard politicians who picked the wrong Goorie to steal from. What's good for the goose is good for the gander, pal. Ninety seconds later, Kerry was parked three shops down from Patterson Real Estate.

She left her keys in the ignition and went to the window she'd checked out two days ago. Except woman plans and God laughs. A note had been tacked to the sliding front door since then.

Strictly No Cash. All rent from February 27 is to be paid by EFT or direct deposit. By order of Management. Have a wonderful day!

I'll give you have a wonderful fucking day.

Kerry swore at management and at direct deposits, and at her lousy fucking timing too. She swore at the ads in the window offering prime country retreats for a million plus, and she swore at the ratty shotgun shacks of Durrongo on sale for a quarter of that. She swore about muddying her expensive bike chain for nothing at all, and then she swore that she would make Jim Buckley rue the day he stole her backpack if it was the last thing she ever did. It was daylight fucking robbery, that's what it was. Robbery with Violence, in fact; never mind Brenden Abbott or Ned Kelly or Willie Sutton, try locking up the real criminals of the world who ... *Willie Sutton.* Kerry caught her breath.

I rob banks because that's where the money is. What was she thinking? Buckley's overwhelming passion, the thing that really made him crack the fat to end all fats, was being the mayor. She'd seen him preening in the role, week in and week out. Every issue of the *Herald* had him swanning around and pontificating on the prospects of the shire. Hadn't he swelled like a toad when Black Superman called him Mayor Buckley at the funeral? Kerry grinned widely. Robbing the real estate had been the obvious, lazy approach. If you want to kill a snake, you kill the head, you don't waste time mutilating the body. She laughed out loud as she accelerated up Nunne Street, with visions of the council chambers burning to scorched bare earth behind her.

On the other side of town, caution was called for: council would definitely have cameras, and it would be on the security patrol's route. Kerry found a large green industrial bin to park behind and checked that the bike was invisible from the street. No cars around. No sound of engines, just the sound of the disco off in the distance, echoing over the tin roofs. Careful now, girl. Head down, helmet visor low, walk shoulder-swinging like a man. Find the torch in the side pocket of Donny's old red schoolbag, cos the fucking visor makes it midnight. Kerry pushed the hard plastic edge of the visor up a bit. Enough to see three meters in front of her. It'll do. It'll have to do. Looky there, a security firm card already folded into the front doors to mark their first visit of the night; beautiful. But quickway now, don't fuck around. Bust the high toilet window, scrape them sharp window fragments out. Helmet tossed deep into the bushes and feed yaself inside, become a brown snake like Pop, travel head first like a skinny person always can. Torch in ya teeth, hands down, down, down now bracing flat on the loo seat: hold my weight ya plastic bastard, hold my weight . . .

In at last! Inside the council building. Listening, on all fours, over the hammering of her heart. No sirens. Nothing. Adrenaline surging through every cell now, back on the job after how long? Yeah, baby! Like riding a bicycle. Never forget. And never forget the thrill, either, the fucking awesome aliveness of stealing back what's yours.

Getting to her feet in the bathroom, Kerry looked and shied backwards in sudden fright. Ned Kelly was gazing at her from the mirror. A narrow rectangle of her face showed through the black balaclava. She grinned: it was another sign, but a better one this time. Good old Ned, good on ya mate, good on ya digger! Appreciate the support, Unk. But no time to linger. She opened the bathroom door, and soon found herself in the main foyer.

Expecting at any moment to hear sirens and a blaring cop loudspeaker telling her she was F.U.C.K.E.D. *fucked*, Kerry hopped over the reception counter and began ransacking the open-plan workstations. She flung aside bits and pieces of useless stationery, diaries, pens, USB sticks, a hundred packs of aspirin, photos of council-worker holidays in Bali and Thailand, tampons, gold coins, silver coins. She pocketed a few tens and twenties, but otherwise, to her great dismay, the drawers contained nothing, nothing, nothing. If there was jack-shit here for her, she really would torch the fucking joint, truesgod she would. One way or the other Buckley would feel her wrath.

She looked up at the clock on the wall, breathing hard, sweat running from beneath the balaclava onto her neck. How the hell could it be eight thirty already? She tried another workstation. Locked drawers on this one, much more promising. Kerry fumbled in the red bag, found a flat steel bar, and jemmied her way in, the chipboard splintering easily beneath her tool. Ho ho! Bingo, dingo! Two top drawers that were actually tills— But instantly she dropped flat to the carpet, put her hand over the torch beam as a car drove past just on the other side of the massive glass front wall of the building. Don't be a cop. Don't be the security patrol. Heart pounding in her dry mouth, the thudding telling the driver: *Keep going, keep going.*

They did.

She leaped up again, scooping twenties and fifties into the open mouth of her bag until the tills were empty, even of gold coin. Was it enough? She had no idea how long they would need the QC. Every court case she'd ever seen was done and dusted in under half an hour.

Eight forty-five.

Calculate ya risks, girl. Think, think hard! Blue Light Disco, all the Patto cops looking for smuggled vodka and perving on drunken children . . . she had fifteen minutes at best. Then it would be time to spark up this poxy joint and run like hell.

Bent low, nerves pumped like she was on crank, Kerry made her way over the corridor to the internal council rooms. Would Buckley have stashed the backpack in his office? Could she be that lucky? She took a deep breath at the thought and kept on going.

At the far end of the corridor stood a plinth in a low beam of light. It held a small sculpture of Andrew "Cracker" Nunne, noted philanthropist and only son of the first white settler in Durrongo Shire. Kerry paused. Three generations of her family before her had worked for the Nunnes, building their cattle empire for them. This patriarch had been a hard, clever bastard, by all accounts. The sculpture had him wearing an Akubra, arms on his hips, with a coiled stockwhip clasped in his right hand. Yeah, that'd be about right. But it was brass and brass was valuable, even if Cracker Nunne was not. She weighed the statue in her hands. It'd be missed immediately, but Kerry didn't give a rat's. It's not like it was gonna take council all day tomorrow to find out their cash floats were empty. The goonah was going to well and truly hit the Patterson Regional Council fan in spectacular fashion at 9 a.m., twelve hours from now. Assuming it didn't explode a lot sooner in a panorama of sirens and flashing lights.

Kerry glanced down the corridor to the offices, and then out at the dark street. Nine-oh-three. Well past time to get the fuck out. The odds of the backpack being here at council, she told herself, were minuscule. And like the song says, the secret to a long life is knowing when it's time to go. Kerry headed towards the rear door. Before she reached the exit, though, she stopped. Her face drained to gray and her knees weakened and buckled; she groped with an unsteady hand towards the nearest wall.

Standing before her was Grandad Chinky Joe, six foot four in his worn canvas trousers. Her ancestor wore a felt hat over his straight black hair. In his hand was an unlit corncob pipe, like the ones she'd seen in old cartoons as a kid. Seeing what Kerry held, Grandad Chinky Joe frowned. Trembling, she quickly shoved the statue of Nunne down into her bag until he was submerged in the illicit cash there.

Kerry straightened up. She tottered a couple of steps backwards, then took off her balaclava. Her great-grandfather had recognized Old Man Nunne, but would he know her? How could he? And how much English did he have, anyway? Was this Old Man going to growl her now for stealing? It was Aboriginal Law: never take what isn't yours. Not goods, not time, not dignity, not freedom. *Nothing.* Stick to your own fire and keep to your own business. But it *was* their business, what council did on their land. The dugai were the thieves, not her. She was just effecting a few choice personal reparations. If Grandad Chinky Joe knew she was here to protect the island he would understand, Kerry was convinced of that. Didn't stop her mouth going dry, but. She felt light-headed, as if she might vomit.

"I'm trying to save Granny's island," she croaked. Grandad Chinky Joe nodded minimally, as though he already knew, and didn't much care for further explanations. Then the tall figure stepped further inside the corridor and beckoned her to follow. Feeling the gulf yawning between her and the intoxicating freedom of the back door, Kerry staggered after him. She should have been fleeing as fast as the Harley could take her. But instead she followed the Old Man past a huge portrait of Buckley shaking hands with a conservative prime minister. You sleazy fucker, thought Kerry, wishing she had a knife and forgetting for an instant to be frightened. She could improve the painting Zorro style, slash slash slash.

When Grandad halted, Kerry found herself in front of an imposing steel cupboard bolted to the rear wall of Buckley's office. Grandad placed his left hand on its smooth gray steel and gestured at the padlock. Kerry glanced up at the wall in panic.

Nine-oh-eight. Time's a-wasting. But what if the backpack was in the cupboard? Her breath caught in her throat.

"Ngaoi need cash, bungoo, kami!" she whispered urgently. "If there's yugam bungoo here then ngaio gotta yan, onetime . . . yan! Yan!"

Grandad looked at her and his words were thoughts.

"Yugam yan. Yugam yan." *Don't go. Not yet.* He patted the cupboard like it was a favorite horse.

"In the cupboard?" she asked frantically, and he nodded.

Filled with fresh hope of finding the backpack, Kerry got out her jemmy and attacked the padlock. Metal screeched against metal, but she was past caring about noise; very soon it wouldn't matter what

Buckley had hidden away behind these closed doors. She had to clear out fast or she'd be locked up for longer than Allie. But when Kerry finally yanked open the top drawer inside the cupboard she gasped and forgot all about the backpack. The tray hidden inside the drawer—glass-topped and lined with soft velvet like the ones in museums—was full of very old, carefully preserved relics.

An ochred dhili bag in exactly the same weave Pretty Mary had used for Pop's ashes. Convict handcuffs, a tag telling of their discovery during the building of the Caledonian River bridge in 1889. A souvenir program from a Nigger Minstrel Show in Casino in 1907. Two big lumps of ochre—one white, one brown—and a curved stone axe head right beside them. And in pride of place in the center of the tray, one more thing, faintly gleaming. A silver object pinned by a beam of yellow light falling from a carefully positioned globe.

Black velvet underneath the object, glimpsed through several jagged holes.

What?

Kerry fought bravely to hold on to what was real, fought to distinguish atoms from ghosts and whispers. But it was hard, so hard, for she felt all at once as though she had no lungs inside her, and no heart. No substance at all. Whatever she was at her center had drained away, and her thin gloves clasping the front of the tray were empty sacks. She looked to Grandad Chinky Joe, who gazed down at the kingplate, just once, and then bared his teeth in triumph. The Old Man breathed out onto the glass top of the tray, a long deliberate breath. Faint and trembling, Kerry looked down into the drawer again. She felt as if she was fading fast, observing the scene from afar and on high, floating rapidly away. Was this what it was like to die? Was she even alive? Before she could contemplate her mortality further, she felt her lungs fill with one gigantic intake of breath and her body returned to the room. She was strong now, flesh and blood and guts; she was real. And the object beneath her was real too: she hadn't imagined it.

A palm-sized crescent moon with a dozen bullet holes, slung on a metal chain, inscribed with the words: *King Bobby Saltwater.*

Granny Ava's necklace.

Fearful, Kerry hesitated. She looked to Grandad Chinky Joe, who nodded urgently and gestured at her neck. *Take it. Wear it.* Kerry picked up the silver crescent, felt the weight of the metal. Somebody, sometime, had attempted repairs—several of the metallic chain links were ordinary iron. She gingerly put her head through the loop and rested the punctured plate on her chest. She touched it warily, wondering if it was the badge of a king or of a slave.

A broad smile spread over Grandad's face. Then he pointed to the tray and made an emphatic sweep of his arm, speaking several rapid sentences, mostly Bundjalung. The only words Kerry caught were "ngaoi" and "wiya." *I give.*

It was nine fifteen. She could hear cars outside, the buzz of traffic building now as parents drifted to the hall. It would be madness to linger, but when she went to leave, Grandad blocked her way, insistent she empty the drawer. So Kerry moved fast, grabbing at those things that would fit in her half-full bag—the handcuffs and lumps of ochre, the dhili bag and some quartz pebbles—and shoving them on top of the statue until the bag straps strained. That'll do. She had to flee. There was no time left to burn the building and now, with Granny's kingplate around her neck, not the same inclination to, somehow. She had come looking for revenge but was leaving with the most precious object imaginable. For tonight, that was more than enough.

———————

Kerry bolted outside, blind and deaf to everything other than the crescent that hung around her neck like a circle of fire. The fingers of her right hand pressed exultantly into the sharp edges of the shotgun holes. As if by clinging to those murderous metal ridges, her fingertips pricked by them, she was holding on to her mother, and *her* mother, and *her* mother, binding the generations of Salter women tightly together in one secret act, one secret place. She gave a cry of triumph as she ran to the Harley: this wasn't just fighting back. Tonight, they were winning.

Kerry flung herself onto the bike and kicked it to roaring life. As she reached for the throttle she saw red running down her hand, and shivered. More than a century later, and still the kingplate was wet with their blood. Yet Grandad Chinky Joe *wanted* her to take it. He wouldn't have shown her otherwise, wouldn't have come to her tonight. Wouldn't have beckoned her into the private chamber where four generations of history lay inert behind a locked steel door. The kingplate had saved Granny Ava's life and in doing so had very nearly marked her death—the glory of stealing it back was worth any risk. It would make an exquisite birthday present for Pretty Mary.

Kerry revved the bike.

She had fat wads of cash in the bag on her back.

She had Old Man Nunne and his bloody stockwhip in there too.

She had Granny's Ava's kingplate around her neck and a clear road home, and when she dropped her wrist, the Harley took to that road like the clappers, as if Hell had opened up behind her.

Chapter Eleven

The smoke penetrated everybody's clothes and hair. It drifted in a white cloud past the house jack and the stacked timber, and came to rest in a low blanket above Stockman's Creek, just beyond the Marsdens' back fence. Smoke filled the XD, where Donny sulked, dragged from his computer by an aunt determined that he would see the light of day. Pretty Mary's clapsticks rattled softly to end the ceremony; as the sticks fell silent, the only sounds were the tinkling creek, the distant crows, and the low wheezing of the pregnant Jasmine Marsden.

Pretty Mary beamed as she turned to her clients. When she had discovered that Jasmine was not only having a little girl but was also turning thirty-five, the same age as Donna, Pretty Mary had grown sentimental, and lowered her normal fee by fifty dollars.

"You won't have no more trouble," she reassured Jasmine, who was sucking on a blue asthma inhaler. "I've explained ya not here to make trouble or to disrespect the country." Pretty Mary laid green gum leaves against the wooden stumps of the shack. "Our Pop's been visiting you, that's all. My father-in-law, God rest him. Wanting to see who's here now he's passed."

"Thanks so much, Aunt Mary," said Jasmine, grateful, as her coughing eased. "Now we might get some sleep at last."

Two waark in the paddock across the road flapped their wings at the scene, helpless with laughter. Pretty Mary shot a warning glare at her totemic siblings through the thick smoke haze, but it did no good. Proper cheeky, them crows. She resolved to growl them if they got any louder.

"We want to do some creek regen once the house is fixed," Ryan Marsden offered, looking proudly over their ragged five acres. They had put in mangoes and paw paws, a chook pen was underway, and a new fence made from old pallets now alerted the wallabies to the presence of the veggie garden. With Mount Monk only two paddocks away and the creek burbling beside the house, it was a lovely spot for a young family to dream about the future. Or would have been, if not for the poltergeist.

The spirit world had been causing all manner of difficulties for the Marsdens. They would lie rigid in bed until the early hours of the morning, hearing the groans and murmurs of the poltergeist echoing around them. Their marriage, already severely tested by the shock discovery of a massive termite infestation in the stumps and beams, frayed further with every sleepless night. Now Ryan put an exhausted arm around his wife, hoping her optimism was warranted.

"Ya replacing the stumps—good. If ya gonna do something, may's well do it properly, eh?" Pretty Mary gestured in approval at a dozen concrete beams lying beside the stacked timber. She had decided she liked the Marsdens. They had their heads screwed on right. "Pop's not angry with youse," she went on, lighting up a fag from the coals in the smoking drum. "Just having a good old dorrie at what youse are up to. You might have seen the story about him in the paper a while back? Pop Owen Addison?"

Ryan confirmed that they had indeed seen pictures of the teenage Pop holding a large boxing trophy, and another photo of him, much older, with the eyepatch he took to wearing after moving to town, where a puckered Goorie eye socket was cause for consternation.

"Queensland junior champion he was. Silver Gloves," Pretty Mary bragged, stashing her clapsticks in a Crazy Clark's bag and folding it into her brown vinyl handbag. "During the war. He did the lot: boxing, rodeo, timber-cutter, stockman. Gang foreman for years. Ended up elected to ATSIC, would ya believe? That's how we got our place, see. Bank manager turned nice as pie when he seen them pay slips . . ."

Decades later, Pretty Mary was still agog at the three miracles of Pop's middle age. His sudden elevation to ATSIC councillor, with a jaw-dropping salary that they had at first assumed was an accounting error; then the invitation for Pop to go sit in an air-conditioned office with his Grade Three education and discuss the complexities of a mortgage with Matty Nunne's brother Russell. And the third, culminating miracle: the house on Mount Monk Road itself. A place of their own that no mission manager could waltz into in search of lice or dust or dissent. A house where a person could plant a tree and not be told that it was the wrong tree, or in the wrong place, or that he had to rip it out because permission had not first been sought from the cow-cockie's missus. A home where a family could be raised, free of the awful fear of being moved on when the work dried up or the dugai goodwill had drained away. The house had come too late for her mum's generation, booted from island to mission and then back again. But for Pop and Charlie and Pretty Mary, there had been a brief window in the nineties when the miracle of home ownership had become possible. If he had sometimes pissed in the sink after a night on the turps, if he'd given her a sore jang more than once, if he'd made the young lives of Ken and Donna something of a misery, Pretty Mary would never, ever forget to praise Pop's name for walking bravely into the Commonwealth Bank that day and making their home a reality.

"That's Pop in the middle." Kerry held out her mobile. "Between Mum and Dad."

"How did he come to lose the eye?" coughed Ryan, made bold by the discreet passing over of an envelope containing two crisp hundred-dollar bills. Pretty Mary paused to blow out cigarette smoke, adding to the general murk.

"Well." She hesitated, tapped her durrie against the XD's side window, ashing the ground below. Screwed up her mouth and scratched behind her ear. Kerry and the others waited patiently, but Pretty Mary was weighing her words with great care. The crows hung intently on her answer, missing body parts being of keen professional interest to them.

"Took a fall off a horse," Kerry finally answered as the silence stretched out awkwardly. "Mustering, hey Mum? His eye socket was crushed. No ambulance, course, back them days. No doctor either, if ya worked for Old Man Nunne. Just bush medicine, a few swigs of rum, and a couple days' rest if you was lucky, then back into it."

"Geez, that's interesting," said Ryan. "I'd love to find out more about the local history around here."

Kerry and Pretty Mary exchanged a look.

No, you wouldn't, thought Kerry.

Jasmine had sucked her breath in sharply. "They call them the good old days but they weren't always, were they?" she said.

"Tough as nails, though, them old bushies," offered her husband with a half smile.

"He had to be tough. If he couldn't work he would have been sent back to the mission," Kerry answered sharply, stung by the idiot's half smile, "and coulda lost his kids."

"No, bub . . ." Pretty Mary said, smoothing her hair in the sideview mirror. She tucked some stray wisps back into her hair band.

Ryan swivelled, jumping at a chance to escape Kerry's acid.

"We told you that mustering story cos youse was only little," Pretty Mary said, finally coming to a bold decision. Pretty Mary folded her arms tight around her handbag and leaned back against the car. She shifted around until she found exactly the right place for her hip to rest, just below the rear passenger door handle. From inside the car, Donny squinted at his grandmother's torso blocking out the late afternoon sun.

"It was Old Man Nunne cost Pop his eye."

A wave of disgust rippled through Kerry, and her face contorted. *Of course.* The Marsdens stared, baffled. The ghost of a smile still hovered around Ryan's lips as he waited for her mother to elaborate. Pretty Mary raised her right arm and made an odd, emphatic snapping gesture, as though casting a spell. She gave a dry laugh.

"Oh, he was pretty flash with a stockwhip, that old mulaga. Crack the eye outta ya head any day of the week—he was known for it. Plenty of one-eyed Goories round ere back then. Cracker Nunne, they called him."

Cracker Nunne, cried the crows enthusiastically. *Cracker Nunne, Cracker Nunne.*

There was a moment of dawning comprehension. Then Jasmine jack-knifed, vomiting onto the ground beside the stacked timber. Stinking wet drops splashed onto the planks of the new-home-to-be.

Two bright red patches appeared high on Ryan's cheeks.

"Why would you say that to a woman who's thirty-eight weeks pregnant?!" he objected hotly.

Pretty Mary held his gaze and very nearly smiled at Ryan's masterful extraction of victimhood from her story. That took some front, that did.

"You asked." She was unapologetic.

"Jesus! It's revolting." Ryan ran stiff fingers across his shaven head and grimaced. "And now I suppose we have to worry about a one-eyed Aboriginal ghost who—"

Dry retching, Jasmine flapped a hand at her husband, telling him to shut up, he had said enough, and for Christ's sake give her the inhaler.

"Give her that thing. And I already told ya, Ryan. Pop won't be bothering ya no more. You might wanna get them corner stumps out, but. They're ready to let go any old tick of the clock, and there's rain coming," Pretty Mary said, climbing into the XD and banging the door closed with two careful hands. "Make tracks, dort. I've gotta see a man about a kangaroo."

Kerry glanced at Ryan, who was copping a quiet diatribe from his wife in between her deep sucks from the pale blue plastic cannister.

"Cheerio, neighborinos," said Kerry brightly, stuffing the folded envelope of cash into her bra. She drove away, shaking her head at Pretty Mary's transformation into a straight-up history warrior. Amazed, too, that she had lived her whole life not putting two and two together. Every Goorie knew what sorts of things happened on them old pastoral stations, yet she had spent thirty-three years accepting a pretty childhood fable. Pretty Mary's words rode a dizzying roundabout in her mind. *Cracker Nunne, they called him. He was known for it. Cracker Nunne, they called him. He was known for it. Cracker Nunne . . .* Until, driving past Mount Monk, she saw the wallaby mob grazing in the slanting afternoon light. Their quiet peacefulness was a mercy and sparked the memory of that long-ago day when Pop had taken her to the foot of the mountain and told her to beware the savages.

By Christ, 'e was a hard man, Bob Buckley . . .

It seemed there had been a lot of hard men in Pop's life. Hard men with stone hearts, bent on turning the country into their own clenched fists.

"You give them something to think about, anyway," Kerry said to her mother with a shout of laughter, wishing she had a cold beer to wash away the lingering scent of Jasmine's vomit.

"Yeah, well." Pretty Mary chuckled. "I was gammon, really. But it's good to jar em up while they're new. Make better neighbors outta them."

"Hey?" Kerry's brow wrinkled and she slowed despite her raging thirst. "Do ya mean it wasn't Cracker Nunne?"

"Oh, naw, that part's true alright. Pop went to work for him straight after he won his Silver Gloves, and Pop wouldn't back down for any mulaga them days, stockwhip or no stockwhip. But maybe he shoulda backed down. Ya can't box with one eye, can ya?"

Nunne had finished Pop's career with one stroke of his whip, then. Ended his dreams of the Golden Gloves, and what might have followed.

"As for Pop hanging around—didn't we smoke him at the river, proper way? Didn't we lay him to rest where he wanted? Didn't we sing him into the ground?" Pretty Mary interrogated Kerry, index finger hovering in admonition. Yes, Kerry agreed warily. Everything had been done the right way at the river for the cantankerous old bugger, to keep him from hovering about the place.

"I'm not following ya," Kerry said, still puzzled.

"Seen them house stumps?" Donny leaned in unexpectedly from the back seat. "White-anted to buggery?"

Kerry gazed at Donny in the rear-view mirror. Why was her nephew grinning from ear to ear? She had been distracted by the ceremony and the smoke and hadn't paid that much attention to the old house.

"Why would Pop wanna come over this side and annoy dugai people for?" Pretty Mary asked, grinning along with Donny. "Ain't no mooki been near that house."

"Are you telling me they're not even haunted?" The corners of Kerry's mouth twitched. Pretty Mary, up to her old games again.

"Course they ain't haunted—they just bin hearing the termites chewing that old place to the ground in the dead of the night!" Pretty Mary gave a sly giggle.

"That's their poltergeist?" Kerry guffawed. "*White ants?*"

"Proper scary, them ants," said Donny, deadpan.

"Oh, they be frightened for Pop all hours now," Pretty Mary laughed, screwing one eye closed and peering around. "Waiting to see old one-eye Goorie looking in the window!"

Kerry dragged the envelope out of her bra and waved it at her mother in delight.

"Two hundred bucks," she hooted, "to exorcise termites!"

"Ssshh," Pretty Mary said, wobbling a palm at her daughter and only holding it together long enough to get the words out. "Careful, bub. If they don't get them stumps out, Pop might come back!" She raised both arms, making high, wailing ghost noises, then exploded into raucous cackles. Kerry pulled onto the footpath and crumpled against the car door, crying with laughter and begging Pretty Mary to shut up before her bladder let go.

Pretty Mary recovered first. She wiped her eyes. Then she put the envelope of cash into her handbag, where it nestled between her smooth wooden clapsticks and her bottle of Gaviscon.

"That'll square us with Telstra and still leave twenty dollars towards the party," she said, blowing her nose and clipping the handbag shut with satisfaction. "I call that a good afternoon's work."

"If Scummerlink'd do their job, you could buy yourself something for a change," Kerry said.

In the back seat, Donny had tuned out of the conversation. He put his head out the window, resting his temple on his folded hands so that the breeze blew back his bleached locks. All of Donny was yearning for the blue Pacific.

Extravagant flashes of lightning brightened the kitchen. Long chords of thunder rumbled across the sky; big rain was coming off the Margin Ranges into Durrongo. Pretty Mary's lounge room curtains, bunched together with blue bailing twine since the hot weather arrived, billowed like yacht sails as the wind gusted violently over the creek flats.

"Hope the roof holds." Even as a kid Kerry expected the rusty tin panels to catapult down Mount Monk Road every summer. The louvres rattled in their frame, the one made from rough-sawn plywood adding a discordant lower note.

"How much should I put for exorcisms, Nan?" Donny sat cross-legged on the lounge room floor, creating a website from pirated software. Pretty Mary's attention was split between him, Savannah's kids, and the cards in her hand.

"Oh, I dunno, two fifty, I s'pose. Leave that, bub! Put it up

in the sink for me, darling, he can't have it, it's got chilli in it—"
Dr. No had been about to taste-test some leftover hamper. "Go play
with your toys, you sod of a kid. Ken, drag that toy box outta the
back room for them, will ya?" But Ken was asleep in front of the
cricket. Dr. No tried to climb into Pretty Mary's lap, reaching for
her playing cards with sticky fingers. Seeing Pretty Mary's growing
irritation, five-year-old Rosie hauled her brother away and plonked
him in the middle of the lino. His mouth trembled, threatening a
tantrum.

"Charge what the market can bear," Kerry advised. She had been
schooled in business homilies from the drug dealers in Brisbane
Women's: buy low, sell high, haha. Be clear on your target market
and differentiate your product. And so on.

"Just put by wossername. Negotiation," Pretty Mary told Donny,
rearranging her hand as Kerry went to drag out the toy box. "That
way we can yarn em up, see. Gotta suss out if they got bungoo or if
they on the bones of their mooya. And listen, bub," she told Kerry,
casually fanning a royal flush onto the table, "the Gift isn't for making some huge profit off of. I just want to cover me bills and have a
little bit left over."

"Well, that's a relief," Kerry shot back. "We wouldn't want to go
exploiting the Gift and becoming millionaires, would we?"

"Bills including back rent for 214 years, Mum," Ken suggested,
springing to consciousness. "We're not gonna save anything by acting all Mother Teresa."

"Ya got that right, bruz," Kerry agreed as she recalled sliding
headfirst over broken glass into the pitch-black of the council bathroom three days ago. The story of the break-in had led the news the
next morning, and Pretty Mary had narrowed her eyes at the TV,
declaring that the local kids responsible needed a good flogging.

"Ya don't mind me being Mother Teresa when it comes to shouting you grog price, though, do ya, son?" Pretty Mary said pointedly.
Black Superman was the one in her good books today, along with

Donny for helping her on his computer. Ken had been relegated. He grunted a noncommittal grunt and turned to the Windies, who shimmered on the TV screen with a violent flaring as the power surged.

Then the house dimmed.

"Oh, no way!" cried Donny, who, lacking a computer battery, had just lost all his work. He slammed the laptop shut and glared ferociously at the bare lightbulb that swung above the kitchen table. Dr. No stomped joyfully on a tower of Duplo, sending primary-colored plastic shooting into every corner of the kitchen. He giggled with satisfaction as his older sister painstakingly went to pick them up again.

"That's Mother Nature for ya," said Kerry cheerfully, throwing in her lousy hand. "The cranky old cunt. Whoops," she added, remembering the kids. Not that they hadn't heard it all before. Pretty Mary joked that they could set the clock by Sav's screaming at the kids at seven thirty every morning, as she tried to get them to daycare and herself off to work.

"Wet weekend and a house full of bloody jahjams," complained Ken. It was pissing down, his petrol tank was empty, and he had no bungoo for the pub. He began to scroll on his phone. "Toyota Camry, black, electric windows, 190,000 clicks, VGC, three grand. Could flip that, make a grand easy. Anyone got three grand lying around under the bed? Hey? Didn't think so, ya pack a tightarses."

Everybody laughed merrily. Three grand, good one, Ken.

Three grand, mused Kerry, try three hundred. Not even, since she had left herself the princely sum of two hundred bucks out of the cash she'd retrieved from council. The rest had been deposited in Black Superman's Ubet account yesterday, and a text sent: *For the QC, love K*. Black Superman had sent her two texts in reponse—an open-mouthed emoji and a long string of question marks. Her response was three words long: *Silence is Golden*. All day she had been forced to bite her lip and listen to Pretty Mary praising him up.

Black Superman's commitment to the family. The way he had gone the extra mile to borrow thousands of dollars from Ezy-Cash Payday Lenders, hiring the QC, giving them all fresh hope. Ken was making out like, yeah, no biggie, he had always expected his brother to come through. But Pretty Mary's ecstasy was boundless. Once again, her youngest son was the Golden Child. Kerry's ribs still ached from scraping across the sharp aluminium sill of that toilet window, but she couldn't say a damn word about it. Such is life, she told herself severely, suck it up, but her mood remained dark.

"Aw here we go, here we go!" Ken leaped up. "Nissan Pulsar, 2001, 230,000 K, minor hail damage, seven hundred and fifty!" Pretty Mary pursed her lips, hoping that Ken wouldn't humbug her too hard in front of Kerry.

"Oh, gimme a break! Any idiot can *buy* cars. But how many have ya sold?" Kerry snapped, not much caring if her brother blew a gasket just because she, a female, had the fucking temerity to question him about the bombs multiplying in the yard. It wouldn't be so bad if he'd mow the lawn, but it was like Jurassic Park out there. Ken's ancient rustbuckets grazed among the hip-high paspalum, providing free housing for brown snakes, bush rats, and giant huntsman spiders, none of which cared to distinguish the inside of the house from the outside. Kerry had been forced to shift a coiled night tiger from the laundry tub only last week, and she was well and truly over the fantasy that was Gunnagunna Motors.

Ken's fingers twitched as he stared at his sister. Whatever was rising in his body—adrenaline, testosterone, some other cellular transformation—was palpable. Every fiber of him screamed instant antagonism. Muscle memory in his right arm and fist told Ken exactly what it would feel like to smash Kerry and her big mouth to the floor. Male and female, they all fall the same, ya hit em right. He hung by his fingertips on to the ragged ends of his self-control.

"Oh, you're the fucking expert now, are ya? Then how about ya sell one thing? Hey? Like a *bike*. Or else get off my case, ya smart-

mouthed bitch! Think I haven't got enough problems without listening to you yap on all the fucking time?"

"Settle down, Kenny," Pretty Mary said in alarm. "She didn't
mean nothing—"

"You been hitting the crack pipe, bro? Nobody's gonna buy a
fucken Pulsar with hail damage. And as for me selling . . ." Then, as
Dr. No tried to climb Kerry to sit on her lap, "Can you bloody not!
Jesus Christ, these fucken kids."

She rose abruptly, tumbling Dr. No harmlessly onto his plump
little arse, and went to stare out the front door, as far away from Ken
as she could get. Slanted rain was sweeping through the veranda,
driven by howling gusts coming off the mountain. A few miserable
cattle in Scruffy McCarthy's paddock stood with their heads lowered, their rumps to the tempest.

Inside, among the scattered toys, Dr. No began to sob with re-
jection. Kerry scowled over her shoulder at him, and then at her
brother, who had volunteered Pretty Mary for babysitting duty
while Savannah and Aunty Val went to Tweed for tests on Val's bad
heart.

"Eeyah, look now. Youse two wanna knock orf!" said Pretty
Mary, annoyed, as she righted the howling Dr. No with a swift up-
ward haul of his arm. Rosie ran to build her brother another Duplo
tower in consolation.

"Nan," Rosie asked Pretty Mary in a cautious whisper, "is Aunty
Kerry a baddie?"

"Bloody oath she is," said Ken sourly, lighting one of his
mother's smokes. Pretty Mary laughed and asked Rosie what she
meant. The story came out: Uncle Neil had warned Rosie away
from Kerry, saying she was a Bad Lady and that she shouldn't talk
to her. Aunty Kerry had been to jail and *everything*. Kerry shook her
head in faint amazement. Like Ken hadn't? And Pop? Even Black
Superman had seen the inside of a watch house. And since when
did going to jail make somebody a villain, for Christ's sake? But that

was dugai logic for ya. Steal a million acres and you're a pioneer hero with a brass statue in the council chambers, but pinch a car or a mobile phone and you're some kind of fucking monster.

"Aunty Kerry used to be naughty," Pretty Mary reassured Rosie, "but she isn't naughty anymore . . . *Are you*, Aunty Kerry?"

"Unfuckenbelievable," Kerry told the rain, then swivelled to face her mother's judgment. "Yeah, bub, I used to be a little bit naughty, but I tell ya what. I never knocked me girlfriend's teeth down her gob. I never started a stupid fight at the Durrongo pub that ended up with two people in Emergency. And I *certainly* never "borrowed" a shitload of funeral money off my poor old grieving mother and made out to everyone like I hadn't." She put quotation marks around *borrowed* since Blind Freddy could see that Pretty Mary's funeral payment—no longer mysteriously missing in the Centrelink system—would not be winging its way back into her account any time soon. It had mutated into the ruined sedans that ringed the leopard tree.

"Keep yapping," said Ken, nodding rapidly. "If ya wanna start something, just keep it up with ya big fucking gob." Kerry's guts squirmed, but she was determined to show no fear. The great overgrown thing, standing over their mother for every cent he could squeeze. If he got a hit in, well, she'd get up off the floor and smash him straight back, the dead dog.

"It's my bungoo!" flared Pretty Mary. "I can lend it to whoever I want! So settle down, the both of ya!"

"Who knocked your girlfriend's teeth down her gob?" Rosie asked Kerry.

"Eeyah, don't go worry about all that sorta business. Do me a drawing, bub." Pretty Mary distracted the kids with biros and paper. She searched for an unused tea bag and flicked the kettle on.

Kerry stomped down the hall to go jull, discovering in the dim light of the toilet that her period had just arrived. That's where she'd gotten the nerve to stand up to Ken, then.

It explained, too, her white-hot fury at yesterday's Centrelink letter confirming that Pretty Mary had received Pop's funeral money two months ago. If her bed in Trinder Park had been empty, Kerry would have wiped Durrongo and everyone in it, but the bed was long gone. Kerry had taken her impotent rage to the gym instead, and been persuaded by Steve to stick around a little longer in New South Wales.

Another long rumble of thunder, and the TV shuddered to life. Ken turned back to the Windies. At the kitchen table, Dr. No started drawing a picture of himself and Kerry riding the Harley.

––––––––––

"Grab me gun, Donald," Ken ordered later that afternoon, leaning into Donny's bedroom from the veranda. Savannah swayed gently in the hammock, just back from the hospital where the tests on Aunty Val's heart weren't looking too flash. Donny came out holding a small cardboard carton.

"Change ya mind yet, Rambo?" Ken asked as he took the box. Donny shrugged, hating his father for the mockery, but at the same time deeply shamed by fear. Ken and Savannah both laughed.

Their conversation drifted into the quiet house.

"Don't be a pussy," Ken taunted. "What ya waiting for, the Second Coming?"

Donny shrugged again.

"It's not that bad," Savannah told him. "Here." Donny accepted a beer.

"I can't stand to see that lubbly white skin going to waste," added Ken, plugging the tattoo gun into the only electrical socket on the veranda without blackened scorch marks radiating from it. "But I'll put a bitta color on ya one day, lad."

"Alright. Do it." Donny surprised everyone, including himself. Kerry lifted her head. From the lounge she could see Ken nodding at the chair facing the backyard wilderness. With a tea towel folded between his teeth, Donny sat while Ken went to work.

Half an hour later, giant beads of sweat rolled down the boy's forehead. There was no cushion of fat on his scrawny arm to ease the pain, and he could no longer hold in his moans. Flies buzzed, tantalized by the delicious coppery scent of the boy's blood.

"Take a break, bud," Ken said, straightening up and looking for baby wipes. Donny peered in the round mirror Sav held up. His upper arm was red and angry-looking, but visible beneath the smeared blood and inflammation was a breaching humpback whale. He glowed, turning his arm this way and that. Ken had managed to exactly replicate the picture Donny had sketched last year from an old Byron Lighthouse photo.

"Deadly. You're a fucken hectic tattooist, Dad!"

Savannah handed him another beer. The kid had guts. Who knew?

"Keep going?" Ken asked, gun pointed to the ceiling.

"Dunno. I'd like it to have a calf, down here. But it canes, eh," Donny replied, still admiring his arm. He was nauseated, and the beer wasn't helping. Nor did he want Ken to bugger up what was already the perfect tat. Ken grunted. He put the gun down and pulled off his Jackie Howe, revealing a mishmash of tats. Across the top of his shoulders stretched the only piece he'd paid cash for—an elongated Goorie flag, fluttering around a gray nurse swimming up a cross-hatched river.

"Try something this size if ya want to know about pain," Ken told him, pointing over his muscled shoulder to the black infill of the flag. "Four hours straight in the chair at Mullum." Donny was silent. All this agony and still he didn't measure up. Something wriggled in his guts, then, something alive with anger and hurt pride.

"Gorn then, Old Man," he said, looking Ken fair in the face. "Give her a baby." Do ya worst. Ken turned the buzzing machine back on and bent to the job.

But at the exact second the needle met Donny's flesh, Pretty Mary bellowed inside the house.

Savannah jumped and raised her eyebrows: Ken usually did all the yelling around this joint. In the kitchen, Pretty Mary's voice grew more and more heated. Ken chuckled and shook his head.

"Fuck me, what now?" he muttered to himself.

"I already lost one daughter! But nah, you mob don't care 'bout that. Selfish!" Pretty Mary yelled. "Ya can bugger off elsewhere if ya still wanna go doing crime." She clutched at a stick-figure drawing of her daughter wearing a scribbled black balaclava.

"Selfish? I did it to save the fucking island. Black Superman didn't just suddenly pull three grand out of his fork!"

At the words "three grand" Ken paused. The ropy muscle of his right forearm stood out while he listened, motionless, the gun pointing at the floorboards of the veranda. Donny exhaled loudly as the sharp pain stopped. Inside, Pretty Mary was still going for it at top note.

"You blooming myall or what? What if the cops shot ya? What if *you* get locked up for five years? What then?"

"Someone had to do *something*, specially if you're gonna hand over all your pay to that useless fat prick outside!"

Kerry appeared on the veranda, wild-eyed, with the red school-bag over her shoulder and her chest heaving. She squinted at the pelting rain. Fine spray ricocheted up off the top of the back stairs, dampening the front of her jeans. Rainwater gurgled loudly through the house's ancient guttering and spurted horizontally from holes in the rusty downpipes.

"Whaddya doing tormenting old ladies?" Ken asked. It was the first time he'd asked her what she was doing since the day she'd returned from Queensland, Kerry reflected bitterly as she placed herself carefully for a quick getaway. Her movements, her thoughts, her feelings, none of these were normally of any consequence to Ken. He had been a mongrel ratbag of a kid, but since going to prison at twenty-one, her brother had lived in a world where what he did and thought and felt was at the epicenter of all things. What

Kerry did or didn't do—that was no skin off his big black ring. But the man's curiosity had obviously been piqued by Pretty Mary's volume. There was also the small matter of *three grand* somewhere in the equation.

"Ya mum's fully cracking the shits, hey?" joked Savannah carelessly, nursing a cold beer as she reclined in the hammock. Fuck me, boiled Kerry, we still in slavery days are we?

"You arseholes are unbelievable," she snarled, reaching deep into the schoolbag and pulling out the kingplate.

Donny gaped. Ken let out a wordless noise and lunged towards the silver crescent.

Kerry jerked it away, then strode back inside to slam the kingplate down on the kitchen table hard enough to rattle the cutlery stand.

"*Granny!*" Pretty Mary cried out, her eyes fixed on the damaged kingplate. "Where did that come from?" In shock, she lifted her gaze to Kerry, who stood above it fuming. Pretty Mary edged closer, examining the kingplate without daring to touch it.

"Happy fucken birthday. I was waiting till tomorrow to give it to ya, but if ya don't want me here ya may's well have it now," Kerry told her mother, before storming downstairs to the yard. And you can shove it up your judgmental arse, she only just managed to refrain from adding. Sitting on the growling Harley, she looked up at her brother and his poxy bush pig. "And you can go to buggery too, pal. I'm off doing crime to save the island and all the while you bin ripping Mum off for her fucking pay. Ya the scum of the fucken earth, far as I'm concerned."

Ken let out a roar as he leaped for the stairs. But Kerry was fishtailing up the length of the driveway, spraying wet gravel behind her as she blasted away, bareheaded, through the sheeting rain.

Chapter Twelve

Next morning, Kerry lay breathless on the futon, wearing only a sweaty grin. It was a glorious day, the royal blue of the sky heralding the final gasp of summer. A gentle breeze buffeted the window blind, making it tap rhythmically against the top of the glass window.

At the same instant, she and Steve both laughed, exultant, and rolled inward to face each other. Kerry's dark eyes were soft and vulnerable. Enchanted, Steve reached out a finger to brush the hair off her face; she caught it neatly between her teeth and growled at him, being Elvis. Bloody Steve, making me like him so much. Grrrrr.

"Bad dog," he teased. "Lie down. Roll over!" Kerry growled louder, bit a little harder. Steve yelped in pain.

"That's the second time in twenty-four hours I've been called bad," she said wryly, releasing him and falling backwards to stare at the ceiling. "Am I that bad?"

"My girlfriend the axe murderer," he said. "Get a grip. I wouldn't want you here if I thought you were a psychopath."

"Oh, I dunno. I'm pretty hot," Kerry joked. They hadn't had The Conversation or pledged undying love, or any other sort of love for that matter. But last night they agreed that Kerry would grab her stuff from Pretty Mary's and come camp at the gym. Not forever, given the risk to Steve's business, but for the next little while, until Kerry found somewhere else to crash.

She peered up at the cavernous ceiling where the freshly painted blue walls met rectangles of grimy foam, installed in the nineties and now stained by fly spots and water damage. There were cobwebs up there in the highest corners where Steve's vacuum didn't reach. Daddy-longlegs roamed the unseen beams, constructing silvery cities of sticky thread. All these secret insect lives were going on, far from human care or observation. The high corners didn't bear looking into too closely, but then, Kerry wondered, what did? Everybody hides some things. That was just human nature.

"But you're not my boyfriend," she added swiftly. "I never signed any contract, remember."

Steve gazed at her, his calm exterior hiding the hurt. They slept together, hung out every weekend he was in Patto, spoke on the phone daily when he was up at Burleigh with his daughter. Kerry had all but moved in. What the hell was she, if not his girlfriend?

"Yeah, okay, whatever." He finally shrugged and sat up. "But I'm not risking all this"—he gestured around at the gym—"if you're just mucking around, having a good time before you go back up north. Is that what this is? Be honest."

Kerry got up too. "Yes, at first. Kind of. But not really, not anymore." She struggled to explain, and as she struggled her face told Steve everything he needed to know.

"Right," he said, shaking his head. "I thought this was something more, but that was my dumb mistake, I guess."

"It's not that I don't . . ." Kerry began, then stopped. Why did things always have to be so *complicated*?

Steve ran his fingers through his hair and heaved a loud sigh. They'd borrowed Sav's hairdressing clippers just after Valentine's Day and Kerry had run them over his head, exposing the pale scalp beneath. For a week she'd teased him, called him the only skinhead in the village and never tired of telling him he looked like a lamppost. Now the cut had grown out into a short, dense halo of curls. Steve folded his beautiful arms at her and set his jaw.

"I dunno if you moving in here is such a good idea," he said abruptly.

"*Christ*. You remember Pretty Mary's basically booted me out?" Kerry asked him. Kerry M. Salter, unwanted in every State of the Union.

"Hey, don't make me the bad guy. You're asking me to risk everything I've got."

Kerry put her face in her hands. Typical. She should have just lied, told him she was madly in love, ready to make babies—all that shit that men want to hear. Given the arse from two houses in twenty-four hours, that's some kinda record. There were flop places she could crash for a day or a week, but they weren't exactly safe. And she wasn't up for the kind of crap addicts always had going on anyway—the lying, the violence, the madness. Uncle Richard's place, an hour away outside Lismore, maybe, but his maddening stepson who never shut up about his university crap was there. Oh God, no, she'd end up stabbing him, truesgod. Girl, Kerry told herself, you've fucked things up well and good this time. Could it have been only last October that she was shopping at Logan Central Plaza with Allie and talking about buying tickets to Mardi Gras? Jesus. That was another century, another life. Another fucking *dimension*. Kerry drained her coffee cup, put it down on the floor by the mattress, and watched the last brown drops slide smoothly to the bottom, pooling there. Down, down, down.

"I feel like a fucking idiot, Kez," Steve told her, his bottom lip dragging there, la. Oh Christ. A wave of guilt crashed over Kerry and she touched his shoulder.

"Well, don't. I think you're great. But—"

"Oh, right. *But*," Steve interrupted sarcastically, putting quotation marks around the word with his fingers. Kerry soldiered on.

"Let me finish. Growing up, I didn't worry that much about color. Us Durrongo kids just stuck together. Then I hit Patto High. That was bad enough—"

"I know," Steve interrupted. "I was there, remember?"

"Yeah, but you weren't there long, and you weren't the target, were ya? Anyway, then Donna went missing in Year Nine and no white cunt in Durrongo Shire gave a shit. Think about that for a second. The Patto cops laughed at us, reckoned she'd just gone walk-about with some bloke in a Mitsubishi Magna. The dugais she was drinking with that day didn't give a rat's arse. I had to lie in bed at fourteen and hear Mum cry herself to sleep, and wonder where in the hell my big sis had gone, if she was alive or dead. And then when Dad had his heart attack a few months later, I thought: Fuck em all, stick to your own kind. And till now, I always have. So . . ."

Kerry spread her arms wide: *So, here we are. Nothing's simple, or easy.*

She pulled on her jeans as Steve watched, the ground beneath his feet turning to a quagmire as the truth dawned.

"So after everything, I'm still some kind of enemy?" Steve was incredulous, then angry. "All those jokes you like to make about whitefellas—they aren't jokes at all, are they?"

Kerry shrugged and looked away. Dugais had no idea. No fucken clue what was at stake when you walked out into the world wrapped in dark skin. And if you told them the truth it was always boo hoo, poor me.

"I'm going for a ride," Kerry told him, picking up her keys. *Any doubt, clear the fuck out.*

————————

Kerry rode through the cane fields and the low foothills of the Margin Ranges. She leaned the bike into the long sweeping curves that fell off the sides of the mountains, using instinct and muscle memory to ride as she contemplated the mess of her life.

It was her mother's birthday, and to have any chance of staying on at Shitkicker Flats, she'd definitely need to show up at the party. Would Steve still want to come? Did she want him to? How dirty

was her mother going to be after yesterday? And above all, would
Ken still want to kill her for giving him lip? She still felt like flogging him, the prick. All them old heaps in the yard—useless, rusting
evidence that her mother's funeral money was gone, gone, gone. She
dwelt unhappily on the idea of fronting up at the party solo. In the
past weeks she'd grown used to having Steve around for backup. Her
brother put joking shit on kickboxing as a faggot sport, but Kerry
knew that he was wary of her fella. Nice guy or not, you only had to
meet Steve to see that he could do you some serious damage. There
was no telling if Ken's caution would disappear when she walked
into his territory alone after—

FUCKING HELL YOU MOTHERFUCKING—

A big kangaroo was directly in her path.

There was no time. No time to react, to make things better or
different. Kerry heard the long, loud scrape of the animal's hind
claws skidding on the tar beside her. It was the sound of a life drawing back from the edge of the abyss as the roo shifted course, jerking
away to leap parallel to the bike. She felt the brush of the animal's
taut haunch against her leg, touching her jeans, softly softly. And
then: nothing. Just the roo's ears and back and tail rising and falling,
the most natural sight in the world, as it bounded back towards the
paddocks.

Her blood leaped wild in her chest, threatening mutiny.

The danger had evaporated in the blink of an eye. Kerry pulled
the bike over and turned the engine off. The road curved empty and
innocent ahead, a black-gray strip of normality edged with eucalyptus and paddocks. Cicadas roared in the trees. Puddles lay in the
grassy gutters from yesterday's storm. A placid Hereford rested on its
knees, chewing the cud and wearing a white egret perched between
its horns. The contrast between what was and what could have been
stunned Kerry.

She panted, close to tears. Everything could have ended ten seconds ago on this sunny back road and the Hereford would still have

sat there chewing, the cicadas would still have been thrumming. Only, she would have disappeared. Kerry shivered as she realized that Pretty Mary would have received yet another dead daughter as a birthday gift.

———

From where he sat at his dining table, Jim Buckley saw his pig dog loping, very tired and very sore, across the lawn towards him. The *Patterson Herald* fell from his hands onto the floor. He rocketed to his feet and marched outside to the veranda where the dog stood, her sides heaving.

The pig dog lifted her nose, hoping for a pat, or a treat. At least some encouragement. It had been a very long day for her, and an unheralded one. But Jim could only gape as the dog's smooth white tail gave an uncertain wave. He slowly circled her, speechless, before putting his mobile to his ear.

"Patterson Police."

"Nunny? Jim Buckley."

"Yep, how can I help you, Mayor?"

"I'm gonna send you a photo in a minute. Photo of my dog. I want you to find out who's responsible. Start with that smart cunt Kenny Salter."

"A photo of your dog?"

"Yep. You'll see what I mean," Jim spat. "Top priority, Nunny. And let me know when you've brought him in."

"No problem at all," answered Senior Sergeant Tony Nunne, a man who knew just how high it was wise to jump when the mayor used your primary school nickname. "I'll grab Luke Chin and head over there shortly."

Jim paused. That wouldn't work.

"Ya might wanna leave Luke out of it," he advised. "I'm not after a quiet word in Ken's ear this time. That black cunt's pushed the envelope a bit too fucking far for his own good."

Kerry bought a pie at the Sugarloaf to celebrate her ongoing existence. The hot mince gave off a tantalizing aroma when she peeled back the pastry lid. All those times at high school, smelling the white kids' tuckshop pies and never having the bungoo for a bought lunch. Hot pies still smelled like luxury to her. And while she had a little bit of the council cash left, Kerry intended to live like she meant it. Adrenaline coursed through her, making her jumpy. She felt like sprinting up the street, screaming that she was ALIVE! She wanted to grab someone and tell them how she had nearly died, wanted to smash windows and punch out some arseholes who really deserved it. Wanted to stand barefoot in the main street and howl her victory to the sky.

Her next stop was gonna be the pub for the biggest bottle of vodka they sold, because once she got home she was getting wasted. Chug-a-lug, baby, oh yeah. Ken would be on black cans at the party tonight. So yep, she'd buy a ginormous bottle of vodka and make a night of it. If Ken wanted any drama she'd go down swinging.

Waiting for her pie to cool, Kerry wandered along the footpath and stood in front of Patterson Real Estate. She really should chuck a brick through that fucking window one of these nights. She looked below the riverfront acreages to some ads for waterless weekender blocks serially abandoned by disillusioned townies. Opposite those were the rentals. Kerry read wryly as she bit into the pastry. Everything in Patto was laughably out of reach, three and four hundred bucks a week, but a couple of places in Durrongo were cheap on account of being both ancient deathtraps and also for sale. Kerry took another bite. Chewed. Tried to imagine staying on in New South Wales, having her own place. Living by her own rules. Working the markets for rent money. Maybe get Donny to share with her, he could chuck in for food, or else cuzzie Chris with his missus Shakayla and their kid. No Ken grinding her gears with his bullshit. A place where Steve could visit, or not, as he pleased. Not forever. Just till she could work out what could be done to save the island.

She chucked her pie packet in the bin, wiped her mouth, and snorted. Not very bloody likely that they would give her a house, especially once they realized she was a Salter. But fuck it, she could have been lying dead on the asphalt five clicks from town, so what did she have to lose? The worst they could do was tell her to fuck off. Kerry pushed open the door.

Three minutes later, Kylie shoved a form at her.

"If you could sign here, and here," she said without warmth, "to confirm that you understand there's no liability to us if anything breaks or falls down on your head. They're pretty old, those places. I think this one might actually be a converted milking shed . . ."

Astounded, Kerry signed on the dotted line. This was what it was like, then, to not hear *Get back to ya, humpy* or *That one's just gone.* She looked at her arm. Yep, still black.

"I'll just go out the back and take photocopies," Kylie said, picking up Kerry's license and Medicare card. She either hadn't noticed or didn't care that the Queensland license had expired years ago. "The agent's got the keys, so if you don't mind waiting, she shouldn't be too long . . ."

Still laughing in disbelief, Kerry told her she was in no particular hurry. Alone in the front office, her gaze fell on the other side of the counter. Bit of a pigsty. A cold, half-drunk cappuccino had grown a wrinkled skin. Hand-scrawled notes: *Ring Mandy re netball.* Plumbers' quotes for working on drains at a block of units. A menu from Thai Kingdom. At the top of Kylie's in tray sat a manila folder labelled *375 Mount Monk Road.* The poltergeist house!

Grinning at the memory of her mother's scam, Kerry opened the folder just a crack. Bought by "THE PURCHASER/S" Ryan and Jasmine Marsden of 10 Tibouchina Street, Gloucester, from "THE VENDOR/S" James William Buckley trading as Patterson Real Estate. Buckley's fingers in every fucken pie in town, that'd be right.

The Marsdens had paid him three hundred and twenty grand for the termite palace on five acres. Kerry began mentally to multiply the number of acres in Durrongo Shire by three hundred and twenty thousand, and then divided that number by five. Stymied, she soon gave up on estimating what her family was owed by the Australian state. The number of billions didn't matter much. It wasn't like they were ever going to fucking get it back.

Idly she scanned the rest of the contract until she got to the witnessed signatures at the bottom. Then she blinked.

No.

What?

Hang on.

What!

It couldn't be there, and yet it *was* there.

Kerry flailed in a giant, dumping wave. She fought to break free of the choking water that surged around her, threatening to drag her down to nothingness, as she read and reread the nonsense words at the bottom of the contract. Impossibly, stupidly, across from the Marsdens' two signatures, beneath a third, illegible black scrawl, someone had typed:

Donna Z. Salter, NSW licensed agent 80451.

"Excuse me, you can't be looking at that." Kylie snatched the manila folder away and snapped it shut with a glare. "That's commercial-in-confidence!"

Kerry didn't apologize. Didn't even step back. She remained rooted on the spot, gaping and blinking, staring through Kylie as though she hadn't spoken.

Kylie peered at her, like she was wondering if Kerry had gotten drunk or high in the couple of minutes she'd been photocopying. She put the manila folder into a steel drawer, then shuffled the papers she held into a neat rectangle, hesitating over the keys to 402 Mount Monk Road. *Just get anyone in there,* Martina had told her a fortnight ago. *It doesn't matter who, they're all basically condemned shitholes anyway.* Two lots of prospective renters had come back shaking their heads.

"Hello? Can I get you some water or something?" Kylie was beginning to worry.

All Kerry heard was roaring in her ears. She sank down onto a chair beside the door and leaned forward. Put her head in her hands, trying to fit the broken pieces of the day back together. Had Jim Buckley stolen her dead sister's identity? Was it him who had murdered Donna, all those years ago? Or—extremely unlikely but possible—could there be two Donna Z. Salters in northern New South Wales?

She looked up to find Kylie offering her iced water from the fridge, and to call someone.

"Who sold that old house on Mount Monk Road?" Kerry croaked, water slopping over the rim of her glass to fall in bright clear blobs onto the impermeable blue carpet. "To the Marsdens?"

Kylie hesitated. She was beginning to worry that this Abo chick was some kind of nutter. Then, to her relief, the back door of the agency swung open.

"Holy Jesus Christ on a biscuit," said Martina softly, walking in and recoiling. She switched instantly to battle mode. "Kylie, can you take a couple of hours off and go out, love? I'll manage things here. Quick sticks!"

"But—what are you—I mean, are you—are you going to be okay?" Kylie grimaced. Are you going to be alright with this aberrant black body in the office, she meant. *Safe.*

Kerry's face had turned the color of mangrove mud at low tide.

"It's fine, just go," Martina insisted, ushering Kylie towards the door with five fingertips stiff in the small of her back. Though of course nothing was fine, not anymore. "Come back at one."

Jesus shitting Christ. Another fortnight and she would have been back at Rose Bay. Two miserable little weeks.

With a confused shrug, Kylie headed out the door. In three fast moves Martina had flipped the office sign to *Closed*, snicked the lock, and switched the office phone to message bank.

"You'd better come through," she told her little sister.

———————

Dazed, Kerry followed Donna to the rear corner office.

"Drink?" Donna reached low beneath the polished mahogany of her desk to slop golden liquor into two squat crystal glasses. The solid thunk of the Johnnie Walker bottle landing on top of the desk snapped Kerry back to reality. She looked at Donna's left wrist.

There it was, the faint scar from Ken's ten-speed racer, the day he failed to brake when Donna had stood in the way demanding her turn.

Donna threw back a neat mouthful.

"It's you, isn't it?" Kerry was bewildered.

"Drink. It'll help."

"Why . . . why didn't you let us know you were alive? What were you . . . where have you . . . *Jesus, Donna, why the fuck?*"

"Why am I here now? Or why did I stay away? Bloody sit down, will you?" Donna answered, gulping two more fingers before refilling her glass. She pushed the second tumbler across at Kerry, who gave it the briefest of glances. The scent of whisky sickened her. It was the stench of winter 1999, when Pretty Mary had handed her troubles to a Higher Power and gotten sober, and Dad Charlie had perversely taken to the bottle for the first time in his life.

"Sit down, Kez," Donna repeated, calmly crossing her legs.

Kerry fell into the chair.

"Why not let us know you were *alive*?" she blurted furiously. "For the love of God! Do you know what you put Mum and Dad through?" She shook her head. Pulled out her phone and began to stab at the keypad.

"You need to wait," Donna said urgently. "It's really important. Before you call anybody . . ."

Kerry looked across the desk at this glossy stranger. Donna had different hair—straight now, and layered, with blond highlights, making a kind of expensive ashy effect. The nose was different too, narrower and with more of a peak. But it was her sister, alright.

Whenever Kerry had imagined Donna alive it was as a weathered version of the teen who had left the pub in a stranger's Mitsubishi. A middle-aged woman still wearing those girlish cut-off jeans and a Bon Jovi tank top. But Kerry's picture was all wrong. Donna bore the years lightly, even considering the nose job. She was fit, arms and legs toned, not much different in the waist than she had been at sixteen. Oh, she had the lined cheeks of a drinker if you looked closely, but there was nothing much else to say she was anything but your ordinary Aussie chick. Terribly, terribly ordinary. That olive skin had let her slip away and become somebody else altogether. Who would I be, if I wanted to disappear, Kerry wondered? Somebody Kumar, somebody Garcia. A black American from Atlanta, Georgia: Kerry M. Washington, at your service, ma'am. All Donna had needed was to get a nose job and break her family's hearts.

You stone-cold bitch.

"Please. Just wait one minute—"

Kerry lowered her phone.

"Is this all you've got?" She nodded at the cut-glass tumbler in front of her.

"It's Johnnie Walker Red."

Kerry grimaced. Held her nose closed with two fingers as she sucked half the vile fluid down. She shuddered as it hit her taste buds. Breathed out loudly in disgust and wiped her mouth.

"You're obviously not an aficionado?" Donna raised her eyebrows. Kerry just looked at her. Was Donna making a *joke*? Expecting her to—what? Laugh? No. I'm not a fucking *aficionado*.

"Go on, then. But this had better be good," she said tightly. Because what could Donna say that would help? What could take away the years of not knowing, the tortures they had imagined? Those hideous nights when Pretty Mary sobbed on the other side of the bedroom wall, while the top bunk above Kerry stayed forever empty—a sheeted, pillowed grave—and Dad Charlie raged at everything in his terrible grief till it felled him.

Donna toyed with her glass. Swirled the scotch in a circle to the left, then to the right.

"So, I left after the big fight that day, when Mum booted me out . . ." she said, then stopped. "What do you want to know, exactly?"

Kerry snorted. What did Donna think she wanted to know? Her fucking bra size?

"Why didn't you let us know you were *alive*, one. Where the fuck have you been and what have you been doing for nineteen years, *two*. And why disappear into thin air in the first place? Try that, for starters . . ." Kerry was beginning to yell. She felt like rising up, a force of nature. Felt like smashing everything in this fancy office. She could pick up the heavy office chair she sat in and slam it through the internal window. Could hurl the desktop computer to the carpet, watch it explode into fragments of gray plastic and wire and glass, then take Donna by the arm and sling her into the plaster wall . . . and if she did all those things, then maybe, just maybe, all the stuff on the outside of her would match the stuff inside her, to the tiniest degree, and some kind of balance would be restored.

But Donna was mouthing something else now, something about stabbing Pop, and the scissors getting stuck in his chest. Her sister was coming in and out of focus.

". . . and afterwards, I didn't know if I'd killed him or what . . . there was no Facebook back then, remember. And the longer it went on, and when nobody came looking, the more . . . normal it felt. To stay gone. To just be someone else." Donna's voice was clipped. "And after a couple of years, I *was* someone else . . . I became a different person, Kerry. I don't expect you to understand, but I'm not Donna Salter anymore. Except for my passport and my real estate license. I'm Martina Rossi. I've been selling houses in Sydney for fifteen years, and I'm bloody good at it too."

"Well, that's lovely," Kerry said sarcastically, "and I'm truly happy for ya, *Martina*. Only you didn't kill him. He died at home in bed a couple of months ago. And your mother's having her sixty-fifth birthday party tonight and she thinks you're as dead as he is." Kerry made Donna look at a picture of Pretty Mary at Sandy Beach lagoon. Smiling up for the photo real happy way, her first good day since Pop passed.

"Here. Ya mother. Remember her, do ya?"

The photo winded Donna like a rabbit punch to the guts. She had thought so many times over the years about Pop and Dad Charlie. About Black Superman, and the others, yes. All of these populated her imagination—obsessively in the first months, then less and less as the years sifted by. Even last year she had found herself idly wondering, once in a blue moon, who they had become, whether she would recognize them, encountered at random on a Sydney street. But Donna had known immediately back in '99 that in order to survive she would have to forget the stringy brown woman aghast in the kitchen, screaming about what was to become of her if she didn't mend her wicked ways. There had never been any question of remembering that. Pretty Mary had been surgically excised from Donna's consciousness from the beginning. Asked by acquaintances if she had a mother, she routinely replied no and wasn't even lying. A guillotine had fallen between then and now, and everything on the other side of that shining blade had been put away forever.

Donna contemplated Pretty Mary's image for a long moment, then put the phone facedown on the desk. Her mouth stayed grim, but her eyes were moist.

"She's alive, then."

"Yep. And you need to be there tonight. It's the least you can do."

Donna drained her drink with a shaky hand and put the empty glass down. She was desperate for a smoke, but her cigarettes were in the Mazda. Without thinking, she poured again.

"Do ya wanna slow down a bit with that?" Kerry asked, seeing the tremble in Donna's hand and misinterpreting it as the DTs.

"Will Dad be there?"

Kerry realized how very far Donna had wandered. "Dad's ... Dad had a massive coronary in the kitchen a few months after you took off. Fifth of June 1999. Sorry." She berated herself for the *sorry*. She had nothing to apologize for. It wasn't her who'd fucked off and killed their father with worry. "Ken's divorced. Got three kids that we know about. Two little girls with a Torres Strait chick who went back home with em. And Donny's the oldest, he's nineteen. Mel's boy, lives at home. Mel's dead. Aneurysm."

"Donny?" she winced.

"Named for you. And Black Superman's been in Redfern for years. Him and his partner, Josh, just took on a couple of Uncle John's great-grannies. But they're struggling, and now Mum's talking about taking them kids on, as if she hasn't already raised enough bloody kids for other people ..."

"Did Mum remarry?"

Kerry shook her head no, and paused. "What about you—got any kids?"

"He told me he thought he was gay, just before I left," Donna said, thinking of Black Superman. Her voice grew harder. "Pop flogged him till he wasn't sure of anything much. And no, I wasn't what you'd call the maternal type. I went to the Tweed clinic and got rid of one, but."

She stared at Kerry, chin up, waiting for condemnation.

"Yeah, well. You and me both." The two women eyed each other. No winners, no losers. Just a bit of reality finding its way in between the cracks.

"You with anyone?" Donna asked. Kerry gave a strangled laugh.

"I'm gay. But it's complicated. Just get your stuff and follow me home now." Kerry stood up. It was gonna be a bombshell when she brought Donna to Pretty Mary, hopefully the good kind. "I better ring Mum first, but. I don't want her having a coronary too."

Donna stayed seated on the far side of the desk. Fiddled with the lid of the scotch bottle, tightening and then loosening it. The tinny sound of the metal lid circling around the grooved glass filled the otherwise silent office. Kerry jingled her keys.

Donna refolded her legs as she turned to half face the side wall of the office. When she spoke her voice was low, but clear.

"I can't."

Kerry smiled in incomprehension. "What?"

"It's been too long."

"All the more fucking reason to come now. That's the very least you owe us. You broke Mum and Dad's hearts, Donna."

"You think I owe—" Donna began to cough violently, as though her body refused any debts owing in Durrongo. When the coughing didn't stop, Kerry fetched a cup of cold water from the office cooler. On her return she stumbled, sprinkling the blue carpet with more silver drops, which sat on the surface reflecting the fluorescent lights overhead. She shoved the half-empty glass across the desk and waited with arms folded. Donna drank, wiped her face, and then wrapped both hands around the glass of scotch, interlocking her fingers.

This time she chose her words with the utmost care. If she got this right, nobody had to suffer any more than they already had. She could be safely back home in Sydney in a fortnight with a big bonus in her bank account. Her life didn't have to change one iota, if she was smart enough now.

"I can't just go back and play happy families," she said, speaking slowly so there could be no misunderstanding. "It's been too long and I'm not the person you think I am. I realize this must be a big shock, but, Kez, it's better that things are left the way they are. I'll be gone in a week anyway."

"Better for *who*? Everyone thinks you're dead."

"Better for everyone," insisted Donna.

Kerry stood, trying to process this dizzying proposal, but Ken was roaring down the stairs after her in the pouring rain, a kangaroo was flying out of her peripheral vision directly into her path, and simultaneous with these, in front of her, defiant and implacable and alive: *Donna*. She really needed to sit back down, for her legs were feeling strangely disconnected from her body. But sitting down would signal the beginning of some kind of defeat; it would be the first move towards accepting that Donna wasn't about to walk out the door with her and follow her home.

On the desk, Kerry's mobile buzzed and lit up with the word *Steve*. After half a dozen rings Donna grabbed the phone and handed it to her. Kerry hit *End Call* and shoved it in her pocket. Steve was no longer her most pressing problem. She rested her hands on the chairback, its tartan fabric rough under her palms. Mindlessly staring at it, she rotated the chair slightly to the left and then to the right. *Rock-a-bye, baby, on the treetop, when the wind blows* . . .

"So what the fuck am I supposed to tell Mum?" she finally said. "Happy birthday, and oh, by the way, Donna's alive but she's turned white and doesn't want to know us?"

"You don't need to tell her anything," Donna answered, quickly sidestepping the landmine of *turned white*. Fifteen years in real estate had taught her that some battles could never be won, only dodged. "She's lived with me gone for nearly twenty years. She must have come to some sort of . . ." *Closure* was such a dumb word. "Uh, resolution. She looks happy in that photo, so why not just let her be happy? Why stir things up?"

Kerry pulled her ponytail back with trembling hands and tightly retied it. Looking down, she slowly shook her head. The silver drops of water still lay on the carpet. Nope. It was too cruel. And it didn't even make *sense*. Alright, so Donna had gone off and made a flash new life for herself with a blond hairdo and a corner office. And good luck to her, cos at the end of the day who was she to fucking judge? But to stay away, even now? And to ask her to lie to their mother? No. That was just too cold. It was fucking bullshit. And if the mountain won't come to Mohammed . . .

"Mum's still got a *daughter*. We've all got a sister, and Donny's got an aunt he's never even bloody met. You've got the perfect opportunity tonight. Everyone'll be there. So if that's all you've got . . ."

Everyone will be there. Oh, how absolutely perfect. Christ. But Donna knew this was a situation that needed careful management. *Discipline.* Only discipline had allowed her to survive this far. Only discipline would see her leave this nightmare far, far behind. There was a problem, though. Discipline wasn't working as perfectly as it normally did.

The image of Pretty Mary smiling, far older, hair grayer, holding an armful of freshly cut greenery, was already refusing to leave Donna. For many years she had managed to hold the woman at bay. There had been no Pretty Mary, no idea of a mother. Just smooth, painless scar tissue. Now, though, she was being tormented by two mothers at once—the bloodied one screaming at her in the kitchen in 1999, and the older one smiling on the edge of the lake—and the two were beginning, horrifically, to blur into each other. Or was that the tears?

Kerry took out her phone and looked at her sister. Well?

But Donna needed to clear her head of this. These rushing, blurring pictures of what she could no longer ever be part of. She'd do anything to be rid of the maddening images and to get back home to Sydney.

Her phone rang. Her eleven o'clock appointment.

"Fuck, I need to take this."

She held the phone in her hand, hesitating, mirroring Kerry. Then she let her hand drop.

"Alright, alright, I'll come tonight. Leave me your phone number and I'll call you back after I see this client." Donna stood up, to move Kerry out of the office and out of her life. She was Martina Rossi, and Martina Rossi owed nobody in Durrongo Shire a damn thing.

Kerry gazed at her, suspicious. Short of physically knocking Donna out and kidnapping her, there was no way to force her to come home. Her sister would have to return voluntarily or not at all. Her own mobile buzzed in her hand. Steve, again.

"Right. Well, I can see meself out. But if you don't show tonight," she warned, writing her number down on the back of a real estate card and flicking it to Donna, "don't be too surprised if this office is full of angry blackfellas first thing tomorrow. Mum deserves a proper fucking explanation. We all do."

Chapter Thirteen

"Bitch, call me. It's urgent!" Kerry beseeched Black Superman's message bank. He hadn't answered her earlier calls and texts, and if she didn't tell somebody about Donna—*right fucking now*—her head was going to explode. She would go stark raving womba. Donna's little secret was going to land like a nuclear missile on Mount Monk Road, and she had to get ready for the fallout.

Steve could give her his perspective, she knew, yet Kerry discovered she was loath to call him. The bare fact of Donna's disappearance was bad enough, but to not want to come home, nearly twenty years later . . . What the hell was so wrong with her family? Kerry sat with a bottle of Stoli at a picnic table in the Patto park, and gazed dumbstruck at the grassy slope that led down to the river. She needed help. Needed to yarn to someone who would understand this clusterfuck of a day. Allie knew how grassroots families worked, but ah, where was Allie now, in her hour of need? Kerry found herself almost hating Allie for being in prison.

Her phone began to ring with "January 26." Black Superman, at last.

"Finally, fuck ya!" Kerry answered in huge relief. "Listen—"

"Sissy, it's Josh."

Black Superman's fiancé. His voice was unusually fast.

"Michael asked me to call and ask can it wait till tonight cos we're in a big blue with Family Services. Brandon's fucked up and they're talking about taking him. We've gotta try and sort it the hell out before we head to the airport."

"What's going on?" Kerry asked, lowering her head to the grimy timber of the picnic table. Black Superman had stepped up last year to try and yank Brandon off that well-worn path to Family Services. But maybe he had stepped too late.

"The neighbors reckon he tried to kill their cat," said Josh in a defeated voice. "Half drowned it."

"Christ! He wouldn't do that, would he?"

"I dunno, the psych reckons he's done stuff to animals before, apparently, so—"

"Ya neighbors blackfellas or what?"

"Coconuts. They'll prosecute him, the gammon uptown cunts." Josh spat. A tortured cat was a tortured cat, and he was proper sorry for it, yeah, but a Koori kid stolen away was something else altogether. Brandon ripped away by Family Services was a picture that solved exactly nothing.

"Oh Jesus, Josh, I'm so sorry." Kerry was gutted. Everyone knew Brandon was troubled, but they thought they'd got him in time. Eleven was young enough, just young enough, if you put a lotta love into a hard-headed kid. Maybe.

"Youse still coming up?"

"Yeah, yeah, ya brother's hell-bent on making it," Josh said tiredly. "I gotta go, sis, they want me inside."

Kerry hung up and thought wretchedly about throwing herself into the swollen brown serpent of the river. It was wide, it was wet, it was constant. It would carry her through town and down to the saltwater at Bruns if she floated long enough. She could make herself into a fallen branch and close her eyes, just drift. The bliss of it. Surrender to everything except the power of the water. Let all the bullshit of Donna alive, and whitefellas-who-weren't-boyfriends-but-suddenly-wanted-to-be-boyfriends, and foster nephews headed for short, violent lives in jail—let it all just fall away. She would melt into the water and everything hard would melt with her . . . The river was immeasurably older than she was. It was the Elder. Let it decide whether she lived or died. Maybe she'd sink like history. The pull of the current felt irresistible. The idea of surrender filled her mind, till she could feel the wetness on her skin, the change in temperature as she slowly submerged . . .

Yet in the end Kerry found she lacked the will to chuck herself away. Her legs were trembling and her heart hurt like a bitch, but she wasn't quite defeated, not yet. She took a large swig of vodka and rang Steve.

"I need to talk to you, if you're talking to me," she told him, taking another mouthful of fiery medicine. "Something huge just happened."

"Same," said Steve. "I'll be here waiting."

"That was local trio The Butcher Birds with their single 'Nobody Saw Me,'" announced the ABC presenter. "Now, Mayor Buckley, I believe you've got an update for us on the Ava's Island development?" Anna smiled as she said this, not from any malice towards the council but in relief that the mayor was phoning in his weekly chat. Fond of letting his gaze linger on her cleavage, and far too prone to brush up against her in the doorway of her radio booth, today Buckley would have to harass her over the airwaves instead. She and Gary, her producer, had spontaneously high-fived when Buckley's PA let them know the mayor was working from home, suffering a touch of the flu. *Flu my arse,* Gary told Anna, *he was sinking piss like there was no tomorrow at the game last night.*

On the back deck of his riverside home, Jim Buckley lifted his bare feet onto the railings and reached beneath his dressing gown to scratch himself. A glass of Berocca fizzed on the table next to him.

"Absolutely correct, Anna," he answered in a voice oily with spin. "The proposal's well on track to provide around two hundred new jobs over the next few years. The sad fact is that Grafton prison simply can't cope with increasing demand, and we are very well placed in Durrongo to meet the need once the appeals have been overturned."

"There are some bones of contention, though, aren't there, Mr. Mayor?" probed Anna. "The Greens are questioning how many permanent jobs are actually going to be created, and locals are appealing the development on both cultural and environmental grounds—"

"Look, I'm very confident that the Land and Environment Court will see the clear benefit of hundreds of skilled jobs," Buckley quickly butted in. "Our legal advice says there isn't a snowball's chance in Hades of it being stopped. And at least five percent of jobs at the new facility will be earmarked as Indigenous. So I hardly think frivolous concerns about so-called sacred land, land that has been used for primary production for well over a century, I might add, can be taken as anything but stirring by professional rent-a-crowds, Anna. Those people who are taking us through this expensive and drawn-out appeals process are simply wasting everybody's time. They'd be better off thinking about the local jobs they're putting at risk."

"Strong words there from Patterson mayor Jim Buckley," commented Anna, wrapping up the interview, "who appears very confident that the proposed prison will get past increasing community objections. And now for the latest report on the traffic in the lead-up to the school holidays . . ."

Anna muted her mike and turned to Gary.

"Buckley could sleep on a corkscrew." She shook her head. "It'll get up. But if there's two hundred jobs in it, I'm Oprah Winfrey."

"What's got me buggered is why ICAC isn't sniffing around," Gary agreed, cueing up the next song. "He leads a charmed life, our Fearless Leader."

———

At her desk in the real estate office, Donna flicked off the radio. Went to the bathroom and wet her face. She stood in front of the mirror, shaking. So her father had been dead for nineteen years. Of the men she'd grown up among, only her two brothers remained. And now there was this unknown nephew named for her.

Donna began to fight for breath. Rushed back inside the office to grab her keys before light-headedness overcame her. Safely in the Mazda, she leaned onto the steering wheel. The grief of loss ripped through her for the first time in decades. She bent over and began silently sobbing, her mouth making ugly twisted shapes behind her hands.

She couldn't lose the images. The photo of her smiling mother. Ken that last afternoon, the things he'd called her. Her, sobbing in the back bedroom, going to Pop for comfort when he arrived home from work when she would have been better off asking the cat for help, or the chickens. Dad Charlie, dishing up the leftover birthday cake later that afternoon. The scissors in her hand, appearing out of nowhere, and Pop, flailing backwards, his mouth opening wide as bright red flowers appeared on his business shirt.

And Pretty Mary's high, hysterical accusations.

I don't know how I could have produced a poisonous little bitch like you. Fuck off, nobody wants ya! You don't belong here!

And now, nineteen years later, her sister thought she had stayed away for money, for what was on offer in the white world. And maybe that was a part of it. Moneyed and passing for white was protection. Moneyed and white meant a life with doors that locked out the evil bastards who delighted in destroying women. Girls. But she'd also stayed away in terror that it wasn't the grog talking that night. The terrible question at the center of her life. Had her mother really meant it, and would she say it again to her face the first chance she got? Would she, Donna, be instantly sixteen again, with a world of pain inside her head and absolutely nowhere safe to go? She sat tormented by the smiling picture of Pretty Mary and torn by an urge she couldn't understand to turn the key in the ignition, to head down the highway to Durrongo and find out the answer, once and

for all. Asked, Donna would not have been able to say which she was
looking for: welcome or revenge. Perhaps in some mad way she was
hoping for both.

"You first." Steve spat out his mouthguard and gnawed at the plaster
strapping on his hands. His tank top was soaked through. Sweat
dripped from his chin and made dark spots on the lino. Kerry
gestured to let her rip the tape off, and Steve stuck out both fists
as though he was wearing invisible handcuffs. His teenage boxing
students ogled Kerry and commented to each other beneath their
breath.

"Can I help you?" she asked them acidly.

"Knock that off, you lot," Steve chipped the boys, who giggled
and ran to the changing room.

Kerry let it go. Silly moogle kids. But any adult who gave her shit
would be seriously trying their fucking luck, cos she was close to the
edge. Grandmaster Flash had nothing on her today.

Kerry described what she had uncovered at the real estate office,
as Steve leaned back onto the ropes of the ring. When she was done,
he let out a whistle.

"Fucken hell. Whaddya reckon'll happen? Tonight, I mean.
What's the worst thing that could happen?" He worried, rubbing at
the adhesive left on his hands.

"The worst thing would be if Mum drops dead from shock
when Donna arrives outta the blue," Kerry answered. She would
never, ever forget her father lying on the kitchen floor, her mother
screaming, *Get up, Charlie, get up, don't do this to me, Charlie.*

"Well then, you need to tell her first," Steve began, but Kerry
overrode him.

"Second-worst, *close* second, I tell Mum Donna's alive and then
she doesn't show. And we all have to go out looking for her like it's
fucking Groundhog Day . . ."

"Ah." Steve sucked his teeth as this sank in. Not as bad as a fatal heart attack, but almost as complicated. And nearly as painful for Pretty Mary.

Kerry paused too, calculating more woe. "*Plus*, whether she turns up or not, there's still a pretty good chance Ken's dirty with me for giving him lip yesterday. So he might decide to lose his shit and crack me onetime." Too much lip, her old problem from way back. And the older she got, the harder it seemed to get to swallow her opinions. The avalanche of bullshit in the world would drown her if she let it; the least she could do was raise her voice in anger. Give the arseholes a blast, then stand and defend, or else run like hell.

Kerry frowned at Steve. Some birthday party this was gonna be if the planets didn't align.

"Not while I'm around he won't." Steve grimaced. Kerry blinked as a delicious warm feeling spread through her chest.

"Does that mean you're still coming tonight?"

"If you want me there."

"You'd jump in?"

"Bloody oath I'd jump in." Steve crinkled his forehead at her like it was the dumbest question he'd ever heard. Kerry didn't really know him at all if she thought he'd just sit there and let anyone . . . *For fuck's sake, Steve, tell her.* No guts, no glory.

"You'd wanna be sure, but," Kerry warned. "Knuckle up to Ken and the whole mob might double bank ya." Cousin Chris could punch on like nobody's business, and there was no telling what the others might do under duress. A worrisome picture came into her mind of Savannah swinging a wine bottle. It was followed by a more pleasing one of Kerry taking the bottle and clocking her with it, knocking Sav sideways off the veranda into the snaky waist-high grass. That still left her and Steve knuckling up against Ken, Chris, any randoms who felt like blueing, and possibly even Pretty Mary herself. But ah, it wouldn't come to that. Ken should have cooled off by now. Hopefully.

Steve smiled a pained smile.

"Let's cross that bridge later. And if that's your big news, this is mine: you might not have signed any contract, girl," he said, putting his palms on either side of her face, "but I'm fucked if I'll stand by and watch anyone lay a finger on you, Kez. I'm crazy in love with you, babe—donchya realize that?"

Steve blushed beneath his stubble, a deep red that reached his collarbones. Kerry's heart thumped and banged, threatening to bust out of her chest altogether. Oh God. This life of hers, this crazy fucking life. She was such a fool. They say life has to be lived forwards and understood backwards. Yeah, well, whaddya know, they're bang on the money there. Because, she now realized with a flash of blinding insight, she had comprehensively snookered herself. Had played silly buggers with Steve, acted exactly like any girlfriend would act, in the belief that his white skin would protect her heart. Had gambled that it would be enough, in the end, to let her dismiss him. No matter what they did together or how attached she might become, she could go running back to Queensland with her conscience clear. Because with *whitenormalsavages* there was always an escape hatch sitting there. Always an exit door marked in big black letters: *only a dugai*, and therefore not completely human. Certainly not to be taken seriously in anything that really mattered.

But, Kerry now understood with a blend of horror and joy, you can be wrong about these things, comprehensively wrong. Being in love with this whitefella was impossible, but there you fucking go. Because it turned out she did want to be Steve's girlfriend. She wanted to grab him tight—his calm sanity, his eruptions of laughter, his firm belief that bad things could be made better and that survival was assured either way—and never let him go. This one's on my side, she thought, in astonishment. For once in my damn life I'm not kicking against the pricks alone.

"That calls for a drink." She grinned, producing the vodka bottle.

Chapter Fourteen

"Us mob need to start a revolution, dead set," Ken announced to the party as he basted the lamb sizzling in front of him. A mighty cheer erupted from everyone, even the strays from the pub. Encouraged, he went on. "A blackfella revolution from Durrongo to Darwin." Ken wiped his forehead, happy about his decision to go with cuzzie Chris's homemade spit rather than dig a kup murri. Ah, nothing like it. A gathering of the mob, a charge, and a bloody good feed in the great outdoors.

"Oppressed peoples must be the agents of their own liberation," agreed Zippo, owner of the cigarette lighter at the protest. "But real revolution takes in the economic struggle too, brother." A weathered Metis grandfather, Zippo had taken to Ken's haphazard political theories with intense interest. The two men had argued like cats and dogs for a week, then bonded over a shared hatred of the prison-industrial complex. Between them they were in imminent danger of developing a recipe for a new Australian democracy.

"Sovereignty's gotta be the priority, Hairyman," Ken counselled. "Treaty first for the Goorie man. Then we can talk socialism."

"Oi! Goorie women too!" Savannah joked on her way upstairs, for Uncle Neil had last night revealed a great-grandfather born on the third mission south of Rivertown. It was startling information that nobody except Pretty Mary was quite sure what to do with. *You're not Black,* cousin Chris had informed Savannah furiously. *It takes more than just finding an ancestor, girlfriend. Nah, one-drop rule,*

Pretty Mary disagreed; if their family was here before Captain Cook rocked up, then they blackfellas and that's an end of it. Ken had scratched his head at the discovery. He'd erupted too loudly and too often about Johnny-come-latelys to agree aloud with Pretty Mary, and now when he looked at Savannah, his affection was diluted with chagrin. She and he wore matching red T-shirts that read: *Protect Our Sovereign Waters.* Ken, like every other Salter, knew with crystal clarity—had always known—that the waters around Ava's Island belonged to their Bundjalung mob. Just exactly who constituted that mob, though, and who now fell outside of it, was a little less clear than it ought to be. Ken frowned and turned back to the coming revolution. Savannah might have morphed into a conundrum, but he, Kenneth Edward Salter, was bred Black, born Black, and raised Black. He was as Black as the mooya of a black budigan at midnight, and he had a Black agenda to be getting on with. He wasn't about to be distracted.

"If the Land and Environment Court fucks us with no lube," he continued, "we go direct action. We rip that gammon fence down as often as they wanna put it up. We go camp on our country and bloody well fight for it!" He glanced up at the house, where the kingplate hung, invisible from the road, nailed to the beam facing the rear door. The ancestors were with them again—the ragged bullet holes in the plate were simply more evidence that the Salters were indestructible when they stuck together. Ken knew in his bones there was no stopping them. All he had to do was fulfill his manifest destiny. The prison was as good as dead.

While Ken and Zippo plotted, Pretty Mary sat on the veranda with Aunty Tall Mary and gazed down on the yard. Cousin Chris had raked up eight full buckets of dried pods from under the leopard tree. The men had driven, pushed, or towed all the bombs to the back corner of the yard and parked them in a neat line, just like a real car yard. Then Ken had spent the morning on Uncle Neil's ride-on, leaping and yelling every time toads and snakes wriggled out from under the wheels. Aunty Val helped Aunty Tall Mary and Helen mop the house out; Kerry and Steve were due any tick of the clock with a couple of roast chooks and some big news (hopefully that they were getting engaged). Pretty Mary beamed. Not only had Kenny sold two—*two!*—cars yesterday, he had promptly shouted her a fresh carton of durries plus, incredibly, the lamb price that she had been planning to somehow scrape up out of the bill money. Now, after doing the Patto markets, she was just about square. And oh, she told Tall Mary, wasn't it the best feeling in the world, getting rid of them awful bits of paper scolding her from the door of the fridge? An hour ago she had fed them with great satisfaction into the fire crackling beneath the lamb. Disconnect the power, my arse. She smiled as she sipped at the homemade finger-lime cordial Aunty Tall Mary had brung over from Casino. She wondered if it would be wise to do a reading for her, given Doris's never-ending dramas on the ice. Best leave it, she decided.

"Where do ya want these, Mum?" asked Sav, coming past with potato salad and coleslaw. Behind her, Aunty Val staggered beneath a load of crockery and sauce bottles. Uncle Neil—whose rich brown tan above his Aussie-flag board shorts had taken on a brand-new significance—was helping cousin Chris move the trestle table under the leopard tree.

"Chuck everything on the table next to Pop," Pretty Mary instructed Sav. "And keep that bloody warrigal chained up or he'll be into it before we can blink." Elvis lay disconsolate at the far stretch of his chain, which manacled him halfway between the lamb's glorious aroma and the house. He put his nose between his front paws and brooded on the severe injustice of his situation.

"Next to Pop?" Sav wrinkled her nose.

Pretty Mary looked at her blankly.

"You said next to Pop . . ."

"Oh! I mean next to Ken." Pretty Mary laughed, realizing her mistake. "Pop always used to cook when we had a kup murri."

Kerry sat in front of the shop, checking her phone. No texts. No missed calls. She should have insisted on getting Donna's number rather than just handing over her own like some kind of simple cunt. Their sister always had been a cunning bitch and consummate liar, according to Ken, and it was starting to look like he was right. Maybe Donna had already made tracks, left the clan high and dry a second time. Another bloody good reason to say nothing to Pretty Mary, Kerry decided, as Steve emerged with a hot chook clutched in either hand, claiming to be the wind beneath her wings.

He lifted each chicken shoulder-high, swaying side to side on the footpath and doing his best Bette Midler.

"Can you shuttup and get on?" Kerry asked. Steve simply sang louder, hamming it up for the locals gossiping in front of the notice-board. A couple of the young women began laughing at his antics. Kerry wondered how she would go arriving at the party alone. Caruso and his chickens could walk.

Steve came closer and yodelled louder.

Kerry rolled her eyes. Steve had showered and shaved and pulled out the black polo shirt she'd last seen at the funeral, but he obviously hadn't registered how bloody tricky the party was going to be if Donna showed. And if she didn't. Kerry had lain in bed all afternoon racking her brain for a good way to tell Pretty Mary that her other daughter was alive. Steve advised her to just spit it out. Knowing better, Kerry wavered in an agony of indecision. Depending on Ken's mood, the simple fact of keeping quiet about Donna for an afternoon could be considered treachery. Everybody knew that information was power. And she—his younger sibling and a female to boot—had knowledge of something that he—the oldest and a grown man—had been left ignorant of. That's how Kenny Koala would likely view her revelation. As a crime against nature. But unless she was willing to risk seeing Pretty Mary's world crumble for nothing—and she wasn't willing; the thought was just too cruel—she would have to gamble on Donna not showing her face.

"You okay, babe?" Steve said, finally chucking his leg over the bike. He rested his chin on her left shoulder, and their helmets knocked together with a soft clunk. Kerry shrugged.

"I can't risk telling her. Not on her birthday."

Steve was quiet for a moment.

"Well, you know I got your back."

"Yeah. Just wish you didn't have to."

This decision still nagged at Kerry as she rode down the drive, where Mick Jagger was howling in dissatisfaction from the caravan. It wormed away in her brain as she gave stiff-necked Ken and his lamb a wide berth and went upstairs, and the news sat on the very tip of her tongue as she grudgingly apologized for doing crime while living under her mother's roof.

"Apology accepted," said Pretty Mary primly, demanding a kiss on the cheek from Steve. To Kerry's amazement, no gruelling lecture followed. No enumeration of the many ancestors on high rotation at her bad behavior. It was astonishing what a mown lawn and a carton of smokes could do, she reflected. Maybe it really was as Pretty Mary said—with the kingplate finally returned to the family, where it belonged, the powerful blessing of Granny Ava was radiating out into every tiny nook and cranny.

Her mother was as happy as she'd been in years. Steve was now officially Kerry's boyfriend. Kenny—unbelievably—had just sold two cars to a Lismore punter whose brother was interested in a third. Uncle Neil and Sav and Sav's kids had turned out to be another long-lost distant piece of the upended Goorie jigsaw. And Pretty Mary's favorite son was on his way to see them any moment now with an update on how his QC was gonna outsmart Jiminy Cricket and save Granny's island. All this good fortune came through the mystical agency of the kingplate, according to her mother, and since it was Kerry who had—albeit nefariously—delivered the kingplate back to the mob, Kerry was to be forgiven her other transgressions and misdemeanors.

It was like some kind of ancestral miracle.

With a dozen shots of vodka in her, Kerry heard Donna's voice echoing from that morning: *She looks happy. Why not just let her be happy?*

Why not, indeed.

Kerry kissed Aunty Tall Mary, briefly gave some cheek to cuzzie Helen, then made tracks to sit in the darkest corner of the veranda. To tell or not to tell, that was the question. She waited for Donna's text for twenty long and fruitless minutes. Then Kerry heaved a sigh, took the Stoli, and silently toasted Helen, who was four months pregnant and off the grog.

Bottoms up, cuz.

———

"The city slickers are ere," Ken shouted with a grin some time later. "Lock up ya sons!" Kerry emerged from the house to see Black Superman and Josh pulling in. Both kids in the back. Thank fucking Christ. Brandon hadn't been hauled away to juvey. And since a problem shared was a problem halved, she could now unburden herself. Black Superman would listen and not go ballistic or make things worse by instantly spilling his guts to Pretty Mary. As she waited for her brother, Kerry noticed Donny hauling next door's blow-up pool into the yard. Still half full, the rectangular pool sloshed and jerked over the grass. Was it her imagination, she wondered, or was her neph putting on a tiny bit of weight? She had spied a stringy muscle lurking beneath the skin of his left forearm.

"Uncle Richard here yet?" she heard Black Superman ask.

"On his way from Grafton," Ken told him. "He had that funeral."

"Eh, which way you mob!" Kerry called out in relief. "Here's trouble!" Brandon and Lub Lub were racing to join the other kids clustering around the pool.

"Oi, Donny, empty that out! You'll bust the seams," ordered Ken.

He went over and made Donny tip out half the water he had just hauled all the way from next door.

"Come on, tip er again," Ken insisted. "You can easy refill it with the hose."

"Nuh. S'here now," Donny panted, with a final heave that delivered the sloshing pool to the edge of the leopard tree's shade. As he hauled, his T-shirt sleeve rode up, exposing the humpback newly etched below his shoulder. That arm was definitely a millimeter wider.

"Nice whale there, lad," Kerry observed, coming downstairs to check it out. Ken had long urged her to put Ned Kelly on her abs, but she was skeptical of his talent; she wanted Ned Kelly there, not Marge Simpson. But Donny's whale was impressively realistic. The lad glowed as he explained what he wanted the full sleeve to look like in time, taking in all his totems. Whales cruising across the top, flames below, and then maybe Granny Ava's hoop pine growing up through it all from his hand. Donny was keen for the tree, but Ken had insisted he wasn't near ready for shit like that, the kid reported ruefully.

"How about a Dell lappie instead, with the mouse cord coming down, wrapped around yer forearm?" yelled Ken, with a wink at Sav. "And a big Google symbol over the top?" Sav pursed her lips and slapped at Ken. Leave off tormenting the poor lad.

"Ya think ya fucking hilarious," Donny replied, going to grab the ice from beneath the house, "but ya not, eh." Kerry smiled wryly. Donny, putting on weight, talking up to his father—wonders would never cease. Ken laughed the laugh of a man who had sold two cars at a tidy cash profit, and turned back to basting the lamb. Donny upended the bags of ice into the pool, then began ripping open beer cartons and putting the cans into the water. The kids took this as a signal to strip off and plunge in too, pushing and shoving against the clinking cans and each other for territory, and soon enough shivering while vehemently denying that they were in the least little bit cold.

"Watch Dr. No, won't ya, bub," Aunty Val called out to Rosie from her chair on the other side of the spit.

"She knows," said Savannah, organizing the salads. "She's an awesome big sissy, aren't ya, beautiful?"

———————

The sun hovered close to the horizon for what seemed like hours as the lamb was carved and enjoyed. Steve put his fatty meat aside. Kerry, who by now was neither drunk nor sober, happily scoffed it as well as her own. Then she undid the top button of her jeans, groaning, and resolved to begin a twenty-four-hour fast first thing in the morning. When everyone else was happily complaining that they, too, had eaten too much good tucker, Black Superman stood up, looking exhausted but hopeful. He cleared his throat and reported that the QC was optimistic about their chances in court. He thought there might be enough dodgy paperwork in Buckley's council to bring the prison proposal tumbling down.

"I knew my prayers was gonna be answered!" Pretty Mary exclaimed. "Our Old People are watching down and they're proper happy with you, my son. Praise God!"

"Why not praise Biame up if you gotta be praising any god?" asked Ken, who was getting more cultural by the day.

"How 'bout praise my big black dot," Kerry snapped, still dirty about the funeral money. "Or Black Superman's. Anyway, don't count ya chickens, Mum."

"This prison business was never in the cards," Pretty Mary answered insouciantly, "and I gotta good feeling 'bout this QC fella."

"Chickens!" said Steve, jumping up to retrieve the forgotten chooks from the kitchen. Sav cleared a few plates, then quickly followed him into the house, Kerry noticed with displeasure. When Steve reemerged a minute later she assessed him carefully for evidence of infidelity. But he looked at Kerry, then rolled his eyes at Sav with a horrified expression. Kerry frowned hard. Shuttup man, shuttup! If Sav had been coming on, Steve needed to keep his mouth well and truly closed. The fucking roof would come off if Ken found out. But luckily Ken was distracted by an arm wrestle between Chris and Josh.

"I'll verse the winner," he announced, lacing his fingers together and flexing his arms above his head.

The party clustered around to see the young men have it out. Cousin Chris was bulky, but Josh was a chippie who also lifted four times a week, and in the end it was Chris's hand that got slammed onto the tabletop. But Josh's triumph was short-lived.

"Fuck, I've pulled something," he said, bending over and clasping his arm. Annoyed, Ken looked around. It was no good versing the injured loser. What would that prove?

"You give us a go, Scotsman," he demanded of Steve, who declined with a smile.

"You know I'll win, that's why, hey?" Ken teased. "Whitefellas can't never stand losing to a black man . . ."

"I've got a big match coming up, bro. I can't risk getting injured," Steve said mildly. "But after that, sure, I'll show ya how to arm wrestle, if ya want a lesson."

Ken snorted and went looking for a match among the pub strays instead. Kerry carefully assessed her brother's mood. Clearly still on a high from selling the cars and providing the lamb, Ken had let several things slide that afternoon. He hadn't reacted when Donny cheeked him. Even a dispute about Brandon being made to see a white psychologist twice a week—the condition of him remaining free—had seen Ken mocking rather than enraged. Kerry took another mouthful of liquor and stood up. It was time to try and get Black Superman alone and talk to him about Donna.

———————

The kids stuffed themselves with lamb and chips and birthday cake, played Grand Theft Auto at Aunty Val's, then circled back for a second crack at the cake and the plastic pool. Chris cranked up Chisel and played along on his six-string, accompanied by Zippo banging away with drumsticks on an old Mazda engine, his gray dreads flying in an attempt to impress Pretty Mary. Brandon whined so long and so expertly that Kerry caved in and took him for a burn on the Harley, which of course meant that all the kids then needed a ride. After Kerry dropped off the last grinning passenger, she threw caution to the winds, gunning the Hog in a wheelie along Mount Monk Road past the front gate, to the whooping and cheering of the entire party. That was the best thing about Pretty Mary's: no neighbors. You could let rip.

With the bike parked under the house, and the spit roast officially over, the adults settled back, full of tucker and goodwill, to yarn. From time to time Chris and Zippo disappeared into the van with some of the pub strays and reemerged red-eyed and coughing, grinning at the world that had become that little bit easier to take. Kerry was delighted to see the bucket bong in action. If things did kick off, Chris would be that much less inclined to punch on in support of Ken, and that much less competent if he did. Smoke up, cuz, she thought, get stuck into it. For herself she had decided to just nurse her Stoli. No yarndi for her today. Cos loose lips sink shits. *Ships*. Get a grip, Kez. She checked the level. Third of a bottle left. Not sober, but not legless neither. Loooong way from legless, girl, she told herself, looongest way, suddenly remembering that she had planned to get, and then stay, sober. Oh well. She would slow down a bit. But Ken was still as happy as Larry, anyways. Thought he was some rich cunt now. Biggest hotshot businessman cos he sold two cars, yeah, good go.

"Niece! Don't get me started on Father O," said Aunty Tall Mary to Kerry, with a doubtful side-eye at Steve to see if he was worthy of the yarn. "Remember about the time he locked ya Pop in the morgue?"

"Get away!" Kerry answered, startled. It made her uneasy to realize how little she knew of her grandfather's life. In her memory Pop had always been part of the furniture, first living briefly in the house, and then exiled to the van because of his legendary snoring, and perhaps, truth be told, in punishment for his gambling as well. But just because you live with someone as a child doesn't mean you know them.

"Truesgod. You've heard what the Rivertown mish was like." Aunty Tall Mary raised her eyebrows dramatically. Kerry nodded. There were so many horror stories. "Terrible cruel, under Father O. He was a mongrel, not like Father Morrison was. Well, this one weekend they reckon your Pop visited old Uncle Shorty Henderson on the mish, see, and talk about bold! He'd not long come back from Queensland with that Silver Gloves trophy, all of fourteen, and Pop thought he was as good as any man, black, white, or brindle. He give that much lip to Father O, knuckled up to him and all, they reckon! Father cracked the shits. He woulda bin thinking, right, I'll fix this cheeky little half-caste. So Father grabs him by the collar and slings him into the morgue, onetime." Aunty Tall Mary swung her arms in demonstration. Clapped her hands, loud way. "Locked the door. Left him there all night on his own."

"Are you serious?!" said Sav, horrified.

"Truesgod," claimed Aunty Tall Mary. Beside her, Pretty Mary nodded.

"Father O left him in there with the dingoes howling and the wind whistling off the range through them old slab walls." Tall Mary's voice dropped to a dramatic whisper. "There was dead bodies in there too, bub, a mum and a newborn who'd passed away before the doctor bothered to come out from Yamba. Left him in there with em all night. Eeyah, look your man—he got biggest eye, la!"

Aghast, Steve was looking to Kerry to confirm that Aunty Tall Mary was pulling his leg. Everybody laughed.

"Nah, that'd be right" was all Kerry said, taking another mouthful of vodka, drowning the arsehole missionaries, drowning every white genocidal dog up to and including Jim Buckley, and drowning her non-texting, non-phoning gammon coconut of a sister while she was at it.

"So next morning they unlocks the morgue. Father O says to him, *Ya gonna give me any more lip, son?* In front of the whole mish, mind you. And your Pop just went, *I dunno, Father, am I?* But he said it sorta weird, not being cheeky, more like he really didn't know the answer himself. And his hair had gone all white here"—Tall Mary touched her temples—"at fourteen. But afterwards, when Pop come good, it turned out he had very little fear left. They done their worst and he survived. And them old uncles on the mish, Uncle Robbie and Uncle Tony and them, Pop told them he felt the spirit of Death go into him that night. He took it real serious too."

Hair stood up on several brown arms.

"That's . . ." Kerry shook her head, but whether at the missionaries' cruelty or her Pop's conversion wasn't clear. It was a hell of a story, if it was even half true.

"I don't know that he ever come good really," Pretty Mary chimed in. "Pop always said it made him responsible for a lot of vengeance, having that spirit in him. For the massacres. Stolen ones, too, when they died, their spirits flying around looking for a safe place to rest on their own countries. Well, he was stolen himself, see. It tormented him all his born days that he couldn't name his true country; the shame of it haunted him. No wonder he drank."

Behind Pretty Mary, Black Superman curled his lip and twirled a finger beside his right ear. Womba, he meant. Black Superman firmly believed that their grandfather had been driven as silly as a two-bob watch by missionary brutality, and had taken it out on the rest of them.

Kerry sat, pondering what it would be like to be locked up all night with dead bodies at fourteen. It would change the course of your life. Would be the making of you, or the ruination. And then not long after, Pop was sent to work for Cracker Nunne. Jesus wept.

"But that's dugai culture for ya, eh?" Aunty Tall Mary added, with another significant glance at Steve. "Hurting people, locking little kids up with dead bodies! All their evil ways."

"Father Morrison was different," Pretty Mary began.

"Speaking of vengeance," Ken interrupted her from where he was scraping the barbecue plate clean, "anyone seen the mayoral pig dog lately?"

Pretty Mary frowned. Beside her, Black Superman stiffened.

"No need to look like that, Mum," Ken said airily. "Old mate might be getting a taste of his own medicine, is all. He wants to keep a closer eye on his property if he doesn't want it getting damaged."

"Whaddya mean, 'damaged'?" asked Black Superman in a hard voice, swinging around to check that Brandon was still playing in the pool.

"I just mean a little bit improved, bruz." Ken lowered his eyelids. "Don't stress, ya fucken great pussy, I didn't hurt it. Well, not much."

"You know Brandon nearly went to juvey today for animal cruelty, donchya?" Black Superman's deep-set eyes glittered angrily. "I don't need him hearing that hurting animals is some big fucking joke, bud."

"Brandon needs a good belting," Ken snapped. "That'll smarten his act up real quick. Spare the rod and spoil the child." He gave the barbecue plate another spray with Ajax and sipped at his drink.

Black Superman stared at his brother, nostrils flaring. Oh, here we go, thought Kerry, clutching her Stoli by the neck. There was a quarter bottle left, but she'd gladly sacrifice it if necessary.

"Fuck me gently. You think Brandon's been spared the rod, do ya?" Black Superman rolled his eyes in contempt. Kerry frowned and flapped a wrist. Leave it, bruz. He's charged up. No good arguing with drunks, you know that. But Black Superman was too wild to leave off.

"That kid's had the shit bashed outta him since he was in nappies, brah. Any junkie what come through that crack house coulda done Christ knows what to him and his sister, and on top of that his poxy stepfather kept a length of garden hose handy to flog em with. I seen the photos with me own eyes—five years old with fucking hematomas all over him. Maybe ya wanna think about that before dishing out fucken free advice on fucken child-rearing."

"Nyorn, poor little bugger," Kerry said in horror. "That's too cruel."

"Shocken cruel," agreed Chris, deeply disgusted. "Anybody done that to my kid, they'd be shark shit the next day."

"Any juhm, Mum?" Ken asked as though Black Superman hadn't said a word. Pretty Mary tossed a cigarette to him. Ken lit it with the barbecue lighter.

"We gotta protect our jahjams," Aunty Tall Mary burst out, slapping her palm on the arm of her chair. "Dugais going and hurting our kids like that!"

"These are blackfellas I'm talking about, Aunty." Black Superman swung around. "No good pretending. This is some of our own mob."

"Well, then it was dugais what taught them how to do it." Tall Mary's eyes flashed in rage. "You know what they've done to us mob. It's all gotta come out somewhere."

"Yes, of course it's trauma. But that's no excuse, eh," Black Superman said sharply. He was sick to the marrow of hearing people defend the indefensible, or deny it even existed, when the evidence was right there, clear for anyone to see. "What matters is what we do for our jahjams now. About breaking the cycle."

"They wanna be tied to a tree and flogged," Ken announced. "Black, white, or brindle. Fucking junkie scum." Beside him Sav nodded in vigorous agreement.

"Cos more violence is the answer," said Kerry.

Ken squinted at her.

"Got a better idea, do ya, smartarse? Our Old Law says you do wrong, ya pay the penalty. People going around bashing little kids, it's fucking criminal."

This from the bloke who ten seconds ago had proposed flogging Brandon into submission. And what exactly, Kerry wondered, did the Old Law say about stealing from Elders? From your own mother? Standing over old people for their pensions, humbugging your sister for her last two dollars? Don't wanna talk Law there, I bet.

Kerry was ready to gamble that having Steve nearby was enough insurance to ask these questions when loud wailing erupted from the pool, and her bladder contracted in fear. Black Superman shot out of his seat like he'd been fired from a rifle and hurtled over, closely followed by Josh, Kerry, and Pretty Mary. All the kids were screaming by the time Black Superman seized Dr. No by the upper arms and swung him out onto the lawn, away from the jagged glass glinting beneath the shallow water of the pool. Ken winced and went to stand under the house next to Elvis. The sound of kids in pain touched a raw nerve in him; it always made him want to hit out, and do something—anything—to stop it. Ken turned away from the party and focused instead on untangling Elvis's chain, wrapped multiple times around a concrete house pillar. He did his best to pretend nothing was wrong, took a last draw on Pretty Mary's durrie, and waited, nerves jangling, for the screaming to stop.

"Stand real still, youse kids!" Black Superman ordered as he checked Dr. No for damage. "Nobody move a muscle." Satisfied that the child's cut wasn't serious, he handed Dr. No to Sav, then reached into the pool to carefully retrieve three jagged pieces of a broken Bundaberg rum bottle. While the other kids held still, obediently frozen in place, Lub Lub broke free. She stumbled out of the pool and fled onto the lawn, where she squatted, shaking and sobbing.

"Sissy, wait!"

Brandon broke away after her, dived onto the ground and bundled his sister into his arms. Lub Lub's teeth were chattering, but her reaction wasn't from the cold, Kerry thought, snatching a dry towel off the Hills hoist to wrap around the kid. She examined each small brown limb under the spotlight. Everything seemed in order.

"What's wrong, bubba?" she asked repeatedly with a hand gentle on the kid's back. But Lub Lub kept sobbing against her brother's chest. Kerry gestured to Donny to bring Elvis over from beneath the house. Where humanity failed, the animals would cut through. Elvis wagged his half-a-tail at Lub Lub and bumped her face with his moist black stub of a nose. Her wailing grew a little less frantic.

"You're not bleeding, baby," Kerry reassured Lub Lub. "And Dr. No's just got the one cut, it's not too bad. You're not hurt, sweetie, you're okay."

"It's not that," Brandon said. "It's the smell of the rum. It frightens her."

"Seeing grog wasted has the same effect on me," Uncle Neil wisecracked. "I cried meself to sleep for a week last time I broke a longneck!"

But Pretty Mary was more somber. "Poor baby. She's seen too many grog parties."

"Wanna give her to me, bud?" said Black Superman, squatting down with his arms extended.

Brandon shook his head. "Fuck off!"

Black Superman nodded. "I know you wanna look after sissy, bud. But she'll be safe with me." After a long uncertain moment, Brandon relaxed his grip on Lub Lub, whose sobbing had subsided to an intense snivelling.

"Good lad," Black Superman said, squeezing Brandon's shoulder. He stood and carried the whimpering girl to sit with him on the veranda, where he wiped her face gently with unused napkins and talked to her about Elvis, about kindy, about anything other than the smell of rum and what it conjured up. Directly below them, underneath the house, Lub Lub's misery grated on Ken like fingernails on a blackboard. It was all he could do to stop from jamming his fingers in his ears like a kid himself. Ridiculous! He was a grown man, for Christ's sake—why let a howling kid affect him? Ken clenched his fists and resolved to ignore it. Then he looked into the yard to see

Donny chucking the busted glass into the wheelie bin. *Tinkle, tinkle, tinkle* went thirty-six dollars' worth of Bundy, gone now to the shit. He hadn't even opened the bloody bottle. And—with fast-rising irritation—what genius had put it in the pool in the first place? Rum didn't need cooling down. Any moron knew that.

"Get ya shit in a pile, son, and get the rest of em outta the pool!" Ken yelled in a sudden rage. Donny flinched. Then he obediently started removing the remaining drinks from beneath the feet of the remaining kids, lining the dripping bottles and UDLs up along the trestle table. Ken exhaled loudly.

"Are you a fucking moron? Get them kids outta there!" he growled. "The grog isn't gonna bust itself, is it?"

Donny sighed. Without answering, he shooed the kids away and methodically began returning the cans to the pool.

In his sanctuary beneath the house, Ken stood next to the Harley, brooding over his losses.

Chapter Fifteen

The breaking of the bottle marked a turning point in the mood of the party. The kids, rattled by Lub Lub's reaction, grew fractious. They began arguing over nothing, needing attention every minute or two. The adults never recovered the easy pleasure of the yarning circle, and as the night wore on Ken grew more and more aggrieved about the lost rum. Kerry stopped checking her phone. She focused instead on helping Black Superman and Josh manage the kids. It was obvious that Donna had played her for a sucker. The question now was what to do about it, and for that she needed her brother's counsel. But the kids weren't making it easy. It was nearly ten and somehow Kerry still hadn't found the right time and place to unburden herself.

"I might take my lot back to the motel," Black Superman said in exasperation after separating Brandon and Rosie, feuding over the trampoline, for the third time in ten minutes. His handsome face was haggard, and there were prominent rings beneath his bloodshot eyes. "Brandon, start packing up, buddy."

"Hang on," Kerry hesitated. "There's something I've been trying to tell ya all day."

Her brother turned to her with bone-deep weariness etched into his face. His shoulders, normally square and upright, slumped like those of an old, old man. Kerry saw how deep her brother had had to dig that week to keep Brandon at home and out of the clutches of Childstealers. He had met the challenge, but now her brother was a shell of his real self. He drew her aside.

"Sis, they reckon Brandon's got signs of schizophrenia. Like, saying all this weird shit, that he wasn't killing the cat, he was killing his stepfather. And so now Josh is freaking out about it all, he doesn't know if he's up for being a parent, and I'm kinda freaking out too . . . So can it please just wait?"

"Schizophrenia—what a load of bullshit!" snapped Ken, overhearing. "All these fucking headshrinkers want to get their hands on our jahjams and give em fucking stupid labels. Don't call him womba, that's what they fucking *want* us to think. Like we're the problem! All he needs is some time in the bush, away from them screens."

"They're not saying he's womba," Black Superman answered wearily, bending to put the kids' clothes into their bags. "They just reckon he needs more help, that's all. And any time you wanna pick up some of the load and take him bush, brother, just say the word, cos I'm fucking exhausted. I'm going back to the motel, soon as we say goodbye to Mum."

A sharp wail came from Rosie, who had been shoved off the trampoline yet again.

"For Christ's sake, knock that orf!" Black Superman exploded, hoiking the kids' bags onto his shoulders. "Get in the bloody car, that's it, we're going."

Kerry stood, trapped into silence.

"Okay," she said, turning away with great reluctance. "I'll tell ya in the morning."

————

When Kerry went inside the house, a card game was in full swing. She pulled up a kitchen chair and Pretty Mary dealt her a hand.

"I've still got them old dresses of Taneesha's that'd fit Lub Lub," Pretty Mary went on, having just announced her intention of taking the kids off Black Superman's hands. "Sixty-five's not too old, not with the dort here now to help me out . . ."

Kerry made a horrified face at Steve. Appearing in the doorway, Black Superman shrugged, too tired to argue the merits of Pretty Mary's proposal. Possibly not even wanting to. Would he really give the kids up? Kerry suddenly recalled the dance troupe Black Superman had abandoned after their third public performance, and the way Ken had had to step in when coaching the under-elevens basketball had become tedious to Black Superman partway through the 2002 season.

"We're off," Black Superman broke in, leaning down to kiss Pretty Mary on the cheek. "Happy birthday, ya old duck. See ya tomorrow." He disappeared quietly down the stairs.

"Haven't you raised enough jahjams for other people, my sister?" Aunty Tall Mary asked, recalling various foster kids Pretty Mary had given a roof to over the years. She picked up two jacks. "You really want more kids to make more heartache for you?"

"Oh, don't beat around the bush, Aunty," said Kerry, offended. "Say what ya really mean."

"They's our mob. And anyway, the only real heartache I ever had come from Donna," Pretty Mary declared. Kerry sprayed a mouthful of vodka all over the kitchen table and roared with incredulous laughter. Steve grinned. Kerry had recently made a game of listing Pretty Mary's complaints about her before falling asleep in bed at night. So far the list was up to one hundred and two specific transgressions against Pretty Mary personally, the family in general, or both.

"Can I quote ya on that? Can I have it in *writing*?" Kerry goggled.

"You might of buggered off and hardly ever come back to see us. But at least ya not a crazy bitch going around stabbing people with scissors," said Ken, flicking an ace into the middle of the table. No matter how drunk Ken got, his card-playing skills never seemed to leave him, even with Sav sat on his lap, grinding her arse in an effort to get his attention. "You're just a slack cunt. Donna, she was as fucking mad as a cut snake. Jesus, can ya knock off, Sav?!" He pushed her away. Sav went and stood to one side of the card game, her arms crossed, sulking. Then she very gradually began edging her way closer to Steve.

"Don't talk about my daughter like that!" Pretty Mary frowned, though whether it was Ken's vehement accusations or his use of the past tense that bothered her wasn't entirely clear.

"Ya can't polish a turd, Mum," said Ken, collecting the cards from the center of the table and shuffling. "And ya can't go around stabbing old people and then make out like there ain't some serious fucking mental health issues there."

"So hang on, let me get this straight. Donna's a womba bitch cos she stabbed Pop, but Brandon's not crazy, after nearly drowning an animal the other day?" Kerry challenged, made brave by vodka and the bulk of Steve behind her at the sink. Donna had seemed many things to her that morning but crazy wasn't one of them. She grew sarcastic. "Oh, that's right. I forgot. Women are always crazy when we don't do what men want."

"You haven't got a clue." Ken's scowl from across the table clearly said: *Shut up now. Or else you really are crazy.*

"And yet somehow you magically know it all. You realize calling someone crazy is control-freak shit, eh?" Kerry hit back.

"Not if they really are crazy . . ." Savannah muttered.

"You mob wanna all stop calling my daughter crazy," snapped Pretty Mary, losing her temper. "Nobody's crazy!" Arguable, thought Kerry, but kept it to herself.

Ken gazed at his sister as he tapped ash off his cigarette, and then he grew very still. Everyone in the room recognized this stillness. It was the calm before the storm. Sav froze. Pretty Mary and Tall Mary exchanged a look.

"Your deal, Ken," prompted Pretty Mary optimistically. Ken ignored her. He'd had nineteen years to refine his low opinion of Donna and wasn't about to have Kerry question it. Particularly not in public, and *especially* not in front of Sav.

"What you don't know about Donna would fill a book," he spat at Kerry. "So I suggest you shut the fuck up right now, little girl."

Little girl? Kerry laughed in his face.

"Why's that? It's not like ignorance ever stopped you flapping ya gums," she shot back as she threw down her cards and took another slug of Stoli. "Anyway, I might know a lot more about Donna than you think, genius."

Steve took a sharp breath.

"Kez . . ." he warned.

"Come on now! Knock orf arguing, youse two! Ken, it's your deal," ordered Aunty Tall Mary.

"Nobody cares what you think ya "know", ya smart-mouthed bitch," snarled Ken. Then he swivelled to address Steve, who was leaning against the sink. "Ya wanna keep ya missus quiet, pal. Teach her some fucken respect, or else I will."

The room fell completely silent. A moment of decision had arrived.

"Ah, ya said it yourself, bro." Steve made light of Ken's threat. "Bitches be crazy!"

All the women except Kerry laughed in relief, much louder than the quip warranted. Their laughter was a plea. It said: C'mon, Kenny, chill. See the joke, man. Steve doesn't want to punch on. There's no need for any blueing, not tonight.

"Not in this house they don't," said Ken, unsmiling. "You wanna shut her up, I'm telling ya. Or I'll hold you responsible for the stupid fucken shit that comes outta her mouth."

Steve straightened up from the sink.

"Kez, 'bout time we made tracks, eh?" he suggested. "Where's the bike keys?"

"I speak for myself, you arsehole!" shouted Kerry at Ken. "Leave him out of it! Unless ya really want ya fat arse kicked. He'll wipe the floor with you, ya fucken great overgrown—"

Ken stood abruptly, sending his chair skidding into the fridge behind. He leaned across the table to swipe at Kerry. She shied back out of range and kept going, falling heavily to the floor. Having missed his sister, the trailing end of Ken's backhander caught Pretty Mary fair on the jaw. His mother cried out in pain and fright. Then, ashamed, she put her hands over her face as tears sprang into her eyes. Aunty Tall Mary put an arm around Pretty Mary's shoulders and glared at Ken.

"Oh, that's just bloody lovely that is, Ken!" she accused at top note. "Hittin' old people? You wanna apologize, right now!" Ken wavered for a fraction of a second. He hovered between white-hot rage at Kerry and genuine remorse for hurting Pretty Mary, who was never his target.

"Hitting ya own mother," Kerry sneered from the floor, grabbing her vodka bottle by the neck as she rose in fury. "Real fucken big man you are, eh?"

"It was an accident!" Ken roared, stepping across his fallen chair to sort his sister out once and for fucken all.

"Your whole life's one long accident," Kerry told him, weight on the balls of her feet as she brandished the Stoli.

"Oi! If ya really wanna do this, then let's take it outside," Steve said, jumping into Ken's path and pointing at the back stairs.

"Get the fuck outta my way," Ken snarled, throwing a sloppy roundhouse punch, which the younger man easily ducked. Steve kicked Ken's fallen chair to the edge of the room, clearing a space to fight.

"Chris!" Pretty Mary screamed out the window at the van. Then, "Sav! Go get Chris! See if Black Superman's still here—Kenny! Knock orf!"

"You really wanna punch on here? With two old ladies in the room?" Steve asked, incredulous.

Sav fled outside, calling to the men for help.

"Stop talking and sort the prick out," Kerry urged Steve, waiting for the right moment to leap forward and bottle Ken. Tall

Mary, unsuccessful in dragging Pretty Mary to safety, had joined the others on the veranda, peering in. And so it was Tall Mary who first noticed the flashing lights of the police car silently heading down the drive, blocking Black Superman's exit. She bolted back into the kitchen, crossing her forearms and plunging her fists towards the floor in urgent demonstration.

"Gunjies," she screamed. "Gunjies ere! Ning! Ning!"

The veranda was suddenly overrun with blue uniforms and noisy accusations, and the pulsing colored light of the cop car throwing its authority over everything. The instant Tall Mary screamed, Kerry had fled behind her mother's bedroom door. She flattened herself against the wall, cursing her warrants and praying for Elvis to bite Senior Sergeant Tony Nunne on his withered white arse. The sergeant stood on the veranda, hands braced on his hips, with an overwhelming confidence filling his person. This confidence came from growing up the son, grandson, and great-grandson of the district's pioneers. Didn't the very main street of Patto bear his surname, and didn't the thousands of acres surrounding the dreadful shitbox where he now stood constitute the land his pioneer forebears had opened up? The sergeant stood, content in the knowledge that no matter how many piss-soaked friends and relations were clustered around Kenny Salter on this Friday night, both he and his partner had pistols to hand, and he himself had a taser, not to mention tacit approval from the wider community to use them just as they saw fit. Their matte-black weapons gleamed in the dim light shed by the veranda's dusty lightbulb.

Nunne made an inaudible comment to his partner as he adjusted his Oakley sunglasses, perched permanently on top of his head no matter what hour. The men looked around in disgust. A dozen empty bottles and cans had been abandoned on tables and upturned milk crates; several chip packets fluttered on the floorboards, tossed by the kids as they hurtled between adventures; three dinner plates bearing lamb scraps and smears of potato salad had been forgotten behind the hammock. What they didn't see was the kingplate hanging on the beam, directly above the top of the stairs.

Ken's arms were folded tight as he weathered a fusillade of Nunne's questions. He repelled the standard inquisition like drops of water hitting a hot frypan. A bit of a sizzle and nothing to show for it afterwards.

"So ya don't know anything at all about this break-in at the council chambers?" the sergeant repeated for the third time.

"Nuh," Ken replied. "Why would I?"

"Right, so a DNA test won't show it was you doing criminal damage in the mayor's office?" continued the sergeant, bringing loud titters from Pretty Mary and Tall Mary.

"I think I'd probably remember if I broke in and took a dump on Jim Buckley's carpet." Ken grinned at the mob, who hooted with laughter, right on cue.

"Good one, Uncle Ken," giggled cousin Helen, catching the sergeant's eye for the first time. He smiled pleasantly at her. Then he turned back to Ken, still smiling.

"Pretty girl."

"Say that again and see what ya get." Ken unfolded his arms.

"You gotta understand—we don't know about stealing. That's your department," interrupted Black Superman loudly as he made his way back upstairs. "You wanna go talk to whitefellas if ya wanna know about stealing." The cops swung around, instantly suspicious of an unanticipated black body in their midst.

"Or the government, eh," Steve said from the far end of the veranda, deadpan. The police turned back around. "That's their specialty—stealing."

"You said it, bruz. In receipt of a whole stolen continent, that lot," Chris agreed as though this was simply the commonest of common sense.

"Darnt. I feel sorry for whitefellas, going around thieving all the time. They need help. Shame nobody ever tries to get em back to their culture." Black Superman shook his head in deep, patronizing sorrow.

"I blame the parents," interjected Zippo from the back of the group.

"Yeah, bruz, true, eh," Ken said to Black Superman. He chastised the cops. "You mob wanna take these whitefellas round here up to the city. Show em some of their sacred sites. Shopping malls and factories and shit."

"And for God's sake, can't ya get em back to their old ways? Give em some workshops on how to hang, draw, and quarter people. And witch burning!" Black Superman had hit his stride. "Ya can't go past a bit of good old-fashioned witch burning to turn a troubled white kid around!"

"They wouldn't know how to begin to use people as slaves on cattle stations, these days," Pretty Mary added. "You'd need to teach em that part, Nunny."

"How to invade other people's countries and murder em, and call it civilization . . ." Ken couldn't remember when he'd enjoyed himself this much.

"Child-stealing 101." Black Superman nodded enthusiastically. "Interventions for fun and profit."

"Globalized capitalism for the one percent," Zippo called.

Sergeant Nunne appeared to swell beneath his tight uniform shirt. The mayor was on the money here. Fucking smart cunts. He let his right hand fall onto his belt, sorely tempted to see how mouthy Kenny Salter was with taser strings hanging out his fucken eyeballs.

"Ya gonna tase me now, are ya, Nunny?" Ken asked, raising his chin and readying himself to go down swinging. He'd take this dugai cunt out with pleasure, no worries at all. "Is someone filming this prick?"

"Way ahead of ya, brother," replied Zippo, who had pulled his phone out the instant the cop car arrived in the yard.

"Everyone in the shire knows you've got a vendetta against the mayor, pal," Nunny said to Ken. "Busting down fences, threatening him at council. Breaking in and trashing the chambers. Not to mention what happened to his dog."

"What's this about his dog?" Pretty Mary asked skeptically.

Nunny stuck out his hand, and his partner gave him a phone showing a picture of Buckley's dog. She was freshly tattooed with *FUCK MAYOR BUCKLEY* on one shaven flank and *NO PATTO PRISON* on the other. A giant red swirling dollar sign embellished the top of the dog's crinkled forehead.

Pretty Mary stuck her tongue in her cheek, but her eyes were laughing as much as everyone else's.

"Bugger me," Ken professed with Oscar-winning innocence. "Who would do such a thing to a dumb animal?"

"Whitefellas," said Chris, leaning in and tut-tutting.

"Whitefellas," agreed Black Superman.

"Definitely need them workshops," Ken advised the sergeant.

"You lot think you're comedians," said Nunny heavily. "But it won't be so fucking funny when it gets out that your little land rights campaign cost Patto two hundred jobs. What do ya reckon, Kenny? Might even find an angry mob on your doorstep. Not that you're gonna stop the prison. It's happening, sunshine, whether you like it or not."

"Two hundred jobs? More like two—yours and Jim Buckley's," argued Pretty Mary, stepping forward into the light. Nunny immediately noticed the purple bruise swelling angrily on her jaw.

"Oh, my job's pretty safe. But has someone given ya a smack, Mary? Wouldn't have been this bloke, would it?" Pretty Mary was struck dumb. Nunny smirked at the *Sexy Senior* sticker heaving on her chest. "Wanna lay charges, Mary? No? You'd just cop it twice as bad once he got back home, wouldn't ya?"

The sergeant turned back to Ken, and as he spoke, his voice grew cold with menace.

"You coulda been someone in this town once, Kenny, but take a look at ya now! Pathetic. You're not a tenth of the man your grandfather was. And I'll give ya the drum: the mayor isn't about to let a bunch of half-caste dole bludgers tell him what he can and can't do. So get that through your head before somebody gets badly hurt, pal."

"If yer not gonna arrest me," Ken warned, stepping so that he stood toe to toe with the sergeant, "then how about ya go tell cunt-hooks his dog's still on heat. And tell him from me, if he wants the bitch rooted I know just the dog for the job." The tall Goorie man and the aging cop eyeballed each other with the strange intimacy of true enemies. The taser lay, hard and smooth and poisonous, beneath the fingers of Nunny's right hand, and Ken knew it. As he stared into the sergeant's face, noticing the deep crevices falling away from his enemy's pale gray eyes, Ken felt the lash of Cracker Nunne's stockwhip rippling down through the decades, snaking towards his grandfather's face.

"You pull that thing out, Nunny," Ken taunted the white man, as history ran boiling through his veins, "and let's see how much fucken good it does ya."

Ken slowly stretched his arms towards the roof, towards the king-plate, and then cracked his knuckles together like rifle shots. Black Superman and Chris came up to stand on either side of him, so close that their shoulders touched. The three men made a solid wall of flesh between the uniforms and the family, who were clustered in a horrified semicircle behind them. Silently, Steve walked over and joined them. Then Uncle Neil materialized out of the shadows to find his place beside Chris. The men stared at Nunne and his partner. Two pistols. One taser. And five brothers standing their ground.

A muscle twitched in Nunny's cheek.

"Still filming," Zippo reminded the sergeant.

Nunne's partner cleared his throat in terror as his radio crackled with an indistinct blur.

"Youse gunjies can clear orf of my veranda," ordered Pretty Mary, finding her voice and pointing to the gate. "Ya not wanted here. Not now, not ever!"

Moments passed. Then, with a look of pure hatred for Ken, Nunne took his hand off the taser. Telling Pretty Mary curtly that they'd be back in the morning to follow up, the police beat an ig-nominious retreat down the stairs. Ken watched them go and curled his lip in triumph as he reached down to the volume control on the CD player.

"Yeah, you keep right on walking, Nunny," he called, then howled like a dingo when the sergeant didn't react. As the doors of the squad car slammed shut, The Angels joined the party, "Am I Ever Gonna See Your Face Again" blasting out shockingly loud into the night.

The family, standing beneath the kingplate, had the chorus ready, and they roared in joyful unison at the departing cop car.

NO WAY—GET FUCKED—FUCK OFF!

"Fuck the gunjies!" Ken shouted at the end of the song, his clenched fist high. "This is OUR land." Chris ripped the scab off a fresh beer and handed it over in tribute. Ken stepped onto the top stair and hoisted his beer up.

"Here's ta us mob," he boomed, gulping the stubby in one joyous hit. "They can send as many fucken pig cars as they want—we'll give the gutless pricks the fight of their lives!"

The veranda exploded with laughter, cheering, and backslapping. Ken gazed around at the love shining out of everybody's faces—love for him, their leader. He had forgotten what that felt like, how big you got inside with it. Like winning a grand final, when you did everything right on the field and so could do no wrong off it. The way life was supposed to feel—him, king of his own domain, on his own land, living by his own rules. *I fought the law, and the law lost.*

In the next hour or so, the sensational victory was reworked and savored a score of times. It was analyzed by some and embellished by others. The yarn grew and grew. Glenrowan had nothing on Durrongo, the party agreed. Chris grabbed his guitar and improvized a twelve-bar blues number in celebration. Zippo told passionate stories about battling the cops on Turtle Island, making eyes at Pretty Mary while he did so. Far from ruining the party as it should have, the encounter with the gunjies was instead the making of the night. The celebrations were so raucous that nobody noticed for a full minute when a red Mazda6 arrived in the backyard and its owner stepped out onto the lawn.

Chapter Sixteen

Other people had children or hobbies. Donna had financial goals, goals she met with unbending hard work and pinpoint accuracy. Ambitious, yes, but those in the game who talked about her killer instinct didn't understand shit. She wasn't driven by the understandable anger of other top women agents, or by the competitiveness of the average prick-measuring realtor in a suit. No. She was different.

Nobody in real estate knew she was black; there were some days she almost forgot it herself. But each morning when she woke and looked in the mirror at her Mediterranean skin and dark eyes, she remembered. And so every sale was powered by a deep vein of Aboriginal fear.

With each new commission Donna was fleeing a little further from Durrongo, still running from the troopers, hurtling through the scrub with her barefoot great-grandmother towards Ava's Island. With each sale she managed to push down a little further her terror of ever again having to rely on another human being for safety. Donna owned three houses and a unit, and no white man was ever going to lock her inside any of them.

———

Forewarned is forearmed. Of all the mob, only Kerry kept her cool when Donna made her way over to the house, bearing an elaborately wrapped birthday present and an unreadable expression.

Now, there's a gifting challenge, thought Kerry. Buying for the woman who has nothing after letting her think you're dead for twenty years.

Seeing Donna standing alone at the foot of the stairs, the entire family gaping at her first in confusion and then in shock, Kerry felt a bizarre stab of sympathy. Her poor, stupid sister, thinking she could buy forgiveness with an enormous pink and gold beribboned gift box. Donna's present was fancy but her eyes were wild, cornered, the pupils shrunken black pinpoints. The last time Kerry saw eyes like that was in Brisbane Women's. But Donna had arrived here tonight purely of her own free will. She's that much of a Salter, at least. Ten outta ten for guts.

"Mum," yelled Kerry. "Come out, quick! Donna's here!"

"Come up in the light where I can get a good look at ya, girl," ordered Aunty Tall Mary, not trusting what her eyes told her.

"What? *Who?*" Pretty Mary emerged from the kitchen, and promptly fainted on top of Elvis.

When the yelping stopped, Pretty Mary got to her feet and started crying on Donna's neck that she was sorry, so sorry. Donna burst into tears too, echoing her mother's words.

Kerry realized right then that she had completely misread the situation.

There would be no recriminations for this prodigal daughter, none of the accusations of abandonment or treachery she herself now took for granted every Christmas. If you went AWOL for a year, it seemed, that was a criminal offense against Salterdom. But bugger off altogether for decades and become a ghost? Well, all is forgiven, sister, come home.

Kerry stood beside a perplexed Donny, who had emerged, blinking, from World of Warcraft to find out what all the fuss was about. What he discovered was halfway between a wake and a birth. Pretty Mary bawled with helpless joy as the others reeled around the house like stunned mullets. Through her frowning silence Kerry did her best to tell Donna that she hadn't spilled the beans. For Christ's sake, don't put me in it, she thought. Though that problem seemed to have been overtaken by events.

Nobody had a single thought for anything other than the sister miraculously alive on the veranda.

"Why are *you* here?" Donna gaped at Steve, as though his arm curled around Kerry's waist wasn't explanation enough.

"He's with me," Kerry said.

Donna's face crinkled in confusion and Kerry remembered telling her she was a dyke. Ah well.

"Siddown, tidda, siddown," urged Black Superman, his eyes and nose streaming with emotion. He gestured to the most respectable of the folding chairs.

"Do ya drink?" Kerry asked meaningfully, thumping a couple of cold UDLs onto the table. Haven't seen you for years, sis. Wouldn't know ya from a bar of soap.

"Only on days ending in Y," Donna answered, giving Kerry a tiny conspiratorial nod. She accepted the UDL but remained standing. Folded her arms and hugged the cold can against her chest to hide the tremor in her hand. She wiped at her eyes. The reality of what she had just done was beginning to dawn on her.

No going back now.

Pretty Mary was a mess, and so the others took it on themselves to piece together Donna's missing decades. Dad Charlie was finished, Black Superman told her, and so was Pop. Only two months ago, you just missed him. But Uncle Richard and his mob are still going strong, and the Westville crew are mostly okay too, all bar Doris running amok, cracking out on the ice, and chucking her kids at Aunty Tall Mary to raise. But had she heard the bad news about Granny's island, this terrible prison business? Yes?

Finally Tall Mary, standing in the doorway with her arms folded tight, lost patience. Enough beating around the bush. She voiced the question throbbing on Kerry's tongue: Where on earth had Donna *been* all this time? Was she married, or divorced, or what? Were there kids and grandkids? And the sixty-million-dollar question: Why hadn't she ever, even once in twenty years, made a simple phone call, let them know she was alright?

Donna took a deep breath. Stepped onto the tightrope of her life story.

"Because I wasn't alright, for a long time," she told her drink. "I went to Sydney, hit the drugs, then ended up living with a psycho prick for four years. Never allowed to leave the house except for work. GPS tracker on the car. All my phone calls recorded. He vetted my friends—no men, no mob, nobody he hadn't met. They had to be girls, preferably ones married to his mates. And even then . . ." She unconsciously rubbed at the hinge in her jawline. It was the same movement Kerry had seen Steve do when his false teeth bothered him. It came to her in a blinding flash that her sister's new nose wasn't about vanity.

"It wasn't pretty," Donna summarized.

"No kids?" asked Pretty Mary through a sodden tissue.

"Nah. I lost a couple from being bashed. After the second time, I told the doctors: fix me up."

"Was he Goorie or white?" asked Black Superman, his mouth a grim cave.

"Oh, white." Donna gave a short, bitter laugh. "A white man in a suit. I escaped when the house next door caught fire," she continued. "I thought if I don't take me chances now, I'll be leaving in a coffin. So I bolted. The firies got me to a refuge on the other side of the harbor . . . The year after, I got my real estate license and started selling houses in Wollongong." She gestured at the Mazda gleaming on the lawn beneath the moonlight. "The franchise asked me to come up and be stand-in manager at Patto Real Estate for a few weeks. Then I'm planning on going back to Sydney to buy my own agency." There was a flash of the old proud Donna as she said this. Chin up, ready for anything. Lookout, world.

The family took a second to digest this. Then, as the rags-to-riches story sank in, they slowly began to chuckle, and then the chuckles grew into gales of laughter. A black Goorie woman, in charge of white people's housing! Telling dugais where they could and couldn't live! And, best of all, making good money off the back of it too—driving a red sports car. You wouldn't read about it.

Watching the hilarity unfold, Donna smiled a tightly stretched smile. In fifteen years she had sold enough houses to make two or three Durrongos, and now, heading towards forty, this was simply who she was. She lived and breathed real estate, and often she dreamed it too.

Right then the phone rang. There had been unexpected delays, and Uncle Richard wouldn't make it till the morning. Black Superman told him who was sitting on the veranda and grinned as he handed the phone to Pretty Mary, who burst into a fresh round of tears. Uncle Richard had a few brief, astonished words with her, and then with Donna, making Donna dab at her nose and sniff.

"Are you actually working in Patto?" Black Superman frowned. Trying to sound matter-of-fact, Donna revealed that she had been staying at the Scrub Turkey Motel while she looked after Jim Buckley's office.

Pretty Mary looked up, horrified.

"Just temporary, like?" she asked quickly, from among a mountain of discarded tissues. "Nothing more than that?" No, Donna reassured her, she was only doing it for two or three more weeks and then she would be off. Pretty Mary breathed a silent sigh of relief, let her unspoken terror subside.

"We could've run into you at reception." Black Superman goggled, for he and Josh were staying at the Turkey as well. Kerry wondered if he was going to put two and two together any time soon. Her and her "big news."

"Well, it took ya long enough to come and see your mother." Tall Mary sniffed in aggravation.

"She's here now, that's all that matters," Pretty Mary said, leaping to Donna's defense. "But you sure you got no jahjams? None at all?"

Donna shook her head, pausing as she wondered whether, or how, to explain.

"Half ya bloody luck," interrupted Aunty Val, getting a sharp slap on the arm from Sav and loud peals of laughter from everybody else.

"Sorry, Savvie," Aunty Val said. "But when you get knocked up at fifteen in the back of a Holden panel van, it don't give you a lot of time to enjoy your youth."

"Gee, thanks, Mum," Sav shot back. "Sorry for ruining your life and everything."

"I never said that," Val soothed unconvincingly.

"Fifteen," joked Uncle Neil. "Val was the oldest virgin in Murwillumbah High in 1977."

"I reckon I was the only bloody virgin in Murwillumbah High in 1977." Val corrected him with a gravelly laugh. "And then, just my luck, the first bloody time and I hafta get pregnant."

"I was twenty when I met Dad Charlie," Pretty Mary reminisced. "The best looking man at the Lismore woodchop by a country mile, and I seen him and said, *I'm gonna marry me that Goorie fella.* And that's just what I done. Chaperoned all the way, mind. No try before you buy for Charlie boy. Granny Ruth woulda knocked him into the middle of next week if he as much as thought about it."

"Bet that didn't stop you thinking about it, but," said Val, grinning coarsely.

"I didn't think of nothing else!" confessed Pretty Mary with a toss of her head. "Wedding night couldn't come quick enough for this little black duck." Pretty Mary and Aunty Val both laughed. Chris looked at his feet.

"How about you, Kenny? You're being pretty quiet." Val seized on his transparent embarrassment. "When was your first time? Come on, spill the beans!" But Ken was silent and scowling, and Val was forced to turn to the girls instead.

"Oh no, bugger the third degree, I forget," Donna protested in real horror. Kerry had to rescue the moment by inventing a liaison with a Chilean athlete at the Sydney Olympics.

"You're so full of shit," Black Superman scoffed. "I remember standing next to ya down the bloody pub watching Cathy win gold."

"After the closing ceremony, I mean," Kerry claimed, unfazed. "Juan was in Byron on holiday."

"Which way? He any good in the sack?" Tall Mary asked, interested. Kerry began heaping praise on her fantasy lover.

"I'm gonna go whack the kettle on," Chris blurted, fleeing from the terrible frankness of the women. He headed inside for tea he didn't want. The family gradually drifted in after him, making a cheerful circle around the Laminex table.

Donna looked around.

"There's not much changed in here, Mum," she said, picking up a familiar brown dinner plate and running a finger around the rim. The fridge magnets—*Zero to Bitch in Ten Seconds, Support Our NORCO Farmers*—were different, and the calendar. One of the glass louvres had been replaced with plywood, and the mold speckles on the ceiling had expanded into billowing clouds. But otherwise she was looking at the same yellow cupboards, the same net curtains, the same cracked gray lino beneath her feet as the night she left.

"Yer father's gone," corrected Pretty Mary. "And yer Pop. That's what's changed." She thrust the funeral booklet at Donna, who hesitated before taking it from her mother. The man on the front was old, really old, Donna marvelled. A relic of another time, almost of another world. This worn-out pensioner was a far cry from the man she'd stabbed at sixteen.

Well. Ashes to ashes. And what's done is done. Donna handed the booklet back to Pretty Mary and let her think her daughter's silence was the silence of grief. Which in a way it was.

"We need a photo of us mob all together again," cried Black Superman, still astonished about the motel. The cry went up for photos all round. Donna nodded at the pictures on top of the TV cabinet.

"Have I changed that much?" she joked. What a night that had been, a night to live to forget. Sweet sixteen and kicked to the curb.

"I never, ever gave up, dort. Never lost hope. I knew you'd come back," said Pretty Mary, hauling herself to her feet to clasp Donna around the waist and grip her hand tight, breathe her in. The incredible fact of her daughter—her daughter alive—finally home, where she belonged. The comment was as close as Pretty Mary had come all night to any kind of accusation, Kerry thought. Very strange. It didn't fit at all with her idea of her mother, a woman to whom judgment was the breath of life. They say every child grows up in a different version of the same family. Perhaps it was Donna's disappearance that had tainted her own childhood. Maybe before Donna left, Pretty Mary had been happy to live and let live, a veritable little ray of sunshine like the one now gazing adoringly at her eldest daughter. But no, that wasn't what she remembered of Pretty Mary's drinking years, those times before Donna went away. There had been laughter, yes, but plenty else too. Take them memories out and the picture would be Swiss cheese. The transformation in her mother each day as the piss went steadily down. The resentment and the arguments of the adults, spiking and blurring into each other, the very same arguments month in and month out, bedded down by periods of sobriety and then reliably resurrected by yet more grog.

Those years after Granny Ruth died had been hard ones, Kerry knew, the family scratching about to survive. There were good weeks. A month here and there, when Pretty Mary had been terrified by the threat of Family Services into returning to AA, or had been hauled off by Dad Charlie to Westville to dry out, but then there were the other months, when chaos was one cask of Fruity Lexia away. Times of raised voices, of glass smashing at midnight. And the next day plodding to school exhausted, coming home to find Ken or Donna poking about in empty cupboards to conjure dinners that didn't exist. Followed by the cascading apologies. The tears. Pretty Mary's weeping promises to make it up to them. Only Dad Charlie had kept Childstealers away; only he had known how to make a little kid feel loved among the chaos of Pretty Mary on a bender, the times she'd drag any old drunk home from the pub to keep her company. *Drinking buddies*. Sweet Jesus Christ. The sight of a whitefella with a handlebar moustache still turned Kerry's stomach. Suffer the little children, and spare them the drinking buddies, Kerry thought, seeing in her mother's adoring eyes for Donna the same expression she remembered from a hundred grog parties. *I larve you, my cuz, I really, really larve you . . .*

And then Pop got elected to ATSIC and everything changed. This house replaced the milking shed they had been renting off old Mr. Nunne forever. This house with its electricity and its lino floor, a fridge full of food. Dad driving the cab five days a week, instead of seven nights. On reflection, it occurred to Kerry that Donna might never have known Pretty Mary sober for more than a few weeks straight. And yet here the old girl was, alive and well at sixty-five. Got sober the winter Donna disappeared, and hadn't touched a drop in nineteen years.

The family clustered around Donna, eager to be in the photos. Zippo was showered with half a dozen different phones and instructions on the best angle to shoot from and don't give me twelve chins and make sure nobody blinks and . . .

"Jump in, Kenny," Pretty Mary encouraged. But Ken was sulking in the far corner of the kitchen, hunkered down and swollen with jealousy, Kerry saw. Someone arriving out of the blue and stealing his limelight. And never much love lost there to begin with. Ken drew his arms in and folded them hard against Pretty Mary's suggestion. His mouth jutted with displeasure.

"Not interested," he said harshly. "Not till she apologizes for what she's done."

"Eh?" Chris raised his eyebrows.

"Whaddya mean, apologizes?" Kerry asked. Hadn't he heard

both Donna and Pretty Mary wailing in each other's arms, telling each other they were sorry, so sorry?

"Oh, don't be like that," Pretty Mary said in loud exasperation. "Let bygones be bygones, son." The family agreed with her, telling Ken not to be so slack, to get in the photo with everybody else. Why did everything with Ken have to be such a big deal all the time? Talk about a Drama King, geez.

Donna felt her chest tighten. Of *course* it would be Ken. It always was Ken, remember, the lounge-room wallpaper told her; the very same blue flowers twining on pale green stems as the night she left. Twining for twenty years while she fucked off and fell through the floor of the world. While Pretty Mary shuffled her cards, her hair turning gray, and Ken sat, year after bitter year, calculating the insults life had dealt him.

"You mob make me fucken weak," Ken said, looking from face to staring face for evidence of support and finding it missing. "Truesgod! Didn't you hear what the bitch said? She's working for *Buckley*."

A moment of awkward silence.

"So maybe she can help us," Black Superman suggested. "Tell us how he operates."

"We already know how he fucking operates," Ken exploded. "He buys people off. Gammon cunts like her." His pointing forefinger accused Donna across the entire width of the kitchen, across the decades. "Well, I'm not having it. You stand with Buckley, you can fuck off outta here, onetime!"

Black Superman caught Josh's eye and gestured with his lips at the kids compressed into the distant corner of the lounge. As soon as Ken had begun to shout, Brandon had grabbed Lub Lub and dragged her away. He was holding her tiny face hard against his chest so that she wouldn't have to witness whatever came next in the world of adults.

Josh quickly ushered both the kids outside.

"Some things never change, do they, brother?" Donna said, putting on a show of calm as she dug in her handbag for her lighter. Making out she wasn't frightened. "And I don't mean the kitchen cupboards. You always were an angry, negative prick. But I'm not frightened of you anymore, pal."

Kerry couldn't breathe. Couldn't move.

"Oh, do ya think I don't know your game, you fucking crazy slut? Ya probably only here to try and con us about the island. Yer lucky I don't walk down there right now and drop a fucking match in yer petrol tank." Ken's chest heaved; fresh sweat had broken out on his forehead. He looked easily capable of arson, Kerry thought.

Donna laughed. Crossed her legs as she lit her cigarette and smiled mirthlessly around the room. Alright then, brother, if ya wanna have a go, let's hear it. Donna's heart was achingly sore, but now another, deeper part of her was bent purely on revenge, and was beginning to thrum with wild satisfaction. That epic day had arrived again, dead on time. Unfinished business that had never gone away, had only been buried. Perhaps that was what she had been looking for without even knowing, agreeing to take the job in Patterson: 1999 roaring in at her in all its ferocious glory. But this time she wasn't sixteen. She was a grown woman with four properties, money in the bank, and a fucking score to settle. She tapped ash into the ashtray, half humming, half whispering the lyrics from "You Got Nothing I Want" which had popped into her head. Ken definitely didn't have anything she needed.

When she spoke, her measured voice sounded like someone calm, someone who wasn't about-near ready to pick up a pair of Pretty Mary's scissors and finish exactly what she started twenty years ago.

"*A fucking crazy slut* . . . funny, that's exactly what you called me the day I left, remember? And a shamejob too. An embarrassment to the entire bloody family. *Donna the Donut with her very popular hole.* Ya sound a bit like a broken record, Kenny." Donna swung around to face Aunty Val, and her blond mane swung against her neck with expensive precision.

"Twelve."

"What?"

"Val, isn't it? Well, Val, I lied. I do remember my first time. Remember it pretty damn well, in fact. It was right down there in the end room." She gestured at the hallway with her cigarette, the smoke rising in a tendril above her pointing fingers. "Twelve years old, getting screwed by my grandfather cos I stayed home from school with mumps. He must have decided it was high time I graduated from head jobs—twelve. Or maybe he was just being considerate, what with my sore gob and all."

Stark silence. Then Pretty Mary let out an agonized sound like a balloon deflating, and there was uproar.

"Shut yer hole!" roared Ken, striding over to thump the table and make the whole room rattle with his fury. "Can't ya stop lying through yer hole for once in yer miserable cunting life? Coming in here and stirring up trouble again with yer bullshit and yer filthy lies. Don't listen to her, Mum!"

Pretty Mary had her eyes closed, hand to her head. *No, no, no.*

"As if she would," cried Tall Mary, enraged. "Your Pop was a good man!"

"Oh, there's plenty of lies in this family, alright," Donna said, refusing to show the terror that was streaming through her, coloring the very air around her. "But it ain't me telling them, brother. Ain't me."

Gazing at Donna standing there with her angry red mouth, her stranger's nose, Kerry felt nauseated. Weirdly frightened, and definitely far too drunk to think about her grandfather's prick sawing in and out of her sister's mouth. Oh, the chicks in BWCC were full of stories, nearly every last one of them, black, white, and brindle. They laughed about it sometimes, the fucking pandemic of it. Boyfriends and husbands. Fathers and stepfathers. Uncles. Cousins. The great pulsing cock of the world that beat time in all their lives. But it wasn't black men who had raped her, no, no, no. And as for Pop— Pop never touched her. He had been absent most of her childhood anyway, had been at work, or off at meetings in Canberra, or down at the TAB. He hadn't done a thing; that was a clear, indisputable fact. And Donna—Donna had been dead for these twenty years. What would it mean, to believe a dead woman's story, to give credence to these dark mysterious creatures winging out of her mouth?

"Pop never did nothing to me," Kerry said slowly. "He never even tried." Ken grunted in vindication. But Donna wasn't stopping.

"Well, that's something. He threatened to, if I told. Said he'd kill Mum and Dad and me and then he'd keep going with you anyway. Twelve years old, made you what, eleven? Ten? Great fucking childhood I had."

Kerry blinked and the rest of the family came back into blurry focus. Everyone stood stiffly at the edges of the room, flung back against the walls by the force of Donna and her terrible claims. Steve didn't know where to look. Donny's face had gone sheet-white with strain. If what Donna said was true, then her childhood must have gone in protecting mine, Kerry suddenly realized. But how could it be true? Pop was an Elder. Violent when push came to shove, maybe, but not a fucking pedo. He was always helping people. How could he have— Kerry stared at the kitchen lino, which swam beneath her, a wobbly gray sea. Possibly she was drunker than she realized. Possibly very, very drunk indeed. Possibly this would make more sense in the sober light of day. Or not. Kerry closed her eyes and immediately wished she hadn't, as the darkness began to spiral around her.

"How *dare* you?" hissed Tall Mary. "How *dare* you talk like that about an Elder of this community!"

"She's possessed," Pretty Mary declared suddenly. "Lucifer's using her as his vessel to spread evil." Pretty Mary began praying aloud for the Devil to leave her house.

"Oh, for fuck's sake, Mum." Then Donna homed in on Black

Superman. She wasn't crying, exactly, but mascara was slipping from her eyes in thin black streaks, the liquid collecting at her jawline in murky gray drops. "What about you—which way you gonna jump? Was Pop the Elder of the century for you too? Or is that where you learned to crack fats?"

"Get her out," Pretty Mary screamed, hands clamped over her face. "I don't want the Devil's filthy talk in this house! Get her out—*now*!" Ken rose, but Tall Mary got there first, her open right hand lifted high in silhouette against the bare light globe. She brought it down and slapped Donna hard across the face, bending her in two, the air whooshing out in a sharp cry of shock and pain. Then Tall Mary seized her niece by the forearm, to drag her outside and give her the flogging she so richly deserved.

Pretty Mary plunged forward. Instinct told her to protect her daughter, but a lifelong loyalty to Tall Mary got in the way, complicating and confusing things, and so she faltered. In the end Pretty Mary stood kneading her hands in panic, praying for divine intervention to end the nightmare her birthday had become.

Donna wrenched her arm back from Tall Mary. *My arm, not yours.* She stood panting hard with the mark of her aunty's fingers clear for everyone to see, outlined on her pale cheek. Her left eye had already reddened and swelled. Kerry had a clear view of Donna and her mother facing each other, their hearts on fire, both their faces freshly bruised. Oh, this family. This fucking family.

"Kerry," said Steve. I'm here, he meant. We can go, any time ya want. But Kerry didn't hear him. Couldn't register anything more than what was in front of her face: Donna. Tall Mary. Pretty Mary. Ken, who had skidded to a halt and was waiting to see what happened between the women before lashing out again.

Donna's eyes flashed around the room in marvellous contempt.

"The more things change, eh? Don't touch me again, Aunt, I'm going. And I'll fucking drop ya if ya try, old lady or no. But ask yerself this, Mum. Why would a sixteen-year-old girl stab a man if he'd done nothing wrong? Talk about the Devil in me? I'd be more worried about the Devil you welcomed into your home for the past thirty years."

Pretty Mary stared at Donna, her face contorting in anguish. Sensing a moment of possibility, Black Superman inserted himself between Tall Mary and Donna, and managed to shepherd his sister outside and down the stairs.

"I'll come check on you later at the motel, sissy," he said quietly as he walked her over to the Mazda.

Donna really did begin to cry then, great juddering sobs that rocked her as she poked at her face with her shirt sleeves. From the veranda, Ken flung Donna's handbag onto the lawn, where it lay pathetically among the party detritus, its contents spilt across the grass. Donna stopped to collect it, frantically piling her belongings back in.

"This—this is why I never came back," she spat towards the house, flinging a half-empty beer can at the house in fury. The can hit the stairs halfway up, then bounced back down to the bottom step, where it spun in a circle, coming to rest in a small puddle of its own spilt liquor. Other houses have welcome mats, thought Black Superman with a great weariness.

"I know, sis," Black Superman told her. "I know. It's okay. We'll talk later."

"You believe me, don't you?" she said, her face messy with tears and snot.

"Yes," he told her. "I do. But you better make tracks—"

"Fuck that lying slut off outta here," Ken said, looming up behind them, "before I do. The little troublemaking cunt of a thing."

Vomiting in the toilet, Kerry was dimly aware of the Mazda pulling away up the drive, her sister roaring away and leaving her outrageous story behind to bounce off every wall in the house, ricocheting from Salter to Salter, stirring up trouble between them forever and a day. Maybe that was what Donna had intended all along, to distract them from their campaign to save the island. As

Kerry tried to think through the implications, she was dimly aware of something else rattling in her brain that just wouldn't settle into hard fact. Something to do with Steve. There was a piece of the story that could jolt things into place if only she could manage to pinpoint it. But most of a bottle of Stoli said, *Not now, sunshine, leave it. It's time to collapse into the land of nod.*

She staggered out of the bathroom, too grogsick to even sit pillion on the Harley. Instead, Steve poured her into the XD and drove her home to the gym, where his futon spun in nauseating circles and nightmare images plagued Kerry in her sleep. Pop hung the corpses of Cracker Nunne's working dogs from the leopard tree with the lash of Nunne's own stockwhip. White men roamed the streets of Trinder Park with sawn-offs. There were sirens and gunshots and nothing she could do to save either her or Allie, waking in a sweat as the dugais cornered them deep in Karawatha Forest. Just before dawn, the skeleton of the snake-headed crow looked at her through the mesh of a prison window, its frame of white bones glistening in the early light. The waark spoke sternly to her in angry, rapid Bundjalung, which Kerry couldn't follow. I'm sorry, she told it again and again, I'm so, so sorry. But she apologized knowing all the while that the bird couldn't understand her English, and that it—whatever *it* was—was never her fault in the first place.

———

Well before dawn, Jim Buckley drove very slowly past the Durrongo pub. He angled right at the crossroads, then turned off his engine near the top of Pretty Mary's driveway. He leaned out the car window and let go a couple of low howls at the setting moon.

Jim could no longer bear to look at his defaced dog, but gazing straight ahead through the windscreen at the Salter house, he reached out a hand and caressed her velvet ears. The dog gave his arm a grateful lick. Beneath the house, Elvis woke. Woofing, he trotted up the gravel drive with a sharp sense of grievance, to sort out whoever it was that thought they could park on his road and start howling any time they felt like it. *The bloody nerve.* As he got closer to the LandCruiser, Elvis recognized the tantalizing scent of the pig dog bitch. The wonderful memory of fucking her three days ago blossomed across his doggy mind. He forgot all about intruders and wagged his stumpy tail in wild, enthusiastic circles as Buckley set the tattooed bitch down on the ground beside him.

"Have a crack at that, son," murmured Buckley. "It's your lucky day."

Chapter Seventeen

At 6 a.m. the household twitched in fitful sleep. Pretty Mary and Ken had spent half the night staring at the ceiling, after arguing for long hours about Donna, and Pop, and the years of Donna's absence, which stretched behind them now like a kind of golden age. The argument wore itself into a groove, round and round. Ken stuck to his guns. Donna was womba. Donna was an evil bitch, born that way. Quite likely Donna had come at Buckley's bidding, allowing herself to be used to destroy their campaign. But Pretty Mary resisted this interpretation. She knew that it was the Devil's work they had witnessed. "Not her fault, bub," she said repeatedly, "it's not her fault," until the others began to wonder just exactly who she was exonerating. The family tore frantically at the incident, snatching fragments of meaning where they could through the small hours. By three, exhaustion was universal. By four o'clock, after a couple of Valium and a river of tears, even Pretty Mary had finally managed to reach unconsciousness.

It was Donny who got up to a silent house. He had left the arguing early to go online, before sleeping and dreaming of war. His night was filled with massive multiplayer carnage, machine guns and bombs and loud pistol shots, dreams of himself in a band of brothers overcoming the enemy to advance to the next level. These sounds and images, all very normal, didn't trouble Donny in the least. But a wisp of anxiety hovered around him as he took his first piss of the day. The wisp built into a thunderhead as he remembered what he'd heard and seen at the party, the look in his father's bloodshot eyes when Donna faced him down. And those clouds were still building when some unnamed instinct sent him, bleary-eyed and stumbling, to the top of the gravel drive.

As he neared the open gate, the boy froze. Elvis had been slung roughly across the top bar with his head pointing at the ground and his tongue grotesquely slack in the gentle light of dawn. A bullet had made a small dark cave in his temple, its meaty edges raised, the white hair blackened by gunpowder. He had been shot at point-blank range. At some time in the night, blood had trickled out of his right ear and made its way down to his upper lip, where the flow had stopped; the trickle had dried in a horrible parody of a lipsticked smile. Flies now walked this red line and crawled over it up into the dog's nostrils. After several minutes of blank observation Donny found it in himself to move. He eased Elvis off the gate into his arms and walked down to the house, numb, unaware of the gravel biting at his cold feet or the magpies calling the day into being over at the creek. Blind, deaf, mute, Donny carried Elvis underneath the house where, with the dog held fast against his chest, he collapsed among the dusty cardboard boxes and broken furniture. He curled himself around Elvis's limp form, closed his eyes, and told himself that none of it was real.

"We can't just up sticks and bugger off to Queensland," Steve protested over his third coffee of the morning. "I mean, I get it, but you can't just run away and pretend you don't have a family, for Christ's sake."

"Why not? Donna did."

"And look what's happened. Anyway, I've put everything into the business, Kez. Be realistic, for fuck's sake."

Despite his protests, Steve wondered for one ridiculous moment if Kerry was right, if they should just bail and head north. Wave goodbye to the impossible burden of starting a business from scratch. There were opportunities in Queensland. Definitely a lot fewer crazy bloody Salters to worry about too. But no, it was ludicrous. Behind the door of the locker room, Kerry bent over the basin to heave up the coffee she had tried to substitute for breakfast. Steve winced at her groans and retching. What a clusterfuck the party had turned out to be. Happy sixty-fifth, Pretty Mary; yeah, right. He retrieved a plastic fruit bowl and put it next to the futon.

Kerry zombied out of the locker room and back to bed, hoping to sleep for a week, or to wake with someone else's sober head on her shoulders. But what got her up instead, an hour later, was a terse call from Ken. A family meeting had been called. Uncle Richard was on his way.

"Gah," Kerry said, closing her eyes again. "Murggh." Why did her phone still have battery, today of all days?

"Want any?" Steve asked, showing her that he was cracking eggs into a pan.

"You sound proper grogsick," Ken said, and bit his tongue. "Gimme Steve."

"Yep. Uh-huh," said Steve, after putting his eggs aside and taking the phone. "Shit. Elvis?"

"Arrrrggh, gerh." Dry heaving at the idea of eggs, Kerry flung herself into the shower to become human. *Family meeting.* Yeah, good luck with that. Uncle Richard would want to be some kind of fucking miracle worker this time.

———

"The island, I mean," Black Superman said, standing in the doorway of Donna's motel room. "I wouldn't ask ya to go back to Mum's. I'm not myall."

Donna sat on the unmade bed with dark rings beneath her swollen eyes, not really watching the morning television. Scrolling under images of lawyers and their clients outside a Sydney courtroom was

news from the royal commission. Scores more victims of priests and
sports coaches and teachers were coming forward to break their
silence, to be heard at last. One cluster of faces were from out west,
where a very highly paid school principal had just been revealed as
a serial predator. Donna clicked the television off. *People just ain't no
good.* She didn't call that news.

"What'd be the point?" Donna asked, finally meeting Black Superman's eyes. "I'm going back home next week. Leave this"—here
she waved a furious hand at the motel, at Jim Buckley's sleazy little
empire, at her mad relations—"behind me, once and for all. I've got
a shot at buying my own Sydney agency. Do you know how huge
that is, for a woman? A woman like me?"

Black Superman eased inside and sat down on a scratched plastic chair next to a cane coffee table. Fiddled with the two standard motel biscuits. Orange slice and choc chip, both soft beneath
his thumbnail. Should he offer to take Donna out for breakfast?
Should he tell her again that he believed her? Or jump straight to
the crux of things, that despite last night's fiasco, they still needed
her help to save Granny's island. Fat chance of that. He rubbed at his
face. Someday things would be different, he told himself. Easy and
straightforward. Just him and Josh, enjoying their lives. Weekends
in Port Douglas. Annual leave in Japan. But that day was not today.
He forced himself to sound enthusiastic about Donna's imminent
departure.

"Yeah, I get it, sis, it's massive. And good for you, why shouldn't you
have your agency, when you've worked so hard for it? But the thing
is . . ." he began, then came to a halt. The truth, perhaps . . . When in
doubt, just spit it out. Be fair dinkum.

"Thing is, you run now, after last night, and it'll haunt you forever. You can go as far away as you like, but the past always comes
along for the ride. I should know." He discovered that for some reason his voice wasn't working properly. Big lump in his throat. The
world blurry outside the motel glass.

He folded his arms and told the carpet his tale.

"You asked me if he touched me. And all I can tell you is I don't know. There's these giant blanks. Mainly what I remember is being flogged half dead that time. I'm kind of fixated on that, I suppose, and on this one other thing. I remember seeing Ken on the kitchen floor. He was maybe ten. Lying like this"—Black Superman curled, mimicking the fetal position—"and yelping like a fucking animal, scrabbling round in a circle, trying not to get kicked in the guts by Pop. I would have been three or four, I guess . . . And if I try to go any further, remember more than that, there's just this awful blank hole. Nothing, no memories . . . and so I don't try. But I don't kid myself, sis. I might live in a flash Sydney unit, but some part of me is always gonna wake up sweating in the middle of the night and hear Ken screaming on the kitchen floor. Probably why I wanted to take the kids on, I suppose."

Donna shifted uneasily where she sat and ran her hands through her hair. Black Superman's story made her jaw ache with the memory of her own beatings. And below that, something else stirred. Call it rage, or fear, but it was more than either of those. It thrummed in her constantly, like the waves of sound that humans can't hear but animals can. Below consciousness. A vague hum in her muscle and bone. Alerting her to danger everywhere around her, always, unless she was drunk or high in the safety of her own locked home. It was a cool morning, but tiny beads of sweat broke out on her upper lip.

"And you wonder why I'm going?" she asked.

"I just reckon it might help to go to the river one last time," Black Superman said quietly, seeing her react. "And then you could take one good memory with you, when you go, at least." He waited. Breathed.

Please, please.

Donna flicked the TV back on, the sound still muted. She had deliberately not returned to Ava's Island since Jim revealed his plan with New South Wales Corrections and the Yang Corporation. The deal he described was words on paper and lines on a map, that was all. Nothing to do with Granny Ruth or with Pretty Mary or Dad Charlie. Certainly nothing to do with the place she had been happiest in her life, before Granny Ruth died. Because she was Martina Rossi and she had no past, no family, no history at all.

"I've got enough memories of the island," she said dismissively.

"For me, then. Please. It'll be just us two." Black Superman was begging. Let her go with him, let her see what would be destroyed. Let her see that the river still knew her; that she was still a part of it, despite everything. He wheedled, he argued, he joked and cajoled. He had always been her favorite, the one who got her; he told her over and over, until, in the end, Donna reluctantly allowed herself to be persuaded. She would go to the river with him, but later, in a week or so, not today. Then she would pack her things, and she would drive south to Sydney and she would never come back again.

Black Superman stood alone beside the river. The day was glorious, but fatigue built an invisible wall between him and his surrounds. He vaguely registered the leaves of the eucalyptus and the pine gleaming in the morning sunshine; he saw the river, sparkling like an avalanche of crushed diamonds as it swept down in its hurry to meet the sea. He saw these things, but had no capacity, today, to enjoy any of their beauty. He was almost spent. With his last fragment of strength Black Superman straightened, and he began to chant in the old tongue:

Grandmother, Grandfather, come to us, your blood,
Grandmother, Grandfather, show us the straight path through.

From an unseen tree on the island came the sound of crows. Then the swish of the breeze picking up and changing to a strong, steady wind against his face. The hoop pine began to tremble and sway. Black Superman noticed this, and sang even harder. The wind strengthened. It buffeted the tops of the trees, flinging the crown of the pine from side to side, its massive trunk creaking with the effort of resisting the forces at play on it. A small dust spiral formed on the dirt track, lifting leaf litter and twigs high into the air before dropping them on the rocky edge of the current, near the boulder where Pop's ashes had been scattered. Okay. So you can hear me, but Granny Ava, Grandad Chinky Joe, Granny Ruth, that's not enough, not today. Tell us what to do, what to believe . . . and help us to protect our country, *please*.

The wind gave one last violent gust, and Black Superman flinched, half expecting a branch of the pine to come plummeting down on top of him. But the tree remained intact, and then the wind gradually eased. The sun shone even brighter, casting his shadow onto the surface of the water. Around him, the birds of the forest went about their business as usual, chirping and hopping from branch to branch in search of bugs. A small family of wallabies on the island had heard his song and paused in their grazing, alert to strange sounds they had only heard talk of from their grandparents. Now they bent to the ground once again, but anxious this time, their ears flicking nervously back and forth as they began to nip at the grass with their sharp front teeth. Something was awry. Something was going to happen here soon to upset the order of the universe.

Black Superman waited for a further sign, but no sign came.

Slicing through the Pacific Ocean, far out to sea beyond the Brunswick heads, The Doctor had the sudden tug of an idea from nowhere at all. The idea was that she should turn and head upriver again to the distant waters around Ava's Island. Something there required her presence. The shark nosed her way around and instinctively began heading towards land, finding herself eventually working against the powerful outgoing tide. The swaying of the huge fish beat a rhythm into the ocean, as though she were playing a watery instrument, her entire body the bow. *Stroke, stroke, stroke.* Silver flashes streaked away from her path everywhere she travelled. When The Doctor reached the river mouth, spoonbills and herons developed a wary watchfulness as she passed them by. The grasses on the riverbanks swayed and tossed in the easterly breeze, but below the surface of the water, all was calm. There was no hurry to the shark's pace. Just the slow, steady metronome of her pointed tail, drumming its way upriver to keep an appointment with a very old friend.

———

"I still can't believe you left my keys with him," Kerry complained, gingerly swallowing her last bite of vegemite toast as she and Steve hammered down the highway in the XD. Tiny black fragments of burnt cane swirled past the car and those that didn't landed on the ever-expanding spider-crack in the windscreen. Steve flicked a lever, tried to wash them off, but there was no water in the XD's reservoir. All he succeeded in doing was smearing the specks across the windscreen in long gray semicircles. They drove on, seeing the world through ashes.

"What if he's taken it up the Goldie and flogged it?" Kerry had a horrifying vision of Ken walking into Jupiter's Casino with a fat roll of green hundred-dollar bills. And a blank space under the house where she had parked the Harley yesterday.

"Doubt it. And anyway, if you weren't legless on Stoli I wouldn't have needed to leave them with anyone," Steve pointed out, irritated. Kerry made a low sound. She was too sick to deal with this. With her head resting on the glass of the passenger window, she closed her eyes against Steve's indisputable logic, then opened them again as nausea bit hard. She kept them open this time, watching the cane fields blur. Someone on the radio was going on about the royal commission into child abuse. Beaudesert BoysTown topping some national fucking table for sex crimes against kids. A school principal out west, just as bad. Kerry stabbed the radio off with a rigid forefinger. Do yer fucken head in.

"I was listening to that," Steve said.

"I just hope it's still in one piece," said Kerry. Anxiety sat in her gut like a toad.

"I'd be more worried about your sister being in one piece," Steve muttered, wondering what a family meeting entailed, and what his own role in it might be. "She was pretty upset when she left last night."

"Yeah, her and everybody else! Ah, she makes me weak," Kerry said heatedly, wild with the disruption Donna had brought and the unknowable consequences everyone would now have to bear. "It was easier when we thought she was dead."

"Nice."

"Well, Jesus, *what the fuck*? Turns up out of the blue and then half an hour later dumps that steaming pile of shit in all our laps! And for what? What did she think was gonna happen?"

"Maybe she's been wanting to get it off her chest for twenty years," Steve said feelingly.

"So why not wait a bit bloody longer, then? But no. She had to run her mouth at Mum's birthday, onetime. Right in the middle of our fight about the prison too. It's all a bit fucking suss."

"Babe, you're forgetting one thing—she didn't come to you looking to cause trouble," Steve contradicted. "If you hadn't stumbled across her at the real estate yesterday, she'd still be missing and nobody'd be any the wiser. Unless you somehow think she engineered that as well."

Kerry fell silent. That was true enough. Twenty-four hours ago Donna was still dead. It was she who had resurrected her, by going into the real estate in the first place. So—looked at in one cockeyed way—it could be Kerry who was responsible for last night's catastrophe. She gritted her teeth. If only she'd stayed on the bloody footpath yesterday morning. Ah. *Woulda, shoulda, coulda.*

"You sound like you believe her," she accused. Steve shrugged awkwardly. He could say so many things in response and struggled to find the one that would do no harm.

"Why would she lie?" he finally asked.

"You didn't know Pop. He was an alcoholic, and he could be violent, but he wasn't a fucking pedo." Kerry's voice rose in protest, but before Steve could remind her that he had met Pop, he was drowned out by the wail of a fire engine overtaking at high speed. Steve eased the XD to the edge of the road, and the engine quickly overtook, disappearing down the highway in front of them.

"Cane fire's gotten away." Steve squinted at the large plume of dark smoke rising a kilometer to their left. A constellation of hawks had gathered above the fire, black shapes hovering high above the flames. Seconds later they passed the pub billboard—*Old-Fashioned Country Fun*—and Steve slowed for the turn into Durrongo.

"At this time of day?" said Kerry, sitting up and forgetting to be hungover. "And that's not cane smoke."

Chapter Eighteen

Kerry knew that her entire family, barring Ken, would have perished in the fire. Donny, Pretty Mary, Chris, Tall Mary, Elvis. All gone. The Harley too, parked beneath the house, would have exploded fast into ugly twisted metal, burnt beyond recognition. She pressed her hands flat onto the dash and leaned forward as Steve sped down the gravel towards the terrible column of smoke and ash. She needed to get the first lacerating look over and done with, get it behind her. This, then, was the "lots to talk about" that Ken had alluded to on the phone—carnage on an unimaginable scale. Buckley had sent more than cops this time round. He had sent murder.

But the truth at the other end of the driveway was less catastrophic. Steve pulled up under the charred leopard tree, rising now like a blackened and admonishing finger from the singed lawn. They emerged from the car to an odd tableau. Not only Ken and Sav but Uncle Richard, and Aunty Val, and Donny and Chris too, were standing on the lawn, dishevelled but unharmed. The Harley was parked safely on the far side of the chicken coop. A ten-year-old fire alarm was emitting an anemic beeping from the lounge. Dr. No had been up at the crack, said Sav, and this time his howling had saved lives. Pretty Mary was there, fully alive and unhurt, her face loose in a way that was horribly familiar. Laughing at the joke that was her life. Not even trying to hide the bottle in her hand.

"Gimme that shit," Kerry said, snatching at the grog. Pretty Mary swung the bottle away, got loud. Protested her rights.

"You can't bloody talk. You was rotten yerself last night, didn't know yer arse from yer elbow. Coming round ere, acting like bloody Mother Teresa . . . good go." She lifted the bottle and took a long, defiant slug.

Kerry swore under her breath. Trinder Park was three hours away. So was the moon, so was Mars.

"Maybe don't worry about it, just at the minute," murmured Aunty Val.

Three firefighters—one a Murri fella with a plait who Kerry recognized from the funeral—were hosing the smoking timbers at the front of the house. The blaze had destroyed half of the veranda and a good chunk of the kitchen as well so that, to the family standing where the stairs had been, the shack looked like a doll's house with half the front wall lifted away. The fridge, scorched but with magnets still intact, remained in its normal place next to the sink. Beyond it, the lounge room, smoke-damaged and soggy, was exposed to view. All the world could have watched TV there now if the plasma screen hadn't been totalled by a piece of fallen roof iron that lay, twisted and steaming, in the middle of the carpet.

Home smelt of smoke, Kerry realized, and not the good clean eucalyptus juhm that cleansed and healed, but juhm tainted with firefighting chemicals and singed lino. Somehow the place reeked strongly of failure and despair as well. Were they cursed to always have bad luck, her mob? Was it about luck, though? Or was this Buckley's doing, sending goons in the night to enforce what the cops hadn't been up to? Maybe Ken was right. Maybe Donna had returned to wreak vengeance on the family who'd rejected her a second time. She had signed her death warrant, if so. But nah, Kerry's money was on Buckley. The prick had form.

"That'll do it," called one of the firefighters, turning off his hose and signalling to someone on the fire truck to rewind it.

Uncle Richard stood alongside the others, his Akubra pushed well back from his forehead. His brow was creased like a much-folded certificate kept safely in some bottom drawer, and the skeptical expression that the palsy lent his face seemed even more appropriate than usual. Off to the side, Ken was telling Sav that the nasty jagged cut above his right knee was nothing, don't fucken worry about it.

Something caught Uncle Richard's eye, something distinctive among the debris, and he frowned even harder. He stepped forward, poked at the charred wood with a steel-capped boot. The wet ashes stirred and broke at his touch. From the dry wood beneath, a tiny plume of smoke made its way to the surface.

"Gimme that pole, bud," he ordered Chris, who retrieved a length of green bamboo that had held a light above the barbecue. Uncle Richard stepped back from the blistering heat of the ruins. From a distance, he tried unsuccessfully to lever something out from beneath the glowing veranda beam.

"Too hot," he finally said, letting the pole drop. "It'll have to wait." He turned to Pretty Mary. Beside her sat Donny, hugging his knees, expressionless, in one of yesterday's folding chairs. Uncle Richard pulled his sister close. His movement unknowingly mimicked that of Brandon last night. The big brothers of the world who care and protect. They do exist, alright, Kerry thought with a rare flash of self-pity. Just not for this little black duck.

Uncle Richard kissed the top of his sister's head and then used both his thumbs to wipe tears from the inner corners of her eyes, eyes that were no longer laughing. His left thumb ran down her cheek and unexpectedly met a lump bulging on her jaw.

Pretty Mary flinched away. Uncle Richard peered closer, trying with the same thumb to rub the purple-black ash mark off her face, but she snatched his hand away. She took a step backwards, with the mark unchanged on her face. He narrowed his eyes. Pretty Mary groaned faintly as she looked at the fire truck, barely managing to hold in her shame.

"Don't ask. Just don't."

A moment's silence. Then Uncle Richard let go a deep rumble of discontent. When he spoke his voice had a sharp edge.

"Who wants to tell me what the hell's been going on here?"

When nobody answered he swung around to face the Murri firefighter. "Ya know me?" Uncle Richard quizzed the man.

"Yeah, course, Uncle."

"Was this an accident?"

"Hard to say, Unk."

"Don't come the raw prawn with me, son."

Uncle Richard eyeballed the younger man with the authority of his sixty-seven years. His gray hair insisted on an answer.

"You're a Brown," he informed the man suddenly. "Pop Owen got you into TAFE, years back, when you left school."

"Yeah, that's right. Otis is me dad. Maureen's me mum."

"I went to Tranby with Otis back in the day. Went out with his sister for a bit too. Sandy. Well, brother, was this an accident or not?"

"I'm not supposed to say, Unk," said the firefighter uneasily. "But see the way the flame's bolted up there, la? Could be accelerant. Maybe. It wasn't me what told ya, but."

"Accelerant. Well, we can talk about that later, I reckon."

"I'm supposed to inform the police if there's any—"

"Oh, no need for the gunjies here, I don't think. You blokes were just leaving, eh."

The man looked at Uncle Richard, then glanced over at his workmates. They were coiling hoses, wiping down equipment. It was a sunny blue Saturday. The swell was pumping at South Golden. His kids were at home, waiting for him to take them surfing. He twisted his mouth.

"Yeah, I reckon we'll head off dreckly."

"Good lad."

Uncle Richard clapped the man's shoulder, then turned to the business of the house. Someone had wanted the shack gone, and hadn't been too worried about the people inside it. Someone had been prepared to chuck accelerant beneath sleeping bodies and throw a lit match in after it. Who would do that in tiny, insubstantial Durrongo? There were fresh 4WD tracks near the front gate. And Buckley was rumored to be getting desperate as ICAC got more and more interested in the island development. But the mayor wasn't stupid.

As Uncle Richard walked back to Pretty Mary and Ken, he looked around curiously. His sister was there, safe enough for now, and his niece and nephews. Kerry's new fella. The neighbors, all present and accounted for. Tall Mary and Helen had shot through after some big blue last night, Ken said, and even the orange cat was okay, sitting on top of the chook pen, washing its paws and utterly scornful of humans who were silly enough to let their homes burn half to the ground.

The third firefighter had at last got the sickly smoke alarm to shut up, and a blessed silence fell. No crows cawing. No bulls bellowing. Not even a dog losing its head at all the excitement.

"Where's Elvis?" said Uncle Richard.

Donny flinched.

Uncle Richard discovered that nobody would look at him, let alone answer the question. The charred leopard tree, Aunty Val's Hills hoist next door, even the gums lining the creek—all were far more intriguing to the gathered clan. There was a distinctly dog-shaped hole in the picture in front of him. And a Donna-shaped hole too. Uncle Richard put his hands on his hips and spoke slowly.

"What aren't you mob telling me? Where's Elvis, and where's Donna? And why isn't Black Superman here?"

The heavy silence didn't change. Kerry bummed a smoke off Pretty Mary. She took a long draw. Then, seeing that nobody else would, she described her version of the previous night. How the cops had arrived to do Buckley's dirty work for him, and gotten short shrift, and how Donna then turned up out of the blue making everything far, far worse with her strange and shameful stories. Probably Black Superman was with her. As for Elvis, that Kerry couldn't say.

"He's dead," Ken told her. Shot in the night by the same vicious arsehole who'd tried to burn them all alive in their beds.

Kerry stared at her brother. Elvis—dead? *Does not compute.*

Uncle Richard's head flung up in alarm.

"So where's Donna now?"

"Who fucken cares?" spat Ken, instantly furious at the sound of her name.

"She's been shown the door," Kerry told Uncle Richard. "She's probably in Patto, I think. At the motel."

Uncle Richard raised his eyebrows at Pretty Mary. A daughter found and lost in one night.

"That right, Mary? She been shown the door?"

"That's right, my brother. I can't be worrying about . . . I gotta think about what's best for us mob. I can't . . ." she trailed off. How to even speak of such hideous things?

"And the dog—shot dead? Is that definite?"

"Yep, Donny found him up by the road, first thing this morning. Can't get much clearer than that, can ya?" Ken said bitterly.

"Well, that's a damn shame, and a worry. Where'd ya put him, nephew?" Uncle Richard asked.

From the folding chair, Donny merely blinked at the blackened ruins in front of him. Words a universe away. But he knew Uncle Richard understood silence. Would get his meaning, would know that the death of Elvis had been . . . not altered, no. Not reversed. But at least cleansed, a little, by the roaring flames. *Ashes to ashes, dust to dust.* It was only right and proper. Elvis was floating in the air, all around them. He would always remain safe at home now. He could never be taken away more than he already had been.

Uncle Richard tilted his head a little, looking at the boy.

"Here?" Uncle Richard pointed his lips at the ruins.

"I think he might be in shock," said Kerry, finding her own legs beginning to quiver. She could have woken up an orphan, if things had gone just a little differently, and she would never see Elvis alive again. Ken nodded as he limped heavily towards the XD. His right leg was awash with blood from the knee down. Somehow this was appropriate, Kerry thought vaguely. Elvis was gone. A line had been crossed. It was a day for blood and flame. And retribution.

"Shock. That's exactly right, sis. Shock and awe. Dugais knocked them black houses down in Byron in the fifties. Well, Jim Buckley's got exactly the same bloody idea. Only the cunt's gone straight to attempted murder." With difficulty, Ken reached in and took his keys out of the Falcon's ignition. He leaned all his weight against the car, wincing and batting Savannah away.

"Can you just fuck off out of it," he said irritably. "There's nothing wrong with me." Blood made a slick red sock of his foot.

"You need stitches, idiot," insisted Sav, with Dr. No clamped onto her hip.

"Which part of *fuck off* are you having trouble with?" Ken snapped.

Sav sighed heavily. Went over to Donny, took his chair when he stood up to offer it.

Uncle Richard beckoned Donny over to him.

"I'm real sorry you had to find him like that, son," Uncle Richard said. "He was a deadly fella, old Kumanjay, even if he did insist on pissing on me boots every time he seen me. Now listen." Uncle Richard put his right hand on Donny's left shoulder. His straight arm made a dark bridge between the youth and himself. Uncle Richard gazed steadily at his nephew and in the dark pools of his uncle's eyes Donny found somewhere to be. He came back to the world, then, shivering and afraid.

Kerry saw the shivers. Tossed a picnic blanket from the barbecue over the boy's thin shoulders. It went over his head, at first, blinding him for a moment. Then Kerry pulled it down around his back and tucked it into the neck of his shirt, transforming it into a cape. Better than nothing. Donny stood, cloaked in dirty wool, facing his Elder.

"Nephew," said Uncle Richard, very quiet. "About this fire, now. You done it, eh?"

Donny's face crumpled.

"Cos of yer puppydog?" Uncle Richard asked gently.

Donny bawled. He had no clear memory of anything after walking up the drive and seeing Elvis hanging there with his red tongue drooping out his mouth . . . Until the fire engine—also red, a fact that was somehow important in a way Donny couldn't understand—had come and the hoses began to blast at the inferno. If they said he did it, then he must have. As for *why*. Reasons were nonsense. All he knew was that death meant smoke and it meant flame. Elvis—a constant presence all his life—was dead. His Aunty Donna—a constant absence—was alive. And, as ever, he was so very alone in the world.

"Grief comes out in all sorts of strange ways, son, but ya can't be burning houses down," said Uncle Richard, wrapping his dark arms tight around the kid. Holding on, holding on. Let him know with his man's muscle and blood that he's safe. Let him feel a part of something good. Something stronger than he himself is.

Donny kept apologizing through hiccuping sobs.

Uncle Richard shushed him. Told him it was going to be okay. He would be okay.

"Are you fucking seriously saying that . . . *Fuck!*" Ken limped in circles. Flung his hands about as it became obvious that this was not Buckley's doing. "What in the fucking name of fucking Christ has got into the kid—"

"Will you take that lad home with you, my brother, and help him, *please*? Take him and teach him; he's growing up all back-to-front here. Got no respect, no culture . . ." Pretty Mary pleaded. Uncle Richard's face hardened. When he spoke, still holding Donny close, he made sure the boy heard him.

"You talk like this child's the problem, Mary. In front of him."

"If he's burned half the fucking house down, I'd say that is a problem," blurted Kerry. "I mean, come on, Uncle."

"Yeah. And so who owns that problem, bub? Who made him who he is, to go burning houses down?"

The family stared sullenly at Uncle Richard.

"This lad is one young fella in a family," said Uncle Richard. "He's got a father, doesn't he? And a Nan. Aunts and uncles. Cousins. We're all a part of this. Not just him."

Kerry fell silent. Recalibrated.

Ken limped towards the back fence, gesturing and swearing at Mount Monk in disbelief. He didn't know what the fuck Uncle Richard was on about. His retarded son might have burned the veranda off the house, yeah, but it was all Buckley underneath it. Buckley had thought up the prison, had murdered Elvis. Buckley had set in motion every terrible thing that smoldered in front of him today. There was a problem alright—and every problem has a solution close to hand.

"Don't you worry, son," Ken called out. "We'll put old mate in the ground and then I'll go sort that cunt Buckley out once and fer all. He'll rue the fucken day, truesgod."

"Meaning what?" asked Uncle Richard.

"Meaning I'm gonna fight for our rights, not die yapping while they pick us off, one by one."

"Yeah, okay. We need to fight. But first I think you better come to Men's Camp this weekend. Get yer head clear, neph. Manage yer anger so you use it, not it using you."

"Fuck all that anger management crap. I *need* to be angry to defend our island!" spat Ken, staring back at everyone with wild eyes. "Angry's all I've fucking got."

Uncle Richard adjusted his Akubra. Pushed his tongue around behind his lopsided mouth as he gazed at Ken.

"There's been a death here, Kenny. And a shooting death at that, serious business. Course you're angry. We all are. So this is what's gonna happen. You'll get that leg stitched. Then you'll come bush tonight, with yer son. Me and Uncle Kev. Uncle Les from up Tweed way. Uncle Moke, plus a few other brothers from Lismore, with their kippers. We'll siddown on country and we'll yarn this business. And after that, if you still think ya need to sort Jim Buckley out, well, he'll be walking around next week just the same as he is today."

"I'm not talking about next week. I'm talking about *now*," said Ken as he clicked open the boot of the XD and lifted out Pop's hunting rifle. The air shifted and thickened around Ken. He was blurred and enlarged by the presence of the gun, as it came into focus above all else.

"Oh, here we fucking go," muttered Kerry, catching Donny's horror out of the corner of her eye.

Without any warning, she was utterly enraged. Had had it up to here with Ken. With all of it. And she discovered she was done with being afraid.

"Justice delayed," said Ken, closing the boot with his bent elbow, both hands glued on the rifle stock, "is justice denied. I'm sick of being denied."

Kerry sidestepped Steve and headed straight towards Ken.

Fucking macho bullshit.

"Better put the gun down, Ken," said Uncle Richard carefully, "and just yarn with me here a minute."

Yeah, good luck with that, thought Kerry.

"Show us," she said, as though the .22 was a new phone. "I thought that was long gone. Is it loaded?"

But Ken kept a firm hold of the rifle. Rivulets of blood had made their way from his gashed thigh down to the earth. Twisting crimson snakes threading down his dark leg. His jinung glossy against the grass. The stock of the rifle was an old, scratched thing. Pale yellow wood. Scraped with years of use, years of putting tucker on the table, and a few times giving the worst of the Durrongo rednecks pause. Kerry had thought it pawned years ago, or stolen; hadn't seen it for so long. Had never even thought of it still existing. Yet there it was, resurrected.

"If it ain't loaded now it soon will be," Ken said. "I'm sick of fucken talk, talk, talk."

"But can I just feel it?" Kerry asked, reaching down. Ken swiftly swung the barrel behind him, out of her reach. Then he held it even closer, cradling it to his chest as he paced the lawn. Ready to aim and fire. His striding momentum nearly enough to make it happen. Kinetic energy, surging from foot to leg to arm to index finger.

Nigger, nigger, pull the trigger.

"Don't fucken play silly buggers," Ken told Kerry, breathing fast and shallow. His blue eyes were pinned to dots. Holding the gun like this was the Second Coming. Ken squared his shoulders, looked up to address Uncle Richard, and the family, and the whole fucking world that was arrayed against him. "Buckley wanna send cops with tasers to *my* door, shoot *my* dog? Fuck him, he'll pay."

"Kerry . . ." said Steve, terror jangling in his voice. "Can you just—"

"Then we'll all pay, brother." Kerry let out a harsh bark of laughter. "Shoot him and we're all fucked. We'll lose the island for sure. And you'll die in jail an old man." A stupid, vain old man, she wanted to add, but Ken had raised the barrel of the rifle and cut her words in half.

"Kerry," said Uncle Richard. "Come away back here please, bub."

Come away back. What am I, a sheepdog? She hesitated, not done yet with Ken and his gammon Big Man act. Then saw with horror that Steve was about to venture out and rescue her, like all she needed was another fucking hero.

"Shoot Buckley and we'll all pay, bruz," she repeated over her shoulder as she walked back to the others. Steve fell on her, dragged her away. Joined with Pretty Mary: What the fuck were you? Do you think you're bloody? Don't you ever dare.

"I'm tired of being shit on!" Ken shouted. "If nothing changes, nothing fucking changes."

"Steve," said Uncle Richard, his voice still easy but his gaze locked on the rifle. "I want you to take the women and Donny and go next door. Chris, you stay." Uncle Richard gently shoved Donny sideways to Steve. Nodded at Neil's F100 next door. Get in and clear out, he meant.

"Got it," said Steve. "Should I call—"

"Don't do anything. Don't call anyone," said Uncle Richard. "Just go."

"I'm not leaving till he's put that bloody gun down," said Kerry. She was steaming about Elvis, poor Donny, the smoldering house. Donna. The island, fast slipping away into history as the family turned on each other. The whole stupid bullshit of life this side of the border. But ah, Jesus. Her uncle was right, and this unholy mess belonged to them all.

"You'll go and you'll go now," said Uncle Richard to Kerry, all his softness vanished in an instant. Stung, Kerry shrugged Steve off. *I'm not a child.* When Uncle's back was turned she peeled away, stomped under the house. Squinted through the cracks in the scorched wooden battens, waiting to see who got shot first.

When Steve had taken the women and children next door, Uncle Richard and Chris glanced at each other and did a surprising thing, both of them sinking down in the middle of the lawn with no words needed. The two of them folded cross-legged onto the dirt as though choreographed, as though some magnetic force had drawn them earthward a dozen steps away from Ken. Uncle Richard slowly opened his palm above the burnt grass. Ken didn't accept the invitation. He remained standing, the rifle dangling now in his right hand, the barrel parallel to the ground. My big brother, the human compass. Which way will he swing? Where exactly is true north?

"I know ya wanna shoot him, nephew. But the word on the street is Jim Buckley's gonna get what's coming to him soon enough,"

Kerry heard Uncle Richard say. "ICAC is very bloody interested in his dealings. It's the big boys in Sydney, and it's not going away this time."

"Yeah, I've heard that before," Ken argued. "He's protected."

More talk followed, indistinct and low. Squatting on her haunches, Kerry shuffled closer until she was in the spot Elvis had inhabited for most of the party. His steel chain was still tangled around the concrete house stump. The empty clip on the end of it a terrible sorrow.

Talk from the men about Donna, mutterings that she couldn't make out. Ken yelling again, pacing, throwing the rifle around. He looked like a lunatic. If Steve had stupidly called the cops that'd be it. No other excuse needed: bang bang bang!

Oh my God, they killed Kenny.

Kerry found that her teeth were clenched. Her jaw was granite. There was no way for this to end well. She peered through the wooden slats at the three men.

"—lying through her hole exactly like she did twenty years ago!" Ken was shouting. "And you believe her! You of all people, Uncle. Why?" His right arm straight down, his fist clenched beside his knee, rigid. The gun horizontal against it. Seen in silhouette from where Kerry crouched, a crucifix. Or a crosshair.

"I want you to put the rifle down, Ken."

"This rifle stays right the fuck where it is."

"Okay. Okay. My nephew, you need to listen to me now. I love you, you know that. That's never gonna change. And you're right. I do believe Donna," Uncle Richard said heavily, waiting for Ken to lift the rifle and fire. Because God only knows. He took a big breath. "I believe her because I've got good reason to, Kenny. And I reckon you do too. It wasn't your fault, son."

Ken's face spasmed, became unrecognizable. He turned and bellowed at the thin spirals of smoke rising from the ruined house. Put the weapon to his shoulder and pulled the trigger, shot at the smoke haze, at the chicken coop, at the white thumbprint of the moon sitting above the western range. The shots echoed off the mountain, sounding like a whip cracking across the distant pasture. He reloaded and fired again and again. Then finally stood, heaving for breath, still looking like murder.

"Pop Owen," Uncle Richard said quietly. "Cold comfort, or maybe none at all. But terrible things happened in his life. Things that warped him, Ken. He never talked about it much, it's easier to drink than talk. But he was hurt bad. Not a couple times. Again and again and again. Being taken away, never really knowing his family, the shame of that. Then the mish, O'Sullivan, and all the rest of the scum that the church protected. The station too. He lost his eye, lost his dream. Some of that pain had to go somewhere. There's no shame to you in it, my nephew. It wasn't your fault. Not Donna's fault either. You were the innocents in it all."

Ah, Christ, thought Kerry, swept by a tide of wild knowledge.

"I love you, my nephew. We all do. And we can get through this. Just put the gun down now."

Ken swayed where he stood, his mouth opening and closing. Every thought but one left him. He upended the rifle where he stood, turned himself into the Unknown Soldier. For a long moment he didn't move. Then, quivering, he sank slowly down onto his good knee. Leaned forward over the barrel, his head bowed, his body shaking.

Uncle Richard and Chris lifted from the ground like eagles. Chris sprinted, slid in to kick the rifle away from beneath Ken's chin, sending the weapon whirling into the cloud of dust and ash he had just raised. Uncle Richard arrived a moment later and enveloped Ken in a bear hug until he crumpled, put his hands over his face, began to sob. And beneath the charred and broken house, in the dusty yellow light streaming through the bars of the battens, Kerry suddenly realized that her own face, too, was awash with tears.

Chapter Nineteen

Uncle Richard sat at the wheel of his rattling HiLux, Ken stitched and bandaged beside him. Kerry and Steve stood on the grass with Pretty Mary, both of them still filthy from the day's burning, dragging, dumping, and sweeping.

"You be right till Tuesday, my sister?" Uncle Richard said. Pretty Mary made a face and gestured at the house with her wineglass.

"Be a lot better if you mens was gonna stay and fix this," she said acidly. *In vino veritas*, thought Kerry.

"That's sorted," Uncle Richard said, putting the ute into gear. "Black Superman and Josh are on it." The volume of the rattling went up several notches. "Sure you won't come?" he asked Uncle Neil, who shook his head, dubious on Salters since hearing about Ken and the rifle. Uncle Neil had taken the rebel flag off his ute, but still. Sixty years a white man. A bloke had every right to stop and think. Maybe he wasn't pure white, but he didn't feel like much of a blackfella either.

"Gotta work, mate. And find Mary a new set of stringers."

"Next time then, brother." A handshake, a man's short nod.

Just then Black Superman and Josh drove in.

"We better get cracking first thing," said Josh. "Lots to get at Bunnings by the look. Couple days to fix the kitchen up and fit the new stairs. Veranda's gonna hafta wait."

Uncle Richard climbed stiffly out of the HiLux, hugged Black

Superman, the kids, Josh too. Shook Brandon's hand and told him he'd heard all about him protecting his sister, good ways.

"Who done it?" breathed Brandon, his big eyes swelling at the house.

"We don't know yet," lied Black Superman. "C'mon, shift ya stumps, we gotta go to Bunnings."

"But whose fault was it?" Brandon insisted, removing three lollipops from his mouth for clarity.

"There isn't always someone to blame, bud," Black Superman told him. "Sometimes things just happen. You move on."

Brandon put the lollipops back in and looked skeptical. Nobody was ever blameless in the world he'd come from.

"Nan, promise you won't bury him till we're back," said Donny's blond head, popping out from among the eskies and swags. For the corpse of Elvis had been found, not even scorched, beneath the charred remains of Ken's old surfboard.

Pretty Mary grimaced. "E's gonna be proper ripe by Tuesday, son."

Uncle Neil came to the rescue. "Use my fishing freezer. You're staying next door anyway, more the merrier."

"Oh! I nearly forgot." Steve went over to a pile of burnt wood and shuffled around in the ashes. Picked something out and rubbed most of the muck off it before folding it in a rag and giving it to Pretty Mary, who held it out to her brother.

Uncle Richard squinted beneath the rag at the kingplate. Sucked his teeth in alarm.

"You bring it when we bury old mate, Mary, and we'll put it back where it belongs. Far too dangerous to be just hanging around. Probably got a lot to do with this." He pointed at the house with his lips. Then he dropped his voice. "And don't let Steve touch it again. It's not for dugais." He handed it back and revved the ute loudly. "Right, let's yanbillilla, now. This camp ain't gonna run itself."

When the sounds of the HiLux rattling and backfiring had faded away to silence, Pretty Mary stood in front of the shack, arms folded, wineglass cold against her left shoulder. Black Superman put an arm around her waist.

"We'll fix it up for ya, Mum, don't worry. Be good as new," said Josh. "Better."

Pretty Mary wrinkled her nose.

"Bloody old dump," she told him airily. "It coulda burned to the ground for all I blooming well care."

"Darnt, don't be like that," Black Superman chipped her.

"I still got me teepee, and I still got me cards." She slapped her vinyl handbag triumphantly with her free hand, for the tarot—at first thought lost along with the kitchen table—had fortuitously been brought downstairs earlier in the night by Aunty Tall Mary.

Upon discovering this, Pretty Mary had promptly hurled away the Miracle Healing Meetings flyer that she had stashed in her bra. "That's all a black woman really needs, somewhere to camp, and a way to feed herself." A large part of Pretty Mary meant it. One version of her wished aloud that the house had burned to ashes, washing away the ugliness of its history. Maybe if the shack were destroyed she'd be able to put away that awful scene in the kitchen, forget the terrible words that had been uttered about Pop. Maybe then she could have lost the memory of Tall Mary's hand raised high in the air before it came crashing down onto Donna's face. A benediction straight from Father O'Sullivan, delivered decades after his death by one of the two dozen Marys he had insisted on naming for the Blessed Virgin.

––––––––––

"Come crank out ten kays," said Steve, lacing on his runners on Monday afternoon. "You'll feel better." Spreadeagled on the futon, Kerry closed her eyes in silent protest. Oh. My. Lord. This fella, truesgod. No matter what mad shit went down, the Energizer Bunny always wanted to go another round, but she most certainly did not.

For Kerry was wrung out, spiralling downward. All she wanted to do was stay in bed. She had grown progressively slacker as the weekend wore on, trying and failing to make some inner sense of her family's story. In contrast, Steve's enthusiasm had surged higher and higher. Nothing blokes liked more than a *project*. Working alongside Black Superman and Josh, Steve had the rubbish dumped by teatime Saturday; the new front wall was already built, and as soon as Uncle Neil brought home the used stairs he'd scavenged from a building site in Lismore, the house would be almost back to its old self. If only people were as easy to renovate, Kerry thought.

"Pass. Bring back a packet of Tim Tams," she said, returning to Facebook, where she learned that Allie's cousin Pryce had just been selected by an American college basketball team. There would be some wild partying in Logan tonight. But she was too exhausted to party. Too tired, too sad, and too broke. The Salters had discovered that afternoon that the Land and Environment Court had denied their appeal. Now Kerry's mind flashed back to a recurring picture: one of roaring yellow bulldozers smashing through the bush beside the river, destroying the big gums and ripping the earth to shreds beneath their sharp tracks. Pictures she had until today flat-out refused to allow into her brain.

"Up the ridge and back, then."

"You deaf? If ya got no Tim Tams, then leave me be, fuck ya."

"Lazy sod," Steve accused, hands on his hips at the end of the bed. He prodded the sole of her foot with his big toe. Tap, tap. Tap. Tap, tap, tap, tap. Pause. Tap. Kerry felt like jumping up and decking him, onetime.

"I thought you wanted to do the Mullum fun run."

"I'm not lazy, ya maggot. I'm in mourning."

Steve tapped some more, knowing she was about to cave.

Kerry eyed him and felt a faint stirring of lust. Check it out. Standing there all muscly and shit with his shirt off. She groaned. Maybe a run would help her to shift this depression. Help her to think more clearly, too, about Buckley, what to do with the disaster that had been delivered to them by the useless arseholes of the Land and Environment Court. She rolled out of bed to get dressed.

"Just as well you're good looking, cunt," she told him, brushing her hair and tying it back.

"I'm so hot I piss napalm, baby." Steve struck a laughing pose in the gym's huge mirrors. Kerry blew a loud raspberry at him and ran downstairs.

"It's funny cos it's true!" Steve called down after her.

They matched their pace on the road up to the ridge overlooking Patto, Steve running a touch slower than usual, Kerry pushing herself that little bit harder. Your body can nearly always do more than your brain thinks it can, Steve had shown her. Don't anticipate the pain of training before it arrives. Work with the reality of now.

Yeah, yeah, yeah. Easy for you. You're not the one bleeding, with a bloated gut and mad chocolate cravings. And anyway, the reality of now is shit, boyfriend. The reality of now is living in a crappy small town where the same corrupt murdering bastards have run things for a hundred years, and if ya don't love it, you're free to leave.

Kerry eventually settled into a rhythm: pace, pace, breath in. Pace, pace, breath out. The running was hypnotic, allowing her to shake off the whirling thoughts of the birthday party, of Pop, of the danger to Granny's island. While they ran past one kilometer of cane after another, climbing steadily onto one of the spurs coming off the distant range, she wasn't stressing about Pretty Mary. Wasn't bereft about losing Elvis to a gun-toting maniac. She wasn't worrying about the possibility of Ken finding himself another rifle to wave around like a fucking idiot, nor agonizing over the chances (slim to none) of Uncle Richard working some miracle on her brother at Men's Camp. Yeah, right. Bunch of blokes out in the scrub telling each other how fucking wonderful they all are, and how hard done by. Steve thought it was deadly, of course, but then he would. He was forever talking about young guys, what they needed, how to help them grow. *They need older blokes to help turn them into men,* he argued when Kerry challenged him. *Well, they ain't gonna turn into fucking washing machines, are they,* she'd retorted. There's nothing ever said about young girls, what they're missing out on, what they need. Always the same old story—the squeaky, violent wheel gets the oil, and the others just get on with it.

When they reached the small park at the top of the spur, Kerry signalled she needed a rest. Her legs burned, and there was nothing around to quench her thirst. She popped a flat pebble in her mouth and waited for the stitch in her side to ease. To her irritation, Steve cranked out twenty fast burpees and then began doing pull-ups on the crossbar of a nearby picnic shelter. Fuck me. Does this bloke ever stop? For even five minutes? She staggered away from him, looked at the country instead, while her wind returned. North was Durrongo, where there were no ominous plumes of black smoke this time. Just cattle country stretching away in all directions, the setting sun glinting on the distant silver ribbon that held Durrongo in its watery embrace. Miniature cars making their way along the highway to the east, Brisbane- or Sydney-bound. A few of them turning their lights on as dusk arrived. I could just jog home now, Kerry told herself, and point the Harley at Queensland, and kiss all this drama goodbye. Then paused, realizing she'd used the word *home* to describe the gym in Patterson.

"You okay?" Steve wandered over.

"Yeah."

"There's Wollumbin way over the back. But is that Mount Monk?" Steve asked, pointing at another smaller peak rising from the same range. The perfect circle of the full moon was suspended above it.

Kerry laughed in disbelief. "For real?"

"I'll take that as a no. But what's that look for?"

"What look?"

"That 'I love you but you sure do drive me up the wall' look."

"Well, as if Mount Chincogan looks anything like Mount Monk! How did white people even *find* Australia?" She shook her head. "Captain Cook musta bin looking for Canada. Or China."

"China's not all that far," Steve retorted. "And how about not putting shit on me every single minute of every single day?"

Kerry blew another loud raspberry.

"Not far? In a little wooden boat? Good go! And you wanna be with a blackfella, ya gonna hear stuff you're not used to, sunshine. Cultural deprogramming. Ya should be paying me."

"You're so full of shit," Steve said, putting his palms flat on the ground and stretching.

Kerry bristled. "You think my culture's not valuable? Compared to oh, I dunno, pissing it up on Anzac Day and going down to Cronulla to bash the wogs?"

"I didn't say that," said Steve. "You're just so fucking rude all the time. The Murries I trained with on the coast weren't like that. Your Mum's not like that. Or Uncle Richard, or Chris. Uncle Richard invited me to the next Men's Camp, actually."

"Huh." Kerry was nonplussed.

"He said I'm doing some of the same stuff with the young blokes as he is. Plus he's got it in his head that we're gonna have black kids together." Steve stopped, embarrassed to present this startling idea to Kerry.

"What a beautiful vision," Kerry said, ironically. "Once I've popped em out we could bring em up here, little Johnny and little Mary"; she swept the horizon with an expansive arm; "and point out the brand-new prison on the river where their ancestors used to live. We can say to them, 'Kids, one day, when we're pushing up yam daisies, absolutely fuck all of this will be yours.'"

"Uncle Richard said it, not me," Steve countered. "Anyway, I'm invited to the camp."

"Yeah, go bush, deadly." She grinned. "You might even learn something about navigation."

Steve squinted at Kerry, standing there mocking him as usual. Grabbed her and put her on the grass, tickled her ribs till her bladder began to fail and she had to quickly admit defeat.

"Okay, so you might be stronger than me," she told him, sitting up and brushing grass off. "But I'm far more intelligent, and better looking. Black too. So it all evens out in the wash."

"Oh, I fucking give up," Steve said, causing another great cackle of laughter to erupt from Kerry.

They ran slower on the way back, Kerry's legs heavy and her breath ragged long before they reached the outskirts of the industrial estate. Steve checked his watch as they walked upstairs past the first of the night's customers. "Just enough time to prepare for the six o'clock pump class," he declared. Kerry showered, ate, collapsed on the futon. Tried not to think about anything.

Chapter Twenty

Deep in the bush, beneath the pale disc of the moon, a dozen men gathered around a yellow-box fire. They murmured, stomping their boots against the cold. It was a long way to the nearest village, over an hour to any real town. Some of the men wore footy jumpers: the Eels, the Sharks, the Dogs. Others were protected from the chill night air by cheap jackets. At the midpoint of the semicircle, Uncle Richard, whose Akubra had been replaced with a woollen beanie, stripped off his red flannelette shirt to reveal the marks of Seniority on his chest. If the cold worried him, he hid it well.

Uncle Kev used clapsticks to bring any stragglers to the fire. Then Uncle Richard went over to where the other boss, Uncle Les, was holding a cut-down two-liter orange juice container by the handle. Without taking it from the other man's hand, Uncle Richard grasped the container's base. Swirled its contents against the opaque plastic sides, satisfying himself that it was the right consistency. Dipped in his right thumb and beckoned the younger men to come up in turn. They thrust their chests out: nervous, curious, proud.

"This," he said a dozen times, drawing his ochred thumb across each Goorie body, "is a ceremony about Love."

"Does Mum know Donna's gonna be there?" Kerry asked incredulously.

Immediately after the horror of her birthday party, Pretty Mary had indulged in several long rants about Donna. But since Ken had dropped his bombshell, the topic of Donna's accusations was well and truly off-limits. If it was raised, Pretty Mary would retreat to her room with a slam of the door, emerging hours later with swollen eyes, refusing to answer any questions about what she'd been doing, let alone what she believed to be true about her dead father-in-law.

Black Superman wrinkled his nose.

"Yeah," he said. "She *knows*, but she's real twitchy on it. Don't go giving her the third degree and buggering everything up. Just let things flow natural."

Kerry rolled her eyes. More tiptoeing. And the main thing that was flowing naturally was cheap Moselle, straight down Pretty Mary's gullet. Ken had come back from Men's Camp smiling and sober; a few of his uglier demons had been exorcised around the yellow-box fire. But as if a quorum of one designated drinker was required at Shitkicker Flats, Pretty Mary was hitting the turps like there was no tomorrow. Refusing to listen to sense or be dragged to any meeting. *When is it my turn,* Kerry had marvelled in amazement to Steve. *When do I get my big chance to lose the plot and be the family fuck-up?*

"Oh," said Kerry now to Black Superman in umbrage, "you got it, bro. I won't bugger it up. Anyway, what could *possibly* go wrong?" Donna and Ken and Pretty Mary, brought face-to-face over the corpse of Elvis to get things straightened out. Now, there was a recipe for family harmony if ever she'd heard one.

"You got a better idea, girlfriend?" asked Black Superman sharply, feeling responsible for the expensive folly of the QC in the Land and Environment Court. "Buckley's ready to start putting the dozers through any day, Zippo reckons. So if you've got any bright fucking ideas on how to stop him, let's have em."

"What's a ten-letter word starting with A, meaning a self-taught student?" called Pretty Mary, screwing up her face over the crossword. She flexed her arthritic ankles beside the crackling firepit that Ken had just built for her between the Hills hoist and the chook pen.

"Autodidact," yelled Kerry through the nonexistent kitchen window. She was stirring curry on Steve's camping stove, which was all they had till Black Superman's child endowment came through. The ongoing house repairs had convinced her brother to take un-paid leave and stay a bit longer. In Durrongo he could live in a T-shirt and jeans; Pretty Mary was right on hand to help out with the kids. He and Josh were planning to rent a house in Patto, test out bringing the kids up on country. There was more to life, he told Kerry, than a government wage.

"We'll be poor but free," he quavered in an old pensioner's voice, as he chucked three swags into the caravan. It was vacant again, now that Chris had moved back in with his girlfriend and kid in Mullum.

"Spare me. Poor, while your tenants pay off your negatively geared unit in Redfern," mocked Kerry, playing the world's tiniest violin. "With a decade's worth of super in the bank."

"Well, yeah, there is that," Black Superman admitted, not reveal-ing that a recent conversation had caused him to withdraw all his super.

"Don't you go thinking about muscling in on the Tarot Teepee," she told him sternly. "That's woman business there, straight up."

"Another dream destroyed," he said, deadpan. "Another vision shattered."

"Boo fucken hoo," Kerry said. "Get a haircut and a real job."

"Never mind 'bout haircuts and jobs," Pretty Mary chimed in, anxious about the funeral that afternoon. "Is my curry ready yet? Was there enough coconut? I don't wanna be sitting on the river-bank with me guts growling like an ol' mission manager just cos youse mob are too damn lazy to cook up a decent feed!"

"Aw, Mum," said Black Superman, hugging her tight. "Don't ever change, will ya?"

"Get orf me, ya great black fool of a thing!" Pretty Mary pushed him away, went to the fridge for a refill of Fruity Lexia.

Some things don't ever change, thought Kerry. And then, some things don't change enough.

———

Kerry was lowering the lid on the simmering curry when her attention shifted to the afternoon news on the borrowed TV in the lounge. The lead story was federal politics, yada yada yada, who fucking cared. But the second segment told of a Brisbane couple who had fled a crime scene after a botched robbery.

Kerry turned the camp stove off.

A botched Sunnybank robbery involving a stolen safe.

She ran into the lounge.

"... the two robbers succeeded in removing the safe undetected," said the news anchor with barely suppressed laughter, "but appear to have come undone attempting to use dry ice to access the contents. When the thieves used a sledgehammer on the snap-frozen safe, both it and the approximately eighty thousand dollars inside shattered into tiny fragments. Police are still searching for clues to the identity of the women, who are both described as being of Caucasian appearance ..."

Kerry could picture it perfectly. Rocky and Peanut, their mouths agape. Frozen cash exploding into confetti around them in the car park at Sunnybank Plaza. She collapsed onto the lounge and laughed till she cried.

Chapter Twenty-One

Black Superman timed their arrival at the river down to the second. Long fingers of autumn sunshine slanted through the gums, and nobody else was there in the clearing to spoil the solitude. The scene—the water alive with diamond sparkles; the tide swirling and lapping at the dark, wet rocks as magpies carolled sweet and long from the island—could have been straight from a movie.

"The jewel in the crown," Black Superman said to Donna as they pulled up.

"My island home," Donna murmured, aiming for irony, only to discover that she meant it. She took a deep breath and climbed out of the car, dazed by the oddity of being back at Ava's Island with someone who knew it the same way she did. Her and Black Superman back after how long? Well over two decades since they'd swum here together, bombed off the rope swing still hanging, tattered, from the high gum branch, cooked their catch side by side over glowing coals on the tiny beach opposite. Where had those years gone, and the versions of themselves who inhabited them? Unanswerable questions. But her clever, persuasive brother had been right about one thing: the river bend was still itself, still as beautiful as it had ever been. You thought you remembered it, had long ago nailed it firmly in the place of childhood memory, when you were off in Sydney or Hong Kong or Ubud. Then you came back, and realized yet again that you'd been wrong—it was impossible to hold it all properly in your mind's eye. The perfection of the river stunned Donna now, just as it had on both of the secret visits home that she'd made since leaving. She breathed in the scent of the gum leaves and the wattle blossom washing across the narrow channel that separated them from the Old People. That faint fishy tang she knew so well, mixed with the earth smell rising off the mossy rocks. The bright couch grass growing down to the very edges of the island. The prettiest place of all, the place where she'd had a childhood while Granny Ruth still lived to show it to her. Donna sucked it all in for one delicious moment, her eyes pricking with tears, before turning back to Black Superman.

"These came," she said brusquely, handing him a wad of legal documents. She turned up the collar of her jacket against the cold breeze coming off the river. Shook her head at him and spoke drily. "You should be in sales, brother." Black Superman grinned and folded the papers into the pocket of his Driza-Bone, his heart hammering with what they were both about to do.

"It's gonna be awesome," he told her, adrenaline flooding through every cell, as alive as he'd ever felt. "You know we're doing the right thing."

Donna, rather less convinced, looked around at the bushland, the river twinkling at her like some favorite uncle who was always pleased to see her but who always had somewhere else to be hurrying off to as well. At the edge of the clearing stood an enormous yellow bulldozer. It pointed, silent and ugly, at the trees it was set to mow down. Switch it on and all this glory—everything their family had once held so dear—would be smashed to smithereens in two hours flat. Nothing was simpler than wanton destruction. Nothing more fragile than earliest memory. Donna turned away, ignoring the machine.

"Lovely day for a funeral," she said, wondering which lucky Salter had scored the job of bringing the frozen remains of Elvis to the river.

"I dunno if I can do this, Uncle," Ken confessed. A muscle flickered on the good side of Uncle Richard's face, and the old man glanced in the rear-view mirror. Chris, Steve, and Donny bunched together in the back seat. Men in the making, and good ones too, but none of them his peers. He steered out of Pretty Mary's gravel drive in silence, passed through Durrongo, and continued on over the highway. Was partway down Settlement Road before he responded, gruff with displeasure.

"We talked about this."

"I know," said Ken. "But it's—"

"I'm not setting foot on the island till this other business is sorted," Uncle Richard interrupted him. "And you know why, neph."

Ken was silent in the passenger seat, looking down at his jeans. He pushed sulkily at the denim with his palm heels, trying to buy more time. Trying to find the magic words that would release him from his unwelcome duty. Uncle Richard sighed, pulled the ute over to the side of the track. He sat still, looking at the damaged weld-mesh fence that lay buckled on the ground ahead of them. Then he turned to Ken.

"You wanna come to the Law, you come to it clean, son. No grog, no drugs. And no debts left unsettled either. Too many blokes are gammon, always looking for shortcuts, but there ain't any short-cuts, see. Most times ya just gotta do a hard thing for the right reasons, before ya ready."

Uncle Richard rubbed at his nose and then unzipped his nylon jacket. Unbuttoned his flannelette shirt a little to reveal the broad scars that ran across his chest, as though some enormous paw had raked at his flesh there. Those shining brown highways where no hair would ever grow.

"You want these?" he asked Ken, taking his nephew's hand and placing it over his heart, ignoring the sudden stares from the back seat. "They don't come for free, my nephew. You gotta earn em."

Ken sat alone in the ute, arguing with himself. He lit a fresh durrie off the stub of his old one and then smoked it down to the stub as well.

The other men had joined the family and were circling the bulldozer in fascinated horror. "I wanna stab them tires," said Kerry savagely. Chris pointed out that bulldozer tires were, unfortunately, built to cope with that sort of thing. "Drop a lit match in the tank, then," said Kerry. But the fuel tank was locked.

Donny was the first to notice the key. Sitting right there, high up in the machine's ignition. Rage rose in him; he ripped the silver key ring out and hurled it into the river with a splash, his throw almost reaching the muddy margin of the island. Kerry blinked in surprise.

"That'll slow em down a bit," she cried in approval, only realizing thirty seconds too late that they could have driven the dozer into the river and left it there to rust.

"Good lad," Chris told Donny with a squeeze of the neck. In the tree above, the smashed camera sat, gazing down uselessly at them.

Off to one side, Uncle Richard and Pretty Mary were deep in conversation with Donna, a conversation that had been going for a good twenty minutes. They formed a secret triad, heads close, and the others couldn't hear what was being said. There was more back and forth between them, until finally the two women embraced. Donna turned away, wiped at her face when she thought nobody else was watching. Once she nodded that she was ready, Uncle Richard brought the two women back to the rest of the family.

"Kenny boy," he called. The door of the ute reluctantly creaked open. There was a very long pause before Ken got out and limped over. It's like part of him's gone missing, Kerry thought. Or, no, not that, not exactly. More as though something that had been covering him up for years had been peeled away at Men's Camp and chucked away into the bushes. Fidgeting in front of her now was the real Ken.

"Here," said Uncle Richard, pointing at the ground. "Next to me." Ken took his place, stony-faced. Black Superman walked around the outside of the semicircle then and stood next to Pretty Mary and Donna. He put his hand on Donna's shoulder. To his surprise, she left it there.

Silence fell. Nobody knew quite what to expect.

"You all know Ken and the lads have been out bush," Uncle Richard said, tipping his hat to the back of his head, the way he did whenever he was thinking particularly hard, or had been put on the spot. "So we's here to do coupla things today. We got old Kumanjay to put on the island, of course"—with a nod to the body of Elvis, wrapped in a stripy nylon bag and waiting for his interment—"but before we do that, we got some business to sort out. Can't be at a Law Place when there's still bad blood between anyone. So I wanna bring sissy back in like she should have been welcomed back in the first place."

He addressed Donna directly. "You been a long time gone, my niece. A real long time. We've missed you. We never forgot you, and this place"—Uncle Richard indicated the river, the island—"the Old People, nobody ere ever forgot you neither. This punyarra jagan, the river, Granny and Grandad's island—everything here owns you, you know? This river your goomera, this jagan your body. I'm just sorry you had to be away so long from your blood's country where you belong. And I'm especially sorry I wasn't there the other week to welcome you home the right way, too, and to tell you I believe your story. So it's deadly to see you back at last, bub."

Donna nodded gravely, twice. Didn't smile. Didn't let on she'd come back to the river twice, over the years. And certainly didn't jump for joy at finally being made welcome. She could forgive Pretty Mary, it turned out. And Black Superman hadn't needed forgiving. As for the rest of em, that remained to be seen.

"Alright, then, nephew," said Uncle Richard. "Say your piece."

Ken cleared his throat. Shoved his fists deep in the pockets of his jeans. *Face your demons. Do a hard thing for the right reasons.*

"I wanted to say. I, ah, wanted to apologize to ya." Meeting Donna's eyes for the first time and seeing the ripples of shock beginning there. "When ya turned up outta the blue, it was a kind of a huge deal, and I said things I shouldn't have ever said."

Ken breathed hard, beginning to sweat under his T-shirt despite the cool breeze cutting across the clearing. Do a hard thing for the right reason, ah Jesus. Pretty Mary was crying into her hanky again; she had turned into a regular firehose these days, the old mother. Bawled at the drop of a hat. Kez not giving nothing away, as usual. Donna looking at him like he was a two-headed calf. Uncle right there, but, steadying him, goodways. And Donny watching too. Yeah. Donny. Do it for the kid. Ken straightened, took his hands out of his pockets.

"More than once I said them things. But, sis, I believe you. I'm your brother and I shoulda helped you—and I didn't. It was like part of me believed you about Pop, but more of me hated you for saying them things out loud. It's too bloody hard to hear, the truth. But really, deep down, I knew . . . I knew exactly what you knew. So there it is."

Ken looked directly at Donna and blew his breath out hard, trying not to break open in front of everyone. Uncle Richard's arms coming around him now as he struggled with the desperate urge to tear away, to cut and run from the shame and weakness. Finally giving up the idea of flight as he realized that his uncle really wouldn't let go. The knowledge thumped Ken hard in the chest like a heavy steel blade. His ground zero, right here with this old gray man, stood beside the running water.

"Good man," said Uncle Richard, clasping Ken's head to his shoulder. "Good man." Then kissed his head and stepped back, releasing him into his new life.

"So, Donna. You've heard your brother apologize. Did you wanna say anything?"

Donna blanched away from the faces that swung to her. The

sharp eyes, judging her as they'd always judged. She felt a crystalline rock form in her throat. Wanted to rip that rock out and hurl it at every last one of them for bringing her here, putting her though this ordeal. She pulled away from Black Superman.

"Sissy . . ." he said.

"Apologies are easy," Donna said in a hard voice. "I spent twenty years alone. I was a fucking *child*. Someone has to pay."

"Yes," said Uncle Richard, his voice grave. "We should have listened better. A crime was committed against a child. And someone should pay. But when the criminal's dead and buried, it's not always so easy, bub. Sometimes an apology is the only way."

Another awkward pause. In the end, Donna gave a shrug, and it looked as though there could be no resolution. Then a fierce cry broke from Pretty Mary. She turned to Donna, her arms folded and her bottom lip trembling.

"Please, dort," she said. "I threw you out that night cos I was too scared to hear it. I'm so sorry, my daughter. I wasted twenty years, lost all that time, for nothing—"

"*You* were scared!" said Donna in amazement. "*You* were scared? Do you even know what fear is? Do you know what it is to be a little kid, always listening in the night for footsteps? To be terrified to go to the bathroom, in case he's waiting? To put up with it, year after year, so he doesn't go after your younger sister and your little brother? While you were down the *pub*?"

Pretty Mary shuddered, and Uncle Richard quickly put his arm around her. It was asking too much, all happening far too fast. Donna needed more time to—

"Yer hard as nails," Kerry accused her sister, swamped by sudden anger. "Okay—it was wrong, and it happened, we believe you. But Ken's said he's sorry. Mum's said she's sorry. What more do you want? Want us to build a time machine and go back to 1999? Rake the old bastard's ashes up so you can spit on them, tell him how much you hate him?" She stared at her sister.

"History's made us all hard, bub," interjected Uncle Richard swiftly. "We had to grow hard just to survive, had to get as hard as that ol' rock sitting there. But the hardness that saved us, it's gonna kill us if it goes on much longer. People ain't rocks. Donna, bub, it was terrible wrong what was done to you. Criminal. But he's gorn now. So all we can do is apologize for not listening. What happens next, well, that bit's up to you."

"Don't ask me to forgive him!" she told Uncle Richard, eyes flashing with rage.

"Nobody's asking that of you, bub," he replied. "That's not what today's about."

As Donna hesitated, Pretty Mary found the courage to speak again.

"You weren't the only one, dort," she said slowly, putting up a palm to stop Uncle Richard's interruption. "I know, brother, I know she don't care—and maybe it's not right to ask her to care. But she deserves to know, any rate. Pop told me when he was dying, cos it was eating away at him, worse'n the cancer was, he said. Three coppers grabbed him in Brisbane as a kid. Fourteen-year-old. Locked him in the cells and took turns at him all night for winning the Silver Gloves when he was supposed to lose."

"Jesus Christ Almighty," muttered Steve.

"So you knew, then," Uncle Richard said to Pretty Mary, tipping his hat back.

"Oh, I know plenty of things, brother," she told him, squaring her shoulders to hide the quaver in her voice. "And I'm proper sick and tired of being quiet about em too. But now, if Donna don't mind, we've said we're sorry, and I'd like to put me old friend in the ground."

"Donna?" Uncle Richard waited. "We aren't talking about forgiveness. That's the dugai way. But can we at least keep on going as a family?"

Everyone watched. Momentarily the world held still.

"Please, sister," said Ken softly.

Donna sighed. Closed her eyes. Opened them again. Saw her blood standing around her.

"Go on, then," she said wearily, and so the funeral of Elvis began.

———————

The river was high and the sun was shining and the mullet were jumping fit to beat the band. Beautiful, but when Ken waded into the current he yelped with the cold, and so the green canoe was heaved off the back of Uncle Richard's ute. After everyone had been rowed across to the island in shifts, the family clustered in the scrub behind the pine tree. Donny and Ken dug a deep round hole next to Grandad Chinky Joe's granite boulder, and Pretty Mary kneeled there on the soft red earth. She took the wrapped kingplate out of Kerry's schoolbag and placed it gently on top of Elvis's small rigid body, before more paperbark was put down and the earth shovelled in on top. "A kingplate for my king," she said, smoothing the soil flat, ready for the shells. "It's only right." Uncle Richard sang then. Pretty Mary's clapsticks rang out over the grave while Donny danced shake-a-leg with his father for the very first time and the sight of it made everybody cry, even Kerry.

"Getting soft there," Ken teased her even as he flung an arm around his son's shoulders, hugging him side-on. "Turning into a girl."

"Kiss my black arse," Kerry told him. Ken laughed loudly, showing the world his broken teeth.

Everyone walked through the smoke a second time, and agreed that their bellies thought their throats were cut. Donny and Steve were sent to gather firewood. Ken heaved the heavy esky up from the water's edge and handed a silver cookpot over the grassy lip of the island to Chris. Kerry's guts grumbled at the sight, craving curry. Cold air always gave her an appetite, and river water too.

"Wonder if Elvis left any pups behind anywhere," Kerry mused aloud.

"I wouldn't be surprised, dort." Pretty Mary smiled at the idea.

"Want a hand with that kai, Mum?" asked Donna roughly, as though her mother wasn't easily capable of dishing out tucker for half a dozen people. Pretty Mary caught her breath.

"Thanks, bub," she said, as though there could be nothing more ordinary than pushing a couple of steaming bowls into her daughter's hands to pass around. Breaking bread.

———

The kookaburra on the branch above peered down at the pot and let out a short experimental stutter. Chris glanced up, threw it a lump of gristly chook tendon, which the bird caught neatly where it sat. Tossed its beak up twice, and the snack was gone.

"Bloody cannibal." Donny grinned.

"You wanna thank old Kumanjay for that," Kerry told the kookaburra. "That dog tried for many a long year to catch that speckled hen. Aw, I'm gonna miss the mad little bugger, truesgod." She grew teary again at the thought of no more Elvis lurking in the backyard.

"Course you will," said Uncle Richard, sucking at a wingbone. "He was family. And you cry for him, too, bub. Us mob gotta learn to cry when we're sober, might stop us killing each other."

Kerry told her uncle that by some miracle she had never killed anyone yet, and barring breaking into council, she hadn't done any crime at all for over a year. She was a reformed character, in fact. Steve immediately leaned in, rubbing his head on Kerry's shoulder as she tried to mop up sauce with a bit of buttered bread.

"Whaddya doing now, dickhead?" she asked.

"Basking," he told her, "in the reflected light from your halo." Everybody laughed, cynical of Kerry's rehabilitation. She threw her bread crust at him and showed him a vertical finger.

"Aw, very funny. Old Grandad Joe come to me that night at council, ya know." Kerry changed the subject to show how little she cared about anything Steve might do or say. "Showed me where the kingplate was, or else I woulda missed it completely." She paused. "Which might not have been such a bad thing." A lot had happened since the kingplate reappeared in their lives, and not much of it good.

"Was ya scared?" asked Ken. "I woulda filled me daks, truesgod."

"Shittin' meself," Kerry confessed. "Too scared to even run."

"Oh, the old fella wouldn't wish any harm on us mob." Pretty Mary smiled. "He wouldn't hurt a fly. Granny Ava, now. *She* mighta flogged ya up . . ."

Uncle Richard frowned as he drew a hand across his stubbled chin, searching for chicken fragments. No matter how kind Grandad Joe had been to Kerry, the damaged kingplate was not any sort of thing for a childless young woman to handle. It just wasn't proper; you didn't summon the moon that way.

"I wondered if all this trouble might be cos I stole it," Kerry admitted to Pretty Mary. "Even if it was stealing from old Jiminy Cricket, and ours in the first place . . ."

"Run us through what happened," Uncle Richard said, blowing on a pannikin of tea, and so Kerry told him the story of breaking into council chambers that night. How she'd found only cash and the statue of Cracker Nunne before Grandad Chinky Joe appeared and insisted on leading her to the cabinet in the back room.

"I went in looking for a big heap of bungoo, enough to save this place," Kerry explained, keeping to herself the exact contents of her missing backpack, which she hadn't quite given up hope of retrieving. "But instead I ended up with the kingplate and some other bits and pieces from Jiminy's office. I've still got em." She indicated the red schoolbag. "Quartz crystals and artifacts and whatnot. I had to grab anything I could and bolt when the—"

"Quartz crystals?" interrupted Pretty Mary and Uncle Richard in loud unison.

"Show me," said Uncle Richard, putting down his tea so fast half of it splashed onto the picnic blanket.

"Granny's clever stones," Pretty Mary whispered, her eyes wide, and a sudden thrill shot up Kerry's spine.

Kerry fossicked in the schoolbag, pulling out and putting to one side the brass statue of Nunne that she had kept to sell. Then she produced a plastic Aldi shopping bag. Two gray heads knocked in their rush to discover what she had brought away from the council.

"These ain't nothing much," said Uncle Richard in disappointment after a minute or two. "Not clever stones, anyway. And I dunno what that is, but it ain't ochre." He pushed the nondescript objects back into the Aldi bag and handed it to Kerry with a glum twitch of his eyebrows. She stashed them away. Some gammon thief she'd turned out to be.

"Aw, ya had me going for a minute there," she said morosely, wishing she had saved that morning's spliff for now. A feeling of sharp dissatisfaction lodged in her chest. With Elvis buried and no joy from the court, there was only more hard and hopeless battle ahead. They held no cards in the saving of the island.

Pretty Mary picked up the brass statue, weighed it in her hand with a thoughtful expression.

"I know a bloke in Murbah who'll pay good money for that," advised Chris, and Kerry brightened.

"So ya made it onto the island after all, Grandfather," Pretty Mary said. "Ya murdering old bugger."

Ken frowned. Donna paused, her spoon halfway to her mouth.

"Whaddya mean, *grandfather*?" Kerry said indignantly. "Grandad Chinky Joe's your grandfather."

Pretty Mary let out a peal of laughter. She stroked at her pecan-brown arm with long, elegant fingers.

"With me this color? I *called* Grandad Joe grandfather, cos he was married to Granny Ava for nigh on thirty years. But Granny Ruth and a score of other jahjams besides her had Cracker Nunne for a father. Who do ya think was chasing Granny Ava that day?"

"Granny Ava ran to save her life—" blurted Kerry. "You said! It was to save her life, the bastards shot at her when they were stealing our land!"

"Oh, they shot her alright," agreed Pretty Mary calmly, scraping the last of the curry into a plastic container, ready to take back to the car. She pressed the hard plastic lid down with her thumbs, clicking it shut, then looked up. "And she run for her life, yeah. But the land was long gorn by then. Use ya brain, girl! Nunne's mob bin here two generations already by 1899. It was all stations and villages. Granny bolted so they wouldn't take bubby off of her, see. She already lost four of Cracker's kids to the gunjies. She told me she'd rather have drowned that day than lose another one. And it worked." Pretty Mary looked about her at the island, nodding with grim satisfaction. "She put up a humpy and scraped a living doing what she had to. Raised baby Ruth while Grandad Joe come and went from the stations . . . till they took Mum later, course. But Mum was twelve by then, she knew who she was and where she belonged, eh, brother?"

Uncle Richard nodded agreement.

Kerry sat stunned. Imagined the life of her great-grandmother, hidden away on the island, far enough from civilization, so-called, to be left in peace with the only child she ever got to raise. And Granny Ruth, stolen from paradise at twelve, only to run back to the island years later with a head full of the catechism and a disease gifted to her by the son of her most recent employer.

Kerry watched the flames of the campfire lick around the dry eucalyptus branches and briefly turn pine needles into bright orange skeletons of themselves. She looked for faces in the rising smoke and didn't know who she was anymore. The family had always been proud of their Chinese blood, and Kerry had long assumed a bit of white convict was floating around somewhere in the family tree. But to descend from the very first land-grabbers, the murdering pioneers?

Half of white Patterson would be their cousins.

Kerry curled her lip. Hell would freeze over before she claimed that lot as kin.

"So we'd have family down south, then?" she finally asked. "Them other four kids?"

Uncle Richard nodded. "If they lived. Well, we know Uncle John lived, cos of finding Aunty Alice mob. We'd have rellos in Sydney, I reckon, probably out west and up in Queensland, too, by now. They took them stolen kids anywhere and everywhere . . . so you wanna be proper careful, any time ya go with a blackfella."

"I was always glad Kenny had his kids with an Island woman," Pretty Mary confessed. "Ya just never know who ya related to."

Everybody fell silent then, reflecting on what had been said.

Pretty Mary put the curry in the esky, rinsed out the pannikins and handed a bag of frozen peas to Ken to whack on his aching leg. Then got to her feet, stretched, and suggested to her daughters that they might like to come with her to the woman place on the far side of the island.

"Woman place?"

"Why ya think Granny run all the way ere to have that jah-jam?" Pretty Mary arched her eyebrows at her daughters. "When she coulda just hidden in the bush anywhere, eh?"

Pretty Mary led Kerry and Donna away through a low pall of the funeral smoke that was clinging to the scrub behind them. As they walked, three pairs of feet and three heads could be seen emerging from a broad belt of gray around the women's collective middle. Seeing this, Ken brayed with laughter.

"Hubble, bubble, toil and trouble," he said, winking at Chris, Donny, and Steve. "The witches are on the march!"

"Woman business," said Uncle Richard, lying down with his hat over his face to catch some shut-eye. "Not ours. Leave em be."

Chapter Twenty-Two

Four o'clock came and went. The shadow of the pine tree slanted lower and lower over the water till it reached the cars parked in the clearing opposite. The canoe was packed with gear, and one final billy of tea set to boil on the coals. Then the family slowly mustered without speaking by the side of the newly dug grave. Behind them, a mob of waark began making a terrible racket in Granny's pine. Kerry shot an irritated glance in their direction. Why did the birds with the most hideous voices always have the most to say? Cark cark fucking cark at top note, the bastards, worse than the rednecks at the pub. Her schoolbag twitched in her right hand. If she could chuck it hard enough she could clean the lot up in one fell swoop. The brass statue alone would stun a Brahman bull. But Pretty Mary wouldn't have a bar of hurting a crow. Waark was one of her totems and so the birds, noisy fuckers, had to be tolerated by everyone in earshot.

"Goodbye, my old friend," said Pretty Mary, waving and blowing kisses at the grave. "Lub you! Ya can forget about my hens now, and going julabai on everybody's blooming jinung. You go enjoy yerself, mustering up them bullocks with Grandad and Granny. And mind them blue dogs don't rip ya, the rotten sods." Then she leaned over, seizing something from the top of the grave.

"Look," she said, excited, waving a spotted feather. "That's from Dotty! Old mate sent it to me, and I'll tell ya why, dort. It's a sign." Yep, thought Kerry, a sign that a pheasant coucal had passed by in the past few hours. But she held her tongue, after Uncle Richard caught her eye and tipped her the wink with a grin. Ah. Pretty Mary tucked the speckled feather carefully into her bra, spirits lifted by the discovery.

The others said their goodbyes silently, patting the mound or touching the shells that formed a large circle on it. Donny made minute tearful rearrangements of them in demonstration of his devotion. "Wonder if he gets his full tail back now, in the after-life?" Pretty Mary mused as the crows' barrage grew louder, almost drowning her out.

Kerry shot the birds another death glare. Aw, truesgod. Some people called em messengers, waark. She called em bignoting arse-holes that didn't know when to be ning.

"Ah, shut ya big black 'oles," Kerry snapped. "Us funeral mob, ere! Show some respect!"

"That's my minya," protested Pretty Mary.

"Funeral mob," chanted the crows in instant delight. "Funeral, your funeral! Cark. Your funeral!"

"Maybe, Mum, but they make me weak," Kerry argued, run-ning at the birds, swearing and threatening them with a giant mock-heave of her schoolbag. To her horror, the bag flew out of her hand. The patch of red canvas sailed higher and higher, to-wards the pine branch, flustering the waark into the air, before the shoulder strap caught on a jagged branch twenty meters above the ground. The crows couldn't contain their joy at this development. They flew in circles above the tree, wracked with paroxysms of helpless laughter when Kerry asked them through gritted teeth to help retrieve the bag.

As Kerry let out a groan, the family began throwing lumps of wood at the branch. A shower of heavy timber pockmarked the riv-er's surface before they finally gave up. Uncle Richard rubbed at his throwing shoulder and grimaced. Everyone agreed: the tree trunk was too hard to climb without ropes, maybe even with them, and the snapped-off branch that the bag hung from wouldn't support the weight of an adult anyway.

"Hafta wait for a decent storm," Uncle Richard advised in the end. "That might knock it off . . ."

"*Fuck*," Kerry spat. "Just my fucking luck. I'm that bloody broke too." There was clearly some kind of backpack curse upon her, the rate she was going.

"Back to the Tarot Teepee for you, my girl," said Pretty Mary censoriously, like Kerry had deliberately thrown away her only worldly wealth.

"At least you still got yer phone," Steve said, handing it to her out of his pocket, for he had used it earlier to film the dancing. Kerry grimaced, remembering that her key card was halfway up Granny's bloody pine tree too, much fucking good it did her, when her account had been empty since December. It was cash all the way for this little black duck. Still, it would have been nice to have the damn thing.

"Sit and have a cuppa tea, sis," said Ken, picking up the boiling billy of tea and swinging it in giant circles. "And then we best head home."

———————

"We should yanbillilla, I s'pose," sighed Kerry. She squinted at the canoe, pivoting with the tide. "You want to go first trip, Mum?"

"Hold on," said Black Superman with a glance at Donna. "Before that, we've got something to—"

"Sister?" interrupted Uncle Richard. Pretty Mary was focused on a plume of orange dust billowing up from a long way down Settlement Road. The buzzing of an engine came closer as the vehicle sped towards the clearing. With a sinking feeling, Kerry remembered the sudden disastrous arrival of Jim Buckley in that exact spot a few months ago. The buzzing was getting louder and louder. Nobody drove that fast for no reason.

"Hey, look out," said Ken uneasily.

"Whoever it is, they's going like a bat outta hell," agreed Uncle Richard.

Pretty Mary reached into her bag and gripped her tarot cards, berating herself for not doing a reading while she was in her full power at the women's place. Oh, the cards didn't lie, but it was hard to keep the faith sometimes, with the odds stacked so long against you in this life of sorrows. She wondered about the prospects of doing a reading now, with everyone so het up and distracted, the energy of the group gone haywire. But there was no time. Once you got old, that was it. There was never enough *time* to do the important things that you wanted to do. Other people's plans were always getting in the way of your own.

"Kombi van," said Ken, listening acutely, one palm raised behind his ear like a miniature satellite dish. "Firing on three cylinders."

"Zippo!" said Steve.

"He's found fourth gear, maybe the Yankees are coming," said Kerry drily.

Zippo was renowned for his glacial pace; nobody had ever seen the man hurrying, or without a joint in his hand. The family clustered together, horribly afraid of what news their friend might be bringing.

Sure enough, when the car rounded the last bend and screeched to a halt it was Zippo who emerged. He ran to the water's edge and began yelling incoherently at the family through cupped hands. It took a moment for everyone to register that behind the hands and the enormous beard, there was a giant grin splitting his face. And it took Zippo three goes before the family could begin to make out what he was on about.

"ICAC's arrested Buckley," he yelled. "Found thirty grand of cash bribes in his house, hidden in an old backpack. Come down on him like a ton of bricks, it couldn't have happened to a nicer arsehole."

There was a second of incomprehension, and then the Salters

began yelling too. They hugged and whooped, looking about them wildly at the island, the graves, the river, the clearing. All safe now. All safe. The ugly yellow mass of the bulldozer on the bank opposite suddenly rendered impotent. "Praise God," said Pretty Mary, sinking to her knees and allowing the tarot cards to fall loosely from her hand. "Praise His Name, the cards never lie."

"That old karma bus, eh?" Uncle Richard laughed, his belly quaking. "It musta gone and made an unscheduled stop at old Jiminy Cricket's place . . ."

Donny let out a scream of joy and ripped his shirt off. Ran and bombed off the bank into the cold river. Immediately climbed out and stood shivering next to the fire with the biggest smile on his dial anyone had ever seen. "Ah, ya moogle and no mistake," said Pretty Mary, but she was grinning fit to beat the band herself.

While the others whooped and hugged, Kerry walked alone in a disbelieving circle. Thirty grand. On its way to an ICAC safe somewhere in Sydney. *Sydney.*

Her.

Thirty.

Fucking.

Grand.

"Ol' Jiminy Cricket be locked up tonight," exclaimed Pretty Mary in ecstasy. "The brothers be throwing him a party too, I bet."

"Aw, flash mouthpiece'll have him home by dinnertime," said Ken, shaking his head, skeptical. "He'll probably send more goons round home too. Try and shake us up."

"I wouldn't be so sure of that," Donna said.

Ken glanced over. Donna had her back to him, squatting down and smoking as she stared blankly into the water, trying to comprehend the giant U-turn her life had taken in the past week.

"Hey?"

"Who do you think rang ICAC?" She stood up and turned around. "I sent them enough dirt on Buckley a month ago to keep him locked up till the Second Coming. That prick's gonna need a walker by the time he gets out."

Ken hooted with laughter.

"Buckley thought I was just some dumb piece of skirt he could rip off," Donna continued. "I was on to him, though. At first I was just gonna make him suffer a bit, make him give me thirty percent of the development deal—"

"Oh God no," thought Kerry, horrified. Seeing her expression, Donna put up a hand to stay her.

"But, nah, hang on. I couldn't bring meself to do it. Plus it didn't take too long to come up with a better idea." She nodded at Black Superman.

"What better idea?" asked Kerry warily.

"Jim's not dumb; he's got a dozen shelf companies. But it's pretty hard to hold a real estate license when you're sitting in Long Bay." Donna blew out smoke, looking extremely pleased with herself.

"Come again?" Pretty Mary was lost. Jim Buckley getting arrested at long last—that had to be a good thing. But she was buggered if she knew why Donna looked like the cat that got all the cream, and the cow thrown in for good measure.

"Will you tell them," said Black Superman, pulling the documents from his pocket, "or will I?" Donna took them from him, savoring the moment.

"I went to Jim three days ago," she said, grinning.

"Only after I talked some sense into you," Black Superman added.

"And made him an offer he couldn't refuse. You are looking . . ." Donna said, carefully unfolding the deeds, "at the new owners of Patterson Real Estate. It'll be us deciding who comes to live in Durrongo from now on."

"And I can tell you right now, there ain't gonna be no medium-security prison involved." Black Superman grinned beside her.

"Partners in crime." Steve shook his head admiringly.

"Well," said Pretty Mary, as realization dawned. "Ain't that deadly! If the two of youse don't take the blooming cake!"

On the other side of the river the Kombi engine roared to life, backfired twice, roared again. "See yez at the pub," Zippo yelled, heading for the celebration that was already cranking up. "The Greens are shouting the bar!"

"Order pizzas!" shouted Ken.

"Shit, five fifteen," said Steve, pulling out his phone. "Pump Class is at six."

"No flies on you, sis," said Kerry to Donna with newfound respect. Maybe you could dismantle the master's house with the master's tools, after all. She could see it now. Donna in the corner office, leaning back in her leather armchair, running the whole shebang. Black Superman smooth as you like in his Italian suit, flogging off houses to the middle class. Both of em raking in bungoo hand over fist as the gentrification tided upriver from Bruns and Mullum. And all the dugai punters having to take a cultural awareness course before they got the green light to buy. *You Are on Bundjalung Land 101*, and the rednecks shown the fucking door!

"Hang on, hang on, before yez all get too happy," objected Ken. "Buckley might get locked up, but he still owns the land, and it's still for sale. So what's changed?"

"Here, bruz," said Black Superman, pointing and reading. "The PURCHASER aforementioned will additionally have the exclusive rights of access to and enjoyment of the PROPERTY known as Riverside Downs for a period of not less than two years from MARCH 18 . . . We made him chuck in a free two-year lease. And anything can happen in two years, eh?"

"Two hundred years be a lot better," said Ken, causing Donna to roll her eyes. "But I suppose it gives us some breathing room."

"I gotta hand it to ya, truesgod," said Kerry wryly. "Ya get the business dirt cheap, ya got a free lease on this place, and yer gonna make a killing selling houses into the bargain. Maybe I should do a real estate course."

"Why not?" said Black Superman, his eyes crinkling with laughter.

"Speaking of killing," said The Doctor, the black triangle of her fin slicing the surface not ten meters away, "there is the small matter of a debt."

The family staggered forward to the edge of the island. They gaped down at the bull shark swaying in the water, graceful with the promise of death.

"Jingeri, wardham nanang," said Uncle Richard formally. "We remember your clan's kindness."

"Punyarra," said The Doctor, with a sharp flick of her tail. "I'm pleased to hear it. As the debt is long past due."

The shark swam in a wide circle, patrolling the channel that stretched between the canoe at the base of Granny's tree and the clearing opposite. Sturdy enough an hour ago, the canoe suddenly looked to Kerry like a child's toy. A joke. When The Doctor swam past, Kerry saw that the shark was longer than the boat, and she shivered.

"What's going on?" asked Donny, making his way over from the fire, pulling his shirt on over his head.

"You know Granny Ava swum across here," Pretty Mary explained grimly. "Well, by rights she should have died. She was shot, and losing blood, but she made it. Bargained her way over to the island when the shark come smelling the blood, see, but there was a catch. She had to promise old wardham something in return for her life: whiteman's meat instead of her own. She tried her best to get the dugais to follow her into the river that day, but they turned back."

"My grandfather died waiting for this debt to be honored," said The Doctor with a snap of her tremendous jaws. She lunged past the watching family at speed, deliberately hitting the bank with a sideways glancing blow so that a trickle of earth poured into the water. The brownish stain of the soil quickly spread and then sank beneath the swirling surface, vanishing from sight. "My mother died waiting. Our patience wears thin."

"Ngali kangani gulgan wahhni," said Uncle Richard stiffly. "We hear your word."

The Doctor swam faster, forcing the wash of the river higher up the bank each time she passed. The clear river water began to muddy with the earth falling away from beneath the Salters. The shark swam so close to the lip of the island that Kerry could have reached down and touched her jutting dorsal fin. Uncle Richard hadn't moved. His face had turned oddly gray, and he was tipping his hat back and forth in agitation. Nobody spoke. Then Ken slowly eased back several steps. He turned and bent to pick up the long-handled shovel they had used to bury Elvis. His eyes gleamed, for here was his chance. A chance to prove himself righteous in battle. Holding the shovel high with both hands, he looked to Uncle Richard, and silently pointed his lips at the shark. He braced his legs in readiness, ignoring the pain from his wounded thigh. One jump. One thrust behind that streamlined head. But Uncle Richard frowned.

"Can't break Granny's word, son. Not here."

Ken's face fell. He lowered the shovel.

"*Blood will have blood.* It is the oldest Law," said The Doctor, rolling onto her side to eye Uncle Richard.

"Yes," Uncle Richard said heavily after a long pause. His voice made Kerry tremble. She had seen her uncle stern many times, but now his face was filled with something more like dread. As though he was deciding to kill something truly beloved.

"If it's blood you're owed, then it's blood you'll have," the old man said.

He took his pocket knife out and tested the edge of the blade against his thumb. It flashed bright in the rays of the lowering sun.

"Ken."

Ken looked up, seared with fierce joy. Held his head high as he went to his uncle. *At last, at last.* The old man shivered to see the look in his nephew's eye. Uncle Richard thrust his knife into the campfire coals, and then took Ken to stand on the very lip of the island.

Ken looked to the sky, steeling himself for the bite of the steel.

"Jala goomera," Uncle Richard said to The Doctor. "Eat blood, and be satisfied."

He slashed the blade across the thick muscle of Ken's upper arm, the cut man grunting with pain as he spurted red into the current.

The Doctor thrashed wildly at the scent of the blood. She bit at the red cloud billowing around her and then leaped high to snap at the riverbank in a rage. Clumps of dislodged grass and dirt flew through the air. The family jumped back in sudden panic as the water boiled beneath them.

"Trickster!" the shark roared in frustration. "We were promised the meat of murderers, not scant drops from your Shark Clan!"

"Step away, now," Uncle Richard said, dragging at Ken. The younger man was staring down as though hypnotized at the fading pink bloom he had just shed. Blood streamed through his fingers where he clutched at the fresh wound. Uncle Richard led Ken over to the fire and slapped a handful of ash on the cut. Then he turned back to where the shark glowered at him in cold fury.

"You have tasted the blood of a Shark Man, Old One, that's true," Uncle Richard addressed The Doctor. "But his mother's grandfather was a stranger of the promised meat. The debt is paid."

"Arrrrggghhh!" The Doctor screamed, leaping high and twisting furiously in midair, snapping her jaws at the unavoidable truth. When she landed, the huge wash slopped against the island, stray drops spattering the family so that the wetness of the river ran down their faces, dampening their clothes and hair. Then the wash surged back down, dragging against the weakened bank and taking away yet more earth from beneath the lip of the island. The eroding force of the wave was finally enough. The jutting tongue of land in front of Granny's pine cracked and slowly sank, the rim of earth collapsing into the river.

The current didn't hesitate. It flowed easily into the new indentation in the shoreline, carving its way yet further beneath the pine, relentless on its journey back to the sea. The river tore at the bank, carrying away rocks and soil and pebbles, drowning trapped insects and myriad other tiny creatures. It ripped at the tangled grasses and reeds, exposing the thick arteries of root that still anchored the pine in place. Mixed with the earth and stones and grasses that fell away into the water were the drops of Ken's blood, still warm, which had fallen on the ground less than a minute ago; drops of his blood, along with the gravelly white ash that Ken had scattered out of Pop's funeral basket on that exact spot weeks earlier.

Everything—grass, stones, blood, ashes—washed into the current and was gone.

"Kingilawanna!" cried Pretty Mary to the sky.

"Kingilawanna," said Uncle Richard wearily, raising his right hand to the setting sun. "It is finished."

Chapter Twenty-Three

Steve gave Pretty Mary a hand to climb out of the canoe and over the boulders into the XD. Heading back to the boat, he deviated in his path to stare at something odd, lying on the very edge of the clearing.

"Check this out," he called.

Exasperated by yet more delay, Kerry went over and peered down into the kangaroo grass. What she found lying there was the skeleton of a bird: a frame of thin pale bones with a few black feathers half rotted into the soil around it. The bird's small angular skull lay white against the ground, and wedged onto the beak, she saw, was the much tinier skull of a brown snake, its curved fangs wedging the two halves of the beak tightly shut.

The hairs on the back of her neck tingled, and she shivered and looked away. Some things are just too bloody dangerous to toy with, even when they look like they're dead and gone. That waark should've known better than to muck around with any mundoolun in its path. Shoulda just kept on going.

"What the hell?" said Steve, gazing around uneasily. "What *is* this place?"

"Alas, poor Yorick," Kerry murmured, then louder, "it's nothing. Just a crow."

She picked up a stick, flicked the carcass into the thicker scrub. Kept on going, and didn't look back.

Donny waited, the last to be ferried over from the island. As the others stood in the clearing, itching to get to the pub, Kerry wandered off for a leak. She squatted behind a soap tree, and the memory came to her of that first afternoon when Buckley had roared up in his ute. She fled from him that day, fearing discovery and arrest, but just look at things now. It was her at the river and Jim Buckley who was locked behind smooth steel doors. A disbelieving smile spread across her face as she stood up and buttoned her jeans. She laughs loudest who laughs last, and ain't that the fucken truth.

"Like riding a bicycle, alright," Uncle Richard was saying to Pretty Mary, puffing as he leaned on the oars. "Bloody hard work."

"See ya, cuz!" Chris taunted Donny from the XD. "We'll come back for ya tomorrow. Maybe."

"What?" Donny had his hand to his ear, looking panicky.

"Aw, don't torment him," protested Kerry. "You mob go. I'll grab him and bring him on the bike. Steve can borrow the XD to get to the gym, eh?"

"No worries," agreed Ken. "So long's he fills the tank. I'll even have a beer for him while he's at work." He caught Uncle Richard's glance. "A light beer."

"Yer all heart, brother," Steve said ironically. "Ya choking me up."

"You know it, bunji." Ken winked.

On the island, Donny sat poking at the ground beneath the pine with a dry twig. He knew that much of life was about waiting, and he also knew that waiting, especially for the youngest son in a big family, was a skill worth cultivating. At the same time, he thought it was well within the bounds of possibility that the others might bugger off and leave him all alone on the island as a hilarious joke, very funny haha. Nobody to keep him company all night but the ghost of Elvis and the ancestors he'd never even met, an idea that gave him the horrors. When Ken turned the key of the Falcon, Donny got to his feet and began collecting firewood to hide his fear. Then in great relief, he saw Kerry get in the canoe and head over to the island, rowing with more energy than skill.

"Let's head. There's a party at the pub. Open bar."

"It feels weird to leave Elvis," Donny said, dragging on his jeans that had been drying beside the fire pit. "I can't believe he's not gonna be at home no more, it's not as if—"

He was interrupted by a loud crack from above. Both Donny and Kerry flinched, then Donny let out a sharp yelp as a blur plummeted past, clipping his shoulder. By some instinct he snatched at the falling object and when he looked, he discovered that he was holding the red schoolbag.

"Eh, fuck off!" he cried, feeling the weight of it, his eyes wide with fright. "That coulda killed me!"

"I reckon." Kerry breathed. The statue inside could have easily brained Donny. "Old Cracker Nunne's still after his revenge, eh." They craned their necks to gaze upwards. The dead limb that the bag had hung from sagged now at a different angle, pointing at the clearing where it had earlier reached skywards.

"Tree must have shifted a bit when the bank fell away," Kerry assessed. "We better make tracks before the whole bloody lot comes down." She turned to leave. The irony of having her skull split open by Granny's tree on the very day they reclaimed her land would be too much to bear.

"*Thanks for catching my bag, Donny,*" the boy bit back, far more shaken than Kerry had realized. "*Well done, neph. Can't thank you enough for saving my stuff . . .*" His thin chest heaved, and angry spots of color appeared high on his cheeks.

Kerry squinted at him, taken aback. This lad, now. Getting proper cheeky. She suddenly laughed, wrinkling her nose and hugging him to her. It was good to see some spirit returning to the boy. That whale on his arm must be doing him a power of good.

"You're right. Ya done real good to catch it, bud. Lucky there's nothing to break." She took the bag and opened it in demonstration. "Brass ain't gonna smash in a hurry. Or bits of quartz, or whatever this is." She showed him the ambiguous lump nestled inside.

Curious, Donny reached in to press a fingernail into its waxy surface. Took it out and sniffed it.

"Ken reckoned the smell of it'd give a baby a nosebleed, but I don't think it's all that bad," Kerry added, turning to the canoe in dismay. "Shit. We're gonna hafta drag this boat up off the river and hide it before we go. I hope ya feeling strong."

"Where'd this come from?" Donny demanded sharply. Kerry turned back around. Her nephew stood very still; all color had drained from his face.

"Council. You know, that night when Grandad Chinky Joe visited me?" Kerry told him. "The label said ochre, but Uncle Richard reckons it isn't."

Donny's expression was feverish. Kerry peered at him.

"What's wrong?"

Donny opened and closed his mouth, twice. Kerry frowned at the thing he held, roughly the size and shape of a baby's head. A horrible thought came to her.

"You're worrying me now, bub."

Donny made an odd gurgling sound, unable to get the words out.

"Come again?" Kerry put a hand on the boy's trembling back as he bent over. After a moment, she realized that her nephew was crying. "Slow down, bub, take a big breath."

Donny sucked in a great lungful of air and straightened up, came to the surface and breached. Looked at her with shining wet eyes and let fly the ten words that changed their lives forever.

"It's ambergris," he told her. "Whale vomit. Worth two hundred bucks a gram."

He pushed the strange, pungent object towards her, and Kerry reached for it in wonder. Their hands met around the dark lump, which resembled not a stone, and not a heart, but something in between both those things. It rested there, smelling of the earth and the ocean, and of hope too, and as her fingers closed upon the ambergris it somehow felt to Kerry like she was holding an island.

Afterword

Too Much Lip is a work of fiction, and the specific locations of Patterson, Durrongo, Ava's Island, and Rivertown exist only in my imagination. But lest any readers assume this portrayal of Aboriginal lives is exaggerated, I would add that virtually every incidence of violence in these pages has occurred within my extended family at least once. The (very) few exceptions are drawn either from the historical record or from Aboriginal oral history. The epigraph refers to my great-grandmother Christina Copson who, as a Goorie woman in Wolvi in 1907, was arrested for shooting her attempted rapist (also Aboriginal). Christina later beat the charge against her in a Brisbane court, unapologetically stating that although she had shot her attacker in the hip, she had been aiming for his heart and she was only sorry that she had not killed him.

Acknowledgments

The writing of this novel was helped immeasurably by the 2016 Copyright Agency Author Fellowship. Thanks are also due to the Australia Council for a New Work grant; Avid Reader in Brisbane, who generously supplied a quiet place to work; and Jill Redmyre for precious writing time granted at Springbrook. Judith Lukin-Amundsen was the most scrupulous of editors—I thank her for her encouragement.

About the Author

Melissa Lucashenko is a Goorie author of Bundjalung and European heritage. Her first novel, *Steam Pigs*, was published in 1997, and since then her work has received acclaim in many literary awards. *Too Much Lip* is her sixth novel and won the 2019 Miles Franklin Literary Award and the Queensland Premier's Award for a Work of State Significance. It was also shortlisted for the Prime Minister's Literary Award for Fiction, the Stella Prize, two Victorian Premier's Literary Awards, two Queensland Literary Awards, and two New South Wales Premier's Literary Awards. Lucashenko is a Walkley Award winner for her nonfiction and a founding member of the human rights organization Sisters Inside. She writes about ordinary Australians and the extraordinary lives they lead.

A Note from the Cover Designer

My elders have taught me that all meaning comes from Land, so part of my practice has always been about highlighting that meaning and importance while drawing attention to the beauty and complex harmony of country. During the process of creating the artwork, I traveled to Bundjalung country, and it allowed me to recall just how special that country is and how intensely alive it is; so embedding that feeling into the piece was important to me.

It was a beautiful challenge to bring Kerry's quiet but strong and thoughtful character to the work. The designs in the Land help to show that magnetic connection between Aboriginal people and our homelands. Even on a flash motorbike, wearing a leather jacket, we belong right there where our ancestors have been for generations, and that's the meaning I wanted to reflect, which is also reflected beautifully in the book.

—Teila Watson

Here ends Melissa Lucashenko's
Too Much Lip.

The first edition of this book was printed
and bound at LSC Communications in
Harrisonburg, Virginia, August 2020.

A NOTE ON THE TYPE

The text of this novel was set in Bembo, an old-style humanist serif typeface originally cut by Francesco Griffo in 1495 and named after 16th century Venetian poet, Cardinal, and literary theorist Pietro Bembo. This typeface was a departure from the common pen-drawn calligraphy of the day and influenced the style of roman typefaces we are familiar with today. The version now commonly used was created by Stanley Morison for The Monotype Corporation in 1929.

HarperVia

An imprint dedicated to publishing international voices,
offering readers a chance to encounter other lives and other
points of view via the language of the imagination.